Abraham Hayward, Henry E. Carlisle

A selection from the Correspondence from 1834 to 1884

With an account of his early life Vol.1

Abraham Hayward, Henry E. Carlisle

A selection from the Correspondence from 1834 to 1884
With an account of his early life Vol.1

ISBN/EAN: 9783743414914

Manufactured in Europe, USA, Canada, Australia, Japa

Cover: Foto ©Raphael Reischuk / pixelio.de

Manufactured and distributed by brebook publishing software (www.brebook.com)

Abraham Hayward, Henry E. Carlisle

A selection from the Correspondence from 1834 to 1884

A SELECTION

FROM

THE CORRESPONDENCE

OF

ABRAHAM HAYWARD, Q.C.

VOLUME I.

A SELECTION

FROM THE

CORRESPONDENCE

OF

ABRAHAM HAYWARD, Q.C.

FROM 1834 TO 1884.

WITH AN ACCOUNT OF HIS EARLY LIFE.

EDITED

By HENRY E. CARLISLE.

IN TWO VOLUMES.—VOL. I.

LONDON:
JOHN MURRAY, ALBEMARLE STREET.
1886.

LONDON:
PRINTED BY WILLIAM CLOWES AND SONS, Limited,
STAMFORD STREET AND CHARING CROSS.

PREFACE.

IN presenting these volumes of Mr. Hayward's Letters to the public, I feel it to be my first duty to state distinctly that they do not pretend in any way to contain a 'Life' of him. Unfortunately, among his papers, which on his death passed into his sister's hands, there were no diaries, or journals, or autobiographical memoirs ; in fact, nothing from which a connected story of his life could be produced ; but from the correspondence found among his papers and from his own letters, courteously placed at my disposal by his friends, I have carefully made a selection which forms the chief contents of these volumes.

I have, where I could, inserted all the most striking and interesting incidents of his life, which are preserved in his friends' memories, or his own writings. Mr. Hayward's own letters possess the remarkable merit of giving us a sketch of the men and women who were his contemporaries, while at the same time they undesignedly disclose a great deal of his own true nature, more especially that kindlier side of it which, if oftentimes masked by the energies of a fiery, combative spirit, was still very real.

Moreover, these letters contain nearly all that can be authoritatively stated concerning his " life." A sketch, indeed, of his early years, prior to the date of the first of the letters, introduces Mr. Hayward to the reader. But with this exception, as little editorial interference as possible has been placed between the public and the letters.

"The threads of human lives," writes Mr. Hayward, "are so closely and marvellously intertwined, that none can be unravelled from the rest without destroying the pattern even of that one. This is the condition of our social existence : we neither live nor die alone, nor can the history of our lives be told alone." Taking these words as my text, as it were, in entering upon my work, I have endeavoured so to deal with the materials before me as would best have met the approval of the great master of biographical criticism had he himself been alive to read these volumes. I trust I have printed nothing that is likely to give pain, and especially to any of those, with whose lives, Mr. Hayward's own life was "intertwined."

At the date of the first letter, Mr. Hayward was thirty-three years old ; he had been ten years in London; he had just published his translation of 'Faust ;' and was about to make his *début* in London society, in which for half a century afterwards he was more or less con-spicuous.

The letters of the first twelve or fourteen years discover to us "a brilliant *tableau* of wits, beauties, statesmen, and men of pleasure about town ; " and many a page sparkles with reminiscences and anecdotes of Lord Lyndhurst, Lord Lansdowne, Macaulay, Lockhart, Lady Dufferin, Charlie and Frank Sheridan, Mrs. Procter, Thackeray, Lady Charleville, Lady Chatterton, Lord Melbourne, D'Orsay, Lady Blessington, D'Este, Rogers, Lord Stanhope, James Smith, Sidney Herbert, the Duke of Newcastle, Mrs. Shelley, Dickens, Disraeli,

Theodore Hook, Sydney Smith, Thomas Moore, Lady Morgan, Dawson Damer, Lord Alvanley, Mrs. Norton, Louis Napoleon, Louis Blanc, Thiers, Dumas, Von Radowitz, Contessa Guiccioli, Manzoni, and many others.

In 1848 Mr. Hayward, having retired from the Bar, was enlisted with others, and especially with the famous George Smythe (afterwards Lord Strangford), as a contributor to the *Morning Chronicle*, at the moment when it became, in the hands of the Duke of Newcastle and Mr. Sidney Herbert, a *Peelite* newspaper. This era in his career is not so distinctly marked in his correspondence as might be expected. But there are sufficient proofs of the ability, the energy, and the usefulness of his work.

On the eve of the formation of Lord Aberdeen's Cabinet, in December 1852, we are able to form an idea, from Mr. Hayward's correspondence, of the anxious "reconnoitreing" which ushered into being the Coalition Government.

At the time of the Crimean War, Mr. Hayward's correspondence with the Duke of Newcastle became more intimate and important. The letters, too, which he received from M. Thiers, giving his views on the preparations that would be necessary in the event of a war with Russia, are of themselves of great interest ; and, besides, they give us the first important occasion upon which Mr. Hayward appeared as, what he so often was afterwards, a "connecting link" between some of our own and leading statesmen abroad ; and, moreover, they reveal the kind of influence a highly cultivated man of a good social position may exercise upon those in whose hands the conduct of a nation's affairs may for the time be entrusted. After the accession of the Coalition Government there ceased to be any basis for active partisanship with the *Peelite* cause ; but Mr. Hayward's friendship with those (except Lord Aberdeen) who were the foremost members of the Party continued in all its strength. When the *Peelites* (who were taunted for being all "officers," without any "rank and file,") began to be, either in a state of abeyance, or more and more absorbed by one or other of the great parties, it is noticeable that Mr. Hayward's association with Lord Palmerston became more frequent and intimate, and the letters disclose some very remarkable instances of the result of this friendship. When three years after Lord Palmerston's death, Mr. Gladstone, in 1868, became the Prime Minister, his association with Mr. Hayward (which long had been friendly) became much more close than before.

But not only in politics may Mr. Hayward be re-garded as a "connecting link" between this country and other nations. His correspondence and association, on the one hand with Macaulay, Lockhart, Thackeray, Stirling of Keir, Lord Stanhope, Sir G. C. Lewis, the late Lord Lytton, Henry Bulwer (Lord Dalling), Lady Morgan, Mrs. Norton, Laurence Oliphant, Nassau Senior, Mrs. Grote, Delane, Chenery, Charles Greville, Lord Broughton, Lord Stratford de Redcliffe, Mr. Gladstone, Mrs. Singleton (Violet Fane), Mr. Froude, Dr. William Smith (Editor of the *Quarterly Review*) ; and, on the other hand, with the Duc d'Aumale, MM. de Montalembert, de Rémusat, Mignet, and Mérimée, Louis Blanc, Pierre Dupont, Guizot, with Don Zarco del Valle, Gayangos— not to mention that at an earlier period of his life with

Madame de Goethe, Tieck, and the Grimms—is sufficient to justify us in seeing in him a link between the
leading literary men of this country and the Continent.

Mr. Bernal Osborne has described Mr. Hayward as
the "connecting link between the political and literary
magnates." This description, true as it is, has the effect
of at once presenting Mr. Hayward to us in the double
character we have already ascribed to him.

The correspondence with Lady Charleville, Sidney,
Lady Morgan, Georgiana, Lady Chatterton, Mrs.
Norton, Lady Palmerston, Lady Waldegrave, Mrs. Grote,
Lady Dufferin, Lady Emily Peel, Mrs. Procter, the
Countess de Florian, Lady Clanricarde, shows that when
writing to women, Mr. Hayward wrote earnestly, in-
tently, and in truth wrote his best ; and that they in
turn appreciated this trait in his character.

In conclusion I have to offer my thanks to Mr.
Kinglake, for explaining to me several allusions con-
tained in the Letters which at first seemed obscure. My
thanks are also due to H.R.H. the Duc d'Aumale, Mr.
Charles Villiers, Lord Carlingford, Mr. Gladstone, Dr.
William Smith, Lord Edward Pelham Clinton, Lady
Emily Peel, Madame de Florian, Lord Emly, Lord
Lytton, Miss Canning, Lord Dorchester, Mr. R. B.
Sheridan, Mr. Beresford-Hope, Sir Herbert and Miss
Lewis, Miss Lewin, Mrs. Procter, Mrs. Singleton (Violet
Fane), Mrs. Cornwallis-West, Sir Charles Wyke, Lord
Salisbury, Lord Wemyss, Mr. Bright, the late Mr. Forster,
Mr. Cardwell, Lord Mount-Temple, Lord E. Fitzmaurice,
Sir W. Stirling-Maxwell, Lord John Manners, Lord
Normanton, the Marquis Casa de Laglesia, Count
Karolyi, Sir Francis Turville, General Bulwer, Sir

Frederick Pollock, Mr. Swayne, Mr. Collyer Bristowe, Mr. John Murray, Mr. A. L. Francis, and other friends of Mr. Hayward who have either supplied me with letters, or with other much valued materials.

HENRY E. CARLISLE.

WOODMEAD,
   LYME REGIS,
      DORSET.
         November 1886.

CONTENTS.

———◆◇◆———

INTRODUCTION.

1801–1824.

CHAPTER I.

1824–1834.

CHAPTER II.

1834–1840.

CHAPTER V.

1852–1854.

CHAPTER VI.

1854–1856.

CHAPTER VII.

1856-1858.

The Peace negotiations—Lord Palmerston and Mr. Hayward—Mr. W. E. Forster on Mr. Hayward—Letter

MR. HAYWARD'S LETTERS.

INTRODUCTION.

1801–1824.

The Hayward family—Birth of Abraham Hayward—Goes as a pupil to Mr. Twiss at Bath—At Blundell's School, Tiverton—Articled to Mr. Tuson, solicitor—Life at the Tusons'—Applies himself to study English literature—Leaves Mr. Tuson's, and goes to London, and becomes a student of the Inner Temple.

THE Hayward family have been settled in Wiltshire for some centuries. In the registers of the parishes of Beechingstoke and North Newton, which record as far back as 1573, members of this family appear as the owners and occupiers of their own small properties in the neighbourhood. The grandfather of Abraham Hayward was the owner and occupier of a small property at Hilcott, North Newton, which in his day used to be known as "Hayward's." Some time after the death of the grandfather, his son Joseph Hayward, the father of Abraham Hayward, sold the property at Hilcott, and went to live at Wilton, near Salisbury.*

* The Hilcott property has since been bought back by the Hayward family, and is now in the possession of — Hayward, Esq., distant cousin of Mr. A. Hayward.

In the year 1799 he married Mary, a daughter of
Mr. Richard Abraham of Whitelackington, in Somersetshire, and on the 22nd of November, 1801, their
eldest son was born in "the stone-fronted house on
the south side of Kingsbury Square," in Wilton, which
they occupied at the time. At the neighbouring village
church of Wishford, in the following February, the child
was baptized, and had given to him the name of
"Abraham," after his mother's family. Little Abraham
grew up at Wilton till he was between seven and
eight years old, when he was placed as a private
pupil with Mr. Francis Twiss at Bath, with whose
family he remained domesticated for the next two
years.

Mrs. Francis Twiss was "the loveliest of Mrs. Siddons'
sisters," very like her distinguished sister, and a very
fine reader. Besides the family of Francis Twiss there
were then living in the house under Mrs. Twiss's care
three young ladies who became, so to say, Abraham
Hayward's schoolfellows. One of these, Miss Searle,
married Horace, the son of Francis Twiss, and when in
later years her old schoolfellow first came up to London
he had no kinder friends than Mrs. Horace Twiss and
her husband, who was then a distinguished member of
the House of Commons and one of the leaders on the
Oxford Circuit, and at their house he was always a
welcome visitor. His intimacy with Fanny Kemble
and her sister Adelaide, Mrs. Twiss's nieces, most
probably dates from the days when they used to stay
with their aunt at Bath, and was renewed when he
frequented their cousin's society in London. Adelaide,
afterwards Mrs. Sartoris, was his favourite, and he de-

scribes her as being "a charming woman, overflowing with mind and sensibility." *

On leaving Bath early in February, 1811, he went to Blundell's school at Tiverton, then under the head-mastership of Mr. (afterwards Dr.) Richards. He remained there till January, 1817. Whilst he was there the discipline and diet are said to have been very severe, and at the outset to have affected his health, so that when he came home after the first half-year, his mother noticed his "blear eyes," and other signs that implied want of food. By keeping her boy well supplied with pocket-money, the mother did what she could to make up for the deficiency of his school-fare ; but her son in after-life always spoke assentingly of his mother's conclusion, that the hard fare had permanently injured his health. But with the exception of the hardness of its regimen, he always spoke well of his school; and in adverting to the course of its studies, to its strong traditions, to its time-honoured customs, and to the age and manliness of its upper-form boys, would oftentimes declare that his old school was "the Eton of the West of England." The studies of the school did not carry him deep into Greek, but made him a good Latin scholar ; and from the rivers of Tiverton—the Exe and the Loman—he keenly learnt all they could teach him—becoming a capital swimmer, an extraordinary diver, and besides a very skilful fisherman. On leaving Tiverton he remained at home for nearly two years, as he was then in indifferent health, and his father engaged a tutor for him to assist him in his studies. It was at

* Mrs. F. Kemble's " Records of her Life ;" *Quarterly Review*, No. 307, p. 117.

this period, it is believed, that he acquired his mastery over the French and German languages, which enabled him in after life to make himself so perfectly well acquainted with the literature of both countries. At the end of September 1818, when he was nearly seventeen, his father articled him to Mr. George Tuson, a solicitor then living at Northover, but subsequently at Ilchester in Somersetshire, with whose family accordingly he became domesticated for the next five years.

In becoming a member of Mr. George Tuson's family young Hayward was fortunate, for he was thus thrown intimately amongst most accomplished and agreeable people; and in Mr. Tuson himself he found a man of cultivated tastes, possessed of an excellent library, which he was only too eager his clerk should enjoy when free from the responsibilities of the office. Mr. Hayward appears at this time to have had little propensity for pursuits which, if they had not unfitted him for, might have interfered with the development of his great passion for reading: whilst from those immediately about him he received nothing but encouragement in any self-imposed education. Thus from seventeen to twenty-two years of age he was able to give free and undisturbed application to the study of English literature. It is difficult to estimate correctly what had been the effect of his pupilage at Bath, in arousing in him an attraction towards the great masters of the English language; or to speculate how far he had been affected by the fine rendering of some of their most splendid passages by the great Siddons' Sister. But it is not improbable that when he found himself at large in

Mr. Tuson's library, the recollection of those days at Bath, when he had sat listening intently to Mrs. Twiss reading, may have allured him at once to the great masters' works from which she used to read. However that may be, it is certain that during this period Mr. Hayward laid the foundation of his knowledge of English literature, for which he afterwards became so remarkable as to call forth the opinion that, for the purpose of actual use in cultivated society, the late Lord Macaulay and Mr. Hayward were the two best-read men in all England. Moreover, it is impossible to doubt, that Mr. Hayward's delight in society arose from this early study of the literature of the past century, when sitting solitary in Mr. Tuson's library, conning the story

> " Of those gay times of elegance and ease,
> When Pleasure learnt so gracefully to please ;
> When wits and courtiers held the same resorts—
> The courtiers wits, and all wits fit for courts ;
> When woman, perfect in her siren art,
> Subdued the mind, and trifled with the heart :
>   *   *   *   *   *
> When all was Fairyland which met the view."

He became fascinated and attracted by the *fine* world of which he read, which seemed ever in variegated and changing clusters—now filling the stately *salons* of a Devonshire, a Holland, or a Chesterfield House ; now congregating at Almack's or at Ranelagh ; now lounging in at White's or at Brooks's, or sauntering leisurely and gaily along the Mall and about St. James's.

In 1823 his articles of clerkship ended, and he was set free from the dull routine of a solicitor's office, from its trammels, its surroundings, and its confinement : free from a life the duties of which, although he performed them with scrupulous care and industry, had palled upon him and given him the feeling of being "cabined, cribbed, confined." Thirsting to taste of that cup of life which he had filled for himself, and, unlike Faust, not irresistibly restrained by the hum of voices in the air, he gained his father's consent to his abandoning the profession of a solicitor, and after a brief interval spent with his family at Weymouth he hastened to London, where, in October 1824, he entered himself as a student of the Inner Temple.

CHAPTER I.

1824–1834.

THERE is so close a parallel to Mr. Hayward in the description he has given in one of his writings of another, that we are tempted to quote it here in so far as the parallel is maintained. "He is not a specimen of a period, an illustration of a calling, or an example of a class. He is in no sense a representative man. He stands alone in his peculiar and personal description of celebrity. . . . He starts with no advantage of birth or fortune, and he never acquires wealth : he produces no work of creative genius : he does not intrigue, cringe, or flatter : he does not get on by patronage : he is profuse without being venal : he is always on the side he thinks right : yet we find him, almost from the commencement to the very close of his career, the companion and counsellor of the greatest and most distinguished of his contemporaries, the petted member of the most brilliant and exclusive of European circles." *

The striking individuality of character he here depicts was at no time more apparent in his own career than at this period of his life ; and perhaps at no other time are we able to realise so fully what must have been his energy, his intellectual power, and the force of his will, as when we find him preparing to cross the Rubicon of his life and set out on his career.

Except to two or three personal friends *not* of the great world, he was then utterly unknown. He knew it. He knew, too, that he had no public school or university education to support him. But his self-reliance was not less strong than his appreciation of things was just ; and conscious of possessing the power to do what he wished, he proceeded to utilise that power accordingly. After passing through his student course in the Inner Temple, he practised as a special pleader till he was called to the Bar in the month of June 1832. Success in his profession he then considered essential, and he set himself steadily and earnestly to work to master its principles.

He had not been long in the Temple before he became a member of the London Debating Society. This Society had been founded in London by McCulloch, John Stuart Mill, George Villiers (afterwards Lord Clarendon), his brothers Hyde and Charles, Romilly, Charles Austen and others, on the plan of the Speculative Society at Edinburgh, "in which Brougham, Horner and others first cultivated public speaking."† But the Society

* " Frederic von Gentz." *Edinburgh Review*, Jan. 1863.
† The present Lord Grey and Mr. C. P. Villiers, M.P., are now perhaps the only survivors of the original founders of this Society.

not having fulfilled its original purpose had become, at the time Mr. Hayward joined it, in the hands of Mr. J. S. Mill and Mr. Roebuck, a platform from which the principles of the "philosophic Radicals," as they were called, could be enunciated with safety, and win perhaps a silent approval from a sympathising audience. But the principles of the "philosophic Radicals" were currently reported to be based upon the teachings of Bentham, whose utilitarian philosophy (misunderstood at the time) was looked upon with horror and indignation by the greater portion of *fine* and respectable society. It was believed that the utilitarian principles were cold-blooded and atheistical, and were similar to those taught by the Radical school in France, which had produced what then used to be spoken of as "the horrors of the French Revolution." Previous to 1830 there prevailed in Society an intense and strong conviction that Liberalism, as it was then beginning to manifest itself, meant nothing, and could lead to nothing but a repetition in England of the French Revolution of 1789. Mr. Hayward then shared this feeling. In his 'Autobiography,' John Stuart Mill has given a description of the debates of the London Debating Society after Mr. Hayward joined it. From it we give the following extract :—

"In the session following 1826–7 things began to mend. We had acquired two excellent Tory speakers, Hayward and Shee (afterwards Serjeant Shee) ; the Radical side was reinforced by Charles Buller, Cockburn, and others of the second generation of Cambridge Benthamites : and with their and other occasional aid, and the two Tories as well as Roebuck and me for

regular speakers, almost every debate was a *bataille
rangée* between the "philosophic Radicals" and the
Tory lawyers; until our conflicts were talked about, and
several persons of note and consideration came to hear
us. This happened still more in the subsequent seasons
1828 and 1829, when the Coleridgeans, in the persons of
Maurice and Sterling, made their appearance in the
Society as a second Liberal and even Radical party on
totally different grounds from Benthamism and vehemently opposed to it; bringing into these discussions the
general doctrines and modes of thought of the European
reaction against the philosophy of the 18th century;
and adding a third and very important belligerent party
to our contests, which were now no bad exponent of the
movement of opinion among the most cultivated part of
the new generation. Our debates were very different
from those of common debating societies, for they
habitually consisted of the strongest arguments and
most philosophic principles which either side was able to
produce, thrown often into close and *serré* confutations
of one another."

This extract clearly shows not only the character of
the debates, but also the influence Mr. Hayward at once
acquired in their course amongst those whose mental
attainments have since become more widely known and
acknowledged than his own.

Moreover, his connection with the London Debating
Society brought him into contact with some of the most
aspiring and philosophic young lawyers of the day. For
the past thirty years, England had ringing in its ears the
sounds of the mighty crashings of falling states, and the
yet mightier attempts at giving birth to new ones.
Right, and no longer custom, precedent, and statute,
was now coming to be regarded as the foundation upon

which all laws should rest, and the study of natural law, so long disregarded by English lawyers, was beginning to attract their attention. The result of this study was to create in many earnest and able minds, a strong desire for the complete reform of English law and procedure. Lord (then Mr.) Brougham's famous speech on Law Reform, in April 1828, promoted among some of the younger lawyers an impulse in the direction he indicated, which immediately led to the establishment of the *Law Magazine, or Quarterly Review of Jurisprudence.*

It was in June 1828, that the first number of that journal was published, under the joint editorship of Mr. W. F. Cornish and Mr. Hayward; when the fifth number appeared Mr. Hayward had become sole editor, a position which he occupied until June 1844. During his connection with the magazine, he undertook the task of reviewing the Reports presented by the Commissioners appointed for the Reform of the Laws, as they successively appeared. "To supply materials for a comparative estimate of the English system of jurisprudence, he also compiled accounts of the codes, courts, and procedure, civil and criminal, of several leading European and Transatlantic states." Under Hayward's editorship the *Law Magazine* obtained more than a European reputation by the brilliancy of its biographical articles, and its essays on commercial law, and legal subjects of passing interest. Mr. Hayward's editorial duties, moreover brought him in contact with many foreign jurists, and with none more than with that celebrated band who were congregated at Göttingen. Frederick Charles von Savigny, a jurist of great reputation, one of this band,

had in 1815 published a tract entitled 'Of the Vocation
of our Age for Legislation and Jurisprudence,' in which
he asserted that all law should be founded on "natural
right." This tract was republished about twelve years
later, and Mr. Hayward having come across it in his
editorial researches, was so much struck by it that he
determined to translate it into English, for the benefit
of those who, though interested in "the great edifice
of general jurisprudence," were unacquainted with the
German tongue. His translation, which appeared in
June 1831, and was very well received, made no small
stir in legal circles, and attracted the attention of the
lawyers to the scholarly and earnest reformer in their
midst. The success his translation had won him at
home perhaps prompted him to visit Göttingen itself in
the same autumn, and armed with his letters of introduction, and in the guise of a staid professor learned in the
jurisprudence of England, he presented himself to and
was received with enthusiasm by his brethren of
Göttingen. Evidently impressed with the interest at-
taching to his visit, Mr. Hayward kept a journal while
he was at Göttingen, which unfortunately only now
exists in a fragmentary form, and is essentially what
follows :—

" 1831. *August* 19. *Hugo.**—English only lately become
fashionable. When Hugo first began, no one hardly
knew it. Hugo, in illustration of Hegel's obscurity, told
me that on his giving a toast at a dinner at Berlin the
toast-master declared himself unable to repeat it, as he
did not understand it.

" *August* 21. *Sunday.*—Went to church with Hugo, sat

* J. R. Ritter Hugo, professor of law.

in the Professor's seat ; only Blume * and Gans † there.
Hugo talked during the beginning of the service—women
separated from the men, and exceeded them in number
by three-fourths. All the service sung, except the sermon.
Received a call from Huren ‡—like a Frenchman of the
old school—found he had not got Mackintosh's § History ;
never heard the name of Macaulay.

"Dined at the *table d'hôte*—music (very good) during
dinner—amongst other things beef and pears together for
dinner. Blumenbach ‖ talked about craniology, seemed
to admire Spurzheim ¶ but not Gall—said it was great
folly to attempt to tell character—the book on his table
was Elliotson's translation of himself, which he said contained a good *résumé* of craniology.

"Supped with Hugo, talked a good deal with Eichhorn**
about law reform ; at supper sat next to Hugo and
Boeckh, who gave me some particulars of the German
Universities, amongst others that the Crown Prince of
Bavaria had been there. The professors talked mostly
amongst themselves in German. There was no general
conversation, the supper very good, the wine excellent,
hock, burgundy, champagne, roasted ducks, crabs, beef or
veal, an excellent [   ] †† and a large bowl of ice carried
round till it was empty—it came three times to me.

* Friedrich Blume, professor of jurisprudence.
† Gans, Edward, jurist, author of ' The Law of Succession in its
Historical Development.'
‡ Huren, Arnold Horman Ludwig, historian, professor of history
at Göttingen.
§ Mackintosh, Sir James.
‖ Blumenbach, Johann Friedrich, distinguished physiologist and
anatomist ; keeper of the museum at the University of Göttingen.
¶ Spurzheim, Gaspar ; and Gall, Franz Joseph ; two distinguished
phrenologists at Vienna. Elliotson, John, a distinguished physician,
mesmerist, and phrenologist.
** Eichhorn, Karl Friedrich, professor of German law at Göt-
tingen.
†† Illegible.

They all rose together about half an hour after supper. Grimm stayed nearly half an hour talking to me about English periodicals, and walked home with us. Made an appointment with him the next morning at the library, went there at half-past nine, found his brother and talked to him a good deal about bibliomaniacs. J. Grimm * came in and immediately brought me some books I wished to see. We afterwards went into the library and talked there for more than an hour, mostly on English literature ; promised to review his book, offered me a letter to Schlegel, and appointed the next morning at nine to bring it. Went to call on Müller,† found him at home and talked to him mostly in German about England and Lewis ;‡ called on Blume, talked to him about antiquities, offered to review his book, which he volunteered to send me.

"*August* 22.—Was obliged to hurry home to be ready for Hugo, who had promised to take us in his carriage. Went with him, told us something of Eichhorn's history, that he had been rather lazy in the early part of his life, and had been a captain of cavalry ; also of Blume ; talked to me of Savigny, said that he himself was the founder of the historic school, spoke of the falling off of the members of his school, said he could not account for it, took us then to the Anatomical School, the professor very polite. Hugo had never seen it, and appeared as much pleased with the novelty as a child. (The numerous contrivances for his carriage, the steps and the iron crook and the cloak, his story about his having had

---

* Grimm, Jacob Ludwig, first librarian to the University of Göttingen. He and his brother Wilhelm Karl together composed the celebrated ' Kinder- und Haus-Märchen.' In 1837 they were dismissed from Göttingen, with other professors, for protesting against the violation of the Constitution by the King of Hanover.

† Müller, Carl Ottfried, professor of archæology in the University of Göttingen.

‡ The late Rt. Hon. Sir George Cornewall Lewis, Bart.

a new cloak made to please a lady. I said his cloak would make a good history. Blume said his sofa had seen a great deal of service, having belonged to a celebrated actress. Hugo said it must be then *malhonnête.*) He expressed disappointment at our not coming to the lecture, said he had set two such nice chairs for us. Accordingly promised to come—hurried off to Blumenbach."

Here the "journal " abruptly ends.

Mr. Hayward did not see Savigny, whose tract he had translated, on this visit to Germany, but later in the year he received a letter from him in which he wrote :—

" The packet has really given me the liveliest joy, and this joy is greatly heightened by the account which my friends at Göttingen have given me of your visit, since you have left there the most favourable impression. How could I be otherwise than rejoiced when a man of earnest exertion and active spirit like you, gives an extended circulation to my views, in an elegant form, in his excellent country, which I so highly esteem. But believe me, it is not merely this selfish gratification which I feel. For a long time it has excited in me the most painful feeling, that your country, in all other branches of knowledge actively communicating with the rest of the world, should, in jurisprudence alone, have remained divided from the rest of the world, as if by a Chinese wall ; and for many years I have followed with attentive pleasure all attempts by which some few men, of a proper tone of mind, have sought to break through this wall. You now occupy a distinguished place amongst these, and thus I cannot but follow your exertions with the liveliest sympathy and the most sincere good wishes ; wholly independently of the circumstance, that you are so kindly mindful of my name

and works. Every communication which for the future
you may make to me of your labours will always be
received with the warmest interest by me. . . . Your
Magazine also has always attractions for me."

The natural outcome of his visit to Germany and
Göttingen was the desire to become better acquainted
with German literature. When Mr. Hayward was at
Göttingen, Goethe was still alive ;* and many of those
he met there were his intimate friends ; and as was then
the way with Germans of the cultivated class, they were
eager to impart to such a person as their English guest
a share of their own interest in the fame of the great
poet and his works. On his return home Mr. Hayward,
acting on a suggestion arising from a remark once made
by Charles Lamb to a friend of his—" that he had derived
more pleasure from the meagre Latin versions of the
Greek tragedians, than from any other versions of them
he was acquainted with "—set about making a translation
of Goethe's ' Faust ' into English prose for his own use.

The translation was the work of leisure hours, but as
it proceeded, the discovery of the inaccuracy and deficiency
of all previous renderings of the great poet's verse into
English, and of the injustice of the prejudices against him
that existed in the English mind, induced Mr. Hayward
to entertain the idea of giving publicity to his own
translation ; and after he had added a preface and notes,
he hoped the publication of his work would "contribute something towards the promotion of German
literature in this country, remove the very disadvan-
tageous impressions that had hitherto been prevalent of

* Goethe died on the 22nd of March, 1832.

'Faust,' and keep public opinion suspended concerning
Goethe till some poet of congenial spirit should arise,
capable of doing justice to this the most splendid and
interesting of his works." Wishing the translation should
first undergo a severe test, he circulated the first impression privately among his friends. Their criticisms
and opinions on his work were sufficiently favourable to
decide him to make the book public, which he did in
February 1833.

By this time Mr. Hayward had been called to the Bar,
and was going the Western Circuit.

In the following incident, narrated by Sir Theodore
Martin in his 'Life of Lord Lyndhurst,' we catch a
glimpse of Mr. Hayward at this period, and of the
position he held in his profession.

After adverting to Lord Brougham's chagrin at the
defeat of his Local Courts Bill by Lord Lyndhurst in
the House of Lords in 1833, Sir Theodore Martin
relates that—

" He (Lord Brougham) had drawn his chief arguments
in its favour from foreign systems of jurisprudence.
When a deputation of the principal agency firms
of London attorneys waited upon Lord Lyndhurst
to ask him to oppose the Bill, he pointed this out to
them, and told them he knew little or nothing of these
systems. On this they undertook to obtain full information for him, and at their request Mr. Abraham
Hayward, who had made a special study of foreign
systems of jurisprudence, drew up a pamphlet, of which
Lord Lyndhurst availed himself, and from which he
showed that his 'noble and learned friend had exceeded
his usual allowance of inaccuracies.' After the Bill was
thrown out, the attorneys waited upon Lord Lyndhurst

to make grateful acknowledgment for the service he
had done them, when with his characteristic generosity
he said, 'Thank Mr. Hayward—he has done it all.' "

The interest which was taken by both Germans of the
cultivated class, and the amateurs of German literature
in this country, in Mr. Hayward's translation of 'Faust,'
and the suggestions and criticisms they afforded him
on his work, induced him to contemplate publishing
a second edition of it. But before he did this he
resolved to " talk over the puzzling parts of the poem
with many of the most eminent living writers and
artists, and some of Goethe's intimate friends and con-
nexions." Accordingly in the autumn of 1833 he went
to Germany again, and was most flatteringly received by
Tieck, Von Chamisso, Franz Horn, the Baron de la Motte
Fouqué, Dr. Hitzig, Retzsch, Madame de Goethe, and
others. From them, and also from Mons. Varnhagen
von Ense, he collected suggestions and notes upon the
original poem and his own translation of it. The translation itself he found, on passing it through a most
severe ordeal, required but little correction ; but he so
profited by the many advantages at his command, that
in the end he ventured to say " that the notes to the new
edition contained the sum of all that could be asserted
with confidence as to the allusions and passages which
had been made the subject of controversy." In January
1834, the second edition was published. It at once
attracted the attention of the most eminent poets and
men of letters in this country. Southey (the " laureate "),
Wordsworth, Rogers, Allan Cunningham, Hallam, and
many others wrote to congratulate him on it ; even

Coleridge, though opposed to the notion of a prose translation of any poem, declared this one to have been done well. On all sides congratulations poured in. His old friends among "the amateurs of German literature"—George C. Lewis, the Austens, and Mrs. Jameson of the number—regarded the work as a great achievement in the cause they all had at heart, of making German literature better understood and appreciated by their countrymen. In Germany the translation was called "word true and spirit true." In later years Thomas Carlyle remarked that of the nineteen translations of 'Faust' then existing, "Hayward's was the best." And a recent writer stated that Goethe's first part of 'Faust' was his best and most straightforward work in poetry, and that "Mr. Hayward's is the best of the translations of 'Faust' for the same reason—because it is the most straightforward." * The translator's fame became noised abroad. Society became interested, and opened its ranks to welcome one who had just received the brevet of "man of letters," and the "Translator of 'Faust'" became known to many of those who helped to people that "world of elegance and ease" of which he had dreamed as he hung over his books in Mr. Tuson's library. †

For half a century longer he kept his place in it, rising gradually and by various means to enjoy "the privilege of mingling in daily and familiar intercourse with the most eminent men and women of the age, and of going at once to the fountain-head of every description of knowledge."

---

* "A French Critic on Goethe." *Quarterly Review*, Jan. 1878.
† 'Faust : a dramatic poem by Goethe, translated into English prose, with Notes.'

Little remains now to be told. The Literary Society
of Berlin made him an honorary member. Lockhart
secured him as a contributor to the *Quarterly Review,*
when he was already contributing articles to the *Foreign
Quarterly,* and to his friend Edward Lytton Bulwer's
Monthly Magazine.

The first ten years (1824–1834) of Mr. Hayward's
life in London were over. We have been able to touch
but lightly on the most interesting events of that period,
but sufficiently, we humbly hope, to illustrate the many
great qualities Mr. Hayward possessed, and to lay an
adequate foundation for the story of his after-life, which
will henceforth be almost entirely told by the letters
that passed between him and his friends.

CHAPTER II.

1834-1840.

Mr. Hayward's 'Home Letters'—His journey across the Alps—Disinclination for a seat in Parliament—His election as a member of the Athenæum and Carlton Clubs—The parties in his Temple Chambers—Letter from Mr. T. Carlyle—Description of his life in London—Letter from Mr. Gladstone—Mr. Lockhart—Mr. Hayward's articles on Lord Durham's Canadian policy—Position of Lord Melbourne's Government—Visit to Paris.

MR. HAYWARD'S Correspondence commences with the letter narrating his journey across the Alps in the autumn of 1834. It is followed by one to his sisters—the first of that series of 'Home Letters' which constitutes the chief record of his life during the next five years.

These 'Home Letters' are very numerous, for Mr. Hayward kept up a frequent correspondence with his family; only a few, however, have been selected, but sufficient, we think, to give a concise and continuous account of his life during this period. It is a peculiar and interesting fact that the Hayward family possessed all things in common, and many passages in the letters fully reveal this to have been the case. The only things Mr. Hayward ever concealed were his personal disappointments and vexations, and whenever the re-

velation of these became inevitable, it was made in so
tender and considerate a manner that his family never
realised the full extent of the annoyance.   No man was
ever more loyal to home ; no one ever performed the
duties of son and brother more thoroughly or more
agreeably.   So solicitous was he for the happiness and
welfare of his sisters, that his sympathy, advice and
help were always at their command.   He was constantly
thinking of what would give them pleasure.   In his letters
home he takes care to mention those things, about himself and affairs in general, which he supposes it will
interest them to know.   Thus he relates his election to
the Athenæum and Carlton Clubs ; he writes concerning
the men and women he met in society, their parties to
which he went and those to which they came at his own
chambers in the Temple.   Occasionally he refers to the
feeling in society on some political question, deprecating
at the same time all personal interest in politics, and
stating his belief that, even if it were possible for him
to be returned for Parliament, a seat in the House of
Commons would be only a drawback.   Here and there
he touches lightly upon his professional doings, while
he dwells with evident satisfaction upon the success of
his articles in the *Quarterly Review.*

Mr. Hayward's account of his journey across the Alps.

Temple, Oct. 14, 1834.

I shall have much pleasure in giving you the best
account in my power of the great storm which devas-
tated the whole line of the Alps in August last, *i.e.* of
the traces left by it on my track, for I did not arrive till
it was over.

I left Zurich on the evening of the 26th August last by the *eilwagen* or mail-coach, which goes along the Lake of Zurich and over the Lake of Wallenstadt to Coire ; intending to proceed from Coire by the celebrated Splügen pass into Italy. My fellow-travellers were two young Italians, a burgess of Coire and his wife (some twenty years younger than himself), and a Pole. As these Italians play a leading part in my adventures, I may as well describe them to you at once. They were young men, about twenty-six or twenty-eight years old, obviously belonging to the cultivated class of society. Both had studied at the best Italian universities, where one had highly distinguished himself, and both were well versed in the doctrines of the civil law, which induced me to suspect that they were advocates ; but as they appeared to be objects of suspicion, if not absolutely proscribed, in Austrian Italy, I made no inquiry as to their rank and station, even when our intimacy had grown sufficient to justify it. In person and character they presented the same sort of contrast as Ravenswood and Bucklaw in the ' Bride of Lammermoor'; the one being short, stout, light-complexioned, and frank ; the other taller, slighter, dark-complexioned, regular-featured, and reserved. At the time of our encounter they were on their return from a tour of amusement in France, Germany and Switzerland. The Italians spoke French and Italian, the Coire burgess French and German, his wife German, and the Pole French. We soon got into conversation, and before breakfast-time the next morning were all of us the best friends in the world. Finding my Coire acquaintance exceedingly communicative, I availed myself of the opportunity to collect information as to my route, and learnt, to my great joy, that the road I had to travel was one of the most remarkable on the continent, and so good withal, that I could easily arrive at Milan a

day sooner than I anticipated. We were to reach Coire
the forenoon after our departure from Zurich ; I accordingly arranged in my own mind to go post the same
day to the village of Splügen, travel over the mountain
to Chiavenna on the next, and endeavour to reach Milan
by the Lake of Como on the third. Rumours, however,
had reached us, that we might possibly be detained an
hour or two by the consequences of a storm which had
just fallen with dreadful violence in our front; and about
six in the morning we received sure intelligence that the
Rhine had risen suddenly, and inundated the valley
through which we had to pass. On entering it we found
that the waters had subsided, but the bridge and several
miles of the regular road were washed away. Instead
of a change of horses, a large boat had been provided
by the postmaster, into which the bags, the baggage,
and the passengers were stowed, to be rowed or rather
shoved over to the opposite bank, not far from which
was a vehicle, by courtesy only to be denominated a
coach, for the conveyance of the bags, the baggage, and
the passengers to Coire, over some miles of road or
track never before honoured by anything of greater
dignity than a cart. And here for the first time I began
to entertain doubts of the practicability of the course I
had arranged for myself; doubts which very soon became converted into certainty. At a post-house about
six miles from Coire, we ascertained that not only the
road over the mountain, but most of the road between
Coire and the village of Splügen, was impassable : on
learning which my Italian companions also began to
look exceedingly blank. To appreciate the difficulties
of our position, you must also bear in mind the peculiar
nature of the journey.

The road winds for nearly sixty miles through a
defile or gorge, occasionally broad enough to afford
room for a village, and occasionally so narrow and

abrupt as to give rather the idea of a single mountain split in twain, than of two mountains approximating. At the bottom of the defile is a river, roaring and boiling like a cataract. When a patch of even ground presents itself, the road is formed like an ordinary road upon a plain ; when the ground is even on one side of the torrent and not upon the other, the torrent is traversed by a bridge, and the road is continued as before ; when both sides of the defile are precipitous, the road is cut into the side ; and when an insurmountable mass of rock presents itself, it is perforated. Thus you find yourself one while aloft on the side, and then again at the very bottom of the gorge, accordingly as the road ascends and descends to take advantage of the varying facilities of the ground. The bridges vary in height for the same reason ; sometimes the arch is only a few feet above the water, and sometimes it is at an elevation from which it is fearful to look down. The overhanging precipices are often capped with snow, and the edges of enormous glaciers are seen peeping over at intervals.

The storm in question was what was there called a *Wolkenbruch* (cloudbreak or waterspout). A mass of clouds, surcharged with electric matter and with rain, had been for weeks collecting along the whole range of the Alps, and came down at last, like an avalanche from the sky. It has been stated that the ensuing destruction was caused by the melting of snow and ice in combination with the rain ; but the effects were far too sudden and capricious for this solution of the phenomenon to be true. Torrents descended from precipices entirely denuded of snow ; streams poured down defiles which had no connection with glaciers ; houses were washed away on eminences which no inundation could have reached ; and so instantaneous was the rush of waters, that three workmen, engaged in roofing a shed belonging to the Splügen posthouse, were engulphed before they

could extricate themselves, though at work not fifty
paces from the posthouse, which was saved. Their
bodies were found two days after, thirty-five miles off,
in one of the branches of the Rhine; all three perfectly
naked, with the exception of half a stocking upon the
leg of one of them. It was believed that their clothes
had been rubbed off against the rocks; yet their bodies
were little mangled, and two were immediately recognised by their friends. The sites of the posthouses had
been so skilfully chosen that almost all of them had
escaped; but three-fourths at least of the cottages com-
posing the villages were ruined, and a full third of the
inhabitants of the district were missing. You may guess
the effect upon the road. In the first place, forty-three
bridges (to the best of my recollection) were gone; and
at every point where the waters had descended from the
precipice, a large chasm in the road had been the consequence. Rocks, too, as big as houses, had rolled into
the pass, which in parts was so completely buried that it
looked as if a whole mountain side had broken on it;
whilst the water, swelling over and so clearing the
obstruction, presented many new, and what in other
countries would be called remarkable cascades.

I have anticipated a little, to make you aware of the
full extent of our difficulties. I must now request you
to return with me to Coire. Here all, of course, was
confusion and uncertainty; neither of the regular
couriers had yet arrived, but rumours were hourly
coming in of the wildest and most startling description.
So far from the convulsion being over, huge masses were
still tumbling from the precipices, and a village not a
league from Coire had that very morning received
warning of its fate, from the incipient trembling and
crumbling of the mountain at its side.

It was so obviously the innkeeper's interest to detain
us, and Swiss innkeepers are such notorious disregarders

of honesty and truth, that after listening attentively to all he had to say about the matter, I sallied forth to collect information for myself. I repaired in the first instance to the courier, whose duty it was to start on the next day but one for Italy. From him I learnt that there was much less of exaggeration than I had suspected in the accounts ; that it was really a service of some risk and great uncertainty, but that he should set out on foot at the appointed time, with the best guides that were to be had, and should highly esteem the honour and advantage of my company.

On my return to the inn I found my Italian fellow-travellers joined by one of their countrymen, who, it seems, had been driven to take refuge in Switzerland from the tyranny of Austria, and was now hovering about the frontier in order to communicate as frequently as possible with his friends. I have seldom seen a person whose manners and address upon a short acquaintance were more pleasing than this gentleman's. He declined telling me his real name, as well he said for my sake as his own ; but finding that we had more than one intimate friend in common, we soon struck up an acquaintance, which I earnestly hope some time or other to renew. Principally through his suggestions and aid, our plan was speedily arranged ; we agreed to start early the next morning, and advance at all events till some invincible impediment presented itself. Accordingly, about half-past six or seven A.M., we set forth. The only striking object that presented itself upon our road was the village already mentioned as on the point of being destroyed. We paused opposite to it for a few minutes, and observed the mountain as closely as we dared. It was still firm and unbroken, but a huge angle was already separated from the mass by a crack, and there was a constant though scarcely perceptible crumbling upon the sides. They told us that so soon as the furniture and the moveable part of the cottages were removed, it was intended to accelerate the fall by an explosion of gunpowder. We arrived at Thusis about eleven, and here for the first time acquired precise intelligence of the present character of the pass.

We found that the road was still passable for carriages to nearly the end of the Via Mala (about four miles from Thusis), but that for the next forty miles at least it could only be travelled by foot passengers, if at all. The postmaster, therefore, proposed to forward us in a *char-à-banc* (a peculiar kind of car) to the first breach in the road, where persons engaged by him were to be in waiting to carry our luggage and guide us to Andeer. From Andeer to the village of Splügen, which we had resolved on reaching if possible the same night, we were to proceed as we best might with such fresh guides or porters as we could procure.

We ordered dinner at Thusis, to give time for the necessary arrangements to be made. The most important regarded the luggage, and I waited in the yard to watch the proceedings of our host. I had only a light trunk, a carpet bag, and a hatbox, weighing altogether less than fifty pounds. The Italian had at least 150 pounds, including a large iron-bound trunk. After duly weighing and deliberating, it was settled, to my extreme surprise, that three men would be sufficient for the whole ; *i.e.*, that each guide was to walk seven or eight miles across torrents and along precipices with sixty or seventy pounds upon his back. I mentioned my apprehensions to the postmaster, who laughed at them ; and I afterwards learnt that the peasantry of these passes are habituated to this species of duty from youth, and that the common allotment on their smuggling expeditions, during which they take by choice the most difficult and least frequented tracks, is forty kilogrammes (eighty English pounds) a man. The Italians subsequently agreeing to leave their heavy luggage to be forwarded, two bearers only were engaged. We left Thusis after dinner in high spirits, which the view of the Via Mala excited to the highest conceivable pitch. This is at once the deepest and narrowest part of the defile, and as the road seems to hang upon the precipice, the traveller may almost fancy himself in the condition of the samphire gatherer. There is one point at which the projecting precipice is more than three thousand feet above the torrent ; and the precipice is projecting in the strict sense of the term, for a stone dropped from the summit would fall into the water at its foot. The Italians burst into a sort of ecstasy, and began apostrophising Nature and her works in a style which might have justified a sober-minded Englishman in mistaking them for mad. But not being, at that time at least, a sober-minded Englishman, I sympathised with their enthusiasm, and admired them for it. After amusing ourselves for some time with throwing stones into the gulf and calculating the depth by the time the sound of the splash took in reaching us,* we advanced to the spot at which our labours and dangers were to begin, which fortunately was a little beyond the narrowest part of the pass, or our onward progress would have been instantly at an end. The first grand obstruction had been caused by the fall of a large slice of the mountain across the road, which was completely hidden under a mass of trees, stones and rubbish, shelving down into the water and forming a precipitous bank. Here we found our

* A chamois hunter told me that the height was 3,600 feet, and that it was the highest sheer descent in Switzerland. It is stated somewhere in M. Humboldt's ' Travels ' that there is no downright precipice in Europe more than 1,200 feet high, and that the highest is in Wales. This is surely an error. Mr. Brockedon describes the mountains bordering the pass as varying between 6,000 and 8,000 feet in height.—A. H.

porters impatiently awaiting us. After assisting to brace the baggage on their backs, and arming ourselves with walking poles, we took our course along the summit of the bank, where the softness of the mould afforded a firm footing, and in a few minutes we came again into the road. The second obstruction, the loss of a bridge, was easily obviated by a plank, though, as the plank in question was a rotten and uneven one, I own I experienced some awkward sensations as I incautiously looked down from it into the abyss which I was traversing. Then, the road had led close along (indeed partly overhanging) the river, and only a strip of it, often not exceeding nine inches in breadth, remained. Again, it was washed in parts into a most wearisome description of rockiness (if I may be allowed such a term), or had been strewed over with ruins from above. But there was nothing very trying either to the muscles or the nerves, until we came in sight of Andeer, which had suffered dreadfully, though, from its standing in a comparatively open part, rather from the effects of inundation than from the direct driving and pelting of the storm. The river had swelled so high as not merely to sweep away a number of houses with their owners, but to work out a completely new current (which it retained even after the flood had completely subsided) for itself, and we found all the surviving inhabitants—men, women and children —employed in a seemingly vain effort to force it back.

We made at once for the posthouse, intending to hire fresh guides and proceed without delay. Some twenty or thirty of the villagers here collected round, out of whom we were at full liberty to choose, but the minds of all of them seemed made up on one point, to make us pay as dearly as they could. I forget the precise sum, but to the best of my recollection they demanded about two crown dollars (nearly ten shillings) a man from Andeer to Splügen, and made it a *sine quâ non* that we should increase the number of our guides or bearers to three. The distance was about nine miles, the whole way up hill. All agreed in stating that the latter part of the journey was the worst, and could not be performed without imminent danger after dusk ; and it was already past four. I therefore was for acceding, without a moment's hesitation, to their terms, and intimated my acquiescence, conditioned on my fellow-travellers' consent. Here, however, I should mention that the principal conduct of the expedition had throughout devolved almost exclusively on myself, the Italians being wholly unacquainted with German, the ordinary language of the peasantry of the eastern part of Switzerland. I was consequently obliged to translate the particulars of the treaty, when an unexpected difficulty arose. The Italians vowed that no power on earth should induce them to be guilty of such extravagance or submit to such extortion. In vain did I urge that the sun was already in the west, that we had not a minute to waste in chaffering, that money was altogether a secondary consideration in the circumstances. It might be, they said, a secondary consideration to an Englishman, but it was no secondary consideration to them ; and an altercation commenced, carried on partly through an Italian who had joined us and partly through myself as interpreters, which lasted full twenty minutes, without producing the slightest prospect of a satisfactory result. Exasperated out of all patience at what I thought the idle folly of my friends, I was more than once on the very point of parting company and proceeding by myself, when an effective mode of terminating the discussion was suggested to me. I drew the two men who had come with us from Thusis aside, and finding that they had suffered little from fatigue, promised them the full rate of pay claimed by the men of Andeer, provided they would pretend to acquiesce in the terms

proposed by my companions, and depend on me for
making good the difference. They jumped at the
proposal, and to prevent the strange Italian from blab-
bing, I hired him as the third. This fellow, however, had
the genuine bandit look, and, unless physiognomy be
all a fable, will some time or other most certainly be
hanged or decapitated. I had taken a dislike to him
from the first, and the manner in which he mingled in
the dispute was that of a man anxious rather to prolong
than to shorten it. As the price of silence, too, the
rascal insisted on my giving them one bottle of wine
before starting. I impatiently flung them a piece of
money, which I afterwards found was sufficient to buy
three, and the mistake turned out an all but fatal one.
They remained, in spite of threats and remonstrances, a
good half-hour in the *cabaret ;* and came forth at last in
a state very ill adapted for travelling amongst precipices.
When I saw the least steady take my portmanteau upon
his back, I bade it an involuntary adieu. As we left
the village, the sun was already behind the mountains,
and sundry hints were dropped amongst the bystanders
as to the foolhardy character of the attempt. We had
proceeded briskly for about a couple of miles along a
road of wild beauty, presenting few impediments though
amply marked by traces of the storm, when the only
one of our bearers who knew the road complained of
faintness and sank down against the bank. The sickness
which followed afforded the most convincing proof that
his complaint was neither more nor less than drunkenness,
and after swallowing about a quart of water, which I
administered to him in his own cap, he revived sufficiently
to resume his load ; but we were obliged to slacken our
pace to favour him, and his pale face and tottering step
kept me in constant apprehension so long as there was
light enough to look at him. But soon after it began
to darken, and just as we were fairly involved in the

most awe-inspiring portion of the pass—with vast
precipices clothed with the darkest, gloomiest and most
suspicious-looking pines on either side of us—a more
legitimate source of uneasiness (such, at any rate, we then
thought it) drove all minor causes of discomfort from
my thoughts. I was turning round to look at the
torrent, which boiled, foamed and sparkled through
the mist about a hundred feet below the level of our
track, when one of the Italians (the shorter and more
vivacious of the two) caught my arm and informed me
in a low emphatic whisper that we were betrayed :—
"That Italian scoundrel (he added) is in league to
murder us, and he has dropped behind to give the signal
to his friends. Listen!"—and sure enough the Italian
guide, who under some pretence or other had kept
constantly some twenty or thirty yards behind the rest,
shouted, and in less than half a minute the shout was
answered or reverberated from an overhanging wood
upon our left. It may have been echo, or fancy, for I
cannot conceive how anybody could have got there ;
but I intend this narrative as a record of impressions as
well as of events, and no impression was ever deeper
than mine at the moment,—that a signal had been
replied to from the height. My friends heard or believed
they heard it too, and we instantly agreed on taking
measures accordingly. We had no weapons except our
walking poles, but we were three against three, and our
guides were encumbered by their loads. So far therefore
we had the best of it, and we resolved on keeping
our advantage. We first ordered up the Italian guide,
and intimated to him, in language there was no mistaking, that no more dropping behind or shouting would
be allowed. The guides then proceeded in a row. I
took my place as often as it was practicable upon their
flank, to prevent them from communicating with one
another, and the Italians followed close, prepared to

VOL. I.   D

knock down the first man who showed the slightest symptom of insubordination or made any effort to disembarrass himself of his load.   The frequent narrow- ness of the track afforded us a great protection when once upon our guard, as every two or three hundred yards we came to passes where a single man might have stood against a troop, and a fragment of rock would have been as fatal as a shot.   Silently and anxiously we moved on till within about a league and a half of our destination, where it was understood the main risk, the precise character of which was unknown to us, was to be met.   The night was dark, neither moon nor stars were to be seen, the rain began to fall thick, and frequent gusts of wind ran moaning through the pass, when the splash of waters immediately in our front gave warning of a new description of difficulty, which I despair of describing with accuracy from the very partial view which I caught of the surrounding objects in the dark. So far as I could judge, the road had originally been raised on a prolonged bridge or causeway along the surface of some rocks, divided by torrents from each other.   The road being completely gone, we had to pass from rock to rock on planks and trees hastily laid across by the villagers ; so hastily indeed that more than one of the temporary bridges slipped and changed its resting- point as I stood upon it ; and as their height varied from six to ten feet above the water, which darted by with such headlong rapidity as often to reach the surface with its spray, a false step or the sliding of a board would probably have proved fatal.   We had three or four places of this sort to cross, besides some hundred paces of road ploughed up into holes and strewn with huge stones, into and over which we fell and tumbled pro- miscuously.   Several times I found myself up to my knees in water, and two or three times upon my face. The bed of the Dart or Teign, in a drought, would give

you a pretty accurate notion of this part of the road.
We advanced, of course, but slowly, and it was more
than half-past ten when at a turning of the gorge, a
solitary light in the distance gave token of the Splügen
Inn, and after another ten minutes' rough walking, we
were there. A few days before, this inn was the centre
of a group of cottages ; it now stood alone, and the
effect on the mind on entering was striking and startling
in the extreme. The whole lower story seems to form a
long, low, hall or vault; a staircase at the farther end
leads upwards to rooms appropriated to guests. A
number of wild-looking men were grouped about in the
gloaming ; for this vault or hall was only lighted by a
solitary lamp on the staircase, which, seen through the
vista, reminded me of Fuseli's remark on a solitary
candle in the long room in the Academy—that it looked
like a damned soul. Here at any rate, thought I, I am
at last in as wild a scene as Mrs. Radcliffe ever painted
—a bit of real, genuine, unsophisticated romance. Unfortunately for my story, though very fortunately for me,
the landlord was not in keeping with the place ; he had
nothing of the Schedoni look, but was as honest, civil,
and obliging a creature as could be wished for in a
civilised community. His chief regular customers being
refugees, he divined at once the position of my friends,
and after giving them his best advice as to crossing by
the Bernardin into Sardinia, he joined with them in
persuading me to accompany them. He represented
that the first part of the road towards Chiavenna was
altogether gone ; that on leaving his house I must
instantly strike up the mountain and take my chance of
getting round by the hunting paths, which might also
have been effaced by the storm. My friends, on the
other hand, dwelt more on the dangers of treachery, for
their path over the Bernardin was understood to present
full as many dangers of the regular description as mine.

D 2

They pressed upon me the ruined state of the canton,
which had rendered the peasantry desperate; the recent
(still uncomputed) loss of lives, amongst which an un-
friended stranger's would not be missed, and the tempting impunity afforded by a border country to crime.
The Italian guide knew of my intended route; he knew
me, moreover, to be an Englishman, and must believe me
from my comparative carelessness of money to be rich:
he had, doubtless, associates at hand or in the inn;
nothing could be more easy than to waylay me in the
pass, fling me into the first ravine, and if (which was by
no means likely) any questions were asked, escape
into Italy or say that I had tumbled from a rock.   This
association of ideas was unpleasant, but I had commenced
the adventure with my eyes open, and was now resolved
to go through with it.   The groundlessness of our late
fears considerably blunted the edge of those which my
companions showed so strong and (I verily believe)
heartfelt interest to instil, and before sitting down to
supper I had declared my definitive resolution to proceed
across the Splügen, and commissioned the landlord to
furnish me with guides.   I also took the precaution of
speaking with the guides who had come from Andeer,
and let drop, as if accidentally, that we had given up our
original intention of separating.

It was past midnight before we went to bed.   My
friends were to start at four in the morning, but as the
first part of my journey was the most difficult, I was
recommended not to attempt it before sunrise, about
five.   My bedroom was within that occupied by the
Italians; knowing, therefore, that I should unavoidably
be awakened by them, I did my best to snatch an hour
or two of sleep; but my nerves were too much shaken,
and the cold at this exalted region was intense.   In the
valleys, at the season of which I speak, the common
covering was a thin counterpane and a sheet.   A couple

of blankets and a very thick woollen counterpane had
been placed without any express direction on my part
on my bed, yet I felt almost frozen, and tried in vain to
warm myself by an accumulation of cloaks. I never
closed my eyes a moment, and when about half-past
three my companions began to be astir, I got up and
dressed myself too. We parted with sincere regret,—on
my part certainly, and I believe on theirs, though I fear
my notions of expenditure had proved rather embarrassing to them ; not that they were in the least tainted by
the silly weakness of wishing to conceal their circumstances ; economy, as they frankly owned to me, was
with them a thing of necessity, not choice, and I did my
utmost in all matters of mere personal indulgence to co-
operate with them. Still there were occasions, as in the
affair at Andeer, where we jarred. On the whole, however, we advanced, in the three days we were together,
further towards mutual esteem and friendship than we
should have done probably under ordinary circumstances
in a month ; and I thereby got rid of another large slice
of my nationality. Step by step, indeed, I have come
to the conclusion, that the cultivated classes of all nations
are essentially alike ; that the few points of contrast are
conventional and on the surface, unmarked or forgotten
in those moments of high excitement which appeal to
the imagination or call out the emotions of the heart ;
and that an Englishman of a susceptible disposition, and
tolerably comprehensive understanding, has as good a
chance of sympathising with an educated Frenchman,
German, Dutchman, Italian, Spaniard, or Pole, as with a
countryman.

My own guides were in attendance at five. One was
a Swiss chamois hunter, the other a native of the Italian
side of the Alps, who, from what I could collect, drew his
chief revenue from smuggling. The one spoke German
only, the other Italian and a little German—so little that

I was often obliged to act as interpreter between the two.
I could generally manage to make them both understand
me, but I confess I was sometimes at a loss to construe
their *patois*. Neither of them knew the track—in fact,
there was not a man in the village who did, no news
having yet arrived of the only party that had preceded
us ; but the chamois hunter professed himself to be
thoroughly acquainted with all the bearings of the pass,
and every four or five miles we were sure of coming
to huts where we could inquire. The distance to
Chiavenna by the regular road was about twenty
English miles.

The first two hundred paces of the journey were
ominous enough. Our course lay across the ruined
village, which now looked like the bed of an exhausted
torrent, strewn with tokens of the ruin it had wrought ;
clumps of thatch, beams, and building blocks being
thickly scattered amongst the stones. As we gained the
turf, the elder of my guides halted for a moment to
point out to me where his own cottage had stood, and
then led the way up the mountain through a forest of
fir-trees and pines. It was tolerably clear of underwood,
and we seldom lost traces of a path. An hour and a
half's hard walking brought us to a level with the
glaciers, amongst and supplied by which they told me
there was a small lake highly celebrated for its trout.
Though an ardent brother of the angle, I felt no inclination to fish for them, and I had much more pleasure in
watching a large herd of cattle feeding only a few
hundred feet below. Alpine cows have a peculiar tact
in clambering, and they are generally quartered during
the three summer months upon the rich patches of
verdure which occur amongst the snow. Before attempting to descend, we proceeded for about two hours along
the ridge, diving into the ravines which intersected it
and reascending as we best could—

On one occasion we walked nearly a quarter of an hour
along the bottom of a ravine up to our ankles in water ;
on another, we had to cross a chasm between two rocks
upon a tree not more than nine inches in diameter. At
length the elder guide conceiving that we had gone far
enough to head, as it were, the impracticable part of the
pass, we seized a favourable opportunity for striking
downwards, and by dint of springing, sliding, and
scrambling, won our way into the road about a mile
from the Austrian custom-house, which is situated a
little over the topmost ridge where the mountain begins
to slope towards Italy. Here, then, all the danger and
(the rest of the road being all downhill) the worst part of
the fatigue were seemingly at an end ; and as my spirits
rose with the sense of difficulties overcome, I internally
compared myself to Sancho in that celebrated adventure
of his, when, after enduring all night the worst agonies
of fear upon the supposition that he was suspended over
a bottomless abyss, he found at daybreak that his feet
were about six inches from the ground.

The custom-house officer kept me waiting for him
rather longer than was necessary, but behaved with
marked politeness when he came. He merely looked
at my passport, and took my word for the rest : that I
had no contraband commodities or prohibited books

* Manzoni, 'Adelchi.'

amongst my things. It was lucky that he did take my word for it, for I had the 'Paroles d'un Croyant,' which I had quite forgotten at the moment, in my bag. We breakfasted on bad wine, black bread, stale sausages and raw ham, at a miserable little inn about a mile within the Austrian frontier, and then walked briskly along the regular road for nearly a league and a half.

You must not suppose that we were smoothly advancing upon the road ; for I can assure you that my expectations as to the speedy termination of my labours were most lamentably disappointed. Again and again were we compelled to turn the flank of the mountains by ascending them, and four or five times we had to thread our way amongst masses of rocks precipitated into the pass, so large and so thickly scattered as to give one the notion, when fairly involved in them, of a labyrinth. These ascendings had one advantage—they varied the prospect delightfully. Thus, after watching the celebrated waterfall near Isola (more than 200 feet high) from the road, I found myself standing on the edge of the precipice from which it dashes ; and, such is the force of practice, I could watch the waters without giddiness as they fell over and hung glittering in the air. What remained of Isola and the other villages in the vale, looked from the height exactly like the houses in the cork model of a town ; so much did height and distance diminish them. We stopped twice to refresh ourselves ; and I had here a striking instance of the fair dealing and correct notions of my guides. Considering that their contract included everything, they invariably protested against my paying for them at the inns. Their rate of pay, indeed, was altogether anomalous, and only justifiable on the supposition of risk. They were to have a Napoleon apiece.

I arrived at Chiavenna about half-past five, having been about eleven hours upon my legs. I started early

the next morning for Riva, a hamlet situated at the
northern extremity of the Lake of Como, and principally
remarkable for the excessive unhealthiness of the air.
To sleep there a single night is pretty sure to bring on a
fever, and I was anxiously warned against indulging in
the shortest slumber in its vicinity. A row-boat starts
every morning from this place to communicate with the
steam-boat at Domaso. Into this I got with five or six
passengers of the lower order, after successfully resisting
an impudent attempt at imposition made by a rascally
Austrian official, who wanted me to believe that it was
his duty to search my baggage unless I paid him a five-
franc piece to go free. I repeated his intimation aloud,
and then tendered him my keys. A search, in fact,
was a matter of perfect indifference to me, for my bag
and portmanteau were very loosely packed, and (having
thrown away my 'Paroles d'un Croyant' at Chiavenna,
for fear of accidents) I knew that he could not detain me
above ten minutes at the most. At the same time I
produced my passport, *visé* by the Austrian ambassador
and countersigned upon the frontiers. My gentleman
looked the very picture of confusion, stammered out
something about not wishing to give trouble, and slunk
away. The same trick was tried with similar success at
Domaso, at Como, and at Milan,—in short, wherever, as
it seemed to me, a change of conveyance took place
within view of any fellow in uniform. Yet such is the
all-pervading influence of corruption and tyranny, that
it would be highly impolitic to resist in any case ; so
that if you have anything that can be called contraband,
and the head official of any post, however petty, insists
on searching, you should bribe.

I arrived at Domaso at nine ; breakfasted there on
lake trout, peaches, grapes, and figs ; went on board the
steamboat at eleven ; reached Como, which lies at the
other extremity of the lake, about five ; got into the

diligence, which was in waiting for the steamboat passengers, immediately, and arrived at Milan a little before eleven. A singular incident occurred to me on reaching the Hotel Reichmann, to which I had been recommended.

On the way from Como a young German and myself had got into conversation about the professors of the University of Berlin, where he had just completed his studies. We had been talking a great deal in particular about Raumer the historian, Hegel the metaphysician, and the celebrated law professor Gans, with whom I was personally acquainted. My new acquaintance had engaged rooms in the same hotel, which as usual was crowded to excess. As we stood talking with the porter, three or four gentlemen entered, and the German turning round exclaimed to me: " Why, there is Professor Gans himself!" Gans sure enough it was, and our meeting was cordial in proportion to its unexpectedness. What adds to the strangeness of the coincidence—Gans and a friend, with two or three others, formed the party who had preceded me across the Splügen, though our routes, as it struck me on comparison, differed much. Some variation was to be expected, as they had travelled exclusively by day. He subsequently introduced me to Raumer, who was also by an odd accident at the hotel.

About ten days intervened before I was again traversing the Alps; but it is not my intention to trouble you with what I witnessed in the interval. I despair of giving the interest of novelty to a description of the cathedral, opera-house, pictures, entrances and promenades of Milan; but Manzoni is personally so very little known to Englishmen, that I am tempted to give you a slight sketch of my interview with him.

Before leaving England, I sought in vain, through the whole round of my friends, for some one who could put me in relation with Manzoni. No one, duly qualified

in this matter, was to be found ; not even amongst
his warmest travelled admirers, not even amongst the
literary men who have made Italian literature their
peculiar study, was a single person personally acquainted
with him discoverable.   I was a little more successful on
my journey ; for a friend at Frankfort gave me a note to
one of Manzoni's most intimate friends, and the Italian,
whom I met at Coire entrusted me with a complimentary
communication to his son.   I was also not totally without a pretence for addressing him, having mentioned
him in a note to my translation of ' Faust.' Unfortunately
both friend and son were absent, and Manzoni himself
was at his country-house at Brussiglio, a village about
six miles from Milan ; so, much against my inclination,
I was driven to the last resource of sending a copy of my
translation, with a note expressing the highest admiration
of his genius, detailing the disappointments I had experienced in my efforts to approach him in the regular
way, and intimating a humble wish that he would suffer
me to dispense with the ceremony of an introduction.
His answer was couched in a studied tone of cold politeness, rather implying than expressing the permission I
had sought, and my *amour propre* being wounded to the
quick, I resolved, by Gans and Raumer's advice, merely
to drive over and leave my card at Brussiglio.   I did so,
and was driving off again, when the servant came hurry-
ing out with his master's most earnest request that I
would alight ; a request with which I need hardly add I
very readily complied.   I followed the servant through a
hall and ante-chamber into a receiving room, where I
found Manzoni by himself.   He advanced to meet me
with flattering *empressement*, mingled with a little graceful
confusion, as he anticipated my apologies by elegantly
apologising for his note.   His daughter (the Marchesa
Azeglio, the wife of the author of ' Ettore Fieramosca,' I
believe) had been taken dangerously ill the day my letter

arrived, and between a conscious unfitness to welcome a
stranger under such circumstances and an unwillingness
to repel, he had blundered out a reply which he had
since begun to fear must be thought exceedingly rude.*
Before mentioning the little I can recall of our conversation, I will try to describe his personal appearance for
you.

Manzoni is about the middle height and size, with an
oval face inclining to length, regular features, and dark
hair plentifully sprinkled with grey. His age must be
about forty-five, but he is a young looking man for that
age. There is a touching expression of melancholy in
his look and voice, and nothing can be softer or more
fascinating than his smile. He instantly led the conversation to Goethe, expressing in particular the highest
admiration of ' Faust,' but avowing a conviction, that the
problem started at the commencement was one beyond
the author's capacity, or any man's capacity, to solve.
He then talked of Goethe's dramas, when I ventured to
express a doubt whether Goethe's genius, with all its
universality, could effectively adapt itself to the stage.
He said that he gave the preference to Schiller in this
respect, and cited ' Maria Stuart ' and ' Don Carlos.' Here
we coincided; but I told him an Englishman could
hardly be expected to sympathise with the enthusiasm
of a people like the Germans, just struggling into liberty,
for the character of the Marquis von Posa.† What he

* Manzoni's general unwillingness to receive strangers, particularly Englishmen, is sufficiently accounted for by the watchful
jealousy of the Austrian government, who, if he received company
like Tieck at Dresden, or Sismondi at Geneva, would probably
withdraw his permission of residence. He made no political
allusion of any sort during our interview.—A. H.

† I saw ' Don Carlos ' acted at the Frankfort theatre in the
autumn of 1833, and the effect produced by the character of von
Posa was astonishing. Almost every sentiment he uttered elicited
a cheer.—A. H.

says to Philip is all very fine and true, but about as new
to a grown man as Mentor's advice to Telemachus. I
mentioned the popularity acquired by Lessing's 'Nathan
the Wise' in consequence of the doctrines of religious
toleration taught in it, as a parallel instance of popularity
arising from time and circumstance. This led him into
a series of reflections, beautifully expressed and illustrated,
upon the manner in which works of real genius often
acquire fame by their defects,—at any rate by their
exciting and (so to speak) vulgar qualities, rather than
by loftiness of imagination or depth of thought. As a
kind of corollary to the argument, he half in earnest
avowed it to be his creed, that, as society became more
enlightened, it would tolerate no such thing as literature
considered merely as a creation of art. On my asking
him if he did not think we should always have romances,
he said he saw no reason for excepting them ; the soil,
he added, was already in a state of exhaustion. I told
him I had been with two other Englishmen to the
Borromean library solely in consequence of the mention
made of the founder in 'I Promessi Sposi' ; but he shunned
the allusion, and I saw or fancied I saw a symptom or
two of the Byronic aversion to be viewed as an author.
He spoke a little of Victor Hugo, and expressed great
admiration for Scott, whose death he said had unfortunately prevented their meeting as he had anticipated.
He does not read English, and avowed an almost total
unacquaintance with our living writers. The author of
'Pelham' was not even known to him by name ; which,
considering Mr. Bulwer's extraordinary continental celebrity, is perhaps the strongest instance that can well be
given of Manzoni's indifference regarding England and
the English.*

* Many instances of the same sort of indifference on the part
of other distinguished foreigners have occurred within my own
private knowledge. When M. de Schlegel arrived in England in

This is a rude outline, but it is all I have retained. The general impression was in the highest degree favourable. The interview lasted about an hour and a half, during which I twice rose to depart, but was detained by him. He evidently converses from fulness of mind and excitability, without any anxiety for display. Indeed he has never been at the trouble of acquiring conversational fame, and is therefore not embarrassed by having any of that sort to support.

I left Milan, to return by the Simplon, on September 7th. Here again all regular travelling was at a stand, and I could only engage a place to Arona. I arrived there in the evening, and had the gratification of seeing a sunset on the Lago Maggiore, which I coasted the next morning by sunrise on my way to Domo d'Ossola, with the Borromean Isles full in view. The unusual warmth of the summer had made the vines more than

---

the spring of 1832, he had never heard of Mr. Macaulay, then in the very zenith of his fame as a speaker and writer ; and M. Charles Dupin, the author of the 'Commercial Power of Great Britain,' had never heard of Mr. Babbage's 'Book on Manufactures,' four months after its publication—a book now translated into every language of the Continent. Again, in an interview I had with Say, the political economist, a few months before his death, I asked him what he thought of Dr. Whately's 'Lectures.' He said the very name was new to him, yet the book was at that very moment in his bookcase, with "*from the Archbishop of Dublin*" inscribed upon the title-page. I picked it out and showed it to him myself, but he had evidently never looked beyond the title page, if so far.

Mr. Bulwer's reputation is highest in Germany, where I have seen critical journals giving him the preference to Scott. But he has forfeited some portion of their favour by his preface to ' The Last Days of Pompeii,' in which he incautiously assumes that no writer has ever yet succeeded in that species of fiction to which his last work belongs ;—forgetting Wieland, forgetting too, as I verily believe, the author of ' Valerius.' The romance itself will certainly not operate in diminution of his fame.—A. H.

ordinarily fertile, and the grapes were hanging in festoons
from tree to tree in the orchards and hedges, and
occasionally across the road ; giving to this northern
angle of Italy, for the season, all the rich glowing
luxuriance of the still more genial climates of the south.
One error, most studiously disseminated by the authors
of tours and guide books, I must notwithstanding take
the freedom to note.   It is not true that the rich plains
of Italy break suddenly upon the traveller descending
southwards from the Alps ; the defiles widen so very
slowly that the effect of contrast never comes upon you
by surprise, and you travel thirty or forty miles after
crossing the summit before the effect in question ever
comes upon you at all.   The descent from the Jura
range into Switzerland from France is far finer in this
respect.

The only serious damage on the southern side of
Domo d'Ossola was the destruction of the fine bridge
six miles from the town.   On the northern side, about
twenty miles of road were injured much in the same
manner as the Splügen road, though the damage was
neither so frequent nor so formidable.   Domo d'Ossola,
however, was only saved by a wall from being washed
away by the inundation, and there was a village, or
rather town, in a neighbouring valley, where more than
a hundred and fifty people were destroyed.   I had made
up my mind to turn pedestrian again, but so many
workmen (2,000 I was told) had been set to work in
filling up chasms and clearing away obstructions, that
the very morning of my arrival the road was declared
practicable for cars, and I enjoyed the honour of being
the second to pass in one.   We alighted at all the rough
places, and the workmen lifted the car over two of the
worst.   At the village of Simplon I found the regular
diligence in waiting : and I started in it for Geneva so
soon as the courier from Milan, whom I had preceded by

about two hours, arrived, accompanied by an English
gentleman homeward bound like myself. We got to
Brigg before dark, and consequently saw the whole pass
by daylight ; but after the Splügen the wildest parts of
it looked tame ; nor do I believe that any one who had
seen both under similar circumstances would ever dream
of instituting a comparison between the two. Nothing
very striking occurred to us on the road, nor shall I
request your attention to Geneva and its lake, though
gemmed round with objects of interest,—the castle of
Chillon, the rocks of Meillerie, the château of Ferney,
the house where Gibbon put the finishing hand to his
history, and that where Byron and Shelley, with the
author of 'Frankenstein,' had resided for a time. It also
still boasts a first-rate European celebrity in J. C. L. de
Sismondi, the admired historian of nations and of literature. At one of his delightful soirées I had the good
fortune to meet the Countess Guiccioli, who has been
described so very often that I shall hardly be called
indiscreet for stating the impression she made upon
myself,—the rather that I never heard her fairly appreciated but by Lady Blessington.

I had been relating some anecdote about Nicolini or
Manzoni to Madame de Sismondi, which she requested
me to repeat to the Countess —— (I did not catch the
name) ; and directly afterwards I found myself seated
by the side of a lively, coquettish-looking woman, with
handsome, expressive features, gold-tinted hair a little
inclining to auburn, a complexion of dazzling fairness,
and, what no one will I am sure deny to her, the plumpest,
firmest, and whitest of busts. Her posture whilst sitting
prevented me then from forming an opinion of the lower
part of her figure, which does not keep the promise of
the rest.

We began upon Italian novels, and I was quite
delighted with the acuteness and justness of her observa-

tions, as I passed in review before her 'I Promessi Sposi,' 'La Monaca di Monza,' 'Ettore Fieramosca,' 'Luisa Strozzi,' &c. &c., for the express purpose of eliciting her criticisms. She was evidently in the habit of thinking for herself, and was nothing daunted by authority. Thus she made no scruple of avowing an opinion that 'I Promessi Sposi' is occasionally very wearisome, and I fancy many readers would avow the same opinion if they dared. She also hit off with unerring precision the parts in ' Ettore Fiera-mosca ' which are too palpably imitated from ' Ivanhoe.' We imperceptibly wandered into sentiment, in which my companion appeared thoroughly at home. You may believe the deceitful character of her appearance by candlelight, when I tell you that, on her remarking that there was nothing worth living for after twenty-five for women nor after thirty-five for men, I hinted that she must have at least three years of happiness to come. She was married at sixteen, and her intimacy with Lord Byron commenced soon after, but she is certainly past thirty. The conversation commenced in French, but on finding that I could follow her in Italian, she adopted it, saying playfully that she could not be *spirituelle* in any other language; and indeed it is hardly ever possible to express the fine shadings of thought (*les nuances de la pensée*) in any language but one's own. All this time I was not aware that I was monopolising the lioness of the night ; and when I was called away to be presented to a foreign jurist of celebrity, I thought it a great bore, and availed myself of the first excuse to steal away to the sofa on which the Contessa was enthroned. On returning to my hotel, I mentioned these impressions to a friend ; and it was not until the next morning that, calling at Madame de Sismondi's, I learnt that my fascinating unknown was the Guiccioli. She was lodging at the Hotel des Bergues with her younger brother Count Gamba. The English who met her at the public table there did not seem to be so much struck with her, and complained of boldness and affectation. But great allowance must be made for her singular position in society, which may well prevent her feeling quite at ease amongst Englishwomen ; and it is hard to condemn the manners of a foreigner for not according with a purely conventional standard of our own.

I merely mention my trip with —— to Chamouni for the sake of mentioning a singular encounter on the way. At St. Martin, where all regular travelling terminates, we found Sir John Bayley, the ex-judge, who, at the age of seventy-four, had just been up the mountain in a car ; he seemed delighted with everything, and begged us to tell his legal friends that he was as well and as happy as they could wish. He had been two days at the inn, where the *ancien magistrat* (as they called him) had become a universal favourite by the kindness of his manners, and the facility with which he accommodated himself to the unavoidable inconveniences of such an expedition.

I had my usual luck in getting acquainted with interesting people on my way back by Lausanne, Berne, Basle, Strasburg, and Paris ; but having now fulfilled the peculiar object of my letter, I conclude.

Ever most truly yours,

A. HAYWARD.

To his Sister.

Temple, Dec. 11, 1834.

I send you my tour or trip at last. Most of it was written at the Inns on my return, but I have been so much occupied that I had no time to print it before. I send you a copy for your drawing-room, and one for use.

I begin to fear it will not be in my power to visit you

at Christmas.   The fact is I have had three briefs in the
last ten days, which have kept me waiting the whole days
in Court.   The consequence is I am behindhand in
other things and shall not be able to spare a week,
and it is not worth while to travel a hundred and thirty
miles for less.   Lethbridge wants me to go to Oxford
with him (he is fellow of All Souls), but I doubt whether
I can even do that.   I dine with Merivale to-day to see
his bride—pretty, they tell me.   Hobhouse is standing
for Aylesbury with a good chance—so he will soon have
franks of his own.   Twiss is gone off to Bridport, contrary to my express advice.   He will simply make a
fool of himself, and spend more money than he can
afford.   Many of my other friends are making fools of
themselves in the same way.   If they get in they won't
stay in, for I think this Ministry * extremely uncertain.
I am told they would give me a place if I chose to risk a
contest for any of the numerous places that are invoking
Conservative candidates, but I would not accept a seat
in Parliament if I could have it for the asking ; nor do I
think it of any use to any man who has not a large independent fortune.   No one young man of my set has made
anything by it but Macaulay, and he is in India.   It is
all vanity and vexation of spirit, and so they will find
out ere long.

Scarlett has just sent me a sort of message to request
the honour (!) of my acquaintance.   As he is as proud as
the devil, and to be Chief Baron and Peer immediately,
this is no bad sign.   We are to meet, I fancy, at Lady
Blessington's, where all the wits and lords of all parties
come together.

* On the dismissal of Lord Melbourne's Ministry by the King,
Sir Robert Peel and the Duke of Wellington formed an Administration.   Parliament was dissolved almost immediately afterwards
(the 30th of December), and shortly after the assembly of the new
Parliament in the following February the Peel Ministry fell.

N.B.—Manzoni, mentioned in my journey, is the chief novelist and dramatic writer of Italy. Guiccioli is the far-famed lady-love of Byron.

Feb. 23, 1835.

I have a pressing invitation from the fellows of Trinity, Cambridge, to spend a few days to meet Sedgwick, Whewell, Thirlwall and Peacock, &c., who are said to form one of the most intellectual societies in the kingdom, and I shall endeavour to go if I can. All goes well with me in law, literature and society. I dine to-day with Baron James Parke, to-morrow with Gurney, who comes the Western Circuit ; and last Thursday I dined with Lord Abinger, so that you see I stand well with the Judges at all events. On the 17th also I received the high honour of being elected a member of the Athenæum Club.*

July 3, 1835.

I am now a regular member of the best London society—by which I do not mean the highest in mere rank—but that which includes all the most distinguished politicians, lawyers, poets, painters, men of science, wits, &c., along with the most enlightened of the aristocracy. I go little to balls, which are too late ; and not very much to dinners, except on Saturdays and Sundays, because I am often engaged in business till nine ; but I can spend every evening in the pleasantest parties if I like, and I do spend a good many so. I dine to-morrow with the celebrated Countess of Cork— aged ninety-two—the friend of Johnson and all the wits of his time. She has all her faculties unimpaired and gives three evening parties a week, to which all her

---

* Under Rule VI., which empowers the Committee (if unanimous) to elect " a limited number of persons of distinguished eminence in science, literature, or the arts, or for public services."

friends go as they like. Sydney Smith has given me
a pressing invitation to spend a day or two at his
living * in Somerset, whilst on the circuit. There is
an article † of mine in the forthcoming *Quarterly* which
will make some stir. It is on cookery and dinner-
giving. I cannot fix the precise day of my coming to
you, but I think I shall start on the 10th. Love to all.

Sept. 22, 1835.

I returned last night. I have been through places
and with people which it would take a week to describe
—Manchester, Liverpool, Birmingham, Preston, Leamington, Dublin, Belfast, Glasgow, Edinburgh, the Highlands, the Hebrides, the Scotch and English lakes, and
heaven knows what besides, and in the course of my
journey I have mixed a good deal with several of our
most distinguished characters.

Whilst in Ireland I went with Babbage, Whewell, and
the Dean of the College, on a three days' excursion
through the county of Wicklow. At Edinburgh I saw
a good deal of Dr. Chalmers and Professor Wilson, the
famed editor of *Blackwood*, with several others ; and in
Westmoreland I was received with great kindness by
Wordsworth, Southey, and Captain Hamilton, the writer
on America, and author of 'Cyril Thornton.' I stayed
a day at Leamington with Dr. Lardner, and after seeing
Warwick Castle, Kenilworth and Stratford, returned
home through Oxford.

Temple, March 29, 1836.

I have taken a fresh set of chambers looking up the
river, and am fitting them up with all speed ; they com-
bine everything necessary for a bachelor residence, and
as my fate seems pretty well fixed I shall fit them up

* Combe Florey.
† "Gastronomy and Gastronomers ;" *Quarterly Review*, No. 107.

handsomely: deep red for the sitting-room. They are at 11, King's Bench Walk,* and Hook, on my telling him, applied Cibber's lines on Lord Mansfield :—

> " Persuasion tips his tongue whene'er he talks,
> And he has chambers in the King's Bench Walk."

I have been elected at the Carlton Club†—one of fifty selected from three hundred and twenty candidates, which adds not a little to my influence and connection. As regards politics, Conservatism now implies merely upholding the present form of government of King, Lords, and Commons, and leaves us open to every other description of reform.

The popularity of my last article‡ is quite inconceivable. It encounters me everywhere, and it is vain that I declare my indifference to eating compared with other matters. The fact is I got up that article just as I would get up a speech from a brief, and I would not eat half the things mentioned in it if they paid me for it. What, for instance, do I know practically of salads? But everything comes from the best London authorities, each of whom I consulted, and most amusing it was to examine them.

Mr. Hayward's new chambers were soon "warmed" by one of those delightful parties, the memory of which maybe still haunts their sombre stillness and lonely tenant.

* Hayward resided in these chambers until he left them for those in St. James's Street.

† His proposer was Lord Stuart de Rothesay, and his seconder Sir Fred. Pollock, M.P. Mr. Hayward took his name off the Club on Dec. 26, 1870.

‡ "Walker's original," *Quarterly Review*, No. 110. This article, together with the previous one, "Gastronomy and Gastronomers," was the foundation of his 'Art of Dining,' published by Mr. Murray.

"They used to include, perhaps three, sometimes perhaps only two, of the loveliest and most gifted women that
London society boasted ; and of men, perhaps about five.
You might meet Lockhart (always less scornful than his
beautiful features proclaimed him), or Macaulay, or
Sydney Smith, or Lord Lansdowne, or Henry Bulwer,
or (when the Peelite times came), Sidney Herbert and
Graham, and the lawless, engaging, George Smythe ; but
feeling the value of novelty, he also would sometimes
provide a new, and perhaps a young hero, a man perhaps
great on the Continent, though hardly as yet known to
London. The chambers were far from large, but there
was one, stern with yellowish law-books, that could be
playfully called the drawing-room ; another reserved for
the dinner ; and this last room, having been furnished
with what at Oxford and Cambridge is called a 'Buttery
Hatch,' the business of waiting was made as quiet as
possible, so as not to interfere with the talking. By
taking unbounded pains—and *that*, after all, is the secret
—Hayward made it a certainty that, however unpretentious his dinners, the food and the wine should be the
best of their kinds. Remembering that he was a host,
Hayward used not to speak at these dinners so much as
he did elsewhere ; and knowing that some of his guests
had come anxious to hear a full sample of some celebrated man's conversation, he would help to give them
what they most sought, would carefully open a channel
for the torrent of Sydney Smith's wit, or—not perhaps
always so willingly—consent to 'give Macaulay his head.'
George Smythe once desiring to know whether he who
was so great in soliloquy could also perhaps converse, laid
hold of a momentary opening, and then, all at once,
flung a paradox across the dinner-table at the head of
Macaulay, saying boldly that tobacco had done more for
the human race than intellect. Macaulay was not a wit,
but his answer, if a little too ponderous for so bright a

society, was at all events ready. 'You prefer,' he said, 'a cow ruminating to Plato philosophising;' and then having regained what in Parliament they call the 'possession of the house,' he went on to make use of his ownership."*

Writing to a friend, James Smith (one of the authors of the 'Rejected Addresses') mentions a dinner at Mr. Hayward's chambers in May, 1836.

"Our dinner-party yesterday, at Hayward's chambers in the Temple, was very lively. Mrs. Norton was dressed in pink, with a black lace veil ; her hair smooth, with a knot behind, and a string of small pearls across her forehead. Hook was the lion of the dinner-table ; whereupon I, like Addison, did 'maintain my dignity by a stiff silence.' An opportunity for a *bon-mot*, however, occurred, which I had not virtue sufficient to resist. Lord Lyndhurst mentioned that an old lady, an acquaintance of his, kept her books in detached bookcases, the male authors in one, and the female in another. I said I suppose her reason was, she did not wish to add to her library."

Mr. Smith is not quite accurate. The joke was made by Lord Lyndhurst ; the story of Madame Genlis's prudery, which gave rise to it, was told by Mr. Hayward.

It was to this dinner Mr. Hayward had asked the celebrated Sydney Smith, whose final refusal was couched in the following terms.

* "Mr. Hayward," by T. H. S. Escott. *Fortnightly Review*, March 1884.

The Rev. Sydney Smith to Mr. Hayward.

33 Charles Street, Berkeley Square,
May 18, 1836.

MY DEAR SIR,

There is no more harm in talking between 11 and 1 than between 9 and 11. The Temple is as good as Charles Street. The ladies are the most impregnable, and the gentlemen the most unimpeachable of the sex, but still I have a feeling of the wickedness of supping in the Temple, my delicate and irritable virtue is alarmed, and I recede.

Ever yours,
SYDNEY SMITH.

To his Sisters.

Hôtel d'Angleterre, Boulogne,
Aug. 17, 1836.

I have been looking about for an opportunity of writing to you for the last four days, and found none till to-day. I was only a night in town, and had not a moment to spare. As to myself, I am here very comfortably settled and working away for the *Quarterly.* The Lockharts are here, and several other pleasant people whom I know—amongst others, Mrs. ——. I met her last night on her way to a Methodist Chapel, to which she invited me to accompany her. The vulgar English are rather amusing, and there are enough of them in all conscience. One old fat woman confided to me this morning that she had lost her purse in landing. I could not help saying, with great appearance of interest, that I earnestly hoped she had saved money enough to take her back; and she said she had a ten-pound note in her stays. It is uncertain when (if at all) I shall go to Paris, for I expect the Frenchmen I wish to see here.

I handed over your letter to Tom* that he might execute your commission, so that I do not know whether there is anything requiring a particular answer from me. The Preserves all arrived safe and are very welcome—but I have only had one party since we met, and hardly know when I shall have another. I don't know what you mean by our kindness. Why, I am afraid we were rather remiss than otherwise; but I do assure you that we were very proud of you both.† I had a long chat with Mrs. Norton last week. She looked very pale and thin, and is now at Frampton.‡ The poem called 'A Voice from the Factory' is by her. On Sunday I saw Miss Martineau and Mrs. Butler (Fanny Kemble that was), who are just returned from America, of which Miss Martineau is on the point of publishing an account.

Mr. Thomas Carlyle to Mr. Hayward.

5, Cheyne Row, Chelsea,

MY DEAR SIR,   Wednesday, [January 11, 1837.]

Certain kind friends are very urgent with me to set about giving a short course of lectures on German literature in the Albemarle Street Institution; that is the thing for me, they say, &c. &c. Without saying yes or no, I determine to ask about it a little. Remembering that you once took me there, I suppose you to be a member; and knowing what otherwise I know, it seems to me I can inquire of no one so fitly as of you. Will you tell me, therefore, something about the conditions and arrangements of such a business in that Institution?

* His brother, Mr. Thomas Hayward.
† This letter was written after his sisters had been paying a visit to London.
‡ Frampton Court, near Dorchester, the seat of her brother, R. Brinsley Sheridan, Esq.

How you get liberty to deliver a course there ; whether you fancy liberty were easily procurable for me ; what the pecuniary *result* is; how you think the enterprise will answer ? Whatsoever you say on it will illustrate it for me ; as at present I am altogether dark.

If you do not know of yourself, then surely you of all men can the most easily get to know ; and no less surely you of all (satirical splenetic) men are the readiest to oblige a man.

When you have time to write answer, pray pack up the Quarterlies along with it ; send your Famulus into Fleet Street, and he will see a Chelsea omnibus ; the cad will bring it me for sixpence within an hour.

I am still busy, but shall see King's Bench Walk by-and-bye. With many excuses for the trouble I put you to,—

Yours always truly,

T. CARLYLE.

To his Sisters.

January 23, 1837.

We have all been influenzaed. Indeed I hardly know a person who has not. The last time I was in Court it looked like a desert. This, of course, has knocked up visiting a little, but yesterday I spent the day with Mrs. Stanhope at Putney ; our party was Colonel and Mrs. Webster, Lady Vincent,* and the Chilian Ambassador ; though it was Sunday there was a good deal of comic singing. Lady Pattison's is the only other house I have been at this age, excepting my *very* intimate friends into whose houses one goes like a pet cat. I have just been writing a long article† on Germany for the next

---

* The wife of Sir Francis Vincent, Bart., and daughter of the Hon. Charles Herbert, R.N., son of the first Earl of Carnarvon.

† " Germany and the Germans ; " *Quarterly Review*, No. 116.

Quarterly, and I expect to get £50 for it. My magazine* comes out this week. Lord Lyndhurst returns this morning, and I am to see him to-morrow about law matters to be brought on in the next session. A dissolution seems to be expected by both parties, yet I do not see what the present Ministry can get by it, as the Radicals would gain more than they. I am quite charmed with the stool-cover. It is quite perfection in its way. I gave my turkey to Tom for one of his fowls, but perhaps I shall aid in the consumption of it. I have not been to the Theatre but once these six weeks. I then went to see the first representation of Bulwer's play: some fine writing, but nothing dramatic.

February 3, 1837.

I send the magazine, and am happy to say that the influenza has not killed us, though it has deprived me of one of my best friends. Caroline, Lady Combermere, is dead from the effects of cold caught at her father's funeral. But it is useless to mourn over anything, though it certainly has saddened me not a little. All visiting is completely at a standstill in Town, and, if a party is given, half are pretty sure to stay away. Political matters are commencing as quietly as need be. There seems to be a general feeling of apathy in all parties, and the common resolution seems to be to wait for the chapter of accidents. I dined with Mrs. Norton and Charles Sheridan† three days ago. I saw Lord Lyndhurst to-day, and he told me that he should not stay wasting his time in London unless something turned up soon. He is as careless about politics as a dandy of twenty. He thinks of nothing but flirting.

---

* The *Law Magazine*, of which he was editor.
† Charles Sheridan, her brother.

April 22, 1837.

I have not visited much lately, though there has been no lack of invitations, but the young ladies complain of a terrible deficiency of balls. It is a pity you were not here last week, for Moore dined with me, and it was not a little amusing to see Lady Vincent and Mrs. Stanhope scrambling for him. They almost quarrelled. Of course I decided the matter by putting him next to my own favourite, which put the others in a rage. The Opera is in full splendour, but horribly dear—a box for a Saturday six guineas. Politics are getting steady again. I do not believe the Ministry have the least intention of going out.

November 13, 1837.

I am very sorry that you should have been put to the necessity of writing. But, as in future the payments will be regular, I hope you will have a balance. If not, let me know without delay, for I have always money in hand. On Friday last I dined with a large Tory party, and walked home with Sir H. Hardinge.* No one knows what is to happen, parties are so equally divided, but Lord Melbourne must declare ere long for the Radicals or the Conservatives, for the Radicals say they will not back him any longer if their favourite questions are to be kept back.† The *Times* I sent contained the best account of the procession, and I saw it from Fleet

* Sir Henry Hardinge, afterwards Viscount Hardinge, G.C.B., Governor-General of India, and Commander-in-Chief at the Horse Guards.

† The general elections which took place after the Queen's accession manifested a considerable Conservative reaction in the country. Lord Melbourne's government in consequence met the new parliament with a reduced majority, and it appeared at one time doubtful if he could carry on the government owing to the demands of his Radical followers, and the opposition of the Tories, without more or less declaring in favour of the Radicals or Tories.

Street. The Lord Mayor's horse kicked out, his atten-
dants judiciously seized him by the legs and so held
him on. Sir P. Laurie galloped backwards and forwards
like an *aide de camp*, flourishing a wand, and ended by
riding over a marshalman. As a show, it was no great
things.*

March 31, 1838.

I am glad you like the silk, Lady Vincent was charmed
with it. I charmed her amazingly yesterday by my report of Sir Francis' "book."† In point of style it is really
admirable, and so far as I have read, the story (laid in
the French Revolution) is very good. It is very highly
creditable to him, and shows him to be still capable of
better things. Poor thing!—she burst into tears when I
told her what I thought of his powers, and has looked
quite buoyant and happy ever since. I spent yesterday
evening there with Wynyard, who, alas! is under orders
for Canada, and must be off within the month. To-day
he dines with Lady Rosebery, and I with Lord Lyndhurst to be introduced to my lady. Monday we dine
together at Lady Stepney's, and Tuesday I am going to
give them and Mrs. Twiss‡ a dinner. My men are Bul-
teel, D'Este,§ Wynyard, Lever, and Vivian. I *must* give
one occasionally, and this is a good time before law
begins. I only intend in future to go to dinner where I
am sure of meeting people worth meeting. I don't mind
the rank, but the dull commonplaces are intolerable.
At Macready's for example,‖ there was no rank, but

---

* The Queen went to the City in state on the 9th of November,
to dine with the Lord Mayor, Sir John Cowen, Bart.

† 'Arundel,' a novel in three vols.

‡ Mrs. Horace Twiss, Hayward's old "schoolfellow."

§ Sir Augustus D'Este.

‖ On the 28th of March (the Wednesday previous), " Mr. and
Mrs. Crawford, the Misses Fitzgerald, Bayley, Cattermole, O'Hanlon,
Hayward, Dowling, Calcraft, Brockenden," dined with Macready.
('Macready's Reminiscences,' edited by Sir Fred. Pollock, Bart.)

there was hardly a person in the room but was worth knowing for something. I don't wonder at all at Mary Anne's making flies* well, for we all can do most things we like. I mean our family, but don't say that out of it. I rode through the park yesterday with D'Orsay to the admiration of all beholders, for every eye is sure to be fixed upon him, and the whole world was out, so that I began to tremble for my character. But he is certainly one of the pleasantest fellows in town.

Here is James Smith's last on ' Coriolanus ' :—

> " What scenes of grandeur does this play disclose,
> Where all is Roman save Macready's nose."

May 23, 1838.

I now dine out little comparatively, and I find I am as well as anybody when I give myself fair play. My horse also does me a great deal of good, and riding is now the pleasantest mode of enjoying society, as one can always join some group or other. I shall give one party, most probably, next week, and that's all. In fact, the fuss bores me to death, but I owe some people the civility. I am asked to-morrow to witness the conjunction of Hook and Sydney Smith at Colonel Webster's, but I would bet odds that one or the other fights shy. I have also accepted an invitation to dine with the Brinsley Sheridans on Monday. They have a house in Grosvenor Square, and are very much attached to each other. You have seen, I suppose, Norton's advertisement that his wife is not to be trusted : a useless insult, as he would not be liable if he made her a proper allowance.

Temple, May 31, 1838.

I am glad to hear you are all so happy together. I wish I were with you, though London is now getting

* Mr. Hayward was an expert fisherman, and his sister, Miss Hayward, was renowned for her skilful manufacture of flies.

very pleasant as the weather gets warm. I have been
very gay this week, and must make up by going out no
more till Monday next. On Monday I dined with the
Brinsley Sheridans. We had the sisters three,* and
Lady Graham, Lord Powerscourt, Lord Melbourne,
Bentinck, Landseer, Fonblanque, and the male Sheridans.
It was very pleasant. Tuesday I dined with the Shep-
herds, with Lady Charleville and some others. Yesterday I had my long-intended party, and a very choice one
it was — Lord Lyndhurst, Hook, James Smith, the
Brinsley Sheridans, Mrs. Norton, Mr. and Mrs. Henry
Ellis, Lady Vincent, and Mrs. Herbert to dinner. Charles
Kean, the Cadogans, and four or five men came afterwards. Some capital things were struck out, but wit is
too evanescent for repetition. Sheridan was saying that
he had been told that it was impossible to get a dinner
at the Temple. "What," said Lord Lyndhurst, "not at
the Chambers of the Gastronomer of the 'Quarterly'"?
"Who," added Hook," has just given us a practical commentary on the article, illustrated by *plates* and accompanied by *cuts.*" They were laughing at me as having
assisted Lady Stepney in her novels (which I never did).
"At least," said Mrs. Norton, "you will not deny that
you taught her 'The New Road to Ruin,' (the name of
Lady Stepney's first book)?" Lord Lyndhurst, who had
to go to the Duke of Sussex's, came with gold-laced
trousers, his dress-coat being left in the carriage. Hook
gravely proposed that to appear with all his glories he
should reverse his position in his chair. Lady Vincent
laughed till she almost cried, as she had never met Hook
before. I have almost filled my paper with this nonsense,
though it is as good as anything else, for I have nothing
serious to tell you, having reserved all such in letters for
Tom.

    * The Duchess of Somerset, Lady Dufferin, and the Honourable
Mrs. George Norton—the three sisters of the host.

November 1, 1838.

I delayed writing until I could send the Magazine, in which you will see I have shown my impartiality by defending Lord Durham.* There is not much going on in the way of visiting at present, but we had a dinner at the Athenæum last week which was rather interesting, being composed of Lockhart, Milman, Talfourd, Henry Ellis, Dickens (Pickwick), and two more. Dickens is no great things, a very commonplace talker at best. The present rumour is that the Duke of Sussex will go to Ireland, and Lord Normanby replace Lord Glenelg.† Heaven knows whom they will send to Canada.‡ There is no doubt their desertion of Lord Durham has given the Ministry a shock. I have not received the jam, &c. I hope it is not lost, for mother's sake as well as my own, for I fear she would be much hurt by such an occurrence.

December 23, 1838.

Thanks for the fowls. I have just been to see the Queen prorogue the Parliament. I thought she looked pale and worn. She walks well, and bowed very graciously to all of us. I went with Lady Murray and Lady Chatterton, and as we had tickets for the interior the sight was really very splendid, for independently of Her Majesty there were lots of pretty women whom I knew.

* Mr. Hayward, in an article in the *Law Magazine* (vol. xx., p. 384) reviewed, and to a certain extent justified, Lord Durham's Ordinance banishing Nelson and his confederates to Bermuda. He strongly condemned the "meanness and moral cowardice" of the Government in disallowing the Ordinance when it was passed.

† Viscount Ebrington, M.P., the eldest son of Earl Fortescue, was called up to the House of Lords, and succeeded Lord Normanby as Viceroy of Ireland. Lord Glenelg resigned the Secretaryship for the Colonies, and was replaced by Lord Normanby; but these changes did not actually take place till the February of 1839.

‡ Poulett Thomson, created Lord Sydenham, succeeded Lord Durham in Canada in September 1839.

The Duchess of Sutherland was the best dressed—her dress was white and gold; Lady Mulgrave's green and ditto. The Canadian question is making a great fuss, and the general opinion is that they will have the best of it, for we have not much more than 2,000 troops there, and can't well get any more into the field for the ice. By the way, the Duke [of Wellington] walked past us, looking, I thought, very ill—he tottered as he walked.

There is a good deal of very pleasant society at present in a quiet way. I dined on Thursday at Lady Stepney's, with Lord Foley, Adolphus Fitzclarence, the Dawson Damers, Lady Morgan, and some more, and I am going to Mrs. Dawson Damer's on Tuesday. I dined with the Chattertons on Wednesday, and was at a soirée there last night with most of the gay people, for her connection is one of the best in Town. He, too, is a very pleasant, goodnatured fellow, not a bit jealous, nor has he need, for that matter, for she is as good as she is clever and agreeable. I am now writing an article on Parliamentary Privilege for the *Quarterly*,* and getting up my own magazine. The actions about the *United Service Journal* † are suspended for the time, but the attorneys have expressed themselves so well pleased with my conduct of the cases that they have promised to back me in future in other matters, and as they are the first in town this may do good. I have also two other cases in hand. Altogether, we are as thriving as need be. I have got a very nice little horse—a thoroughbred mare, rather stylish-looking, and as she is slight and not fit for any work but mine, I got her cheap.

---

* Mr. Hayward wrote an article in the *Quarterly Review*, No. 130, treating of the Privileges of Parliament in the publication of printed papers. The question arose out of the once-celebrated case of Stockdale and Hansard, and after much discussion was finally settled by Act of Parliament.

† He had a special retainer in the *U. S. Journal* case.

In the beginning of 1839 the question of National Education was arresting the attention of many thoughtful minds. Lord John Russell wrote a letter to Lord Lansdowne, President of the Council, proposing a scheme of National Education, and urging that religion should be taught, and "the rights of conscience respected." These last words raised a storm. The Church of England party opposed the government scheme, which in consequence was abandoned. Mr. Hayward appears to have applied to Mr. Gladstone for information and assistance in preparing an article on the Education question.

Mr. W. E. Gladstone to Mr. Hayward.

MY DEAR SIR,   6 Carlton Gardens, Feb. 2, 1839.

I only returned to town the day before yesterday, or your note would have received an earlier reply.

Six months of absence on the Continent have interrupted my acquaintance with the state of the measures respecting education which have been in progress among the members of the Church ; during the last spring and summer I was very much occupied about them, and in the course of a short time I hope to be *au courant* of their present state. But I shall be very happy in the meantime to communicate freely with you, or with any third person at your desire, when I know the specific points on which information is desired. As respects the normal schools, I believe that such institutions are in progress already in more places than one ; but the ground which we traversed last year is too wide to be described in a note.

Believe me,
Very truly yours,
W. E. GLADSTONE.

F 2

Mr. Hayward was, between the years 1834 and 1842, a not unfrequent contributor to the *Quarterly*, of which Mr. Lockhart was then the editor. They enjoyed the acquaintance of common friends, and often met together on some such lively occasion, as the following rhyming invitation suggests.

From Mr. Lockhart to Mr. Hayward.

Feb. 3, 1839.

Nota Bene.—'Tis Friday, the 8th, that's my day,
  When I hope you'll be with me not later than seven ;
In your boots, if you please, but prepared to make play,
  As 'tis Ford * in whose honour the turkey is given.
And except Master Senior †, there's none of the rest
So familiar as you with that shy timid guest.
By-the-bye, what a pamphlet Pierce Stevenson ‡ writes.
  How adroitly Brougham's *noes* and his *nose*, too, he pinches ;
Also those who abandon their spouses o' nights,
  And like Greenhill, the scamp, go a-yachting with wenches.
As for N—rt—n, I always—I'm free to confess—
Thought him little, but now what on earth can be less ?

To his Sisters.

February 16, 1839.

Many thanks for your amusing letters, and I am sorry I have very little to give you in return. I forget whether I wrote since my party, which turned out very well. Lady Vincent and Lady Chatterton both looked very handsome, and Lady . . . was odder than ever. Robert Burrell (Lord Willoughby's nephew) sat next her, and she declares that they fell in love with each other, an account which he is far from confirming. She brought a little stool with her, and explained to the party that

---

* Richard Ford, author of 'Handbook of Spain.'
† Nassau W. Senior, a Master in Chancery, and author.
‡ "Pierce Stevenson" was the name Mrs. Norton assumed when she contributed an article to the *Law Magazine*, " On the Custody of Infants' Act."

unless she "cocked up her right foot" on it, she could
neither talk nor digest. I was obliged to dine out a
good deal last week; amongst the most remarkable
people I met was Sam Slick (Mr. Justice Haliburton, of
Nova Scotia), whom I have since introduced about. I
have also dined this week at an interesting party at Mrs.
Norton's—Lady Graham, Lady Seymour, and Mrs. E.
Phipps (formerly Mrs. C. Norton), were there, and an
American friend of mine said he never saw so many
beautiful women in a room before. I called yesterday
on Mrs. Charles Buller, and had a long chat about
Canada, &c. There is no formal make-up between
Lord Durham and the Ministry, but the understanding
is that the discussion is to be as little hostile as may be,
with almost exclusive reference to the future settlement
of the Colony. Lord Durham's report is considered well
written, but all well-informed people say that it is superficial and *one-sided*, to borrow a German phrase. I
believe his project of a legislative union is about as
feasible as a plan to govern all Europe by a parliament
sitting at Paris. The French Canadians would be not
a bit more satisfied at being governed by an English
majority than by an English governor, and the whole
would end (as in the case of Holland and Belgium—an
exactly parallel case) in a split. I care little about
politics, but this is what is generally said.* There is

* Lord Durham had resigned his command in Canada in
October 1838. Almost immediately after he left Canada the
rebellion broke out afresh, but by the end of the year it had been
quelled. Lord Durham had drawn up a report on the state of
affairs in our North American Colonies, in which he advocated
many measures of reform in their government. Mr. Hayward's
letter no doubt reflects the opinion of society at the time on Lord
Durham's suggestion, that the two Canadas should be united, but,
nevertheless, after some delay and under the enlightened control of
his successor, Lord Sydenham, a united legislature was established
in February 1841.

something quite laughable in the rapidity with which the interest in public questions passes off. The Corn Law cry is thought a failure, and I believe nothing will be done.* I agree with father that it can in no contingency hurt us.† Lord Durham dines with Brougham to-morrow—so much for the quarrels of statesmen. Lord Brougham told a friend of mine it was a reconciliation dinner, yet they do nothing but abuse each other in society. Lord Normanby is Colonial Secretary, and it seems most probable that Lord Clarendon will have Ireland : Lord Tavistock has refused.

March 26, 1839.

I returned Friday, and found all well. My hearing has returned, and the whizzing in my head is pretty nearly gone. I was greatly comforted yesterday by finding a friend rather worse in the same complaint. In fact, there are an extraordinary quantity of ailing people about, which is attributed to the rapid changes of weather. To-day we have a horrible east wind again.

On Saturday I went to Lord Northampton's Royal Society Party. He had sent me a card for four, though I am not a member. There were two Royal Dukes and an infinity of stars and garters. This Irish business will probably strengthen the Ministry instead of weakening them, as their Irish policy is that on which all their people will stand by them. Lord John says he will go out if he does not get a majority of fifteen, but I should conceive he would much exceed it.‡ The best of the

---

* Mr. Charles Villiers's motion on the Corn Laws was on the 19th of February defeated by a majority of 371 to 172.

† This refers to the effect the alteration of the Corn Laws would have upon the family as proprietors of the Haliburton Court Estate.

‡ On the 21st of March, Lord Roden's motion on the policy of Ministers in Ireland was defeated by a majority of 5 for Ministers.

Conservatives hope that the present Government will last, not being at all anxious to have the responsibility of the existing state of things upon their shoulders. To say nothing of America, India, and the Chartists, it seems not very unlikely that Louis Philippe will have to fight for his Crown. I hope you are now reconciled to the addition to the garden. My expectation is that it will be a great improvement. When you have formed your estimate, I can furnish what money is wanted.

May, 1839.

I suppose you have all been much fussified about politics. All is unsettled as ever, as the Radicals refuse to support the Ministry without a change of measures and men. Fonblanque tells me that the Ministry have at length agreed to the following terms. Ten-pound occupiers in counties to have votes—the rate-paying clauses to be repealed—ballot an open question, penny postage, and the abolition of Church-rates. They insist on a minor place or two as a guarantee, and it is said that Spring Rice* must go certainly, and Lord John† most probably. What between the extreme Radicals on one side, and the Conservative Whigs on the other, Lord Melbourne will have some difficulty to keep in. You may consider W. Cowper's letter to the Hertford Electors as the true tone about the Court as to the late failure. The attack on Peel and the Duke is only carried on by the Press. The whole truth is, that the Queen likes Lord Melbourne and detests Peel ; and as

---

On the 16th of April, the debate in the House of Commons, on the Irish policy of the Government, ended in a majority of 22 for the Government.

* Chancellor of the Exchequer; created Lord Monteagle in September 1839.

† Home Secretary.

regards society there is no comparison between the two. As for the Queen's friends, it is all stuff and nonsense; she never knew one of them till put in by the present party. But if I had been in Peel's place I would have dissolved at once, and let the bedchamber people do their worst. I am going to Lady Murray's concert to-night—given to the Duchess of Gloucester—and I have a good many other invitations; last night about eleven I started off to Mrs. Norton's, where there was a splendid collection of wits and beauties, lords and ladies. The first couple I saw were Sir James Graham and Lord Normanby in amicable converse.

June 15, 1839.

The Dorchester assizes are fixed for the 20th; as Coleridge is the senior judge, I am sure of a revisorship. I fancy I shall be obliged to go to Paris again for a fortnight, as I can get no answers in the present state of affairs, and I want both books and information for two or three compositions I have undertaken. I have not been out much, but I have been to two or three amusing things, amongst others to a dinner given to Frank Sheridan* before his departure for Barbadoes at Greenwich on Sunday last.

It was given by Lord Normanby's Irish Staff, and I never laughed so much. I left, however, before they got to the highest pitch, for they ended by putting a quart of cream-ice into one of the guest's breeches-pockets— he having fallen under the table. The Pinneys' carriage stopped at my door last week and left me a dinner invitation for the 21st, which I have accepted, but I keep the scales equal : I dine at Lord Westmorland's to-day.†

* Brother of Mr. R. B. Sheridan and Mrs. Norton.

† Pinney was the Member for Lyme Regis and a Liberal. Lord Westmorland, a Conservative, had at that time very great influence in Lyme.

Sept. 10, 1839.

I passed a very agreeable fortnight in Paris, as Dr. Hawtrey* and I between us knew almost everybody worth seeing that was there. I dined twice with Henry Bulwer, now acting as Minister in Lord Granville's absence, and if I had stayed, could have reached almost anybody through him. I passed one day in going, and three in returning at Boulogne, where I found several old friends. The French were very quiet, and care not a feather about young Buonaparte or any other member of the family, as people keep on saying here. They seem devoted to commerce and internal improvements, and the progress almost daily making in Paris is wonderful. Hawtrey, who had not been there since 1830, could hardly recognise it.

* The Rev. E. C. Hawtrey, Provost of Eton.

CHAPTER III.

1840–1848.

MR. HAYWARD'S letters during these years are still of
a light and varied description. Society and literature
continue to furnish the chief topics of correspondence.
Politics are seldom discussed, but there are some interesting allusions to legal successes.

Since his call to the Bar in 1832, Mr. Hayward had
regularly attached himself to the Western Circuit;
latterly he acted as Counsel to the Admiralty, and for
seven consecutive years he was appointed a Revising
Barrister.

His chief successes as an advocate occurred during the years 1840–1844, and were sufficiently marked to kindle a desire for further triumphs ; the ambition thus awakened is reflected in several of the home letters, especially in one to his father, dated August 1841. But Mr. Hayward's legal career was destined to a somewhat abrupt termination, as will appear in a future portion of the correspondence.

Among his regular correspondents, while editor of the *Law Magazine,* was Mr. Justice Story, an eminent American, author of 'Commentaries on the Conflict of Laws.' Frequent letters passed between them until the latter's death in 1845 ; the following extract is from the only one that has been preserved.

Mr. Justice Story to Mr. Hayward.

[EXTRACT.]

Cambridge, near Boston (U.S.A.),
January 4, 1840.

I beg to return you my sincere thanks for your letter, and assure you that it will at all times afford me sincere pleasure to answer any inquiries or do any acts useful to you on this side of the Atlantic. Allow me to add, that I have long been familiar with your writings, and not only in the *Quarterly Review* but in the *Law Magazine,* and that I have received a great deal of pleasure and instruction from them. It may not be without some interest for you to know, that the *Law Magazine* is taken by the University in this place, and the whole series from the beginning is to be found in our Law Library and is constantly read by our Law Students. I have long thought that the biographical articles, as well as the articles upon Commercial Law, are so valuable and

so generally read, that they would well repay the
publishing if printed in distinct volumes.

Mrs. Norton to *Mr. Hayward.*

Palazzo Boltoni [Bolton Street],
June 11, 1840.

DUTIFUL AND ATTACHED FRIEND,

I send you my new poems, † in confident expectation
that you will be utterly unable to find out their faults,
from the blind admiration which should be the pre-
dominant feeling of your mind to *all* the company you
have asked to dinner on Saturday, and from the general
friendship subsisting between us, and the peripatetic
philosophy which bound us together in that accidental
walk. If I see any review in any magazine in which
translations of Schiller, Goethe, or other German poets
are at all set up as superior to my indigenous verse, I
shall ascribe them to you, and shall view all your actions
distortedly and in base relief through the medium of
my private *Talbot-scope.* (After this sentence, a struggling desire to pay you some strong and startling
compliment in the shape of a laboured pun about
forcing even the sun to cast black shadows, you being
the sun, came upon me, but I resisted the impulse.)
Adieu! Advise all the young lawyers in the Temple to
possess themselves of a copy of these poems; it will
greatly assist their studies. Let them make notes in the
margin of Blackstone and Lewin's Law of Settlement.

---

* Mrs. Norton was the wife of the Hon. George Norton. She
and her sisters, the late Duchess of Somerset and Lady Dufferin,
were the daughters of Mr. Thomas Sheridan, and the grand-
daughters of the illustrious Richard Brinsley Sheridan; they were
no less remarkable for their beauty than for their brilliant intellectual qualities.

† 'The Dream, and other poems,' by Mrs. Norton.

Let Feargus O'Connor have permission to peruse it in prison ; let it be placed in the House of Commons library, in case any more sheriffs should suffer from a mixture of ennui and apoplexy ; in short, do your best to float it on the ocean of popular applause. Resist not, but speedily obey !

Your friend,
HI-SKI-HI.

During Prince Louis Napoleon's residence in England, from 1838 to 1840, " Hayward saw a great deal of him : not merely in the way of ordinary social intercourse, but being consulted by him as a literary man in regard to one of the works on which the Prince was then engaged, and rendering him valuable assistance. Louis Napoleon showed his sense of the obligation which he owed him for these services by leaving with him, before his departure from this country, a friendly note of farewell, accompanied by the present of an ornamental pin of considerable value." *

One day, while engaged with the Prince in discussing some literary point, Mr. Hayward was visited by his uncle, Mr. Thomas Abraham, who was so shocked at his nephew's intimacy with an adventurer, as he termed Napoleon, that he immediately wrote to Mrs. Hayward, begging her to dissuade her son from the society of such a man. In less than two months after the date of the following letter, Prince Louis Napoleon made his descent upon Boulogne.

* *Fortnightly Review*, April 1884. " Mr. Hayward," p. 556.

Mr. Hayward to his Sisters.

Temple, June 16, 1840.

The Dorset Assizes will be about the 18th or 20th, and I shall stay but one night at Dorchester. Uncle Tom is still here ; yesterday he called and stayed for an hour. I offered to get him up a party, but he declined, and two or three times I asked him to dine here ; but it seems they have generally turtle and venison at the Hummums. Prince Napoleon dined here on Saturday, but as the conversation was to be in French, Uncle Tom expressed no wish to join the party, which consisted of Lord Nugent, Sydney Herbert, Lockhart, Mrs. Norton, the Stanhopes, Mrs. Herbert and Lady Vincent. Don't mention it, as he believed the majority to be foreigners. I dine with Mrs. Norton to-day.

Love to all.

When Charles Sumner, the celebrated American statesman and orator, visited England in 1840, he brought a letter of introduction to Mr. Hayward from Mr. Justice Story. As editor of a Law Magazine conducted on the same lines as Mr. Hayward's, he found that they had many topics of interest in common, and, on his return to America, wrote the following letter.

Mr. Charles Sumner to Mr. Hayward.

DEAR HAYWARD,   Boston (U.S.A.), August 31, 1840.

This poor sheet and its pictures* will go by the *Acadia*, which sails to-morrow from this port for Liverpool. What can I write that will not be utterly dull to you of London ? If you still persevere in your intentions

* At the head of the sheet of letter-paper is a vignette of General Wm. Hy. Harrison (President of the United States in 1841), and also a picture of a log-cabin with a cider-barrel standing on end outside the cabin door.

of giving an article * on American eloquence, let me ask
you to read a paper in the last *North American Review*
(July) on Guizot's 'Washington.' You will find there
some six or eight pages, which present a neat and concise
view of *parties* in the United States from the adoption of
the Federal Constitution down to a comparatively recent
period. Its author is Mr. Edward Everett, † recently
Governor of Massachusetts, and now in Europe, where
he purposes passing two or more years. He will be in
England before he returns home ; if so, 1 hope he may
see you. He is, perhaps, the most accomplished man of
my country. The *Whigs*, constituting the Opposition,
have nominated for the Presidency the person whose
head adorns a corner of this sheet. He has in his favour
his good conduct during the war of 1812, and an alleged
victory at *Tippecanoe*, and the vulgar appeal is made,
grounded on military success. This has made him a
more acceptable candidate than Clay and Webster, who
have been serving the State well for years. Harrison
lives in the State of Ohio, cultivating his farm with his
own hands ; and as what is called " help " in that part of
the country is not easy to be procured, his wife and
daughter cook and serve the dinner for the seven or
eight people who daily challenge his hospitality. An
Administration paper alluded to him as "living in a log-
cabin and drinking hard cider." The Whigs at once
adopted these words, and placed them on their banners.
They proclaimed Harrison the candidate of the log-cabin
and hard-cider class. And this vulgar appeal is made
by the party professing the monopoly of intelligence and
education in the country. But it has had its effects.
The country seems to be revolutionised, and the Whigs
are confident of success. The election takes place in

* Mr. Hayward wrote the article "American Orators and
Statesmen " in the *Quarterly Review*, December 1840.
† Afterwards United States Minister in London.

November. The Whigs, in anticipation of success, have already portioned the high offices. Of course all our troop abroad will be recalled, Stevenson leading the dance home. They have republished at Lowell, a manufacturing town in Massachusetts and the Manchester of America, your admirable translation of 'Faust.' I shall send you a copy of this edition by the earliest opportunity. What can I send you from this side of the sea ? Write me soon, and believe me

Ever very faithfully yours,
CHARLES SUMNER.

In his essay on Samuel Rogers, Mr. Hayward relates an interesting incident connected with his visit to Moore, mentioned in the next letter :—" Rogers especially delighted in what may be called rather the musical recitation than the singing of Moore. Nothing annoyed him more than to hear the songs he loved profaned by inferior execution. 'Can *you* stay and hear it?' was his muttered remonstrance to Mr. Hayward, whom he fairly dragged out of the room when an accomplished amateur was throwing as much soul as he could muster into

> " Give smiles to those who love you less,
>   But keep your tears for me."

During this visit at Sloperton Cottage, Moore sang readily every song that was suggested to him, having first announced that he would only attempt those of the more gay and inspiriting kind ; his nervous system having been a good deal shaken by a domestic affliction (the death of his daughter). Mrs. Moore, who watched with considerate affection to see that he did not unconsciously transgress this rule, left the room ; and he

began 'When midst the fair I meet,' but on coming to
the lines just quoted his voice faltered, his hands fell
motionless on the piano, and he burst into tears. It was
to this incident, which had been related to Rogers, that
he referred in his vehement remonstrance." *

Mr. Hayward to his Father.

MY DEAR FATHER,   Calne, September 22, 1840.

I cannot yet say whether I shall be able to come to
Lyme during the next month. The worst of it is, the
journey down always knocks me up for two or three
days. I have nearly done here, and shall leave for
London to-morrow, after revising Marlborough. I spent
Sunday and yesterday at Sloperton Cottage with Moore,
and almost fell in love with his wife, the Bessy of his
songs. Last night he sang for an hour and a-half for
my amusement, and it is just the sort of singing a man
without a musical ear may appreciate—very little voice,
but clear, sweet, and expressive.

Ever yours,
A. H.

Mr. John Murray to Mr. Hayward.

Albemarle Street,
MY DEAR HAYWARD,   October 3, 1840.

I felt much gratified by your kind note on leaving
London, and I sent it on to Lockhart, who appears to
have enjoyed himself to the "very top of his bent" by a
constant flow of most delightful visitors at his brother's
on the Clyde. But the cause of this billet is a visit
yesterday from Mr. Fitzgerald, to communicate some-

* 'Selected Essays.' "Samuel Rogers." Vol. i. pp. 116, 117,
(Longmans.)

thing which he was sure, he said, would be agreeable to
me, viz. : he had heard a letter *read* from one of the
Royal Family of Hanover expressive of the perfect
satisfaction and gratifying delight at the article on Prince
George in the last *Quarterly,** which the writer said
had done more to improve the health and spirits of the
Prince than all the experiments of his physicians. For
certain reasons I thought that this intelligence might
prove equally agreeable to you as to myself, and so I
resolved to send it. Accept my kindest wishes, my dear
Hayward, and believe me to be

Most sincerely yours,
JOHN MURRAY.

Mrs. Shelley † to Mr. Hayward.

[EXTRACT.]

Rue de la Paix, Paris, November 1840.

After a very pleasant tour, I am returned here, where
I hope to stay till Xmas. I left Italy with infinite
regret. Many a long year had elapsed since I had last
seen it, but its aspect, its language, its ways of going on,
its dear, courteous, lying, kind inhabitants, and its divine
climate were as familiar to me as if I had left them
yesterday, and more welcome and delightful than I can
at all express ; it was returning to my own land, a land
and a period of enjoyment, and I was very happy during
my two months' residence at Cadenabbia, on the shores
of the lake of Como, opposite to Bellagio, and close
neighbour to Tremezzio, names rendered classical by
our dear Rogers. He must be in grief for his friend's

---

* In the *Quarterly Review* for September 1840, Mr. Hayward
had written an article, " Prince George of Hanover on Music."

† The second wife of the poet, Percy Bysshe Shelley.

death. The loss of Lord Holland* will be deeply felt, for no man was ever better loved. I had some hopes of finding both Rogers and you here in October, as you were last year, but I suppose the threat of war has frightened you. I let H. Bulwer† know I was here, and he in return left his card, which is a curiosity : it was so dirty I could scarcely read his name. I have two or three old friends in Paris, but I have not been here long enough to make a society. A thousand thanks for your kindness. M. Buchon, from your account, I should really like to see. I like a man who talks me to death, provided he is amusing: it saves so much trouble. Sainte-Beuve I like in his way. French people of a certain kind all know how to talk, and I can always get on with them. He, like all his countrymen, sighs to wash out Waterloo ; they will not remember that they brought Waterloo on themselves ; besides, they think War will prevent Revolution, but I believe Louis Philippe thinks that his dear subjects will beg to have both. How can they have too much of so good a thing as *gloire* of all sorts, foreign and domestic ?—*les jours glorieux de la France dehors et les jours immortels dedans.* The Chambers, however, seem in a body pacific. Louis Philippe was much better received than he expected, which touched him to the heart, so that when he alluded to the attempts‡ made against his own life his voice was broken by tears, and the Chambers had the civility to cheer him. It was strange to see a king upon his throne cry. Fifty years ago Europe had rung with the expres-

* Lord Holland died on the 22nd of November, 1840, at Holland House.
† Afterwards Lord Dalling, then Secretary of Embassy at Paris, and *Chargé d'Affaires.*
‡ On the evening of the 15th of October, a musket-shot had been fired at the King as he was passing along the Quay of the Tuileries to return to St. Cloud.

sions of sympathy. The French take it quietly. I know not why, but the tears came warm and quick into my eyes, and I thought as I looked at weeping royalty of the verse of Manzoni—but you will not recollect the context, perhaps; it means, others besides oneself are and have been unhappy, and that is a kind of left-handed comfort now and then to the suffering. I went to see Soult's Gallery the other day. Have you ever seen it? There is an 'Assumption of the Virgin,' by Murillo, worth ten thousand pictures such as one usually sees. She does not look so beautiful as Raphael's. She looks more like a martyr received into heaven; her almost tearful eyes, soft, upturned, imploring, her parted lips full of sensibility, all appear expressive of painful impressions of horror and death, and gratitude at the reward she is rising to receive; the figure is floating upwards, surrounded by all those foreshortened baby-angels Murillo delights in. She is dressed in white, not usual in a picture, but the colouring is glowing, and, like all Murillo's, is as satisfactory to the eye as harmonious music to the ear. There is a 'Birth of St. John the Baptist,' exquisite from the colouring and truth, but without ideality in the people; a little dog is sniffing at and going to play with a young angel's wing, who turns round to see who is taking the liberty. I should like to see the *Quarterly* and am impatient to see Mrs. Norton's poem. Give my love to her; I like her letters and herself, dearly, as the children say. Adieu! My love to dear Rogers.

Mr. Hayward to his Sisters.

Temple, May 13, 1841.

London is in a strange state of uncertainty, as rumours of dissolution rise and fall with the hour. I rather think there will be none after all, for no strong popular feeling appears to justify it. I do not believe the Cabinet themselves have yet decided. Rational people begin to hope that, soon after the change, a government may be formed so as to exclude the ultras of both sides and defy their influence. There is no doubt many of the old Whigs will support Peel, but his danger lies from the Buckingham and Roden factions. I suppose a Conservative will be started for Lyme, so Pinney had better look sharp.*

The next letter is from Georgiana, Lady Chatterton, whose great literary power was fully recognised by Mr. Hayward. Lady Chatterton was also a good German scholar, and this at once established a bond of sympathy between them. In her diary about this period is the following entry :—

"We had a particularly pleasant dinner yesterday with Mr. Hayward at the Temple. A collection of wits and most pleasant people, whom our agreeable host contrived to amalgamate and draw out, so that they played into each other's hands, and each one said his best. The advice given in his article on the 'Art of Dining' was fully carried out in his own party. We have dined with him several times. Each time we meet different people, and the

---

* In view of the waning popularity of the Government, Sir Robert Peel moved a vote of want of confidence in it. On the 4th of June the vote was carried by *one* against the Government. In the end of June Parliament was dissolved, Lord Melbourne's Government deciding to go to the country rather than resign. The question of Free Trade or Protection was laid before the country. In August the new Parliament met, and decided by a majority of ninety-one that the Melbourne Ministry had not its confidence. Sir Robert Peel returned to office.

last party seemed always to be pleasanter than the one
before it." *

Georgiana, Lady Chatterton, to Mr. Hayward.

Biarritz près de Bayonne,
DEAR MR. HAYWARD,   June 14, 1841.

We have just taken a house at this pretty little sea-
bathing place, and I seize on the first moment of quiet
and leisure which a cessation of travelling gives to write
and tell you something of our proceedings. The heat
soon drove us away from Paris, but fortunately as we
travelled south the weather became much cooler, and we
had no annoyance from it except during the few days
we spent at Bordeaux. The old French towns through
which we passed were very interesting, particularly
Poictiers, where there are some fine remains of Roman
magnificence, and its position is extremely beautiful.
But what has pleased me more than anything I have
seen during this tour was an excursion we have just
made into Spain. We went in a diligence, which
is the only safe, or indeed at all comfortable, mode of
travelling in Spain. Among all the various ways I have
travelled I never happen to have tried a diligence, and
therefore rather dreaded the expedition ; but we found it
all less disagreeable than we expected, and the beautiful
scenery, interesting old towns, and above all the novelty
of everything we saw fully atoned for the jolting, noise,
smoking, and all other horrors we encountered. Indeed,
we are so delighted with the excursion that as soon as
the weather is cool enough we have serious thoughts of
starting *par diligence* to Madrid, and probably go down
as far as Granada and Seville. All the Spaniards we

* 'Memoirs of Georgiana, Lady Chatterton,' by E. Heneage
Dering, p. 91. (Hurst and Blackett.)

have seen say it is much too hot in summer to travel in their most interesting country; but they also maintain that no danger is to be apprehended anywhere *if* one goes by diligence. At St. Sebastian we fortunately fell in with a very interesting religious ceremony and procession—the Fête Dieu, which all the ladies attended in the real old Spanish mantillas, and the peasantry in their gayest costumes. It was a beautiful sight, and the music, both sacred and military, was extremely good. We saw all the different parts of it to great advantage, from having a letter to a Spanish gentleman at St. Sebastian, who took William under his protection and put me into the hands of his sister. For I perceive the ladies and gentlemen in Spain pursue very different occupations, and (as far as I saw) do not walk together or even speak to each other during the promenades. So, during that Fête day I was taken off to hear High Mass early in the morning by two pretty Spanish ladies with fans and mantillas (mine being about the only bonnet in the Church); and afterwards I formed with them part of the procession that paraded through the streets of the town, with bands playing, banners waving, and the houses and balconies all decorated with tapestry and hangings of brilliant colours. Then they took me up to a balcony to see the rest of the procession go by, and in that house we were afterwards joined by the gentlemen, the ladies all sitting round the room in great state, and refreshments handed to them by bowing gallants. I am afraid you will scarcely find time to read this long letter, but I hope you will try and find some to write to me.

Believe me, dear Mr. Hayward,

Yours very sincerely,

GEORGIANA CHATTERTON.

Temple, July 4, 1841.

The Lyme election was not reported, so that your account was the first I heard of it. I have no doubt that I could have turned out Pinney with very little trouble, as I could have persuaded some of his friends to stand neuter; but, if a seat was offered me to-morrow morning, I would not take it, for I could not do the work of parliament as I should wish without giving up everything else. As things are going now, I do not think Peel will have more than 30 majority. At the Reform Club they say 35, but fears magnify as well as hopes. The quantity of bribery on both sides has been tremendous. That and local circumstances have decided most places. London was never pleasanter than during the last fortnight, but my flirting days are over, for I am grown old and steady now, and care more about a brief than a billet-doux. It will not be my fault if I do not become a great advocate, for I make it now my sole object. In fact, I never neglected business in my gayest moods, but one exerts oneself with more spirit when there is a chance. If C—— would die of old age or corpulence, and E—— be made a judge, there would be some chance; but, as it is, I must wait till I am wanted. I get quite enough to keep my hand in here. My plans are not yet fixed as to the Circuit. I shall certainly go to Somersetshire, and perhaps Cornwall; not Wilts, where there is never much business. I don't think there is much chance of my getting anything for the present. Love to all.

Many of Mrs. Norton's letters to Mr. Hayward begin with "Dear Avocat," and she signs herself "C. Client." The explanation of this is to be found in the following anecdote. Mr. Hayward's signature was always and only " A. Hayward." He never signed his full Christian name, for he hated it, and could not bear the least allusion to it. Mrs. Norton was fully aware of this little weakness on his part ; so that one day, when some lady who was bent on teasing him, asked him in her drawing-room what his " A." stood for, " Arthur or Andrew," Mrs. Norton, to cover his vexation, quickly replied to the lady, " Oh, dear no, it stands for ' Avocat,' because Mr. Hayward is a lawyer ; " and " Avocat " she always used to call him afterwards, styling herself his " Client."

Mrs. Norton to Mr. Hayward.

DEAR AVOCAT,   Cowes, July 23, 1841.

I was sorry not to see you yesterday, having (at the risk of the remainder of my reputation here) desired the boatman to row me to the steamers each time they came in, and each time frankly replying to his question " Is it a gentleman friend as you expects, marm ? " " Yes, Clarke." Indeed, but for my boatman I should find Cowes dull, but he is a treasure. The mixture of wheedling and frankness, of shrewdness and simplicity, of great and real kindness to those they believe poor, with a very great approximation to swindling by monstrous over-charge to those they think rich, forms the groundwork of the character of your true boatman ; and if you can cross the breed as in this instance by matching a boatman's daughter with a real sailor, the race produced will be quite in-estimable ; adding to the above primary qualities utter fearlessness of danger, great merriment and humour, and a peculiar readiness of apprehension worth all the intellect and genius in the world; besides a charm of manner quite distinct from taught rules of politeness, and yet as good, if not better. The fact is in our

"Island home," your boatman is the only parallel to the *peasant* of other countries. Farmers want to be gentle-men (and often are, in every sense of the word), trades-men want to be rakes and lords, and tread on the heels of the faults, manners and habits, &c., of the upper classes. Ploughmen are sulky and stupid machines (in general) ; cottagers shy (and often dispirited and distant neighbours) ; your boatman is the only fraction of the English masses who *at once* acknowledges the enormous gulf of distance between his social position and yours, and asserts with cheerful independence his right of brotherhood in spite of that distance. You may make him *duller* by not meeting him half-way, but you can't make him less familiar ; you may make him happier and gayer by conversing merrily with him, but you won't bring him a grain nearer insolence. I take that to be the *peasant* character. I am not sure that in the over-educating of the classes who never can have our *leisure,* what ever else they may obtain that is ours, we have not destroyed all our companionship with them ; they stand too near us for our comfort or theirs ; they climb just close enough to our level to prevent their looking up to us ; they elbow us, and we have no longer room to stretch out our hand in fellowship with them ! Pray don't think I am in love with my boatman. (I have run on so rapidly, I have come to a third page, and blush at perceiving it.) He is sixty, and *very* weather-beaten. Give me the benefit of "whatever doubt may arise in your mind." I don't wish to prejudice my jury, but I must say he showed great sympathy in the non-arrival of my "gentleman friend," and took me (by way of comfort) to see a little deserted schooner that had been towed into port with nothing but a dog and two canaries on board, having been left (supposed sinking) by her crew. It was a common sight to him, but he knew it would be a little treat for me, and did the

honours with a Devonshire House urbanity of its broken
sides, torn sails, and disordered rigging. Good Avocat,
if you can but manage this business,* there will be no
one I shall ever feel so grateful to, and I really think
and hope you will, and I will make my third son "look
up" to you when he is at the Bar, as a guiding star.
Lest I should be tempted to add to my most lengthy
observations on boatmen something on barristers, I
hastily conclude. *Do* you believe shrimps are happy ?
Great naturalists attribute their incessant skippings to
the vulgar mode of expressing rapture commonly
called "jumping for joy," but the new school of
philosophy will rather have it, that they are out of
breath, and trying to reach the water ! On which side
are *you ?* Forgive me pursuing you with these marine
subjects so far inland, and believe me

Ever yours truly,
C. NORTON.

Mr. Hayward to his Father.

MY DEAR FATHER,   Bridgwater, August 1841.

I enclose you a slip of paper† sent to me in Court, a
repetition of what has been said to me by many. Between ourselves, what they call "want of nerve" is the
chief element of my strength. My voice trembles at
the commencement from excitability, and *that* it is

---

* Some private affairs alluded to in this letter.

† "As an old friend, allow me to add my unit of admiration at
the masterly way in which you successfully defended the case of
East v. *Oliver,* and more particularly at your tact in cross-exami-
nation. I prognosticate that you will ere long lead this circuit,
when you have a little more *nerve* (all that you want). My means
of prophecy arise from my having officially listened to every speech
at the Bar in this county (Somerset) for twenty-two years past,
and witnessed the rise and progress of many of your fraternity.

" Yours faithfully,
" H. TUSON."

which makes me impressive when I warm. As Turenne once said at the beginning of an engagement, " I tremble, but it is not from fear." I conducted this case in direct opposition to the advice of all the old stagers. They told me not to read the correspondence for fear of the reply, and I began with it, made it the grand point, and challenged commentary. It proved incontestably that East had commenced and conducted this action solely with a view to costs, and Rolfe at once declared it decisive of the case. I don't suppose it will be reported, but it has been much talked of. I am off to London in an hour, where I hope to find a letter from you.

Mr. Hayward to his Sisters.

St. Leonards, September 14, 1842.

I send you the likeness, but I don't like it at all. I look too set-up, for the sun was in my eyes and I could not keep from winking without an effort. If you don't like it, I will try again on a shady day. I go to Town to-morrow and shall stay a week certainly. We end well, for to-day the fair Rothschilds, and the beauty of the country, Mrs. Lamb * (wife of the eldest son of Sir Charles) dine with Lady Charleville. I have spent two days with the Lambs, who have a beautiful place four miles off. Sir Charles † married Lord Eglinton's mother, Lady

---

* Sir Charles Lamb's house was Beauport, Battle, in Sussex. His daughter-in-law, Mrs. Lamb, referred to as the "beauty of the country," was the mother of Mrs. Singleton, who under the name of ' Violet Fane,' is the author of ' Denzil Place'; the passion, the power, the beauty of which made Mr. Hayward declare " our great laureate outshone by the genius of Violet Fane."

† " Charlie Lamb," as he was familiarly called, whose romantic marriage with the lady referred to caused some sensation at the time, was the " Knight of the White Rose " of the celebrated Eglinton Tournament, in which, as half-brother of the Earl of Eglinton, he took a leading part. He possessed an interesting and original character, and died when comparatively young.

Montgomerie, but I forgot to ask about the Vincents. I am very glad to hear that you have something stirring, and I really hope the father may be brought about again, for he is a thoroughly good fellow.

Yours ever,

A. H.

From the Count Horloge* to A. Hayward, Esqre., Barrister-at-Law.

GOOD SIR AND TRUSTY PLEADER,   A.D. 1842.

I hope you will not attribute to the spirit of intrusion my sudden appearance in your chamber. I belong to the old polite school; and though I have lately suffered much from cold and damp, and also from a pain in my back resembling rheumatism (brought on by the loss of my pendulum which prevented my taking accustomed exercise, and the want of sufficient covering), I should, I assure you, at no time have so overrated my value, as to make sure of a welcome, were it not that I was sent by a lady, and t'would have been ungallant to refuse ; the more especially as she made me the bearer of a message to you, and was the saving of my unworthy self, by causing the very mainspring of my life to be renewed (I being in the hands of most careless strangers, and then suffering under a general interruption of all the vital functions). Sir, you will think me garrulous; 'tis the privilege of age ; and such as you see me I am old enough to have counted out the hours of many lives, and have been accustomed to consider myself of importance. Look in my pale and silent face. Where your eyes are now fixed, many an eye now closed in darkness has turned ; in burning impatience ; in miserable

---

* Mrs. Norton presented Mr. Hayward with a clock, for his services to her in a legal matter. This letter, written by Mrs. Norton, accompanied the clock.

tears ; in listless weariness ; in settled despair. I have not the power to give you their histories ; it is left to each man's heart to write his own sermon on Time, but I should have power to make you *think*, for I have rolled round the last living hour of many men, and, more solemn still, the first hour after death ! *My* life of ingenious mechanism has been the only moving thing in the still chamber, with the quiet corse ; *my* beating has sounded, the only pulse that could break the silence for ever fallen on the master of the house ! But I am too serious. I have heard my donor say that she would give worlds to be able to send you a clock, whose works were warranted to make every hour of your life pass pleasantly, in gratitude for many hours of toil and trouble spent by you in that lady's cause. But since such miracles are not, accept *me* as a friend and companion, and I will endeavour to be a cheerful clock. I consider myself, if not equal to a *man*, at least better than a *Dog*, and there-fore a fitter companion. (A dog moraliseth not ; he lieth " on the rug snoozing ; he requireth food daily ; he dis-playeth his indolence by barking, at the beggar for begging, at the visitor for knocking at the door, at the gardener for digging, at the gentleman on horseback for riding fast, thereby tacitly requiring of the whole world they should copy his do-nothingness. He licketh, indeed, his master's hand, and waggeth his tail, but what of that ? Even the sloth crawleth and eateth leaves.") This is from a great author ; and aptly describes the animal foolishly adopted as " the friend and favourite of man." How much nearer to a man's heart should his clock be than his dog. The clock hath part of his busiest hour ; the dog, not so. The clock, as it were *advises*, nay almost *commands* ; it points, as much as to say, it is time for that consultation with the Attorney-General ; or get you gone to your Courts of Westminster ; or, call your clerk, and get up that case, or those papers will not be copied in time. Can a dog do so? No. Stupidly he lieth, and when his master moves, up jumps Bow-wow, with the single idea that he shall now walk, run, or perchance bathe in the Serpentine! 'Twere as if a clock should always strike " *One*," let what would be the hour! Adieu! Hear me when I advise; that when the circle of Life's great dial is completed, and the ghosts of the Hours accompany the soul into another world, to give an account of its occupations in this, you may recognise none worse employed than those I came to recall; hours kindly, usefully, unselfishly, and I will hope happily spent; hours which are vanished for ever, and have left behind a grateful impression and your old clock,

Yours for ever,

HORLOGE DE TIC-TIC.

Mr. Hayward to his Sisters.

Wiesbaden, September 2, 1843.

I wish you would write and say how you all are, for I shall make this place my head-quarters, and probably stay about a month. Nothing could be pleasanter than our journey, for Damer is a most agreeable companion, full of life, fun, and information; and on board the steamboat to Antwerp we fell in with Prince George of Cambridge, and Macdonald, brother of Lord Macdonald, a man of fame in the London world of fashion. They joined us and we lived together till we got to Cologne, when the Prince was obliged to hurry on. Good-natured and without pretension, he placed himself at once on a perfect footing of equality. He travelled under the name of Lord Culloden, and is on his way to the Ionian Islands. We got here on Thursday. The place is very striking, and I know nothing at any English watering-place to compare with the rooms. There is a

railroad to Frankfort, where I hope to get all the books
and literary information I want without going further.
We are also within a day's journey of Baden, and I really
do intend to pay Mrs. Herbert and Lady Vincent a visit
if they stay. I write and read all the morning, exactly
as if I was in my own chambers. Damer occupies
himself with drinking the waters and walking from
seven to eleven. All external symptoms of his gout
have miraculously disappeared already, and he walks as
well as I do. The fact is, we have never dined later
than four, drunk no wine, and gone to bed early;
which accounts for his convalescence. I cannot help
laughing at the condition of some of the patients. There
is a Dutch count whose head is all on one side, and his
servant comes behind him to put it straight at dinner.
He keeps muttering something which Damer says is
" I'll be damned if I'll pay," and it sounds like it. Next
me are two Englishwomen, who seem to forget that
everything is heard through these thin partitions. Last
night, after talking in the gayest style, one of them
turned to and read a long prayer to their man-servant
and maid-servant.

Mr. Hayward to his Sisters.

Wiesbaden, September 22, 1843.

I was very glad to get your letter, as it assured me that
all were well. I shall leave this place about the 30th, and
be in town about the 6th or 7th October. We pass our
time pleasantly enough here. Lady Gainsborough and
Lady Powerscourt arrived soon after us, and we forthwith struck up an acquaintance. They are certainly two
of the most charming women I have ever met. Lady
Gainsborough was one of the ladies of the bedchamber
under the Whigs. She went away last week, but Lady
Powerscourt still remains, and we drink tea with her

most evenings. Besides her beauty she is very clever
and accomplished, and was just beginning 'Faust' when
we met. Her husband is coming, but does not
mind leaving her to take care of herself and her beautiful
little boy.* Mrs. R.'s brother is not at all the better for
the water-cure, and they are now returning home. I
have just received an invitation from her uncle, Lord
Delamere,† to visit them in Cheshire, but I shall not
leave London again for more than a day or two. I have
read a great number of new German books, and shall
turn them to good account in the reviewing line. We
see the best people who go through, but have seen few
worth knowing. Lord Frederick FitzClarence came
over from Frankfort and stayed two days with us, and
Count —— a Prussian diplomat once attached to the
London Embassy, is very useful. The neighbourhood
is interesting. To-day (Friday) it is the fashion to
go to Mayence and hear the military band, which plays
in the gardens of the town from four till dusk. We
escort Lady Powerscourt and a young German Countess
(the Duchess's maid of honor). We dine at Mayence,
go to the music, and return to drink tea with Lady
Powerscourt. I have been trying the waters, and I think
they have done me good. They are very mild and can't
do harm. A clever young doctor told me that they would
probably suit my stomach, and dispense with the necessity
of medicine, which I cannot bear. Damer has taken the
waters regularly, and is much the better for them. I
have a notion, though, that half the battle is getting up

* This lady was Elizabeth Frances C. Jocelyn, daughter of the
third Earl of Roden ; she married, first, Richard, sixth Viscount
Powerscourt, and, secondly, Frederick William Robert, fourth
Marquess of Londonderry.

† Mrs. R(owley) was the daughter of Lt.-Col. Shipley, by his
wife, Charlotte Watkin-Wyn, whose sister married the first Lord
Delamere.

VOL. I.   H

early and walking about whilst taking them. I have nothing else to tell you.

Love to all.

The Rev. Sydney Smith to Mr. Hayward.

DEAR HAYWARD,

Combe Florey, Taunton,
December 11, 1843.

Do you know anything of the Æsculapius of Lyme Regis ? Does he march in the paths of rhubarb? Can he remove a limb? Does he know his way in the bowels ? Can he see in the cœcum ? Can he remove a full stop in the colon ? Is his practice right in the rectum ? In plain prose, do you know anything about him, and is he fit for the office he is desirous to fill ?

I am here without motive, without excitement, in a state of quiet which I hate, and amongst the beauties of nature for which I have little taste. I envy you the dirt, the hurricane, and malignity, in which (as all London people) you live.

Ever truly yours,
SYDNEY SMITH.

If you come to the West to see your father, or, as the Scotch call him, your *cause*, and will bestow a day upon us, we shall be very glad to see you.*

In 1840 the State of Pennsylvania was declared insolvent. In November 1843, Sydney Smith published in the *Morning Chronicle* his amusing letters on the Pennsylvanian Repudiation. The Americans were very angry at these letters, and their Press accused him in

* This letter has been printed in Mr. Hayward's "Essay on Sydney Smith"('Selected Essays,' vol. i. p. 51), in connection with an amusing anecdote told about Sydney Smith's own Esculapian exploits.

the coarsest language of being exclusively actuated by interested motives.   This was a mistake.   Mr. Hayward sent him some American papers taking his side of the Repudiation question, and received in reply the following letter :—*

The Reverend Sydney Smith to Mr. Hayward.

DEAR HAYWARD,   Bowood, Jan. 8, 1844.

Many thanks for your goodnature.   From the opposite principle, the Dean has sent me all the American abuse. They call me a Minor Canon eighty-five years of age, an ass, and a *Xantippe*, mistaking evidently the sex of that termagant person.   The truth is, that neither Macaulay nor Croker† are like the falls of Niagara.   Macaulay is always rising instead of falling, and Croker has ceased to fall because he can fall no lower than he has done already.   We have had a very agreeable party here.   I return on Monday.

Ever truly yours,
SYDNEY SMITH.

At this period it appears that Mr. Hayward did not limit his literary efforts to the *Quarterly Review*, but became a frequent contributor to the *Edinburgh Review* then edited by Mr. Napier.   In all his social diversions Mr. Hayward never neglected literary work, and was rapidly amassing a store of knowledge concerning European personages and affairs, which enabled him to write and to speak with an authority possessed by

---

* See 'Selected Essays,' "The Rev. Sydney Smith," p. 57, *et seq.* (Longmans, 1878.)

† Sydney Smith and Mr. Croker were always at daggers drawn, and a reconciliation dinner attempted by Parke (Lord Wensleydale) made matters worse.

H 2

few of his contemporaries. "Few Englishmen, indeed,
says Mr. Escott in the *Fortnightly Review*, "have ha(
a larger personal acquaintance on the Continent. Fe\
knew the character of France and Germany better, o
had a juster appreciation and a deeper insight into th
spirit of their literature. Hayward's visits to Paris wer
frequent ; and to the end of his life he seldom crosse(
the Channel less than once a year. He was on intimat
terms with Thiers, Broglie, Dumas, and many other:
Ile introduced more than one French writer for th
first time into England. One of his most interestin;
essays is devoted to Madame Mohl, at whose hous
he was a frequent guest."

Mr. Hayward to his Sisters.

10 Rue Castiglione, Paris, Sept. 7, 1844.

I received Fanny's letter, which was highly satisfactor}
I am now comfortably established and shall probabl:
stay a month, for I can work just as well and amus
myself very profitably besides. This morning I break
fasted with Thiers, the leader of the Opposition, an(
twice Prime Minister, which he is pretty sure to b
again. He is a little, insignificant-looking man till h
gets animated, but wonderfully clever. He said peopl
mistook him much in supposing he wished for a wa
with England, which he thought would turn only to th
aggrandisement of Russia. To-day I dine with th
Countess Merlin, a wit, beauty, and fashionable of th
first water, now staying at Versailles, which I reach b:
the railroad in half-an-hour ; to-morrow with Cousin, th
Minister of Public Instruction, peer of France, &c. I:
fact, I may go just where I like, having just the kind c
reputation which tells here, but unluckily most of th

eading people are away. Let me hear from you in about a week. Love to all.

Ever yours,

A. H.

By the death of Mr. Hayward's father, on Christmas Eve, 1844, a break occurred in that family circle to whose happiness and mutual affection his correspondence bears frequent testimony. The following letter was written only a few days afterwards.

Mr. Hayward to Lady Chatterton.

DEAR LADY CHATTERTON,   Temple, Dec. 1844.

A thousand thanks for your kind note. I got home late last night. Ours was a very united family. We have never so much as known, by our own experience, that a distrustful thought or individual interest meant, and our very property was as good as held in common. My father's death, therefore, though it was to be looked for before many years, is a sad blow, particularly to my mother and sisters, who will feel it hourly. I stayed till they had got composed, but I was obliged to return to town. However, I leave them in the midst of attached friends, and perhaps it is as well to let them accustom themselves to new habits.

Ever yours,

A. HAYWARD.

Mrs. Norton to Mr. Hayward.

'Tis well! I will do so. I did not think to ask Nelly,* but left her to your own unassisted efforts. There is nothing like her—I mean as to agreeability, for I hold myself quite as valuable a companion in the long run, but I

* Her sister (Helen), Lady Dufferin.

don't think I am fit to whisk the dust off her satin slipper in general society. Adieu! It is sure to be pleasant, whoever you ask. You know we have never had a dull dinner in those sacred chambers—"sacred" only to the memory of excellent jests and brilliant observations; otherwise "sacré" or cursed, and lying under the ban of a great legal authority, as not to be rashly supped at by the fair sex. Adieu!

Yours truly,

C. CLIENT,

alias C. de la Griffe,

née Patte de Velours.

Mr. J. G. Lockhart to Mr. Hayward.

DEAR HAYWARD,   March 3, 1845.

I believe there was about as much necessity for an apology from me to you as from you to me—at least we both lost our temper, and it signifies little which soonest or most. I was extremely unwell all yesterday, and therefore hope you will forget all my part of the mischief, as I do yours. With sincere thanks for your prompt and kind note. Since I am writing, let me say distinctly that I used the word 'gentleman' in reference to a most amiable man in its *heraldic* sense only. Though my acquaintance with him is very slight, I believe he is most entirely a gentleman in every other and better sense of the term; and I am sure you never dreamt that I meant in reference to his wife to insinuate that she was not by every personal circumstance entitled to the position which, however, in my perhaps erroneous opinion, she owes to the literary merit generally acknowledged by the world. I was, I own, vexed, under Mrs. Norton's roof, and in the presence of Mr. . . . ., and Sir A. Gordon, to hear a literary man echo the complaint of something like a prejudice against literary men being

entertained among the higher circles of English society.
I don't believe any such feeling lingers among them.
It is, I dare say, very true that people of consequence in
their own province who find themselves of no consequence here, regard with some spleen the ready access
which Science or Literature affords to the fine houses of
which they themselves hardly ever see more than the
outside. But I think, on reflection, you will also allow
that if these rural dignitaries wished to strengthen their
own complaint, they might with perfect justice say that
Science and Literature are flattered by the Aristocracy—
the real Aristocracy—in a degree remarkably contrasted
with their social treatment of the great professions
themselves. If you find, in fact, that a clergyman, a
physician, a surgeon, has made his way into the fashionable circles here, you will find that this has been so
because of his having earned an extra professional
reputation. How many now of the eminent doctors and
divines in this Town can be said to move in the sort of
society you consider as *the thing?* Does any lawyer
mix in it, unless he has made himself distinguished
either in politics or in letters? I have pretty well done
with the *beau monde*, and have no pleasure at all in it,
though I am not so foolish or so improvident (being a
father) as to desire to drop wholly out of it. You are
younger, and will, I hope, long be much gayer than I am.
But I was thinking most of ——, who has just begun to
see the interior of life in the West-end—who enters the
scene with something like *radical* feelings, and whom I
should like to form his own opinion on matters of this
class, without a preliminary impression that we Tories
of his order do scurvily at heart attribute to our worldly
superiors a species of prejudice which I do believe has
no existence whatever—quite the reverse.

Ever yours very truly,

J. G. LOCKHART.

Mrs. Norton to Mr. Hayward.

March 6, 1845.

Sulky, black-hearted Avocat! I have partially re-covered from my amazement that you should say unjust and bitter things about my want of generosity, &c. If this is a *Queen Bee*, you had best say so, and I will go and call and coax her (and we will sit together, as much as she will permit), and ask her here. If you were as gentle as your friend Kinglake, you would have understood better what we all said, and what Lockhart especially meant, and all that I supported of what he said, which you call "going against" you. You don't deserve to be written to, and I only do it because you are my Avocat. I say again, if you have not persuaded her we burnt her in effigy (for you are a gossip), I will go and see the large brown eyes that, like the eyes of all people of im-perfect hearing, have so much plaintive listening in their expression.

Yours, &c.,

C. CLIENT.

Mr. Macvey Napier* to Mr. Hayward.

MY DEAR SIR,   Edinbro', April 12, 1845.

I was very glad to see your hand, but not able to make any reply so quickly as I would have wished. A very severe influenza, which confined me, mostly to bed, for three weeks, threw everything so much in arrear that I can only get out of debt by slow degrees; being still very weak, and not very useful. Miss Berry is so much in your line, that, on seeing the contents of the *Quarterly*, I thought you had given the old concern a *lift*—a supposition which vanished when I saw the article itself. I used to know the ladies well, having years ago met them

* Editor of the *Edinburgh Review*.

at their relation's, Mr. Ferguson of Raith, in Fifeshire*
—one of the best of houses—and afterwards at their own
evening parties. But I have, in a measure, fallen out of
acquaintance with them, owing chiefly to my few-and-
far-between visits to the capital. The book is now old
—very old—and I have some other reasons, which I
cannot properly mention, for not now noticing it. However, I do not put an absolute *veto* upon the proposal,
though rather so ; but of this hereafter. Lord Chesterfield's Letters would do admirably, I should think, for an
Autumn article ; but as it comes within the scope, nay,
the letter of my agreement with Macaulay, I must give
it to him if he claims it. But as I lately agreed to keep
off him for two or three numbers, till Vols. 1st and 2nd
of his History should be out—a most reasonable request,
considering how elaborate his articles always are, and
the time they cost him—I do not think, indeed, am *almost
certain*, that he will wish to decline Chesterfield (Burke
being, besides, his next great subject for an article†) ; it is
most probable it will go into your hands. I will get this
ascertained forthwith, that you may·have it in view, and
in hand ; for it must be a *great* article. So standing
matters, and your views and mine being at one, I think,
I need say nothing more till this is fixed. If you are to
do a short article on Mrs. Norton, that will be all I
could take for next (July) number. If it is to be given
up, we may then think of something else, pungent and
sparkling. If you are still to do it, *short* it must be. No
words almost could express the annoyances I now suffer
from the length of articles, and the accumulation of

* Mr. Ferguson of Raith was the maternal uncle of Mr. Berry,
the father of the Misses Berry, the intimate friends of Horace
Walpole.

† Macaulay at one time contemplated writing a Review of
Burke's Life and Writings (v. ' Life and Letters of Lord Macaulay,'
by the Rt. Hon. G. O. Trevelyan, M.P., vol. ii. p. 152).

matter. If you have aught to say about Mrs. Norton, do say it immediately. Will you tell me—confidently, of course—whether you know anything of a Mr. Thackeray, about whom Longman has written me, thinking he would be ɾa good hand for light articles? He says (Longman) that this Mr. Thackeray is one of the best writers in *Punch*. One requires to be very much on one's guard in engaging with mere strangers. In a Journal like the *Edinbro'*, it is always of importance to keep up in respect of names. Who is ' Eothen¦'? I know he is a lawyer and highly respectable ; but I should like to know a little more of his personal history, and you, I know, can give me that sort of thing knowingly and authentically. He is very clever, but very peculiar. I know he is quite one of Lockhart's men. I do not (honestly) think the *Quarterly* is improving. I regret my long illness will prevent my getting up to town this season. I must go to the country to recruit. One loses, and especially one in my position, by not going to London.

Ever yours,
M. NAPIER.

Mr. Hayward to Lady Chatterton.

MY DEAR LADY CHATTERTON,   Bridgewater,
Aug. 3, 1845.

Don't attribute my long silence to indifference, for it is quite the contrary. I kept the writing to you as a *bonne bouche*—as a resource for a melancholy morning ; and I now congratulate myself on my prudence, for Heaven knows what I should do with or *to* myself to-day if I had not something agreeable to set about. The course of circuiteering brought me to this place yesterday. It is the ugliest and dirtiest you can fancy ; and, being situated on a navigable river, has all the *disagreeables* of

a fishing town without the sea.   Changes of places are
good illustrations of life.   I passed part of Thursday and
the whole of Friday at Torquay, the most beautiful place
in Devonshire, though they have done their best to ruin
it by building.   You should make a tour to Devonshire
and sketch.   This one county could match most continental countries for beauty, and Ilfracombe has something of the sublime.   Apropos of tours, how provoking
it was of Lockhart not to give you a place among the
Lady Travellers.*   I was quite disappointed at the omission, and can only attribute it to forgetfulness.   They
have left out Mrs. Shelley too.   I left London more than
three weeks ago, and the only conversable people I have
met are Sir William and Lady Molesworth far down in
Cornwall, and the Fords at Exeter.   He has at last
finished his handbook,† which is full of pleasant and
instructive matter, but very thick and close printed.   To
illustrate a passage, he produced the other day one of
the knives the Madrid women wear in their garters.   In
case a lover is faithless, they draw it and cut him across
the face, saying : " I have marked you now."   Some lady-
killers would have their faces scored like a hot-cross-bun.
Lockhart reviewed Ford's book in the *Quarterly*.   I also
reviewed Mrs. Norton's poem.‡   The short review of it
in the *Edinburgh* is by me.   Sedgwick's article on the
' Vestiges ' in the *E. R.* has made a noise, but it is too
violent and far from well written.   The most curious
case on Circuit was that of the Brazilian slavers, which
you probably saw in the newspapers.   They were tried
for the murder of their captors, a midshipman and seven
sailors.   I had a brief for the prosecution, and was
occupied three long days about it.   The criminals were
ten in number, each a picture.   Only two looked like

---

* " Lady Travellers," *Quarterly Review*, June 1845.
† ' A Hand-book for Travellers in Spain,' by Richard Ford. 2 vols.
‡ ' The Child of the Islands.'

pirates or murderers. The man who stabbed the midshipman behind the back was a handsome, soft-looking person, and all the young ladies were for saving him. I am not quite sure that some of them were not for rewarding him too. It is not yet known whether they are to be hanged or no. I go to Lyme Regis to see my family in two or three days, and shall be in town about the 18th. I shall stay there about a fortnight. Pray write to me again, and tell me what you are doing and planning, and I will answer on the instant. Regards to Sir William.

Ever yours faithfully,
A. HAYWARD.

Mr. Hayward to Lady Charleville.

Temple,
Oct. 24, 1845.

MY DEAR LADY CHARLEVILLE,

I was delighted to hear from you, though I could almost calculate your movements by the weather, and I think you cannot do better than stay at Malvern during the present weather, and with Wigram and Mr. Lechmere to talk to.

I met Thiers at Lord Mahon's the other morning, and we had a great deal of pleasant chat. He was very animated, and may be described as a Frenchman described Mrs. Norton : "I like her—she is so spirituous and abandoned." He quietly told us of his interview with the Royal family in 1830, when he went to propose the Crown. This is history, and as true as most history —being what the actors choose to be known and nothing more.* The statue list was on the table, Lord Mahon being one of the Committee.† He (Thiers) could not

---

* 'Eminent Statesmen,'—"Thiers," pp. 18 and 19, by A. Hayward. (Murray, 1880.)

† The list of statues to be placed in the Houses of Parliament : and the question was whether Cromwell's statue should be included.

understand any one objecting to Cromwell as a great
man, saying truly that no one had done more to make
the English name respected. He disputed the claim of
Monk, who simply turned opportunely. I quoted what
Guizot says of Monk in his history. "Ah pour ça," said
Thiers ; "J'y mettrois une note, voyage à Gand." * I fear
Guizot was somewhat influenced by the analogy between
Monk's conduct and his own. Milnes was not there,
though the *Morning Post* says he was. Lord Salisbury
was pleasant for a *grand seigneur.* He would allow
Cromwell no merit or greatness of any kind. But there
certainly is a great charm in that bland courtesy and
ease of manner which undisputed position gives. No
one has it who is struggling for a place, either social or
intellectual. Of course we all played up to Thiers, and
said only just enough to bring him out. He was rather
too free with his professions of esteem for England.

Get the Reviews if you can. First, I want you to
read my article on "Chesterfield," * in the *Edinburgh
Review.* You may think me too liberal about Ireland,
but you will agree with me about the rest. Indeed, I
believe that, *au fond,* we agree about Ireland too, for
what you did yourself to reconcile the sects, and do
away with prejudices, is the best possible kind of
toleration and the truly enlightened policy. The proprietors and residents are undoubtedly the only persons
who can understand the country *au fond,* and carry such
policy into practice. If you had lived under Chesterfield's lord-lieutenancy, you would have been taken as
his chief adviser, and have been much such a correspondent as Mr. Prior and the Bishop of Meath. Lady
Holland has been ill, though she did give a dinner to
Thiers and Lord Palmerston. Ledru is here : he went

* Mr. Hayward's statements in this article upon the Irish
Catholics called forth from Lady Charleville some remarks to
which he replies.

to Cheltenham, and meant to look for you *there.* I asked him if he came to marry ; he said, *au contraire.* Regards to all.

Ever yours,
A. H.

MY DEAR LADY CHARLEVILLE,   Temple, Nov. 1, 1845.

I acknowledge your letter directly, because you do not say where I am to address you after Monday. Very probably you do not know ; your tour being like Burns's verses—

> " And where the subject theme may gang
> Let time and chance determine,
> Perhaps it may turn out a sang,
> Perhaps turn out a sermon."

I hope yours won't end in a sermon, though. Shepherd says that the Lincoln's Inn festivity went off very well, and that the Queen looked delighted. Prince Albert was made a student, and with the gown over his red coat, led Her Majesty down the Hall. No invitations at all were issued except to the Royal party, which I think was a mistake. They should have excluded some of their own men by lot, and at least have asked the judges.*

There is not a syllable in your letter in which I do not cordially agree, except perhaps your notion, that I see no evil in the spread of false doctrines. All I could ever mean on this subject was, that I do not think the worse of men for articles of faith which do not influence conduct. If, for example, I thought that Roman Catholics did not think themselves bound to keep faith with heretics (or with any class), I should think them

* On the 30th of October the New Hall at Lincoln's Inn was opened by the Queen.

not only unfit for any place of trust, but unfit for society.

The doctrine, that the end justifies the means, has been used by Protestant zealots as often as by the Jesuits. Cromwell's zealots thought they might commit any crime for the glory of God. *All* the best men in Europe prior to the Reformation were Roman Catholics. Half the best men in Europe are so still. I do not believe that they ever adopted, as an *essential* article of faith, any doctrine that strikes at the foundations of morality. But I fairly own I see very little difference, *as regards morality*, between consubstantiation and transubstantiation. The Roman Catholic takes the words of inspiration in their literal sense ; the Protestant, in their metaphorical sense. As to the essence of the sacrament, and the vital doctrines of Christianity, they agree. Why, therefore, should a man be the worse man for believing transubstantiation ?

It is unfair to tie people down to everything included in their books. Which of *us* believes all the Articles ? Much less all that the Bishop of Exeter, or any other intemperate man, chooses to write and call Church of Englandism ?

I write off this in haste to vindicate myself in your opinion at once, from which you may infer how highly I prize it. It is a bad subject for a letter.

With the exception of a dinner at the Attorney-General's next week, and one to meet de Beaumont (the French writer and deputy), I have no visiting in prospect. What people call a *breakfast* at the Chancellor's, is walking in and making a bow with a full-bottomed wig on : a great bore, but I shall do it on Monday. God bless you all.

Ever yours,
A. HAYWARD.

MY DEAR LADY CHARLEVILLE,   Nov. 23, 1845.

I enclose the letter. How right you are about fools and weak people. Indeed, is not honesty one result of a *sound* understanding, as contradistinguished from what you aptly term "the showy intellect" of a man like Disraeli? Don't all these people miscalculate, and forget that for a temporary advantage and a passing glitter for the many, they are sacrificing the esteem of the select few, who bestow the only reputation worth having?

If the Catholic priests were paid, they would lose their main motive, and best topic. The real use of an Establishment is to keep the ministers of religion steady and quiet, and make them independent, not to teach any particular mode of faith, or why is the Presbyterian religion established in Scotland? If this be so, there should always be a State provision for the ministers or priests of the majority. But you and I perfectly agree in this as in most other matters. The questions, however, will be decided by folly and bigotry for some time to come. I shall be very glad to see the paper you mention. I met H. Ellis yesterday, and had a walk with him. He is uncertain as to stay.

Ever yours,

A. HAYWARD.

I have long considered Lord M. as lost to us, and a sad loss it is. He was so perfectly natural and thorough-bred, a very different thing from well-bred, which refers only to conventional manners. Then the cultivation of his mind was exquisite, and his knowledge wonderful.

Mr. Hayward to his Sisters.

[EXTRACT.]

Dec. 10, 1845.

The Whigs have failed, and Peel is sent for again. The story goes* that Lord Grey broke them up by refusing to sit in the Cabinet with Lord Palmerston as Foreign Secretary, and insisting on strong measures as regards the Church, &c. In fact, one section headed by him wanted to go the whole hog, and Lord Lansdowne, &c., were more moderate. No one, up to this hour, knows what Peel really went out upon.

Ever yours,

A. H.

Mrs. Norton to Mr. Hayward.

DEAR AVOCAT,   Nov. 1, 1846.

I think I am better, though yesterday and all this morning I have been less well; but this evening, for a sick poetess, I may say I feel "pretty bobbish"; my head has been very bad.

LINES TO A LEECH.

Oh, thou dark Leech,
If I could teach
Thee sound and speech,
I'd thee impeach
Of wish to bleach
My cheeks—and each
At once to reach,
Making maids screech !
—But thou, sad Leech,
Hast got *no* speech !
Not even that one—surnamed the "Single"—
By which old Milnes made all ears tingle,

* The truth of this story is to be found stated in *The English Historical Review*, January 1886. "Notes on the Greville Memoirs," by Δ, p. 122, *et seq*. (Private MSS.)

Nor that which was spoken by D'Israeli
(The abridgement of which was " Never say die ")
When he told the M.P.'s who were coming it strong
He'd be sure to make himself heard afore long ;
And convinced *me* at least, when the row was past
That he certainly would be heard at last.
Nor a speech like Brougham's in the prime of his glory
(As long and as sly as an ' Auld Wife's Story '),
Which always sounded when it was done
As if " three single speeches were rolled into one."
Nor like Monckton Milnes, whose famous allusion
Was carried through with so little confusion
That the House could scarcely its laughter smother,
As each wicked sentence begot another.
Nor —— but, it's all my eye
To expect a Leech to speak in reply !

I'm tired of that ode ; but I think an instructive
epigrammatic verse such as this :—

Oh, worm ! from thee, at whom we scoff,
What wisdom may be won—
Who ne'er attempted to *leave* off
Until thy work is done !

Or more playfully, as thus :—

Hark, what a scream ! 'tis Chloë's shout !
Have robbers dared the maid to throttle ?
No, but a leech has just crept out
She put into a half-pint bottle !

I particularly pride myself on the first line. Can
anything be more full of the true instinct of love, or
present more forcibly to the mind that instant recognition of the one dear voice, than the phrase, " 'tis Chloe's
shout "? Excuse me, I thought you would be pleased
at finding the ease with which the proposed subject could
be treated. Don't think me delirious.

Yours ever truly,

CAR. N.

Mr. Hayward had received from Lord Chancellor Lyndhurst, early in 1845, his appointment to the rank of Queen's Counsel.   By venturing to make him Queen's Counsel, rather on the ground of his high qualifications and great abilities, than on the usual ground, that of large practice at the Bar, Lord Lyndhurst placed the ball at the feet of his friend ; but Mr. Hayward was prevented from seizing the opportunity by a vicious attack which he set himself to resist.   It was the habit of the Benchers to elect at once into their body any newly-made Queen's Counsel, and Mr. Hayward was proposed and seconded accordingly, but Mr. Roebuck, by voting against him, prevented him from being elected.   Thereupon Mr. Hayward, justly indignant, engaged in the business of redressing this wrong with characteristic vehemence.   He brought the matter before the Judges, and so far succeeded that they recommended the Benchers, though in vain, to alter their mode of election. In the din of his fight with the Benchers (he had to explain in society, and say, " Who the devil they were ") Mr. Hayward lost or rather abandoned the opportunity of acquiring what would probably have been a great legal practice.*   The following letter indicates the effect produced in Mr. Hayward's mind by the decision of the Judges, and marks the close of his legal career.

Mr. Hayward to his Sisters.

MY DEAR SISTERS,   Dec. 21, 1846.

The Judges have decided, as we expected, that the Benchers are *legally* right and *morally* wrong.   They say

* *Vide* " Mr. Hayward," *Fortnightly Review*, March and April 1884.

that a Q.C. has no legal right. " But they all think that
the mode of election by which a single blackball may
exclude is unreasonable, and they strongly recommend
the Benchers of the Inner Temple to conduct their
elections to the Bench on some more satisfactory principle in future." This is signed by all the Judges, and
is a hard rap on the knuckles, for it says in effect that I
have been excluded by an *unreasonable* method and an
unsatisfactory principle. They are only the more angry,
and we laugh at them. Heaven knows what they will
do, and I am sure I don't care, for every one is against
them stronger than ever. I dine to-day with Kinglake
('Eothen'), with Lady Dufferin, &c., a large party at
Long's Hotel ; to-morrow with Lady Morgan ; on
Wednesday go to Brocket.*

Ever yours,

A. H.

Mr. Hayward to Lady Charleville.

MY DEAR LADY CHARLEVILLE,   Brocket,* Dec. 25.

Everything here is just what you would like—Lord
Melbourne in excellent spirits, and good for four or five
hours of excellent conversation every day. He does not
come down in the morning, but we go for an hour to his
dressing-room. At six he is in the drawing-room. The
dinner-hour is half-past seven, and he does not go to bed
till near eleven. The party till this morning (when Lord
and Lady Cowper went away) consisted of them—Lord
and Lady Beauvale, Mrs. G. Lamb, and Mr. E. Ellice, a
very agreeable and well-informed man, though he is
called *the Bear.* Lady Beauvale is charming, so well-
informed, so graceful and high-bred. Mrs. Lamb also
is very pleasant. I rode over to Knebworth to-day, but
missed Bulwer, who was out with his daughter. His

* Lord Melbourne's country-house.

house is handsome but fantastic, a strong contrast to this, which is plain and brick. There are some good pictures, and the saloon is very handsome. The charm to me, however, of a place like this results from association. I think of the bright days of Devonshire House, and all here are connected in some way with that brilliant period of English social life. Regards to all.

Ever yours,

A. HAYWARD.

Mr. Richard Ford * *to Mr. Hayward.*

DEAR HAYWARD,   Heavitree, Friday, 1846.

I congratulate you on your multiplied successes, legal, literary, and gallant . . . I am coming up to town for a fortnight or three weeks with my eldest daughter, who comes of age. What say you to a quiet Greenwich party ?† It will be a gallant way of pleasing the Hen ; and, if your society is quite proper, I would bring my pretty daughter. I am afraid, however, of the blues as a genus . . . I have this instant sent back the slips of 'Spanish Ladye's love.' The paper, I hope, (if it appears) will be acceptable ; it cannot at all events be so d—d bad as that in the *Edin. Rev.*, as theirs is a soupçon of *Ajo*, and the right thing, but only a soupçon. I envy you mixing among the "gods" during this critical moment of politics. There is no disgrace that Peel does not deserve for his double-dealing and treachery.

I remain, truly yours,

RICHD. FORD.

Early in February 1847, Mr. Hayward was appointed

* Mr. Richard Ford, the well-known author of the ' Hand-book of Spain.'

† The party took place ; and among the guests were the Countess Hahn-Hahn, Mrs. Norton, and Louis Napoleon.

by the Government to inquire into and report upon the Dublin Improvement Bill. He refers to this commission and to the social pleasures of his visit in the following letter :—

Mr. Hayward to his Sisters.

Dublin, Feb. 26, 1847.

Tom says the papers I sent have not arrived, and I believe a good half are lost of those despatched from London for me. So I enclose a report of the close of the open enquiry, a regular Irish scene. Ford is O'Connell's attorney and the Repeal bully. I have ever since been getting up my Report with the evidence, and shall hardly leave Dublin before the 2nd March. Everybody says I have conducted the whole enquiry wonderfully well under very trying circumstances, for the fury of the Repeal party, as the facts began to come out against them, was excessive. I dined last week with the Commander-in-Chief and the Chancellor. This week I have been to one dinner and a ball (last night) at the Castle. There were a great many very pretty women there, but my peculiar favourites are Lady Kathleen Ponsonby (one of the Vice-Princesses), and a niece of Lord Tankerville's, married to an Irish barrister. I am very much petted, and shall be almost sorry to quit. To-night the 13th Light Dragoons give a supper and ball to the Lord Lieutenant, &c., to which I am asked. I shall clear four hundred guineas by the job, so altogether the expedition will answer. I shall be in town on the night of the 3rd.

A. H.

The following letter refers to Mr. Thackeray's lecture on Swift, on which Mr. Hayward had written a notice.

Mr. W. M. Thackeray to Mr. Hayward.

Kensington, May 23, 1847.

O, most kind Hayward! Why do you go for to say that I thought the words "Only a woman's hair" indicated heartlessness? I said I thought them the most affecting words I ever heard, indicating the truest passion, love, and remorse. I said, though Swift announced himself in that letter to Bolingbroke as an *Ambitionist*, and took to the road and robbed—I say that your article just read is a most kind, handsome, and gentlemanlike one, and I'm glad to think I have such good friends and generous backers in this fight, where all isn't generosity and good friendship and fair play. Amongst the company I see that Lord D—— was present; how Lady D—— must have been surprised! But the truth is that lectures won't do. They were all friends, and a packed house; though, to be sure, it goes to a man's heart to find amongst his friends such men as you and Kinglake and Venables, Higgins, Rawlinson, Carlyle, Ashburton and Hallam, Milman, Macaulay, Wilberforce looking on kindly. Excuse egotism, which means thanks in this instance.

Always gratefully yours, dear Hayward,

W. M. THACKERAY.

The Countess of Blessington to Mr. Hayward.

Gore House,

MY DEAR MR. HAYWARD,   May 31, 1847.

I have to thank you for a small volume * of the most graceful and happily-turned verses I ever perused. I instantly recognised the writing, long as it is since I had seen it; but had I not done so, the ease and playful yet tender grace of the style must have set me to guess who this new candidate for poetical fame could be. As

* 'Verses of Other Days,' first published this year.

it is, while greatly delighted with the verses, I am not surprised at their beauty. I am much gratified that I am deemed among the favoured few to whom copies are sent, and take this opportunity of assuring you, dear Mr. Hayward, that I have never ceased to merit the distinction, if a sincere admiration for your talents and a due appreciation of your society entitle me to it. We first became acquainted in 1833 by the gift of your admirable translation of 'Faust,' which convinced me that no one but a true poet could have so well rendered the sense of its great author. The little book, yesterday received, proves how correct was my opinion. I wish it might be the medium of an intercourse, interrupted I know not how, and the cessation of which I have not ceased to regret.

Believe me,

My dear Mr. Hayward,

Sincerely yours,

M. BLESSINGTON.

When a few numbers of *Vanity Fair* had appeared, it was thought that Mr. Hayward might consent to review them in the *Edinburgh Review*. He was very good-natured about it, but happened to be busied about other things, and fancied he could not undertake it. Mrs. Procter, however, kindly undertook to mark the passages which might be usefully quoted, and Hayward thereupon consented, and wrote a review in the *Edinburgh Review* upon the basis furnished by Mrs. Procter in the above letter. The review—because praising a work really admirable, and then only imperfectly known to the general public—had an immense effect, and accelerated the recognition of Mr. Thackeray's reputation and power.*

* Private MSS.

13 Upper Harley Street,

MY DEAR SIR,   July 23, 1847.

I send you 'Vanity Fair,' and I have, as you wished, marked some parts of it. Not perhaps the best, but the most suitable for extracts, as it appears to me. The one quality for which I think Mr. Thackeray deserves the highest praise is the total absence of affectation. He relies, and wisely, upon his own power of describing and interesting the reader in what is simple and true. Like Goldsmith and Sterne he does not elaborate or insist too much upon any feeling, but trusts to our understanding and sympathy.

> " Some natural sorrow, grief, or pain,
> That has been and may be again."

The characters are neither devils nor angels, but living, breathing people. They neither appear through a trap-door, nor change their father and mother in the third volume. One feels well acquainted with all his characters, although they have no pet phrase or peculiar expression, and except in the case of Dobbin's lisp they have no distinguishing habit, or manner of speaking. He has also permitted us to have a story without one of those character-servants who talk as no servant ever did, or would be permitted to talk. Amelia Sedley is charming : she is not an angel, only a good, true, kindhearted girl, who loves an idle, selfish man much better than he deserves (a habit we women are rather given to) :—

> " A creature not too bright or good
> For human nature's daily food,
> For transient sorrows, simple wiles,
> Praise, blame, love, kisses, tears and smiles."

His people are neither above or below one's sympathy, he treats of feelings common to all classes and to all times. And I feel it a great relief, that he has no wish to prove or disprove anything. I rejoice to read again a good old-fashioned love story. He has avoided the two extremes in which so many of our popular writers delight ; he allows that a gentleman may have a kind heart, and does not confine all virtue to St. Giles's ; neither does he make out that all beauty and intelligence are to be found in Belgravia alone. He seems to me to excel in the pathetic parts : the scene between old Sedley and his wife (p. 152), some short passages about Amelia, are expressed with the delicacy of a woman. I send you also " Chronicles of a Drum," * which seems to me very striking. I have not ventured to mark it, and indeed I feel it rather absurd my having attempted to point out what appeared to me merits in *Vanity Fair*, to one so much better able both to appreciate and to praise them.

Yours faithfully,

A. B. PROCTER.

* A powerful piece of verse, by Thackeray, supposed to have been written by an old French drummer, who had lived through the French Revolution down to the time of the death of Napoleon.

CHAPTER IV.

1848–1852.

MR. HAYWARD had begun life as a Tory, but, beyond is contentions with the " Philosophic Radicals," in the

London Debating Society, and the interest he had in listening to the Parliamentary Debates on Catholic Emancipation and on Reform, he had mixed himself up little in active party politics.

We have already mentioned the part he took in promoting the cause of law reform by the establishment of the *Law Magazine.* He belonged at this time, indeed, to that rational, moderate, and thoughtful school of politicians which, while perhaps unpopular with the extreme party, even of both sides, exercises no small influence in English political life.

Before the year 1846, there were a number of young men who were more or less attached to Sir Robert Peel : the Duke of Newcastle (then Lord Lincoln), Sidney Herbert (afterwards Lord Herbert of Lea), Edward (afterwards Lord) Cardwell, and Lord Elcho (now Lord Wemyss) being of the number ; and of whom Mr. Hayward, though not in Parliament, was a personal friend. After 1846, when the Tory party was split up into Free Traders and Protectionists, Mr. Hayward, who had previously accepted the arguments addressed against Protection, adhering firmly to the policy of Sir Robert Peel, and to his personal friends among the *Peelites,* became a very vehement and conspicuous opponent of those Protectionists, members of the Carlton, who wished to turn the Free Traders out of the club. The part he took in these club squabbles drew the bonds of alliance closer between him and that famous band still gathered around Sir Robert Peel, and he thus came to be regarded as a thorough *Peelite.*

In February, 1848, the *Morning Chronicle*, which had hitherto been well known as the exponent of Lord

Palmerston's views, especially on foreign affairs, was purchased from Sir John Easthope by the Duke of Newcastle and Mr. Sidney Herbert. Under their direction, the paper became an exponent of the views of the *Peelites.* Mr. Douglas Cooke was editor, and Mr. Hayward was appointed on its staff. By this appointment he became engaged in direct party warfare.

Lady Dufferin to Mr. Hayward.

39, Grosvenor Place, June 12, 1848.

Rumour has reached me that my private and confidential communications to you have been publicly bandied about, after a banquet at your house, and commented on by astute Diplomats and persons of that dangerous description. I therefore write this in illegible character, trusting that not even *you* will be able to read it, to ask you to dine at my inhospitable board on Wednesday the 21st, when I will take care that there shall be nothing to eat. Fondly hoping that you will not be able to come, I remain, with best execrations, your enemy for life,

HELEN S. DUFFERIN.

One of Mr. Hayward's most constant correspondents was the late Sir William Stirling-Maxwell, Stirling of Keir. Their close and intimate friendship is sufficiently evinced in their letters. They enjoyed in common many friends and many tastes ; and though they differed in politics, they freely exchanged opinions upon political topics of the day, with a certain raciness and freedom peculiar to those who are men of letters as well as

politicians.   At the date of the next letter Stirling had
just brought out his ' Annals of the Artists of Spain,' the
first of his great works on Spain, which Mr. Hayward
had reviewed in the *Examiner.*   Having crossed over to
France meanwhile, Stirling wrote from Paris to thank
his friend for the review, and in his letter describes the
state of Paris after the battle in the streets in the previous
month, in which, after six days' hard fighting, General
Cavaignac defeated the insurgents, restored order, and
was himself proclaimed temporary President of the
Republic on the 29th of June.

*Stirling of Keir** to Mr. Hayward.*

[EXTRACT.]

MY DEAR HAYWARD,   Paris, July 1848.

We arrived here with the mail this morning in due
course of post, seeing nothing indicative of revolution or
outrage, (although they said at Boulogne 1,000 rails had
been torn up on Thursday or Friday), till we drew up
opposite the blackened shell of the refreshment-room at
Pontoise.   The streets were quite quiet as we drove to
Meurice's, and with the exception of a piece of pavement,
in the Rue de Trieste of which the youthful complexion
hinted that it had lately served for a barricade, we saw
and heard nothing that was inconsistent with the ordinary
aspect of Sunday, Paris, and peace.   In the afternoon
we made a tour of many of the scenes of action.   The
Boulevards, as you go towards the Place de la Bastille, get
every hundred yards more disturbed in their roadways
and foot-pavements; heaps of stones piled up out of the

---

* Sir William Stirling-Maxwell was then Stirling of Keir.   He
did not succeed to his uncle's baronetcy till 1865.

way hinder the crowds of passengers; then you see smashed
window or *jalousie*, or a splintered shutter; then a few marks
of balls on the houses, or on the barks of the wretched little
new trees, or poplars of liberty; next, you come on a row
of unfinished houses, with their carved doorways and
balconies sadly gashed : and finally, every house-front
wears a rueful countenance marked like a pugilist's with
severe punishment.   All that cluster of corner houses
which forms one side of the Place de la Bastille has been
severely handled : some have been actually levelled to
the ground; and the rest have their angles here and
there shot away, or two or more windows smashed into
one.   A certain great magazine there with the sign 'Au
Bélier Merinos,' the whole façade of which ten days ago
seems to have been painted a bright chocolate, looked
like a breadth of cloth, tattered with uncertain holes, and
spotted with mud, so effectually have the windows been
confused with cannon-shot, and the wall small-poxed
with musket-balls.   We called it the *Battered Ram*.
The Place was full of people, jabbering and grimacing,
and the top of the column of July crowded with soldiers
and sightseers.   The winding Rue St. Antoine is in
parts almost a ruin.   One of the houses which had
suffered most severely was an " Estaminet-Billard ; " not
an inch of glass was left in any of the windows, and
hardly a window-frame ; but we saw the cigars and the
cues of the players within, making their 'cannons' as
coolly as if revolution and artillery were unknown.   The
Church of St. Gervais had been severely peppered, and
we found in one of its chapels a little crowd visiting and
sprinkling holy water on the bodies of three dead officers,
lying in state there, with bullet-holes and blood-stains on
the breasts of their uniforms.   The Pantheon is not
much punished : the pillars are chipped a little, but so
far as I could see with an opera-glass, the gods and
goddesses in the pediment are unwounded.   The space

in front of it was a bivouac ; and so were many parts of the quays, where a sort of stage had been erected which enabled the poor weary gardes-nationaux and mobiles to sleep in two tiers one above another, like rabbits in a hutch. We afterwards dined at the Café de Paris, and took our coffee at Torloni's in company with a very pleasant socialist friend of Coningham's. The Boulevard was crowded with its usual bearded idlers and un-bonneted grisettes, and I did not see a single face or object to remind one of the fact, that a battle bloodier than Eylau had been fought a few days before in the streets of Paris—except a jolly, laughing beggar with a wooden leg which, he told me, replaced one that he had left in the massacre at Rouen ! Where can the Rachels be, who are weeping for their children, lovers, husbands or brothers? They had not heard the story of Mrs. H—— H—— being taken in arms and men's clothes at the Embassy, so it is no doubt a London lie. Lamartine, they say, is as deeply implicated as anybody in the revolt, which I hope is a Paris lie.

Ever yours very truly,
WM. STIRLING.

Mr. Hayward to Lady Charleville.

[EXTRACT.]

Keir,* Dunblane,

MY DEAR LADY CHARLEVILLE,   Oct. 11, 1848.

Everything goes prosperously with me at present, and I should be querulous indeed if I were not contented with my expedition. My week at Edinburgh was pecu-liarly successful, as I spent a great deal of it with the three men whom every one coming to Edinburgh for the first time would be most anxious to see : namely, Lord

* Seat of Stirling of Keir.

Jeffrey,* Lord Robertson,† and Professor Wilson‡ of *Blackwood* celebrity, who is now as strong as ever. I introduced Stirling to all of them, and they were as glad of the introduction as he was. Jeffrey was delightful as he strolled about his grounds with us ; and we had a very remarkable dinner at Robertson's, at which were Lady Essex, and Miss Johnson, and Lady and Miss Macdonald. They were there the whole week and are now gone to some place near Perth. I passed Sunday (their last) evening with them, and met there de Berg (the Russian) and Major West.

I have been writing two or three articles a week for the paper§ on thoughtful subjects, and have read a good deal at intervals. Pray read, if you can get it, 'Jérôme Paturot à la recherche de la Meilleure des Républiques.' It is an admirable show-up of the folly and nonsense that has been acted and spoken for the last nine months in France. Best regards to Mrs. and Miss Marlay, and believe me,

Ever yours,

A. HAYWARD.

After the French Revolution in February 1848, when Louis Philippe had fled from his throne and France, a Provisional Government was formed and a Republic declared. The Provisional Government, by its 19th decree, virtually guaranteed to all citizens employment, at wages upon which they could exist. The 30th decree,

* Francis, Lord Jeffrey, famous as one of the founders, and for many years the editor, of the *Edinburgh Review*, and one of the ablest of Scotch Judges. He died in 1850.

† Patrick, Lord Robertson, a Scotch Judge, and the author of 'Leaves from a Journal and other Fragments.' He died in 1855.

‡ John Wilson (" Christopher North "), editor of *Blackwood's Magazine*, Professor of Moral Philosophy in Edinburgh University. He died in 1854.

§ The *Morning Chronicle.*

which followed, directed the immediate establishment of
national workshops (*ateliers nationaux*). The violent
socialistic changes promulgated by these two decrees
were attributed chiefly to Jean Joseph Louis Blanc, a
member of the Provisional Government. The horror of
any kind of revolution innate in the large majority of
English respectable society, the unsettled state of
England in 1848, and the dread of the effect of the
Revolution in Paris upon the Chartists and the masses,
filled many people in this country with a fear of the
men who were said to have caused the French Revolution. And when it was seen that the practical outcome
of the theories which had caused one revolution, produced
another revolution even more sanguinary than the first—
for the June insurrection was the direct outcome of the
' Droit au travail ' and ' ateliers nationaux,' inaugurated
after the February insurrection—the feeling of society in
England became more and more incensed against those
' idle dreamers' who, for the sake of a theory, would
upset a throne. In the violent reaction which followed
General Cavaignac's triumph on the 29th of June, Louis
Blanc was proscribed, and fled to England. Mr. Hayward received him when he was in London, and in his
letters to Lady Charleville excuses himself from her
remonstrances. Mr. Hayward, too, mentions a dinner
at his chambers to Louis Blanc. Probably this was
not the only one he gave, for at one both Lord John
Manners and Mr. Quinten Dick were present, and the
following incident occurred :—

" Louis Blanc, fresh from France, was eager for information respecting the constitution of the country which

was sheltering him, and some of the guests endeavoured to enlighten him in rather solid ways. This bored old Mr. Quinten Dick, who at last said, ' Sir, you have heard many explanations of the working of the British Constitution. They are beside the mark. I will tell you how it works. At my last election, I spoke to my constituents as follows : "Gentlemen, my opponent is a very poor man, with a large family. I am a rich man, and I thank God that all I care for in this world, I cover with this hat !" I put my hat on my head, and they returned me. That, sir, is the practical working of the British Constitution.' Those present were all convulsed with laughter, while Louis Blanc looked, as well he might, completely mystified." *

Mr. Hayward to Lady Charleville.

Temple,

My dear Lady Charleville,   Tuesday, Oct. 1848.

I was the first person in England who wrote against Louis Blanc's opinions, and you will see an article of mine against them in the *Chronicle* of to-day, which I send. I believe him to be a thoroughly honest enthusiast, and as much opposed to bloodshed and violence as myself. The evidence regarding his share in the recent outbreaks is perfectly contemptible. But everything goes by passion and prejudice in France. I have not the slightest doubt he will be recalled within a year.

My party consisted of Lord J. Manners, Smythe, Sir A. Grant and D'Orsay. Bulwer fell ill an hour before. Everybody in town is anxious to meet Louis Blanc, with very rare exceptions, and everybody is pleased with him. He knows perfectly well that I am the decided opponent of his doctrines, and so do all my friends. How people get up lies ! M—— has not seen Louis Blanc

* Private MSS.

K 2

since his arrival, and Louis Blanc has no recollection of ever having met M—— at all. We put the question to him yesterday.

Lord Melbourne has sent to say he should like me to come to Brocket as soon as he is a little better. By the way, if men who have planned violence are to be cut, what are we to do with G—— and Lord S——? G——'s letter proves a plan to bring the Birmingham mob to overawe the House of Lords ; and S——, when the party were consulting what was to be done in 1832, said at Brooks's that the King must be sent to Hanover if he held out. Bouverie stated this at Keir before a large party *as no secret.* I begin to think that anybody will do *anything* under the influence of excitement, and that the greatest possible allowances must consequently be made. I am sure *you* would not turn your back on any one whom you in your heart thought innocent, and I am quite sure therefore you will approve my course as to Louis Blanc, with whom I was intimate many years ago.

I have read the whole of the Report of the Committee of Inquiry.* Have those who condemn him read anything but the garbled extracts in the English papers ?

Ever yours,

A. HAYWARD.

Mr. Hayward to Lady Charleville.

[EXTRACT.]

MY DEAR LADY CHARLEVILLE,

Temple,
Nov. 11, 1848.

I hope you bear this cold weather well, or that it is not cold at St. Leonards, for we begin to cry out here. I have sent you two or three papers,† containing articles

---

* On the events of May and June, 1848, in France.
† *Morning Chronicle.*

in which I thought you might take an interest. In the one to-day you will see the state of the controversy regarding the effect of Peel's measures in bringing about recent distress. I have endeavoured to show that there is no ground for the attack, whether those measures should or should not turn out eventually wrong.* There is no chance of a reunion of the Tory party. The leaders of the two sections are wide as the poles asunder, and, of course, Peel's friends will not allow him to be assailed with impunity. Louis Napoleon is considered sure of the Presidency,† but a month is time enough for the French to change their minds half-a-dozen times over. Charles Villiers saw Thiers a few days ago, and says he was very low about the *avenir* of the country, as he well might be.

A book has just come out by a Mrs. Jameson (not the ex-governess), called ' Legends of Sacred Art,' which is very well spoken of, and I should think it would interest you.

I dined with Fitzroy Campbell on Thursday, with the Phipps's, Lord Rokeby, the Hoods, &c. &c. Mrs. Campbell is certainly very pleasant. H. Bulwer marries Miss Wellesley. It is regularly announced. I met him at dinner on Wednesday, and he made no secret of it. I heard from Lady Castlereagh yesterday. They are at Mount Stewart, and go to Powerscourt in December to stay till February. They give me *carte blanche* for a visit during any part of the period.

Ever yours,

A. HAYWARD.

* The *Standard* and the *Morning Herald* were attacking Peel for his abolition of the Corn and Timber duties, and attributing the distress in the country to his premature policy.

† Prince Louis Napoleon was proclaimed President of the French Republic on December 20, 1848.

Mr. Hayward to Lady Charleville.

[EXTRACT.]

DEAR LADY CHARLEVILLE,   Temple, Nov. 15, 1848. ˙

I have not seen Louis Blanc this fortnight, nor am I
likely to be with him. I did what I think right, and I
don't believe a syllable of what his *soi-disant friend* told
you. Why did he remain his friend, or why did he not
remonstrate with him on the use of such language? But
if I am to give up friends because *some* one says that he
heard *something,* I shall soon lose every friend I have,
and lose my own self-respect into the bargain. The
false reports that are spread out of mere vanity, from a
wish to appear to be *au fait* of things, or intimate with
known people, are far more numerous than those told
from malice. You are so truthful, that you never doubt
anything that is told you confidently. *I* doubt everything that has an air of improbability, let the authority
be what it will, and I set the tenor of the life, and the
general tone of thinking against the charge. The notion
of Louis Blanc being bloody-minded is, *to any one who
knows him,* as absurd as that of Lord Ashley and Lord
J. Manners being so, and *they* preach pretty nearly the
same doctrines in the purest spirit of benevolence. Lord
John is dead for the *droit au travail.*

Ever yours,

A. HAYWARD.

Towards the close of 1848 speculation was rife as to
what would happen in the event of Lord John Russell's
Ministry resigning. The need of a strong government
was urgently felt, in the face of the foreign and domestic
difficulties ahead, and of the unsettled state of Ireland.
Mr. Hayward, in his letter to Lady Charleville, states his
objections to supporting Lord Stanley. One of the

schemes (attributed to Charles Buller) for the pacification of Ireland was the payment of the Catholic priests. But, in face of the opposition which the Government felt they would have to contend with in asking money for that purpose, this scheme was never formulated.

Mr. Hayward to Lady Charleville.

MY DEAR LADY CHARLEVILLE,   Nov. 18, 1848.

I enclose you the last note I had from . . . I am glad you liked the article I sent you. I have really no object but truth in what I write, and it is impossible to *admire* Peel as a statesman or a man. But neither can I admire Stanley, who takes the lead with the Whigs in passing the Reform Bill, and actually brings in the Slavery Abolition Act, then joins Peel and votes for the new Tariff, then joins the Protectionists in railing at Peel for the ruin of the West India Interest, the result of his own measure of Slavery Abolition—Whig, Peelite and Protectionist by turns, and the most violent of the violent in each. This is a little too much. I send you a specimen of Disraeli's consistency in a paper of Tuesday last. The article will amuse you, whether you agree with it or not. It had a great success.

I quite go along with you as to what you think right with regard to the priests, but this is to be the new party-cry of the Protection party, and to propose paying the priests *in any shape* would cost any government their places. Yet I can safely say I do not know one thinking person acquainted with Ireland who does not think it is the sole mode of quieting them, and that Ireland never can be governed till they are quieted. The poor law, as you may see from an article in the same paper, has not worked so ill as is thought.

Ever yours,

A. HAYWARD.

The object of these anti-Protection articles was to silence the *Herald* and *Standard*, which were assailing Peel and Lord Lincoln daily till the war was carried into their own camp. The *Standard* had complained of the importation of French turbans and clocks.

Mrs. Norton to Mr. Hayward.

DEAR AVOCAT,   Nov. [6 or 13,] 1848.

Lord Melbourne,* in his letter of this morning, begs me to "persuade you" to come to Brocket. I am sure if you have leisure you will need no *persuading*, and having now become "au fait" as to his odd ways, will simply write him a note saying that I have immediately given you his message, and that you could come down for a few days on such a day if he likes, and *will* come if you hear nothing to the contrary. I feel very dreary and disheartened, what with Fletcher's illness and one thing and another. I can't abide to be talked utilitarianism to (on that account). Adieu, good Avocat! We are off on Thursday at latest for tranquil Frampton.

                         Ever yours,
                              CAR. CLIENT.

Mr. Hayward to Lady Charleville.

DEAR LADY CHARLEVILLE,   Temple, Dec. 28, 1848.

I have been in daily expectation of hearing that your return was fixed. When are you coming back? I was really on the point of running down on Christmas Day, but could not get rid of an engagement for Tuesday.

I have sent you two or three papers containing articles on subjects I thought might interest you. In that of to-day you will find an article of mine on the

* Lord Melbourne died at Brocket on the 24th of November.

Licensing Act, which you, with your literary tastes, may like to read.

The paper* prospers, and we rise in importance accordingly.

I dined on Xmas Day at the Macdonalds', with Lady Essex and some Scotch cousins. Have you read Macaulay yet? It is a brilliant book, but not a good *history*, and there should be occasional simplicity of narrative and repose, which are wholly wanting. This seems to be the opinion of the best judges, and I have no doubt will be yours. How is Tisdale? But, in short, please to write, and tell me all about yourselves. I dined at the Carlton with Lord J. Manners yesterday, and we then went to drink tea at Lady Blessington's, to learn the French news. D'Orsay has got nothing yet,† and does not stir. Regards to Mrs. and Miss Marlay, and Tisdale, and believe me,

Ever faithfully yours,
A. HAYWARD.

The political crisis alluded to by Mr. Hayward in his next letter was the debate in the House of Lords on the second reading of the Bill for the Repeal of the Navigation Laws, the last barrier against Free Trade. The distress in the country at the time, however, had raised the hopes of the Protectionists, for there were many who regarded that distress as the consequence of Free Trade. The debate therefore excited the keenest interest and expectation, and the fate of the Government, and the return of the Protectionists to power, seemed to many to depend upon the division. Lord Stanley made one of

---

* The *Morning Chronicle*.

† When Louis Napoleon was in exile, Count D'Orsay showed him great kindness. The Count in 1852, after the *coup d'état*, was nominated *Directeur des Beaux Arts*.

his greatest and most telling speeches against the Bill.*
Mr. Hayward was present under the gallery of the
House, and

"sat out the debate, and, with a bit of pencil and a few
sheets of note-paper, wrote upon his knees an answer
there and then to Lord Derby's speech, and, walking off
to the Strand with his MS. at 2 o'clock in the morning,
had the gratification to see in print the next day a clear
and conclusive answer to all the arguments of the Protectionists on the previous night.   This article made a
sensation in newspaper circles at the time, partly because
it was the first time anything of the kind had been
attempted, and partly because the article itself was full
of point and argument.   It revolutionised at a stroke
the whole art of leader writing : . . . and statesmen
found all at once that, with a quiet man of letters sitting
in a corner of the gallery with a bit of pencil, they had
to lay their account for prompt and energetic criticism
in the newspapers the next day, concurrently with the
publication of their own speeches, instead of criticism the
day after, when the speeches had done their work." †

Mr. Hayward to his Sisters.

MY DEAR SISTERS,   May 15, 1849.

How are you getting on now ?   I have been hard-
worked during the last week, as I had to write a good deal
during what people called a political crisis, which ended in
nothing.   I have no notion there will be any change
this session.   London gets full.   I dine to-day with the
Chief Baron, and go afterwards to a party at Lansdowne

* The second reading was carried by a majority of ten, and the
third reading without a division.'
† " English Journalism and the Men who made it."   By Charles
Pebody.   The article appeared in the *Morning Chronicle.*

House. Lady Castlereagh and her Lord dine with me
on Friday, when I have also Lady Dufferin, the Sheridans, Lord Lincoln, Sir E. Bulwer, and Lord Mahon.
I hope you get the Paper regularly. All the articles on
the Navigation Laws were mine : not those on the Jews
and Disraeli.

Yours,

A. H.

Prince Louis Napoleon had become President of the
French Republic on the 20th of December, 1848. Odilon-
Barrot formed the first Ministry of the new President.
The Ministry and the President got on tolerably well
together till the Constituent Assembly (which legally
expired May 28, 1849) was replaced by the Legislative
Assembly. The new elections had completely reversed
the position of parties. Power had passed from the
left to the right, the Conservatives were in a decided
majority, and desired the restoration of the Monarchy.
Odilon-Barrot thought that it was no more than fair to
the President to give him the option of adapting his
government to the change. His colleagues agreed with
him, and he accompanied their resignation with a private
letter, pointing out that it was no longer the excesses of
democracy which the chief of the State and his Cabinet
would have to guard against, but the reactionary
tendencies of the opposite extreme. The resignation
was accepted, but Marshal Bugeaud, who was "sent for,"
having shrunk from the responsibility, Odilon-Barrot
resumed office, with a slight but important change in his
Ministry, giving it thereby a more conservative character
than before. The episode of the Edgar Ney letter led
to the overthrow of the Odilon-Barrot Ministry. The

intrigues which brought about the dismissal of Odilon-Barrot on the 28th of October, 1849, placed the Conservative majority and the President in perfect accord in aiming at reaction.* Such was the state of affairs in France when Hayward visited Paris in November, a visit which he has shortly described in the next two letters.

Mr. Hayward to Lady Charleville.

Hôtel Mirabeau, Paris,
MY DEAR LADY CHARLEVILLE,   Nov. 18, 1849.

Perhaps you will like to hear what is going on here. The late change of Ministry frightened people at first, but things are settling down again, and I do not think there is any fear of an immediate *coup d'état* or a fresh insurrection. Louis Napoleon is in a very critical position, but has gained general respect by his firmness and good faith—rare qualities here at the present moment. My own impression is that he will eventually be made President for life, or for ten years, which would amount to much the same thing. The Legitimists are throwing away their chances by their violence and want of principle. More than half of them have actually been voting with the Red Republicans out of spite. I was regularly presented at the last Thursday reception. These receptions are like private parties, and no one goes unless he knows the President or is specially asked by Lord Normanby. The President shook hands, and hoped I was going to make some stay, but I was obliged to move on to make way for others, and had no conversation with him. He looked worn and *distrait*, as if going through a troublesome ceremony, and when a man is contending for empire at the risk of life and fortune,

---

* " Memoirs of Odilon-Barrot ; " *Quarterly Review*, Oct. 1877.
(By A. Hayward.)

it is vexing enough to be employed in paying common-place compliments. In the course of the evening I was introduced to two of his new Ministers, and had some interesting conversation with them. The man who interested me most, however, was Changarnier. He is about 60, and look like a wrinkled *petit maître*. The only English *men* I saw were Lords Lansdowne, Granby, and Holland, B. Cochrane, Ellis, and three or four others. The *réunion* did not shine in women, and Madame Demidoff made a Mrs. Lausada her companion of the night. Lady Ellis and Mrs. Abbot were there, and I also renewed my acquaintance with the Guiccioli, now Marquise de Boissy and a great lady. Lady Normanby sent me a card for her Fridays, and I went to the last. It was rather a brilliant party, more so indeed, than the President's, so far as the female department was concerned. Lady H. D'Orsay was there. To-day I dine at the *Trois Frères ;* Sir W. Stanley orders the dinner. Observe, it is Sunday, and we dine at a *restaurant !* I passed a day and night with the Erringtons at their château. Ellis has been very kind ; I have dined with him once and dine again on Tuesday. I am also asked to each of the Ministerial receptions, and to Tocqueville's, lately Minister for foreign affairs; so I shall stay out the week and go to another reception at the Elysée. The theatres are more crowded than ever, and I see no external change. Best regards to Mrs. and Miss Marlay, and believe me

Ever faithfully yours,
A. HAYWARD.

Mr. Hayward to his Sisters.

Hôtel Mirabeau, Paris,
Nov. 18, 1849.

MY DEAR SISTERS,

I shall stay here till about this day week. I have been to the President's and to the Embassy, and seen

most of the great people. The President receives every
Thursday, and Lady Normanby every Friday, so I shall
go once more to each. The President is playing a
critical game which absorbs all his time and thoughts,
so I don't like to ask for a private interview. At the
reception, he came forward, shook me heartily by the
hand, and hoped I was going to make some stay. I
was then introduced to two of the Ministers, and am
asked to all their receptions. The importance they
attach here to any reputation as a writer, or any connection with the *Times* or *Chronicle*, is extraordinary. We
have a dinner to-day (Sunday) at the *Trois Frères
Provençaux*, a famous eating-house, and our party con-
sists of Lord and Lady Foley, Lord Granby, Lord
Holland, the Baillie Cochranes, the John Stanleys, Sir
W. Stanley, Lady Sandwich and the youngsters of the
Embassy.—Tom tells me you are all well.

Ever yours,

A. H.

Count D'Orsay to Mr. Hayward.

38, Rue de la Ville l'Evêque, Paris,

MON CHER HAYWARD,   17 Jan. 1850.

J'aurois dû vous répondre plus tôt, pour vous remercier
de l'article que vous m'aviez envoyé. J'attendois d'avoir
vu Louis Napoléon. Nous voici de retour à Paris,
établi pour l'Hiver qui est des plus *rudes*. Les affaires
ici vont mal ; l'amour propre en souffrance, fait tous les
grands révolutionnaires en France, il n'y a pas dix
hommes de bonne foi dans ce beau pays ; les gens opposent
dans la Chambre les lois qu'ils avait eux-mêmes
proposées anciennement. Thiers et Berryer, bavards de
profession, sont si versés d'être mis de côté, qu'ils com-
binent une conjuration de Catilina. Les élections de
Paris montreront définitivement de quel côté est le vent ;

en attendant, dans le midi, le gouvernement est obligé de donner son appui à des candidats légitimistes, plutôt que de voir des extrêmes rouges remporter la victoire, c'est bien tomber de Carybdis dans Scylla. Napoléon a le plus grand désir *to run straight,* mais les *crossins* et *jostlings* cherchent à l'empêcher, vous devez vens (?) en apercevoir. Comment avez-vous trouvé le discours de Victor Hugo ? Rappelez-moi au bon souvenir de mes amis d'Angleterre, j'y suis souvent en pensée, et malgré que cela soit toujours avec un grand sentiment de tris-tesse je préfère cela qu'aux gaietés de Paris.

Votre très dévoué,

D'ORSAY.

Dean Milman to Mr. Hayward.

MY DEAR HAYWARD,   Cloisters, Jan. 30, 1850.

I cannot say how much I am annoyed by the failure in my attempt to bring in Thackeray at the Athenæum. But there is no counting on the stubborn stupidity of man. One voice, you know, excludes, and among eigh-teen committee-men that there should not be one self-conceited—I must not fill up the sentence. We are bound not to reveal the secrets of our *Conciliabulum,* but I may say that it was curious to see Macaulay and Croker rowing together in my boat, with Mahon, &c. &c. If I had not thought myself sure of my success, I should not have subjected Mr. Thackeray to the chance of rejection. Pray assure him of my regret and disappoint-ment.

Ever truly yours,

H. H. MILMAN.

Every man whose opinion Mr. Thackeray would value was with him.

My DEAR HAYWARD,   Kensington, Feb. 1, 1850.

Thank you for your kind note. I was quite prepared
for the issue of the kind effort made at the Athenæum
in my behalf; indeed, as a satirical writer, I rather
wonder that I have not made more enemies than I have.
I don't mean enemies in a bad sense, but men conscientiously opposed to my style, art, opinions, imperti-
nences, and so forth. There must be thousands of men
to whom the practice of ridicule must be very offensive ;
doesn't one see such in society, or in one's own family ?
persons whose nature was not gifted with a sense of
humour ? Such a man would be wrong not to give me a
black-ball, or whatever it is called—a negatory nod of
his honest, respectable, stupid old head. And I submit
to his verdict without the slightest feeling of animosity
against my judge. Why, Doctor Johnson would
certainly have black-balled Fielding, whom he pronounced "A dull fellow—Sir, a dull fellow !" and why
shouldn't my friend at the Athenæum ? About getting
in I don't care twopence : but indeed I am very much
pleased to have had such sureties as Hallam and Milman,
and to know that the gentlemen whom you mention
were so generous in their efforts to serve me. What
does the rest matter ? If you should ever know the old
gentleman (for old I am sure he is, steady and respectable) who objects to me, give him my best compliments,
and say I think he was quite right to exercise his judgment honestly, and to act according to that reason with
which Heaven has mercifully endowed him. But that he
would be slow, I wouldn't in the least object to meet
him ; and he in his turn would think me flippant, &c.—
Enough of these egotisms. Didn't I tell you once before,

that I feel frightened almost at the kindness of people regarding me? May we all be honest fellows, and keep our heads from too much vanity. Your case was a very different one : yours was a stab with a sharp point ; and the wound, I know, must have been a most severe one. So much the better in you to have borne it as you did. I never heard in the least that your honour suffered by the injury done you, or that you lost the esteem (how should you ?) of any single friend, because an enemy dealt you a savage blow. The opponent in your case exercised a right to do a wrong : whereas, in the other, my Athenæum friend has done no earthly harm to any mortal, but has established his own character and got a great number of kind testimonials to mine.

Always, dear Hayward, yours very truly,

W. M. THACKERAY.*

Mr. Hayward to his Sisters.

March 23, 1850.

You may tell Follett that if I were not a Free Trader I should stand almost alone amongst the sensible politicians who speak their minds, for *practically* Protection is given up on all sides, though a show is kept up to please constituents. I have not even written on it of late. I dined on Thursday with Cabrera,† the Carlist general, and went afterwards to a party where I was introduced to Lord Gough.‡ Here is a good story for

* Thackeray was afterwards duly elected by the committee of the Athenæum, on the 25th of February, 1851.

† Ramon Cabrera, Count of Morella, after the death of Ferdinand VII. sided with Don Carlos, but being obliged to fly Spain he settled in England about this time.

‡ Commander-in-Chief in India during the Sikh wars of 1845 and 1848.

you. Loudon the gardener wrote to the Duke of
Wellington, to beg leave to see his beeches. The Duke
read it as from the Bishop of London to see his breeches,
and gave a formal reply stating that the Bishop might
see those he wore at Waterloo, as he supposed those
were what he meant.

Mr. Hayward having occasion to go to Paris in May
on business, managed to make his visit one of pleasure
also. In the following letter to his sisters he mentions his
visit to the *Institut* with Lord Brougham, and the dinner
afterwards at Philippe's. But on referring to Mr. Hayward's article on " Lord Campbell's Lives of Lord Lyndhurst and Lord Brougham," we find these two incidents
more fully related, and that one morning Mr. Hayward
called for Lord Brougham " by appointment at Meurice's
about twelve, and found him in a squabble with a Frenchman whom he had engaged to translate a scientific paper
to be read that day at the *Institut*, and whom he ended in
calling *bête comme une oie*. They then got into a *remise*,
and drove to a celebrated optician's in the Faubourg St.
Germain quarter, where Brougham occupied a full hour
in testing an experiment which he had anticipated in
the paper, but which did not turn out exactly as could
be wished. What he wanted to establish was, that
light, falling upon or encountering a flat surface, after
passing through three or four successive apertures in
boards, or pieces of pasteboard placed some paces apart,
would be fringed or uneven at the edges. ' *Voilà les
franges*,' repeatedly exclaimed Brougham. ' *Je n'en
vois pas, Milord*,' invariably replied the optician, who
was himself a member of the *Institut*. To cut the

matter short, (Hayward) gave his voice for the fringes, and all three started for the *Institut* in the *remise*. Before they had gone far, Brougham stopped the carriage, and, in spite of the optician's protest, who said they were already late, insisted on calling to see the Duc Decazes, who was too ill to see him. Their destination was reached at last ; and dragging (Hayward) (who was not even a corresponding member) after him, he hurried into the centre of the assembled *savants*, and began introducing (Hayward) right and left to all of them. This ceremony ended, the business of the day began by Brougham reading his paper, which (barring accent), was not a bad or unsuccessful performance. No less a person than Arago remarked, in answer to a timid inquiry from (Hayward), ' *C'est bien ; mais il n'y a rien d'original là dedans.*'

"On that same day a dinner came off at Philippe's, in the Rue Mont Orgueuil, which had been arranged.for the express purpose of introducing Brougham to Alexandre Dumas, père. Brougham was punctual to the hour, and they were formally introduced by Count D'Orsay, who, observing some slight symptoms of stiffness, exclaimed, ' *Comment, diable, vous, les deux grands hommes, embrassez-vous donc, embrassez-vous.*' They fraternised accordingly *à la française*, Brougham looking very much during the operation as if he was in the gripe of a bear, though nobody could look more cordial and satisfied than Dumas. The dinner was excellent. Some first-rate *Clos de Vougeot*, of which Dumas had an accurate foreknowledge, sustained the hilarity of the company ; the conversation was varied and animated ; each of the distinguished guests took his fair share, and no more than his fair share ; and it was bordering on midnight when the party separated."*

Mr. Hayward to his Sisters.

May 4, 1850.

I got back Thursday morning after a pleasant and profitable trip, having completely succeeded in my case. Lord Brougham was there, and took me to the *Institut* on Monday, where he introduced me to the leading men of science.　On Tuesday I dined with him, D'Orsay, Alexandre Dumas (the celebrated writer), Lord Dufferin, and Stuart of the Embassy.　I went to an evening party at the Duchess of Grammont's, and saw the Duke de Guiche.　Paris was very full.　I do not think there will be a row.　Louis Napoleon has greatly gone down in popularity.　London seems filling, and I am invited to numbers of gay things.　Let me hear how you are.　My case was to examine some witnesses before the British Consul.

Ever yours,

A. H.

Mr. Hayward to Sydney, Lady Morgan.†

My DEAR LADY MORGAN,　　　　Temple, Nov. 2, 1850.

I felt much obliged and flattered by your letter, although I have delayed answering it for two days.　I spent a morning at Madresfield ‡ in the olden time, when I was at Malvern with Lady Charleville, and was much interested in the house, which looks as if the

---

* *Quarterly Review*, January 1869.　No. 251, pp. 57, 58.

† Sydney, Lady Morgan (Miss Owenson), the author of the 'Wild Irish Girl' and other works, was the wife of the eminent physician, Sir Charles Morgan.

‡ Madresfield Court, Great Malvern, the seat of the Earls Beauchamp.

owner had had a great many grandfathers. The present châtelaine would make any place pleasant, and in her present position realises the couplet,

> " The two divinest things this world has got—
> A charming woman in a charming spot."

Lady Charleville read me one of your delightful letters to her, so I was not quite unacquainted with your movements. I have been first to Knebworth with the de Guiches, then to Baillie Cochrane's * with Lord J. Manners, and then two other Scotch places ; and lastly to Mrs. Rowley in N. Wales, where we had Wynns and Glyns and Cholmondeleys by the dozen for the Eisteddvod. What a splendid place Knebworth is ! and how agreeable he † can make himself in quiet conversations, though his loss of hearing (which is *not* worse) lays him under a sad disadvantage in the touch-and-go of a dinner-table. I saw him just now, and he comes to town in December. I dined yesterday with H. Hope, who has done receiving at Deepdene, for which I was too late. Mrs. Norton is in town, escorted from Brussels by Milnes ‡ and Stirling. I went to-day to the Chancellor's breakfast, as it is called, where Lord Campbell asked for and spoke most admiringly of you. Martin is the new judge, although you are not likely to care much about *that*. You will be amused to hear the fuss making about Dr. Wiseman and the Pope. Popular enthusiasm is expected to display itself in the shape of increased bonfires on the 5th. You and I shall look on, or listen, *en philosophes*, and wonder whether this be or be not the middle of the 19th century.§ There is nothing

* Lamington, Lanarkshire.
† The late Lord Lytton.
‡ Monckton Milnes, the late Lord Houghton.
§ Great excitement was caused in England by a Papal Bull, restoring and re-establishing a hierarchy of Catholic Bishops in this country.

worth mentioning in literature, and I do nothing but
read old books, such as Fielding, Scott, the author of
'Florence Macarthy,' &c. &c. Parties remain much
where they were, but Protection is dead, and Disraeli
very nearly, if not quite, forgotten. How soon one of
these puffed-up reputations goes down. It is like a
bladder after the pricking of a pin. By the way, there
is a clever imitation of his novel style, called 'Singleton
Fontenoy,' well worth dipping through. I have no gossip
or scandal of any sort to tell you. Lord Lincoln tells
me that his father's recovery is hopeless—it is only an
affair of months. I have been scribbling with reckless
haste to save the post.

Ever most sincerely yours,
A. HAYWARD.

General Von Radowitz visited England in 1850. He
had been Secretary of Prussian Foreign Affairs from April
1849 until November 1850. As being the virtual Prime
Minister of Prussia, Radowitz had excited much attention when, owing to the state of affairs in Hesse Cassel,
Austria and Prussia were brought face to face, and
seemed to be on the point of going to war, and settling
in a pitched battle their claims to the dictatorship of
Germany. But the Cabinet of Berlin lost heart, the war
party was outvoted, and the Hessians were compelled
to take back their detested Hassenphlug. Immediately
after his defeat and retirement, Radowitz came to
England, and a considerable sensation was produced by
his reception at Windsor Castle, which he visited two or
three times by special invitation. He told Mr. Hayward
that all he needed in the crisis was the moral support of
England. Even an expression of opinion, or a sign of
sympathy, would have sufficed ; but no sign was given,

and he fell.   That the English nation wished well to his cause was notorious.

'Although he did not speak English, the impression left of his conversational powers in the literary, fashionable, and political world of London was highly favourable. His knowledge seemed universal, and his memory inexhaustible.   In him a masculine strength of understanding was blended with feminine delicacy of perception and tenderness of feeling ; and his flow of earnest thought was alternately enlivened by fancy or softened by sentiment, in a manner to exercise as marked an influence on the higher order of women as on men.'

His miscellaneous writings were numerous : so much so, indeed, that it was insinuated his political failure was owing to his literary pursuits.   Mr. Hayward wrote a notice of him in the *Morning Chronicle* of January 2, 1851, which did much to re-establish this distinguished man's reputation as a statesman.[*]

Mr. Hayward to his Sisters.

Dec. 24, 1850.

I have sent a turkey and sausages for your Christmas dinner, or a subsequent one.   I shall not go out of London.   I have struck up a great alliance with the famous General Radowitz, latterly Prime Minister of Prussia.   I dined with him at the Prussian Minister's yesterday, and he dines with me on Monday next, with Bulwer, Macaulay, Lord Lincoln, &c.

[*] " General von Radowitz." ' Biographical and Critical Essays, by A. Hayward.   (Longmans, 1858.)

Lord John Manners to Mr. Hayward.

[EXTRACT.]

MY DEAR HAYWARD,

Belvoir Castle,
December 27, 1850.

Many thanks for your letter, which, being directed to Lutterworth instead of Grantham, has only just reached me.

Proud as I should be to make General Radowitz's acquaintance, I fear I cannot manage to avail myself of your pleasant invitation for the 30th ; and as English is my only conversable language, I should only be a draw-back from the "feast of reason and the flow of soul." Your ecclesiastical news is very cheering. What possessed Bennett * to stand out on those minor points I can't conceive : he held Victory seated on his shoulder, and he knocked her off for the sake of his epaulette. However, if a satisfactory arrangement is now made, I have every hope that church matters will cool down. The ignorance, blasphemy, and twaddle that have over-spread the country like a November fog are beyond all description and defy all criticism. Smythe† has written to me from Brussels, enchanted with the Metternichs and their reception of him. He will greatly enjoy the Dresden conferences.

Yours very faithfully,
JOHN MANNERS.

* The late Mr. Bennett, vicar of Frome, " in consequence of the outcry against his ' Tractarian ' tendencies," was called upon to resign his curacy of St. Paul's, Knightsbridge, and St. Barnabas, Pimlico.
† George Smythe, afterwards Lord Strangford.

3 janvier 1851.

Je vous remercie de tout mon cœur, cher Mr. Hayward, de ce que vous avez bien voulu employer votre élégante plume en faveur d'un nom aussi maltraité par la presse comme le mien. Soyez persuadé que je sais apprécier l'esprit de bienveillance et d'équité qui vous a dicté cet article.

Les réflexions avec lesquelles vous finissez votre article, sont à très peu près les mêmes qui se sont présentés à moi lors de la revue rétrospective que j'ai faite le dernier jour de l'an. J'ai dû en faire une application personnelle. Triste du mal que je prévois, impuissant pour le bien que je désire, je voudrais finir par un peu de repos une vie que je n'ai point épargnée, mais je n'ai pu rendre utile. Ces temps actuels sont difficiles, je dois dire plus, ils sont impossibles.

Votre tout dévoué,
RADOWITZ.

It has been truly said that Mr. Hayward "introduced more than one French writer for the first time into England;" and that at some of his little dinners in the Temple might be found a young literary hero—a man perhaps great on the Continent, though hardly as yet known to London. In the spring of 1851, Mr. Hayward again crossed over into France. The Conservatives, the Legitimists, and Orleanists were hard at work formulating the law of May, by which the suffrage was to be restricted. The Prince-President watched the "Burgraves," as they were called, do his work, and waited silently. The excitement in England over the Ecclesiastical Titles Bill was ridiculed by polite society in Paris. Meanwhile

Pierre Dupont was rivalling the fame of Béranger among
the lower classes of his countrymen. His "Chants et
Poésies" were selling by hundreds of thousands amongst
the French workpeople, particularly in the rural dis-
tricts. Mr. Hayward dined with Dupont, and heard
him sing. "The effect of Dupont's singing is electrical.
It is musical and impassioned recitation rather than
ordinary singing; it is something between Moore and
Mrs. Arkwright. He commonly sings at table without
instrumental accompaniment, and every word is distinctly articulated. His voice is rather husky or hoarse,
till he warms; but when he sees from the kindling
glances of his audience that he is carrying them along
with him, it becomes full, clear, flexible and sonorous,
and lends itself harmoniously to every variety of fancy,
sentiment, or thought. The rank of his company makes
not the smallest difference in his demeanour, nor in his
willingness to pour himself out in verse and music. He
talks with the same ease and *abandon* with which he
sings."* Thus wrote Mr. Hayward of Pierre Dupont in
the *Morning Chronicle* in May, after his return from his
visit to Paris, which he mentions in the following letter:

Mr. Hayward to his Sisters.

Hôtel Mirabeau, Paris,
Good Friday, 1851.

I am passing my time here very pleasantly, and have
seen many people. Yesterday I dined with Lamartine,
and the day before with the new poet Dupont, the Moore
or Burns of France. Louis Napoleon's chance of a con-

---

* "Pierre Dupont." 'Biographical and Critical Essays,' by A.
Hayward. (Longmans, 1858.)

tinuance in power seems very doubtful, but the Legitimists are weak, and there seems no one else fit to put in
his place. The Socialists are strong and numerous, but
I do not think there is any chance of a disturbance this
year. Brougham arrived yesterday, and I dine in his
company to-morrow. People here are greatly amused
at the fuss in England about the Pope. I shall take it
for granted that all goes well until I hear from you.
But write.

Mr. Hayward to Lady Morgan.

MY DEAR LADY MORGAN,   1851.

I send you my tribute to the memory of our dear old
friend.* It was first read and sanctioned in Cavendish
Square. When I once told her I should do something of
the sort, if I survived her, she said, " Then remember to
clear my name from that calumny about the book." I
have been a good deal occupied with political matters,
although the only leading article I have written is one in
to-day's paper—the second—beginning with a quotation
from Brougham. I have not been out this morning, and
am not aware whether there is anything new. The
Duke of Newcastle, Lord Jocelyn, H. Fitzroy, F. Charteris and some other Peelites dine here to-day, but it is
an accidental gathering, no plot. I hope to see you
soon. Under the head of *Ministerial Crisis* in those
papers, I have twice suggested your friend Lord Clarendon as the man for the occasion. You must not be
verbally critical : all these things are dashed off late at
night, when all that can be known is known,

Ever yours,
A. HAYWARD.

* Lady Charleville died in 1851. Mr. Hayward wrote a notice
of her life in the *Times*, which is appended in a note to Lady
Morgan's Memoirs.

Read the review of Lord J. Russell's novel in yesterday's *Chronicle*.

Ida, Countess Hahn-Hahn, at whose house in Berlin Mr. Hayward had in his early visits to Germany been a welcome guest, was the author of 'Faustine,' and half-a-dozen other novels, besides some books of travels and a dramatic poem. In the year 1844 she visited England, and Mr. Hayward heralded her arrival by an article in the January number of the *Edinburgh Review*, in which he introduced her to his countrymen as a German novelist. "Madame Hahn-Hahn wrote a most interesting account of her visit to London, and subsequent tour in Ireland and Scotland. She sent the MS. the following year to Mr. Hayward before it was published, that he might get it well translated into English."* Mr. Hayward lent Lady Chatterton the MS. to get it translated. But just as it was finished, "a great family affliction had befallen Madame Hahn-Hahn, who had requested that the MS. might be returned to her, she having abandoned the idea of its publication." In 1850 Madame Hahn-Hahn joined the Roman Catholic Church and entered a convent.†

Mr. Hayward to Lady Chatterton.

MY DEAR LADY CHATTERTON,　　　Oct. 19, 1851.

The Countess Maugersen has arrived in town, and written to me again for the Hahn-Hahn MS., so I

---

* 'Memoirs of Georgiana, Lady Chatterton,' by E. H. Dering.
† Up to, and for a long period before, 1850, Madame Hahn-Hahn and Mr. Hayward corresponded.

suppose she must have it. Will you, therefore, have the kindness to send it to me. I have been back from my travels about a week. After Powerscourt, I went to Sir John Young's, county Cavan, and then crossed to Scotland by Belfast, spent a couple of days on the Tweed with E. Warburton * and his wife, and a week at Keir (Stirling's) with Mrs. Norton and Lord Lansdowne; very pleasant it was. My next was to Bulwer's, at Knebworth, and my last to Cashiobury.† I hear that the Manners' have reached Milan, and are expected home very shortly. There is hardly any one in town. H. Ellis, who arrived last night from Paris, does not think that Louis Napoleon has improved his chance by his last move. But there will be no *coup d'état* for some time to come, at all events. The Castlereaghs are to winter in town, and she promises to be very hospitable, the fitting-up of the house in Chesham Place being now complete. Mrs. Norton starts for Naples, viâ Paris, very shortly. Lady Dufferin winters in Naples. I have no news recently of Rogers. Thackeray is employed on a novel. He will lecture in the provinces, and then go to America. With best regards to Sir William,

Ever faithfully yours,

A. HAYWARD.

Lord Brougham to Mr. Hayward.

Château Eléonore,

MY DEAR MR. HAYWARD,   Nov. 29, 1851.

I am extremely obliged to you for your kindness, and the interesting information your letter contains. I don't think at all that either Sir James Graham or Lord Aberdeen will separate from the rest of the Peel

---

* Author of ' The Crescent and the Cross.

† Lord Essex's seat.

party. The proceedings of Lord Palmerston respecting the subjects of all Lord Aberdeen's most fixed opinions would make any junction with him, I should suppose, impossible. Indeed I must say that I am somewhat astonished at this which has lately passed, and at the way in which some folks have been carried away by a popular clamour.* The state of things in this country is still very unpleasant, to say the least of it. But as for any outbreak, I don't at all expect it now, and not much even in ———.† You will perceive that the universal dread of it will be in one way or another the means of preventing it. But the blunders—the incredible blunders—that have been committed are not confined to one side, and the shortsighted self-interest which seems to prevail would produce serious damage but for the above-mentioned circumstance of fear.‡

Believe me, truly yours,

H. BROUGHAM.

Prince Napoleon's *coup d'état* took place on the 2nd of December. The following letters from Count D'Orsay are of exceeding interest, as illustrating the effect produced by the Prince's conduct at that time, on one who styles himself " le plus sincère Napoléon qui existe." §

---

* Lord Palmerston's opposition to Austria was well-known, and had been recently manifested by his proposed reception of Kossuth at Broadlands.

† Illegible.

‡ This letter was written only two days before the *coup d'état*, and it is curious to find how so well-informed a person as Lord Brougham was deceived to the very last.

§ This letter was published at 10 o'clock on the evening of the 4th of December, before Napoleon's position was out of danger, and was a semi-desertion of his nephew. (*Vide* also Mr. Kinglake's ' Crimea,' vol. 1, p. 312. 4th edition.) Count D'Orsay despatched a copy of it to Mr. Hayward, as soon as it became known, for insertion in the English press.

MY DEAR HAYWARD,   Monday, Dec. (5 or 6), 1851.

I send you in haste the copy of the letter that King Jerome wrote to his nephew. Have it inserted at once, in some other paper than the *Chronicle*, which is prohibited in Paris. The document is very remarkable, and will interest people at this critical moment. I hope to see you well one of these days. I always think of dear old England, that one must like every day more from what we see everywhere else.

Yours in haste,

D'ORSAY.

'MON CHER NEVEU,

'Le sang français coule, arrêtez-le par un appel sérieux au peuple. Vos sentiments sont mal compris, la seconde proclamation où vous parlez de Plébiscite est mal reçue par le peuple, qui n'y voit pas le rétablissement de son droit de suffrage ; la liberté est sans garantie si une assemblée ne concourt pas à la constitution de la République. L'armée a le dessus, c'est le moment de compléter une victoire matérielle par une victoire morale ; ce que le pouvoir ne peut faire quand il est battu, il doit souvent le faire, quand il est le plus fort après avoir frappé les anciens partis. Relevez le peuple. Proclamez que le suffrage universel, sincère, sans entraves, agissant avec la liberté la plus grande, nommera et le Président et une *assemblée constituante* pour sauver et établir la République.

'C'est au nom de la mémoire de mon Frère, partageant son horreur pour la guerre civile, que je vous écris.

Croyez en ma vieille expérience, pensez que la France, l'Europe, la Postérité vous jugeront.

'Votre affectionné oncle,

(Signé)   'JÉRÔME BONAPARTE,

'Ma.' de France.

'Paris, 4 décembre 1851,
    à 10 heures du soir.'

Count D'Orsay to Mr. Hayward.

MON CHER HAYWARD,   Jan. 2, 1852.

J'ai eu de vos nouvelles par Ranelagh, et je reçois dans ce moment votre lettre. Je vais envoyer celle-ci par l'Ambassade, ainsi je pourrai donc vous parler franchement. J'étais, et je suis furieux contre le coup d'état, car L. N. a perdu à mes yeux un prestige. Je croyais que c'était un homme à ne jamais manquer à sa parole. J'ai la conviction même, qu'il serait arrivé où il en est, par des moyens légaux. Il n'y a aucun doute que la loi du 31 mai aurait été retirée à la 3me lecture, et que, plus tard, la révision de la Constitution aurait été votée ; donc ses 7 millions et demi de voix prouvent que la religion Napoléonienne existe dans le Peuple, envers et contre tous les autres partis. Songez que cette fois, à l'exception de la Bretagne, les Légitimistes n'ont pas voté pour lui ; tandis que la dernière fois, lorsqu'il avait eu 5 millions et demi de votes, ils avaient tous voté pour lui. Je suis de votre opinion, c'est qu'après avoir fait son coup, il devait rassembler une constituante,* enfin suivre les conseils de son oncle Jérôme, dont je vous ai envoyé la lettre. Il est évident pour moi, qu'il n'y a presque pas de républicains en France ; s'il y en avait eu, ils auraient compris anciennement que Lamartine était là pour jouer le rôle du Washington français, il n'a eu à cette époque que 20,000 voix, c'est risible et inexpli-

* A Constituent Assembly.

cable. Quant à la Légitimité, c'est une idée en l'air, et l'Orléanisme, une idée dans les égouts. Vous voyez donc quel beau jeu avait notre homme de rester honnête, sans courir grand risque. Maintenant il dit qu'en arrivant en France, il a fait la méprise de s'appuyer sur les salons et les anciens partis, et qu'il a vu à la fin qu'il fallait s'appuyer sur le Peuple. Donc il va faire du socialisme par en haut, prendre beaucoup des bonnes idées de Girardin sur l'Economie Politique, etc. etc., et se rendre populaire en soulageant le Peuple ; s'il fait cela, il prend racine profondément, et rien ne pourra le renverser, et il est du devoir de tout bon Français de l'aider. Il finit par où il aurait dû commencer, à la vérité, il répond à cela qu'il n'aurait pas pu si bien se débarrasser des Burgraves et autres importuns. Au milieu de tout cela, il faut considérer que Changarnier et Cie avaient un complot bien conditionné pour le flanquer à Vincennes et que La Grange (le Républicain) a avoué, que le tour était bien joué. Vous voyez que je suis juste et impartial, quoique je suis reconnu, depuis 40 années, d'être le plus grand et le plus sincère Napoléonien qui existe. Je voulais que L. N. fût arrivé où il en est, par une autre route, celle que Proudhon lui avait tracée, ainsi que Girardin et moi. Eh bien ! Malgré son succès, je n'ai pas voulu aller le voir, son Oncle Jérôme est venu me chercher pour m'y conduire, j'ai refusé, et je pense de ma dignité de le laisser venir à moi, afin que je puisse faire des conditions dignes de moi, et de mon opinion. J'ai la conviction que vous m'approuverez. Vous ne pouvez concevoir à quel point les gens ici sont courtisans et plats valets ; vanité et succès sont les deux mots d'ordre. On devrait les donner continuellement aux factionnaires. Tout marche à l'Empire. Après le coup qu'il a fait, il serait bête de s'arrêter, il croit à son étoile et à sa mission, il coquettera peut-erre quelque temps, mais le résultat sera ce que je vous dis. Voilà les

aigles sortis de leurs nids, et de l'empaillage du Jardin
des Plantes, pour orner les Drapeaux, et maintenant il
fait donner le nom d'Altesse à ses cousins, il macadamise
la route des Tuileries. Le Peuple désire voir ce palais
habité, et l'armée y tient particulièrement. Selon moi,
il y a longtemps qu'il serait Empereur, s'il s'était appuyé
franchement sur ce même peuple. Eh bien! Que
dites-vous de l'affaire de ce Wykoff? Nous avons
beaucoup d'Anglais à Paris, venez-y donc. Adieu, mon
cher Hayward, faites mes amitiés à Strangford et à mes
bons amis d'Angleterre. Ah! si j'étais riche, je serais
bien vite à Londres. Je suis exilé ici.

Votre très dévoué,

D'ORSAY.

Count D'Orsay to Mr. Hayward.

MON CHER HAYWARD,   Dimanche (Jan. 1852).

Je causais de vous hier au soir avec Stewart, qui a
dîné avec nous aux 3 Frères. Ce matin je reçois votre
lettre et les journaux. Croyez ce que je vous dirai, car
je ne me laisse pas aveugler, et je vous dirai la pure et
simple vérité. Maintenant le coup est fait, nous sommes
la Postérité de cela, c'est à L. N. de s'arranger avec
l'histoire, mais ce qu'il y a de certain c'est que l'armée
est entièrement pour lui. Je le sais de 20 Colonels
différents, et tous sont enchantés que Changarnier,
Lamoricière, Bedeau et Cie ayant été mis en prison (so
much for that pretended popularity of these generals) ils
ont perdu toute espèce d'influence, leurs noms sont de
l'histoire ancienne, assaisonnés de vanité mortifiée, et
d'ambition échouée. Le Colonel Sibthorpe aurait peut-
être plus d'influence sur l'armée française maintenant,
qu'aucun de ces généraux *Numides.* Sibthorpe aurait
au moins l'avantage d'être nouveau, tandis que ceux-ci
sont des Africains usés, dont on a exalté les mérites, qui

consistaient à prendre stratégiquement des moutons, et des parasols. L. Napoléon est planté maintenant pour toujours où il est, c'est à dire, jusqu'à sa mort naturelle, ou un assassinat. La République est aussi enfoncée que la Légitimité, et quant aux d'Orléans, c'est plus qu'oublié. A l'exception de quelques honnêtes Républicains, il n'y.a rien de franchement honnête parmi nous. Ce sont tous des courtisans qui sacrifieraient leurs opinions pour un passe-droit de politique, c'est triste à dire, mais c'est un fait, moi qui me tiens en arrière, je me considère, et je suis considéré comme le plus pur et le plus vrai des Bonapartistes, tel que je l'avais toujours compris depuis 30 années. J'ai l'air d'être dans une opposition, parce que je n'approuve pas la route que Louis a pris pour arriver où il en est maintenant. Enfin je vous écris à la hâte, j'aurai toujours grand plaisir à vous donner mon opinion.

Votre tout dévoué,

A. D'O.

Je viens de lire votre article, qui est extrêmement bien.

The news of the *coup d'état* was followed, before the close of the month, by the removal of Lord Palmerston from the Foreign Office, owing partly to his approval of Louis Napoleon's *coup d'état* to the French Ambassador at the time.

The Duke of Newcastle to Mr. Hayward.

MY DEAR HAYWARD,   Clumber, Dec. 28, 1851.

Many thanks for your constant reports. What a strange affair is the Palmerston kick *à posteriori!* I should think the cause must be one more presentable to the Radical friends of the Government than the interview

M 2

with the men of Islington.* I fancy some intrigue in
France must be the real cause. Be this as it may, his
loss to the Government (which would have been a *gain*
in the days of Pacifico) will now be found most grave,
may be, fatal. I am obliged to you for 'Philo-Landlord.'
I have not seen the *Daily News*, but can judge of its
tone by the answer. I have received many kind and
flattering letters on the subject of my speeches, and I
hope and think in this neighbourhood they have done
some good.

Ever yours very sincerely,
NEWCASTLE.

---

* The Radicals of Islington had waited upon Lord Palmerston,
to congratulate him on his sympathy with the Hungarian Kossuth.

The formation of the Coalition Government of 1852—Mr. Hayward's part in bringing about the coalition of the " Peelites " and Whigs—Letter from the Duke of Newcastle—Mr. Hayward to his Sisters, a dinner to M. Thiers—Letter from the Duke of Newcastle, the Government policy on Free Trade—Letter from Lord Brougham, Count D'Orsay's death—The Duke of Newcastle proposed as Chancellor of the University of Oxford in succession to the Duke of Wellington—Letter from Lord Lansdowne on the coalition of parties—Letters to his Sisters, dinner to the " Peelites "—Lord Palmerston's amendment to Mr. C. Villiers' Free Trade resolutions—Letters from Lord Brougham, on effect of Lord Palmerston's amendment—The state of affairs in Paris, on the experiment of a Coalition Government —The Coalition Ministry—The Duke of Newcastle and the Athenæum Club—Sir George C. Lewis, editor of the *Edinburgh Review*—Mr. Hayward's article on Disraeli—The Charity Commissionership—Letters to Sir G. C. Lewis and Sir John Young—Lord John Russell and the *Chronicle*— Letter from Lord Elcho—The " Eastern Question "—Letters to the Duke of Newcastle from Berlin and Paris upon the feeling in these places towards Russia—The destruction of the Turkish fleet at Sinope—Lord Palmerston's resignation—The Duke of Newcastle and Lord Palmerston's return to the Cabinet—Letters to the Duke.

As the Duke of Newcastle predicted, so it came to pass : the dismissal of Lord Palmerston from Lord John Russell's Cabinet proved fatal to his Ministry ; and with the overthrow of his Government early in 1852, leading statesmen found themselves face to face with a very disorganised state of parties. The Whig or Liberal party, by the differences between Lord John Russell and Lord Palmerston, were separated into two factions, the Radicals hung jealously to the skirts of both, while the " Peelites " stood impassively aloof. The interlude of a Tory Government under Lord Derby afforded experienced politicians the opportunity of attempting to form a coalition among these apparently discordant sections, so as " to produce an efficient Government or an efficient Opposition." By dint of much negotiation, much persuasion, and much intrigue, a coalition was effected ; and when, in December 1852, Lord Derby's Government fell, Lord Aberdeen was prepared to take office, with his various Ministers selected from among the chiefs of the Whigs, the " Peelites," and the Radicals.

Mr. Hayward has himself declared that, after the principal personages engaged in forming the Coalition Government, he did more than any one else to bring it about. Unfortunately, there is little record left of what he did, and no official post was given to him to mark his efficient party services. He lived continually in London, and was a member both of the Carlton and Athenæum Clubs, so that he was " in touch," as it were, with all the chief men of his own party, and was readily accessible when his services were required. There is no 'diary' to detail the interviews at which he was present, or to report the conversations or opinions of the leading men, with whom the crisis brought him in contact. Nothing but a few letters now exist to indicate what was actually the part Mr. Hayward played in bringing about the coalition of the " Peelites " and the Whigs. These, with

such information as could be collected from his surviving
friends, are now printed in the following pages.

It is well known that he devoted himself to "the cause"
of the "Peelites," and worked night and day to make it
successful. Besides urging it in the pages of the *Morning
Chronicle*, he urged it in society, where he was rightly
looked upon as its chief literary 'advocate.' The strife,
the energy, the activity, to say nothing of the ability,
displayed by Mr. Hayward from 1852 to 1855 in
upholding and defending "the cause" of his fellow-
workers in the same political field find, perhaps, some
little trace in his letters, of which not the least interesting
in this chapter are those he received from Lord
Brougham ; and as the chapter draws to its close there
are indications of the coming of the "Crimean War," and
of a closer connection between Mr. Hayward and the
War Minister—the Duke of Newcastle.

The Duke of Newcastle to Mr. Hayward.

MY DEAR HAYWARD,   Clumber, Jan. 15, 1852.

I think Cooke* has kept within the truth in the article
to which you refer, and I have little doubt that the story
of negotiations is not groundless. I do not know that
any letters are to be read in Parliament, but such *may* be
the case—at least I cannot contradict it. I am convinced that if the Government is not broken up at the
Cabinet to-day, Lord John will meet Parliament just as
he is—at least, with only a *shift* or two. I have no idea
that dissolution has ever been seriously considered, much
less decided upon. I am glad you found the Baronet

* Mr. Douglas Cooke, the Editor of the *Morning Chronicle*, and
afterwards of the *Saturday Review*.

so pleasant. Lord Derby seems to be more in his bad books now than ever poor Peel was.

Believe me, ever,

Yours most sincerely,

NEWCASTLE.

Mr. Hayward to his Sisters.

Feb. 26, 1852.

The present Government cannot last more than a month after the new Parliament, which is expected to be elected soon after Easter,* but events are so odd as to baffle all calculation, and the new people are all abroad as to what they mean to do. Their carrying Protection is entirely out of the question, and they want to shirk that question altogether. I have no notion of standing for any place, though I could get in for a thousand pounds. I see a good deal of Thiers,† who dines here next week with the Duke of Newcastle, Gladstone, S. Herbert, &c.

The Duke of Newcastle to Mr. Hayward.

MY DEAR HAYWARD, Clumber, March 12, 1852.

Many thanks for your report of Lord J. Russell's meeting.‡ I think Villiers is in error in telling you that

* Parliament was not dissolved until July. The new Parliament met on November 11, and Lord Derby's Government was out on December 17.

† " When he [Thiers] was in England (1852), being compelled to leave France after the *coup d'état,* a dinner (March 1) was made for him, at which were present : Mr. Gladstone, Mr. Hallam, Edward Lord Lytton, Lord Elcho, Lord Cardwell, Lord Herbert of Lea, Sir W. Stirling-Maxwell, Mr. Henry Fitzroy, Lord Kingsdown, Colonel Damer, and the writer [Mr. Hayward]. The conversation was varied and animated : Thiers had the advantage of language and choice of subject ; but the general impression was that Mr. Gladstone was, if anything, the better talker of the two." (' Eminent Statesmen,' " Thiers," p. 67.)

‡ At a meeting at Lord John Russell's house it was resolved to

there will be no further declaration on the part of the Government on Monday. I feel sure that the hustings speeches and the effect in the country of their evasive conduct *must* force out some declaration, and that a bolder one, at the earliest possible period. Moreover, they know that searching questions will compel them to speak out, and they will make a virtue of necessity, as they also will on the question of early dissolution. I shall be in London on Monday, and expecting a "declaration," mean to be in time for the House.

I am,

Yours very sincerely,

NEWCASTLE.

I think the new Government will have *one* great element of stability. Nobody will like to occupy offices which have once been *so* filled!

Mr. Hayward to his Sisters.

May 6, 1852.

Politics are all abroad, and no one knows what is to happen. A dissolution is far from certain, though highly probable. I hear Lyme is not included in the new Reform Bill.

The present Government is very inferior, yet I do not see how it is well possible to form another that would last. Lord Derby has no chance except by throwing over Protection, and, if he did that, he would soon be denounced like Peel.

Louis Napoleon is getting worse and worse, and has

---

obtain, if possible, a definite statement from Lord Derby's Government of their intended policy with regard to Free Trade. To Mr. Charles Villiers' question, what policy the Government intended to follow, Mr. Disraeli (the Chancellor of the Exchequer) gave only an evasive reply, stating in effect, that the verdict of the country at the coming elections must decide.

nearly made his best friends ashamed of him; at the same time, the violent articles against him are not mine.

I hope you are both well.

Lord Brougham to Mr. Hayward.

[EXTRACT.]

MY DEAR MR. HAYWARD,   Scarborough, Aug. 3, 1852.

I have exceedingly bad accounts of D'Orsay,* and that he is come back to Paris. It is said there is a message every day from the Elysée.

The state of things in this country, as well as in France, is very fortunately that of perfect quiet and great prosperity. If it were otherwise in either country, the consequences would be very alarming, for *here* we have, and are likely for some time to have, nothing that can be called a government; and there, with all the excessive folly of the fête-loving people, any distress would soon put an end to the submission which the alarm not yet forgotten has produced. It is understood—I may say, I am quite certain—that our Government, or rather our Ministers calling themselves a government, are anything rather than satisfied with the elections: indeed, that they are greatly disappointed. Why, what did they—what *could* they—expect?

Yours very truly,

H. BROUGHAM.

I don't believe in an *October* session. I know some of the Ministers say *November.* ⌐ ⸗ ⌐   . !

Mr. Hayward to his Sisters.

Clumber Park, Sept. 14, 1852.

By dint of resolution I got clear of Ambergate, and arrived here by half-past five. This place would beat

---

* Lord Brougham had not yet heard of Count D'Orsay's death, which took place on Aug. 2.

Chatsworth in real magnificence, if a few thousands were
judiciously spent upon it. The dining-room, the library,
and the grand drawing-room are decidedly finer, and
there are more valuable pictures. The best rooms open
on an Italian garden, like that at Chatsworth, and the
garden overhangs a splendid lake, with a regular sailing-
vessel moored in the distance. The park is eleven miles
round, and far wider and naturally grander than Chatsworth. It fails in fountains, in picture and sketch-
galleries, and in the entrance-hall. But I have had no
time to look about me. I go to-morrow or next day to
London, seeing Newstead on my way.* The Duke gives
me a letter to Wildman. Sidney Herbert was here, and
has just left. There is no news. There is a chapel and
prayers every morning at 9, which I missed. The Duke,
however, is totally free from humbug of every sort.
There is no one here but his brother, Lord Robert, and
his sister, Lady Caroline, who does the honours. I am
just going to fish on the lake, where, I am told, I may
catch as many two or three pound perch as I choose.

The Duke of Newcastle to Mr. Hayward.

MY DEAR HAYWARD,   Edinburgh, Sept. 26, 1852.

Many thanks for sending me the *Daily News*, which I
should not otherwise have seen. The article is most
generous and handsome, and does me so very much
more than justice, that if it had come from a political
friend, its tone would have distressed me. I have this
morning heard from Oxford† that the intention of proposing me has been—judiciously, as I think—abandoned.

* Newstead Abbey, once the seat of Lord Byron, then of Col.
Wildman, and now of W. F. Webb, Esq.

† On the death of the Duke of Wellington the Chancellorship of
the University of Oxford became vacant. Lord Derby was elected
Chancellor on October 12.

Of Lord Derby's claims I will not say a word, but I always felt that on my part there were none, and therefore instead of feeling disappointed in failing to obtain the honour, I am deeply gratified by the volunteered tender of support which has been made from all quarters, but more especially from *nearly all* those members of Convocation who are eminent in *any* respect.

I go to Scarborough to-morrow and back to Clumber on Wednesday, having abandoned the Highlands altogether. I shall be in London in about 10 days for a few days. Nothing stirring here. I have not yet read Lord John Russell's speech at Perth,* but Hastie (M.P. for Paisley) told me yesterday it was "very good, and would make a great sensation."

Believe me,

Yours very sincerely,

NEWCASTLE.

Lord Lansdowne to Mr. Hayward.

DEAR HAYWARD,   Friday morning.

I had read the article you allude to in the *Chronicle*, and am confident that if Lord Derby perseveres in his political economy it will not stand fire. I saw also the letter from a correspondent in the same paper. There certainly seems to me to be no good reason to prevent such a cordial understanding between parties as can alone produce an efficient Government or an efficient Opposition, but I look at these matters rather as a spectator than as an actor, which is sometimes a different point of view.

Very faithfully yours,

LANSDOWNE. ·

---

* On the occasion of his receiving the Freedom of that City, September 24.

Mr. Hayward to his Sisters.

Nov. 9, 1852.

Everybody is still in doubt about the ministerial intentions. All the leading " Peelites " dine with me to-morrow
to settle their course, viz., the Duke of Newcastle,
Gladstone, S. Herbert, F. Charteris, H. Fitzroy, Sir John
Young, Cardwell and Lord Ernest Bruce. I have
promised to take Emma and Fanny to the Athenæum
to see the funeral,* and I must get up at six, and I
do not think there can be much to see after all.

Mr. Hayward to his Sisters.

[EXTRACT.]   Nov. 13, 1852.

My dinner went off capitally, and has done great good
by consolidating the Peel party, as there was a rumour
that the leaders were divided. The Government have
been made damaged, but there is no wish to turn them
out till they have shown themselves completely up.

Mr. Hayward to his Sisters.

Nov. 26, 1852.

Palmerston's† interposition has gained the Government
a brief respite, but no one now thinks they can last long,
for sixty or seventy of their men are fatally disgusted
by their adoption of Free Trade.

* Of the Duke of Wellington.

† On the 23rd of November Mr. Charles Villiers moved his Free
Trade resolutions, which, after a three nights' debate, were rejected
in face of Lord Palmerston's amendment by a majority of 20;
and Lord Palmerston's amendment, which virtually was an expression of the House in favour of Free Trade, was opposed by only
53 Protectionists. The action taken by Lord Palmerston while
pledging the present Parliament to Free Trade, left the Government free to proceed on their way to introduce their Budget which
they did on the 3rd of December, but they were defeated and
resigned on the 20th.

It is thought that Lord Palmerston's amendment will be carried by a very large majority. Villiers will probably be beat by twenty or thirty, but this is now of little consequence. Disraeli has put off his Budget to insert some compensation to the land, but if this is of any real value to the agriculturist, it will certainly be rejected, and then the Government must go out. Disraeli is terribly lowered by his detected plagiarisms.* The discovery comes at the most unlucky time for him. The account in to-day's *Chronicle* was given me by Thiers, who is at Lord Ashburton's, where I dine on Sunday.

Lord Brougham to Mr. Hayward.

Hôtel Meurice, Paris.
DEAR MR. HAYWARD, Nov. 27, 1852.

I am much obliged to you for your letter. It seems to have been a difficult matter to decide, and I am not at all sure that the right course has been taken. No doubt turning out the Government before their financial nostrums are produced would have had very bad consequences, but on the other hand nothing is worse than proceedings of parties, or party leaders, which the public cannot comprehend ; and I fear this one will look like an abandonment of Free Trade or a postponement of it to party tactics. At least, it will not be easy to persuade the people that it was both right to make the motion, evidently aggressive in its nature, and right to oppose it because it was aggressive. I don't see how a government can last long which is only saved by its adversaries, and is deserted by the most consistent part of its friends. But the Protectionists will not do the same thing now that they did in 1830.

* The *Morning Chronicle* of July 1, 1848, had published the translation of an eulogy pronounced by Thiers on Marshal Gouvion de St. Cyr. In his eulogy on the Duke of Wellington Mr. Disraeli quoted this translation almost word by word.

There seems a very erroneous opinion here (even among the [August?] enemies of the Government, and who are desirous to prove its incompatibility with peace) that no attempt can be made anywhere for some time, and the great bulk of men, except those personally averse to the Government, hold that peace must be kept, else that Government will be upset. I don't quite agree with them, but delay is favourable to peace in this instance, since it ensures (let us hope) full preparation both for defences and for alliances, *and if that preparation is not complete*, a war would be fatal to the new dynasty,

Yours truly,

H. B.

Lord Brougham to Mr. Hayward.

Château Eléanore, Dec. 23, 1852.

DEAR MR. HAYWARD,

I am exceedingly obliged to you for your bulletin received yesterday. It agrees in all respects but one with my other accounts, and in that respect I believe you to be right, they wrong. The experiment of a coalition is quite necessary, but I remember that of 1806, and nothing could exceed the heartburnings to which it gave rise, not so much among the great as the little ones. When two large bodies meet, the vermin on the surface are crushed. However, I hope at all events the principal persons will show a disposition to yield their claims for the general good. There will be a sad want, I fear, for us law reformers. The worst Chancellor of whom history has left any record will probably be again allowed to extinguish all good measures, besides driving the suitors and the Bar to despair. This will partly be owing to the use he made of his patronage —by which he disgraced himself and pleased the *Court*. It really is too bad that there should be even a chance of this, when you have such men as Page Wood so fit for it, not to mention Cranworth,* Romilly, and Bethell (head of the Chancery Bar, and a good law reformer). I wish to mention a circumstance to you which fills me with some anxiety on account of my old and dear friend Denman, who takes it much to heart. If you have not seen it, pray read his most touching dedication of his pamphlet to Mrs. Stowe—author of ' Uncle Tom's Cabin '—and listen to the secret history of that dedication. I know of my own knowledge what I am about to mention. Application was made to a person of eminence who took an interest in slavery and slave trade, asking him to write a preface to a London edition of ' Uncle Tom.' But as hundreds of thousands were selling and there was no copyright, it was plain that the application was a bookseller's trick to give currency to another edition which was not wanted. Therefore it was at once declined. They then applied to Lord Carlisle—and good nature being hurtful when not accompanied with good sense, he at once agreed, and wrote a preface *taking the wrong view of the very many disputed matters.* Denman was exceedingly vexed, and wished that the refusal had not been given, and that so the mischief of Carlisle's thoughtlessness and ignorance had been avoided. Accordingly, it weighed on his mind so much that he has expressed his sense of C.'s folly in the dedication to Mrs. Stowe of his own (D.'s) tract, but he has expressed his feelings in a subdued tone. However, you will see how strongly he does feel, and I know it is impossible to exaggerate his sense of C.'s folly.

I see he (C.) has been exposing himself again in a lecture, in which he tells the mechanics of Yorkshire that the Duke of Wellington' was an Eton Boy at the time Gray wrote his Ode on Eton College ; but the Duke was born 1771, the year Gray died ! J. Russell has been almost as unhappy in *his* lecture on —— † and

* Lord Cranworth was appointed Lord Chancellor. † Illegible.

his preface on T. Moore. Really, when lords take to literature, they should be a little on their guard.

Yours very sincerely,

H. B.

I don't at all object to J. R. now making a little political capital out of Mechanics' Institutes, for he was long ago engaged in such things along with me. I am much pleased to see the Duke of Newcastle drawing with the Whigs. He is really an excellent as well as most able man, and well fitted to secure confidence. I expect to see him Premier.

Mr. Hayward to his Sisters.

Dec. 28, 1852.

There is now next to nothing to tell, as everything of importance is settled.* The newspaper lists are correct in the main, and the *Chronicle* inserts nothing except on authority. There not being places enough for half the expectants, the discontent, of course, is great amongst both Whigs and " Peelites " who have seats. As Osborne †️ has accepted the Secretaryship to the Admiralty, and

---

* Lord John Russell entered Lord Aberdeen's Cabinet as Foreign Secretary, but on the understanding that he was to resign the seals of that office after a few weeks to Lord Clarendon, and lead the House of Commons without office or pay. Lord Palmerston, partly to please the Liberal party, and partly owing to the persuasion of Lord Lansdowne and Lord Clarendon (whose foreign policy he knew was most of all in accord with his own), after much hesitation consented to join the Cabinet as Home Secretary. Mr. Gladstone became Chancellor of the Exchequer ; the Duke of Newcastle, Secretary for the Colonies and for War ; Mr. Sidney Herbert, Secretary at War ; Sir James Graham, First Lord of the Admiralty ; Mr. Cardwell, President of the Board of Trade ; Lord St. Germans, Lord Lieutenant of Ireland ; Sir John Young, Chief Secretary for Ireland, and Sir Wm. Molesworth (Radical), First Commissioner of Works.

†️ The late Mr. Bernal Osborne.

C. Villiers that of Judge Advocate, hardly a parliamentary man of note, except Cobden and Bright, is left out.
I have no doubt at all that if anything that suited me
should turn up, they would offer it to me, as I have been
of great use to them throughout. But there really is
nothing at present which I should care to ask for, even if
I wanted it.

The following letter from the Duke of Newcastle is an
answer to a request from Mr. Hayward, that he would
allow himself to be nominated for election to the
Athenæum Club by the Committee.

MY DEAR HAYWARD,   Portman Square, Dec. 28, 1852.

I should very much like to belong to the Athenæum
Club,* for the more deeply I become immersed in
political affairs, the less affinity I feel to the views and
general ideas of a political club. A man wants relaxation
from his daily drudgery, and if he cannot find it in a
happy home, he must seek it either in female or literary
society, or in both. At seasons and hours when the
former is unattainable, the library of the Athenæum
must be a great relief to that sense of weariness which
my former experience leads me to anticipate from the
office which I have now had the temerity to enter.† I
should not, however, like to *sneak* into the Athenæum
Club or any other society. I should prefer undergoing
the ordeal of the ballot to coming in under the privilege
accorded to Cabinet Ministers. I should be very glad
to be proposed in the ordinary way, and take my chance.

* The Duke always afterwards made it his club, living there a
great deal, and constantly dining there. Written *correspondence*
thenceforth with Mr. Hayward became, of course, rarely necessary.
† Secretaryship for Colonies and for War.

I am much flattered by what Brougham writes to you. I claim no merit, but honesty and loyalty of purpose. Many thanks for more than one note of useful hints ; I have made use of them. How will the ship sail ? She rides well at anchor.

Yours ever sincerely,
NEWCASTLE.

.

Lord Brougham to Mr. Hayward.

DEAR MR. HAYWARD,   Jan. 3, 1853.

I am greatly obliged by your bulletin, which proved correct in most particulars. The difficulties that beset the new Government are very great, and I only hope they may not prove insurmountable ; for certainly if they should, and the late concern should be restored, the hopes of good people in France may be half realised (that party government is found impossible). One chance the Government may have, I suspect by indications which I perceive that a considerable number of sincere Protectionists have been (as well they might) a good deal disgusted with their treatment, and disposed to fall away from their present leaders—" A bridge of gold to a retreating enemy" is the rule. On the other hand, I don't see the use of extolling the present Government at the expense of all others—for example, the former coalition of 1806. There never was a more honest and patriotic proceeding than that, accompanied no doubt with a direct interest—as most human acts of virtue are. It was in all respects different from the bad coalition of 1784. But both included men superior to the present in their composition, consisting of a race of very much greater men. Therefore, I protest against the puffing of the present as compared with those. Indeed, if it be allowed to be equal or not much inferior to the junction of 1830 (for that, too, was a coalition), it gets abundantly enough of praise.

It is equally injudicious to exalt Lord St. Leonards above all other Chancellors, and I see his secretary has most indelicately joined in the cry. His merits are very great, and he has done good service, because he was in reality adverse to Chancery reform, and yet most ably and honestly gave it effect as soon as he was made to give in to it. (It was like the wheel of the late Government on Protection, but done far more entirely.) But that which he is extolled for is both contrary to the facts and, if it were true, is really nothing at all, viz., his being the only Chancellor who left no judgment undelivered on retiring. If a man goes out six weeks after the long vacation, when he must have finished his judgments (supposing he didn't before the Court rose), he can have none or next to none to give. Truro, no doubt, left judgments in arrear, and was as bad in all respects as a man could be, but he was the only one to whom the *insincere* part of the puff applies. It arises from entire ignorance of what is really, or rather was really, the Chancery evil. It was not a few judgments long undelivered, but a mass of causes unheard, and this the creation of four new judges makes now impossible.

Yours very sincerely,

H. B.

At the end of 1852, Sir George Cornewall Lewis, who was then without a seat in the House of Commons, accepted the editorship of the *Edinburgh Review* in succession to Mr. Empson. Sir George Lewis was glad to avail himself of Mr. Hayward's help, and it was agreed between them that Mr. Hayward should write an article, giving an estimate of Mr. Disraeli's political career, for the April number of the *Review*. The interest which Mr. Hayward took in working up this article is manifested in the following letters, which he wrote to the Editor.

Mr. Hayward to Sir Geo. C. Lewis.

MY DEAR LEWIS,   Temple, Jan. 29, 1853.

The Disraeli biography* which you mentioned is better than I anticipated, and I think a telling article might be founded on it.   I should lay aside all party bitterness, and try to analyse fairly and philosophically his precise position, *with its causes.*   I should simply quote his works as bearing on the formation of his character, but I could interweave some amusing anecdotes ; and his earlier books are new to the rising generation, who would like to hear about them and their origin.   I know every incident of his life, and it was I who furnished C. Buller with the materials of his Disraeli articles in the *Globe* in 1836–37.   What do you think of this ?   What space could you afford, and by what time should you want the article ?   It would have some political importance, as fixing him by a scale of merit against which he would find it no easy matter to struggle.

Ever yours truly,

A. HAYWARD.

It will be very happily timed if it comes out early in April, as his fate is still wavering in the balance, though he is beginning to kick the beam.

Mr. Hayward to Sir G. C. Lewis.

MY DEAR LEWIS,   The Athenæum, March 14, 1853.

I have attended to the whole of your suggestions, and I think there is not a statement which may not be fully

---

* 'The Right Honourable Benjamin Disraeli, M.P.'; a critical biography.   By George Henry Francis.   London, 1852.

substantiated. The whole of Dizzy's adventures of 1832 (including the Bulwer letter, &c.) were printed in a pamphlet to which I have now referred in a note. I myself got that pamphlet for Charles Buller, who wrote the *Globe* articles in 1836. In these articles Dizzy is charged with the introduction to Lord Durham and the Westminster Club. He admitted the Club, and said he did not know its politics ! He was silent as to Lord Durham. The dinner was given by Lady Blessington, and I had the whole story both from her and D'Orsay. Disraeli asked me myself to introduce him to J. Hobhouse as a *Radical.* He got me into a scrape, and I cut him till we met at Deepdene after his marriage. Lord L—— will prove, and so will others, that when the Ministry of 1841 was forming, both Disraeli and his wife gave out that they were to have the Secretaryship of the Admiralty. I can't prove that he applied, so simply said that he *expected.* I have made, I think, a good thing of his eloquence, and I have introduced the most striking specimens quoted by Francis, *all* of which are vituperative. I have left out *all* the social anecdotes, as all are open to the same conventional objection. Time of appearance is most important in periodical publications. If you could get out your number by the first of April, you would do great things. Not because it is All Fools' Day, but because it is four days before the meeting of Parliament. The Government will get into a mess about India if they don't take care.

Ever yours faithfully,
A. HAYWARD.

Dizzy was advertised with Rush * and Louis Napoleon as the latest addition to Madame Tussaud's Repository ; but as I don't know his locality I have struck out Rush's

---

* A then notorious murderer.

name ; although I think the being driven to contradict such a thing would add to the ridicule.

Mr. Hayward to Sir G. C. Lewis.

MY DEAR LEWIS,   The Athenæum, March 16, 1853.

I am not at all sensitive about suggestions or alterations, when there is reason for them, as there always would be in your case.   But it may be best to let me see them.   I take it that if you and I fully agree upon such a matter, we cannot well fail of being right.   Our large experience, as well as our varying modes of training, are a guarantee.   If one takes opinions, one gradually gets into the condition of the man who did not know whether he ought to carry his donkey or his donkey to carry him.   I never yet made a miscalculation about any literary effort after talking it over with a good judge, and I feel quite confident of the success of this article, improved as it is by your suggestions.   There will literally be not a syllable that can *blesser les convenances*.   Send me as many suggestions as you choose.   Lockhart used to say that my best passages were added to the last revise.   I have verified all my quotations.   In fact, I do not think there will be a hitch after I have seen it once more.   His theory of the Venetian Constitution* is what he most prides himself on, and his young admirers (Smythe, with the rest) will be maddened more at the attack of this theory than anything else.

Ever truly yours,
A. HAYWARD.

I had a talk with Gladstone on Monday, and he seemed in good spirits about things in general.

* 'Venetia,' by B. Disraeli ; a new edition, London, 1853.

Mr. Hayward to Sir G. C. Lewis.

MY DEAR LEWIS,   April 12, 1853.

The enclosed may make you laugh. It reached me
through Longman yesterday.   The Disraelites are
phrensied with rage. I hope you saw the *Herald* of yesterday. It is hard if it does not sell a few extra copies
for Longman. Everyone whose opinions is worth having
is dead with us, both as to Alison* and Dizzy.

                                           A. HAYWARD.

Mr. Hayward to Sir G. C. Lewis.

MY DEAR LEWIS,   April 28, 1853.

In treating freely the subject you mention,† we should
be treading on very slippery ground. It would be impossible to review Lord John Russell's administration
without bringing into broad relief the points on which
the Whig section of the present coalition Government
differed from the " Peelites." There is Foreign policy,
Colonial policy (with a Grey episode), the Ecclesiastical
Titles Bill, and finally the quarrel between John Russell
and Lord Palmerston. *I* always deprecated the attacks
on the Whigs in the *Chronicle* ‡ because I thought the
present junction the most natural, but I fear that my
views as a "Peelite" would hardly harmonise with those of
the *E. R.* on such a subject ; and on the whole I am con-

---

* 'Alison's History of Europe since 1815,' was reviewed by Sir
G. C. Lewis in the same (April) number of the *Edinburgh Review*.

† Sir George Lewis had asked Mr. Hayward to review Lord
Grey's book, ' The Colonial Policy of Lord John Russell's Administration.'

‡ It was thought at the time that by " writing down " the leaders
of the Whigs, the *Morning Chronicle* did much to bring about the
fall of Lord John Russell's Government in 1852.

vinced that such an article might give a handle to the assailants of a Cabinet we both wish to last. I should think that what you most want are popular articles, and I think I could write one on the 'Memoirs of A. Dumas.' They embrace everything : politics, literature, drama, &c. &c. I knew the man intimately, as well as most of the notabilities of whom he speaks. In short, I feel pretty sure I could make a good thing of it. If you approve this, let me know forthwith, and tell Longman to send me a complete set of the volumes already out, for I read them at the Athenæum. Sir David Brewster wishes to resume his connection with the *E. R.* Shall I tell him you are equally willing, or could you meet him any day at the Athenæum ?

Ever yours,
A. HAYWARD.

I generally leave my chambers about three, and my best address after that hour is the Athenæum.

In the following letters mention is made of Mr. Hayward's application for a Commissionership under the new Charitable Trusts Act. The letters tell their own tale.

Mr. Hayward to Sir G. C. Lewis.

MY DEAR LEWIS,   July 15, 1853.

I am about to ask your aid, and I know you will afford it if you can. The Solicitor-General* has advised me to apply for one of the Commissionerships under the Charitable Trusts Bill about to be passed. There are three, with good salaries, to be appointed under the *sign manual*, which I take to mean the Home Secretary. There is already a great rush for them, and they are

---

* Sir R. Bethell, afterwards Lord Westbury.

more likely to be carried by *interest* than *merit.* I think
you can conscientiously say that my studies have qualified me for such a place, the duties of which are to
suggest legislative improvements in the system, as well
as to decide litigated points ; and I should be very
much obliged if you would do what you can for me
with Lord John Russell, Lord Clarendon, and Lord
Palmerston. The Chancellor is ready to serve me, so
is Lord Lansdowne, and I may safely reckon on the
Peelite members of the Cabinet, unless their interest is
already engaged.

I have most reluctantly become a place-hunter, but
the plain matter of fact is, that I lost a considerable part
of my small fortune on my brother's death.

Few have really contributed more to the formation
and success of the coalition than myself, with the
exception, of course, of its more distinguished members ;
and I think no one has undergone a greater amount
of personal insult and calumny for its sake. But I
know the world too well to expect anything on this
account. I shall most certainly have an article ready
in ample time for your next number. I think this one
very good.

Ever yours,
A. HAYWARD.

Don't mention the subject except for a practical end.

Mr. Hayward to Sir G. C. Lewis.

MY DEAR LEWIS,   Bodryddan, Rhyl, Aug. 28, 1853.

I have only just received your letter, having left town
for this place (Shipley Conway's) on Thursday last. If
you want the article for your next number, I can finish
it in time, but on the whole, I would rather do it for the

following number. If I had known the full plague of place-hunting, I should never have engaged in it. During my last month in town, I was kept in an eternal fidget about the Charity Commissionership. One day it was uncertain whether the Bill would pass, and the next, who would have the patronage? As soon as my fate was decided, I was obliged to accompany Mrs. Norton to the County Court, which I did simply to prevent her from going alone. No one can be Mrs. Norton's adviser, for she never follows advice. I ended by telling her, in Lady Seymour's presence, that she ought to be interdicted the use of pen, ink, and paper. Still, it was a new worry. My mind is hardly yet settled, and there is a probability of my going to Berlin in the course of the next month as a commissioner to take evidence in the case of Lumley *v.* Gye, an action for inducing Johanna Wagner to break her contract, in which the damages are laid at £30,000. It will be an amusing and profitable expedition if it comes off.

Ever yours,

A. H.

*Mr. Hayward to Sir John Young.**

MY DEAR YOUNG,   Carlton, Sept. 14, 1853.

I should have written to you to tell you the result of my first (and last) serious essay at place-hunting, but I took it for granted that you would hear it from Brewster† (to whom I wrote fully), or Molesworth.‡ But I find that Brewster received my epistle in the Highlands, and

* The Right Honourable Sir John Young, Bart., had been Secretary of the Treasury under Sir Robert Peel, and was one of the " Peelites "; became Chief Secretary for Ireland in Lord Aberdeen's Government.

† Afterwards Lord Chancellor of Ireland.

‡ First Commissioner of Works.

that Molesworth has not been in Dublin at all ; and I should wish you to know what has happened. The appointments to the Charity Commissionerships turned out to be vested in the Premier, and he, Lord John Russell, and the Chancellor * met to consult on them on the 17th August. Besides my more direct political friends, I was warmly backed by Lord Lansdowne and Molesworth (which took off the Peelite character of the application), whilst the Chancellor and the Solicitor-General being my friends (to say nothing of the Irish letters),† I had all that was needed in the way of professional recommendations. That evening Sidney Herbert‡ wrote to me that the choice had fallen on luckier men, and shortly afterwards I received a letter from Lord Aberdeen in which, after regretting that it had not been found "*possible*," to appoint me, he says : " You are aware that the appointment to this office did not, by any means, rest exclusively with me ; but I can say with truth that your qualifications were duly recognised by all concerned." I looked out with some curiosity for the list. It appeared at last, and so unknown are the names that people are racking their ingenuity for the reasons which led to such nominations. Now, if Lord John Russell had claimed the place for H——, or any other party man, the case might have been widely different ; but I cannot admit that any Ministry have a right to give places to private friends from personal motives whilst their party obligations remain unsatisfied. When men work together for a party object, they are all entitled, in their several ways,

---

* Lord Cranworth.

† Testimonials furnished by Lord Chancellors (Irish) Blackburn and Brewster, and by the Attorney-General for Ireland, testifying to the satisfactory manner in which Mr. Hayward conducted the enquiry into the Local Taxation of Dublin in 1847.

‡ Secretary-at-War.

to a share in the advantage of success. Lord Aberdeen might fairly have taken this ground, and Lord John Russell could not have made a quarrel of it, because his original objection to me for old *Chronicle* articles (which I did *not* write) would not bear discussion. Of this Molesworth makes no secret, and I have it in writing from another leading member of the Government. But the truth is, Lord Aberdeen at once gave way to Lord John, and will probably do so whenever the same pressure may be put upon him. Still, I can say with truth that all my friends exceeded instead of falling short of their professions, and I believe the Duke of Newcastle, S. Herbert, Elcho,* &c., were even more disappointed than myself; for, somehow, I had an instinct that Johnny would upset *my* coach.

I must tell you another *Chronicle* grievance which the editor wishes me to mention. Copies of public documents (the last dispatch of Lord Clarendon, published two days since, for example) are uniformly kept back from him and given to the *Times.* This is both unfair and impolitic. The *Chronicle* is the only morning paper that has uniformly supported the Government, and the *Times* constantly turns against it on the chance of gaining any stray ray of popularity, as on the Indian Bill. It is an error to measure utility by circulation. Every one of the leading papers is read at all clubs and reading rooms. Its good articles or arguments are reprinted or reproduced in the provincial papers, or worked up anew in the shape of speeches, and always furnish topics for the friends of the party it advocates. It thus influences constituents, and constituents command votes. Look at the position of a party without an organ during the parliamentary recess ; and the " Peelites " will

---

* Francis, Lord Elcho (now Lord Wemyss), became a convert to Free Trade, and was a Lord of the Treasury under Lord Aberdeen's Government.

be without one if they do not look sharp.   Carry your mind to that period when Gladstone was voting with Disraeli and the Duke of Newcastle abroad.   What then kept up the hopes of the party, or by what was it mainly known?   At some future time I shall be strongly tempted to publish my own articles, with the dates and a preface.   But my individual case is not now the point.   Pray, if you have the means, point out in the fitting quarter the consequences that must ensue from such things.   If the support of any portion of the press is deemed valueless, let it so be understood at once, and then people know what they have to expect, and where they are.   I am writing a long letter because I have not time to write a short one, and you must make allowances for hasty expressions.   Bonham, I am glad to hear, is to have Cane's place : unless, indeed, Lord John Russell should put a spoke in his wheel too.   I am doubtful whether I am going to Germany or to Scotland.   Things still look very awkward in the East.*   Regards to Lady Young, and believe me ever, my dear Young, most sincerely yours,

A. HAYWARD.

Mr. Hayward to Sir G. C. Lewis.

[EXTRACT.]   · Sept. 23, 1853.

I have ascertained that any impression Lord John Russell might have entertained as to my having been his bitter assailant in the *Chronicle* two years ago was completely removed before the meeting at which the

---

* At this time the Porte had declined to accept the Vienna Note, which had been accepted by Russia as a basis for settling the question of Russia's claim to the protectorate of the Greek Church in Turkey. War between Russia and Turkey seemed imminent.

Charity appointments were decided upon ; and, as he did not carry his own friend, I suspect that party claims were laid aside by common consent on all sides.

Lord Elcho to Mr. Hayward.

MY DEAR HAYWARD,   Sept. 28, 1853.

Many thanks for your letters, which are most welcome as they keep me *au fait* of what is going on. In regard to your own Commissioner affair, I hope from what you say in your last that nobody is to blame, but that your failure is owing to some untoward combination of circumstances as yet unexplained, but still such as I trust will remove from the Peelites the charge of ingratitude. I am glad Hayter* has behaved well, as I think him a very good fellow, and I should have been disappointed had he behaved otherwise, especially after his having said to me that he considered you entitled to one of the Commissionerships. I see no harm in the insertion in the *Chronicle* of the letter of which you sent me a proof. It is certainly unfair of the *Economist* to say that the Press were unanimous in favour of a differentiated (that, I think, was the phrase) Income Tax, for the *Chronicle* took up the contrary view and argued it most ably ; and it would be absurd to suppose that those articles did not produce some effect on the public mind, if we admit that the Press is influential in guiding public opinion, which in these days few will be disposed to deny. I am sorry that Cooke is hurt at not having received the Clarendon July despatch at the same time as the *Times*. He certainly is entitled to be treated upon an equality, if not to have a preference given him, in all matters of govern-

* The late Rt. Hon. Sir Wm. G. Hayter was then Parliamentary Secretary.

ment information, for he has certainly been a staunch
friend to the Peelites and to the coalition, whilst our
friend the *Times* is a staunch friend only to the *Times*.
In the Turkey affair, at the stage at which it appears to
have arrived, it will indeed be surprising if the pen has
not to give place to the sword. Austria will make a
mistake if she sides with Russia.*   Lombardy and Hungary are terrible elements of danger to her, and Sardinia,
backed by France, might not be unwilling, in the event
of a general scrimmage, to have another go at her old
enemy. We leave these wild regions on the 10th, and
expect to be in Edinbro' on the 15th, in London on
the 1st.

Yours ever,
ELCHO.

Sir John Young to Mr. Hayward.
[EXTRACT.]

MY DEAR HAYWARD,   Oct. 8, 1853.

I assure you I learnt with no little surprise and great
concern that you were not named to the appointment of
which, when I was leaving London, I thought you quite
certain ; and was proportionately disappointed when
names which I had never before heard turned up as
successful. After a turn so unexpected, it is difficult to
point with confidence to future hopes, and I shall not
attempt it ; but of this I can safely assure you, that
you had well-wishers and strenuous advocates amongst
the best and bravest of our friends, and that I am persuaded they are not disposed either to forget or under-
value one who stood with them in adversity, and in days

---

* On 24th Sept., the Emperors of Russia and Austria had an
interview at Olmütz.

when their scanty ranks were not yet swelled by holyday recruits.

Believe me ever,

Sincerely yours,

JOHN YOUNG.

Is there any chance of your coming here? Both Lady Young and I will be charmed to receive you, so come if you can.

The next letter indicates the early stage of the negotiations which finally ended in the Crimean War; and reflects much of the anxiety that was felt by those in political circles about both foreign and domestic affairs at this time.

Mr. Hayward to Sir John Young.

Pencarrow,* Bodmin.
Oct. 11, 1853.

MY DEAR YOUNG,

Many thanks for your kind letter, which has just reached me here. I came down with C. Villiers on Saturday last, but our host hurried off on Sunday morning to attend the next Cabinet, having missed two (Friday and Saturday) by an extraordinary blunder of the person whose duty it is to issue the summonses. He is waiting in town for the next dispatch from Constantinople, and we are enjoying ourselves in his absence under Lady Molesworth's auspices. Our party here are the Fords, Lord and Lady Vivian, Miss Damer, Fleming, C. Villiers and myself. Villiers and I stay till the beginning of next week, and towards the end of the month it is probable that I shall go to Germany. I

---

* The seat of Sir Wm. Molesworth.

feel pretty confident that the Turkish question will be settled peaceably after all, that is, for the present. And my belief is that the Government will have a very good case for Parliament. They are now popularly judged, not by their own acts and dispatches, but by the vacillating tone and occasionally unprincipled articles of the *Times.* Lord Aberdeen, in particular, has suffered greatly, and I think unjustly, from being everywhere identified with the *Times.* C. Villiers, who has just returned from the Continent, says that the effect is still more palpable there than in England. Monck dined twice with me at the Carlton on his way through town, and everything goes on there as it did before the Carltonian battles.* The Duke of Newcastle and H. Fitzroy have also been dining there. So you may return there, as in the olden time, with perfect confidence. My chief subject of anxiety, politically speaking, now, is the proposed Reform Bill. There is to be an article in the forthcoming *Edinburgh* by Greg, who wrote the one that attracted so much attention. *That* was in a Conservative sense, and depend upon it, the feeling of the country is essentially Conservative. With remembrances to Lady Young,

Ever faithfully yours,
A. HAYWARD.

This is a beautiful property, and a very comfortable house.

In November Mr. Hayward went to Berlin, on a legal commission, to examine witnesses in the case of Lumley *v.* Gye. While he was at Berlin he acquainted himself with the feeling in political circles upon the Eastern question, and wrote home to the Duke of Newcastle

---

* Between the Tory Protectionists and "Peelites," when the former wanted to drive the latter from the Club.

his own impressions of the view taken of it at Berlin.
On his way home he stayed some time in Paris, and
having access to most of the leading politicians there,
he took care to inform himself of the opinion entertained
by French statesmen of the Emperor Louis Napoleon's
policy and good faith towards England, in the event of
war with Russia. These impressions, too, he also com-
municates to the Duke.

Mr. Hayward to the Duke of Newcastle.

Hotel de Russie, Berlin.
MY DEAR DUKE,   Nov. 13, 1853.

I do not expect to be kept here more than a week
longer at the utmost; in the meantime I am making
the best of my opportunities. Notwithstanding the
connection between the Prussian Court and the Czar,
the eyes of the Government here are strongly open to
the dangers of war, and his Russian Majesty has utterly
failed in obtaining the sanction of the Prussian Ministry to his schemes, on which, at one time, he fully
calculated. The Austrians, too, are startled and on
their guard. The language of the majority of the
German papers is now strongly condemnatory of the
Czar. I see a good deal of Lord A. Loftus, and when
one has got over his likeness to his brother, the
Marquis, the impression of his knowledge and judgment as regards Germany is highly favourable. He
says that the Prussian Minister for Foreign Affairs
is most anxious to keep well with England at all
hazards; but it is curious to mark how much our moral
influence has been weakened by the strikes, which
foreigners regard as an unerring symptom that a socialist
revolution is at hand. I tried in vain yesterday to

O 2

persuade Savigny, the greatest of their jurisconsults, and
formerly Minister, that the strikes have very little (or
nothing) of a political tendency, and in one sense are a
proof of growing wealth.

Radowitz is in a most precarious state; during five
weeks he was completely prostrate. Yesterday one
of the Prussian papers announced his death, but the
answer to my inquiries last night was that he was rather
better. Nothing can exceed the kindness of his wife's
family to me. Tell Mrs. Norton that both the wife and
the sister-in-law are formidable rivals, both being handsome, graceful, and fascinating to the highest degree.
They are by birth Countesses de Voss. At the house of
the mother-in-law the other night, I met, amongst other
celebrities, Rauch the sculptor, and Ranke the historian.
White, the *Chronicle* correspondent, went to England a
week since. This is a pity, for he is on the best possible
footing with all the leading people.* Williamson, the
Times correspondent, does not enjoy the same advantages. White has left his duty to be performed by one
of the most intelligent men here, a diplomat, who repre-
sents two or three of the smaller States at the Zoll-
verein. His information is from the best sources. I
have seen several officers of rank, well acquainted with
the Russian and Turkish armies, and depend upon it,
H. R.'s story of the inferiority of the Turks is preposterous. A civilian who compares an army on service
with troops got up for a review, is pretty sure to fall
into the most absurd errors. I take it, there was never
a more ragged-looking set of fellows than the English

---

* In a letter to Sir Edmund Head, Sir G. C. Lewis writes :—
"The *Chronicle* has been for some time a ' Peelite ' paper, and is ably
written—Smythe and Hayward are two of the writers. I do not
know whether any copy of it reaches Fredericton, but its articles
are well worth reading, and its foreign correspondence is remarkably
good, particularly that from Germany." (' Letters,' p. 211.)

army in the Peninsula.   If I hear anything worth telling,
I will write.   With the sincerest regards,

Ever faithfully yours,

A. HAYWARD.

I shall take Paris on my way back.

Mr. Hayward to the Duke of Newcastle.

Hôtel Mirabeau, Paris,
MY DEAR DUKE,   Nov. 30,* 1853.

I came here to refresh my political and literary impressions, and shall stay till next week.

Thiers has been very civil.   He made a dinner-party
for me directly, and begged me to come every evening
to his house (he receives every evening but Thursday)
when I had no other engagement.   It is a good place
to know what is said, or thought, or doing ; and I
was glad to find the tone decidedly favourable to
your government.   On Sunday there was a general
rumour that Lord Aberdeen was going out, and Thiers
was quite delighted when I expressed my conviction
that there was nothing in it.   No one here attaches
any importance to the so-called fusion, and even
the Duc de Nemours' authority for undertaking it is
denied. †

Rather to my surprise, I do not find Louis Napoleon's
good faith towards England, as respects the Turkish
Question, disputed in any quarter, and even Thiers
thinks that a valid and effective treaty might be entered
into.   Louis Napoleon, however, has certainly not succeeded in inspiring respect.   All educated people still

* Wednesday, the 30th of November—the date of the disaster
at Sinope.

† The fusion between the Legitimists and the Orleans branch.

talk of him as a necessary evil. The journals are dull,
and people seem content to take things as they are, and
live without that political discussion which once seemed
as necessary to a Frenchman as the air he breathed.
Lord Cowley returns to-day from Fontainebleau. Lord
Malmesbury brought over all his apparatus for the
chasse, but (I suppose by an accident) has not been
asked to join the Imperial party. The result of my
Berlin Commission has appeared with tolerable correct-
ness in the newspapers. The *Times* is paying dearly
for its vacillations. It is very little quoted by any
foreign journals (German or French), and always with a
sneer or a doubt.

Ever most truly yours,
A. HAYWARD.

Mr. Hayward to the Duke of Newcastle.

MY DEAR DUKE,   Carlton Club,
                              Sunday, Dec. 11, 1853.

I got back late on Friday, and shall hope to see you
ere long, if you are not quitting London directly. The
destruction of the Turkish ships at Sinope, however, can
hardly fail to compel the presence of the Cabinet ; and
in reference to the resulting crisis, Louis Napoleon's real
intentions become of the deepest importance.

During my stay in Paris I saw politicians of all sorts ;
no later than Tuesday last, I dined at Thiers', to meet
some of the leading men of his party ; and I went
afterwards to where were assembled Prince Napoleon,
and several of the ministers. No one doubts that Louis
Napoleon will cordially join with Great Britain in decisive measures (war if necessary) and all his opponents
urge is that he is anxious to precipitate a war, in
other words, to go further than we, instead of (as I

suspected) holding back at a critical moment * and deserting us.   Thiers' last words to me were that the best hope of civilisation lay in a cordial alliance between France and England. "As this will strengthen the Napoleon dynasty," he added, "I need hardly say that my judgment is in opposition to my personal interests and prejudices." The feeling against Russia struck me to be universal, both in France and Germany.

Ever faithfully yours,
A. HAYWARD.

I should say that personally Louis Napoleon has lost ground, but his death, or dethronement, just now would be deprecated by all parties.   He is an admitted, if disagreeable, necessity.

On the 16th of December the *Times* announced the resignation of Lord Palmerston, on the ground of his inability to support the Government Reform Bill.   Mr. Hayward, in his next letter, states his conviction that the disaster at Sinope "precipitated" Lord Palmerston's resignation, and hints that his supposed objections to the foreign policy of the Government lay at the root of the cause of his leaving the Cabinet.

The "peace-making services," alluded to a little further on, relate to the action taken by Mr. Gladstone and the Duke of Newcastle in setting matters in train for Lord Palmerston's return to the Cabinet, which took place on the 24th of December.

---

* What Mr. Hayward had "suspected" proved only too true, but at a "critical moment" occurring a long time afterwards.   See the revelations by the Russian Foreign Office 'Diplomatic Study of the Crimean War,' vol. ii. p. 343, *et seq.*

Mr. Hayward to the Duke of Newcastle.

MY DEAR DUKE,   Temple, Dec. 19, 1853.

You are quoted as bearing high testimony to Lord Palmerston's conduct as regards openness and straightforwardness, and this is perhaps for the best. But facts have come to my knowledge which convince me that his resignation was in reality precipitated by the news of the affair at Sinope, and I very much doubt whether his criticisms will be in a friendly spirit. I shall not mention this to any one else, but it is as well that you should know it, and I assure you I am not speaking from mere conjecture.

What has come over Harcourt? His language about the Government seems borrowed from the *Herald* or the *Standard.* Cooke, too, was getting too bellicose. I had a long talk with him yesterday, and I have written to him again to-day. The articles in this day's paper, however, strike me to be in the right tone. He is a good fellow, and always open to reason, but rather apt to be swayed by men like Harcourt, who, though a clever fellow, is rather too fond of strong language and uncompromising steps.

The Derbyites are more shattered than ever, and to suppose that Palmerston can make a Ministry without the aid of his late colleagues is preposterous. If things turn out, as I hope, his resignation may simply have the effect of accelerating your Premiership.

You will, of course, dissolve if your Bill is thrown out. You need answer none of my notes—indeed, such a note as this is better not answered. Cooke will go on speaking well of Palmerston, and assume as long as possible that he is friendly to the Government.

Ever yours faithfully,
A. HAYWARD.

Mr. Hayward to his Sisters.

[EXTRACT.]

Dec. 26, 1853.

The Palmerston row was made up by the Duke of Newcastle. I dined with him at the Athenæum on Saturday after he had completed the work. It will add greatly to his weight. The only parties to the difference were Lord J. Russell, Sir James Graham, Lord Palmerston and Lord Aberdeen. I have ascertained that Lyme is down for abolition in everybody's list. The Reform is to go on.

Mr. Hayward to the Duke of Newcastle.

MY DEAR DUKE,   Dec. 26, 1853.

I don't know whether you will meet with your usual fate in being frowned at by those whom you have got out of a mess, but I am quite sure that the highest possible estimate is formed and expressed of your peace-making services, both by those who have less directly profited by them, and by the lookers-on.

I sate some time with Molesworth yesterday, and he said that after many talks with C. Villiers and others, they were quite agreed that you must be the next Premier in case anything were to happen to Lord Aberdeen.

I am sorry to find that the Palmerstonians seem very exasperated against Sir James Graham, but the notion of his having done what they think is preposterous. Nor can I believe that he even stimulated the article in the *Times*. Of course, all sorts of assertions are bandied about, as to conditions and concessions. But the best of it is, that the strongest measures appear to have been taken whilst Lord Palmerston was absent from your councils.

I found Lord Elcho (notwithstanding his confidence in his friends) in a great fright lest the Reform Bill should run counter to his conservatism. But I begged him not to cry out before he was hurt. Blackett confirmed to me just now what he had said about the Liberal party, requesting the postponement of the Reform Bill in case of war.

Ever faithfully yours,

A. HAYWARD.

CHAPTER VI.

1854—1856.

The Reform Bill—Letter from M. Thiers on the Eastern Question
and the policy and armaments of France—Letter to the Duke
of Newcastle—Letter from Mr. Sidney Herbert on the probable
consequences of the war—Letter from M. Charles de Rémusat
on the feeling in Paris about the war—Letter to the Duke of
Newcastle on Lord John Russell's Reform Bill—Letter from
M. Thiers—Letters to the Duke of Newcastle on the Stonor
Committee—Letter from Sir William Molesworth—The Duke
of Newcastle and the Secretaryship for War—Letter to Sir
John Young—Letter from the Duke of Newcastle—Letter
from M. Thiers on the expedition to Sebastopol—Visit to
Italy, visit to Paris—Letters to Sir John Young, Lord Palmer-
ston in Paris—State of our army before Sebastopol—Mr.
Hayward offered the Secretaryship of the Poor Law Board by
Lord Aberdeen—Lord Courtenay does not resign, loss of
appointment—Letters to Sir John Young, his Sisters, and the
Duke of Newcastle—Letters from Mrs. Norton and Mr. M. T.
Baines—Foreign Enlistment Bill—Lord Ernest Bruce to Mr.
Hayward—The "winter troubles" of 1854—Mr. Roebuck's
notice of motion—Lord Raglan—Lord St. Germans to Mr.
Hayward—Fall of Lord Aberdeen's Government—Letter from
Sir John Young on Lord Palmerston's position—Letter from
Lord St. Germans on the crisis—Letter from Lord Lansdowne
—Letter to Sir John Young—Letter from Lord Elcho—In-
decision of Sir James Graham, Mr. Gladstone, and Mr. Sidney
Herbert to join Lord Palmerston's Government—Letter to Sir
G. C. Lewis—Letter from M. Thiers—Resignation of Lord St.
Germans—Sir E. Bulwer Lytton's speech on the Newspaper
Stamp Bill—Letter from M. Thiers—Letter to Mr. Gladstone
—Letters from the Duke of Newcastle—Letter to the Count

de Montalembert on his ' De l'Avenir politique de l'Angleterre '
—Letter from Lord Brougham—Letter to Mr. Gladstone,
Count Esterhazy's mission to St. Petersburg — Letter to Mr.
Monsell (Lord Emly).

AT the outset of 1854 a conflict with Russia had
become inevitable. It was of vital importance to the
Government to possess authentic information concerning
the resources of our French allies and the opinions
of their leading men. No one was more competent to
supply this than Mr. Hayward, whose intimacy with
M. Thiers and other prominent Frenchmen enabled him
to render valuable assistance. Apart from the formal
support of his articles in the *Morning Chronicle,* he was
in frequent private communication with the Duke of
Newcastle, upon whom as Secretary of State for War
the main responsibility rested after the actual outbreak
of hostilities.

Thus the correspondence of this period affords some
interesting illustrations of the invisible influences by
which government policy was modified, indicating at the
same time the attitude assumed by that moderate
rational and well-informed portion of Society to which
Mr. Hayward belonged.

Most of the letters bear witness to the absorbing
interest of the Russian War ; among them will be found
some of the series to which Mr. Hayward alludes in his
Essay on M. Thiers, as having been written by the French
statesman " for the use of the Duke of Newcastle "—pointing out not only how the campaign should be conducted,
but what measures should be taken for supplying the
requirements of the troops ; and if his advice had been
followed, both French and English would have been

spared much of the privation and suffering they endured before Sebastopol.*

But although the bulk of the correspondence is occupied with matters political and military, there is sufficient evidence that Mr. Hayward's zest for purely literary work remained undiminished ; and that his trenchant and opportune leaders in the *Morning Chronicle* did not interfere with the preparation of mature and highly-finished essays for the *Edinburgh Review*.

Mr. Hayward to Sir John Young.

MY DEAR YOUNG,   Athenæum, Jan. 5, 1854.

Hayter tells me that on sounding the Liberal members he finds they won't stand the postponement of the Reform Bill, but will (he thinks) be satisfied with a moderate measure. I doubt whether it has even yet been settled by the Cabinet. I *know* that, three days ago, the question of the extension of the borough franchise was *not* settled. There will be a good deal of random talking when Parliament meets, but no systematic or organised opposition. The Derbyites are still all abroad. Palmerston's return shattered their last hope. I for one do not believe that he made any terms. No one can guess how the Czar will take the last formal communication to him of the entry (or intended entry) of the fleets into the Black Sea with orders to coop up his fleet in Sebastopol. Layard (who is now writing by my side) says that to enter for the next two months would be the height of temerity. Perhaps, therefore, the Czar may still try to temporise. Lord Clarendon seems to think that his dispatches will make a good impression

* ' Eminent Statesmen and Writers,' vol. i. p. 55, note. (Murray, 1880.)

when published.   For my part, I believe the Government
will have a very good case.*   With remembrances to
Lady Young,

Ever faithfully yours,
A. HAYWARD.

M. Thiers to Mr. Hayward.

MON CHER HAYWARD,   Paris, 8 janvier 1854.

Je vous remercie de votre intéressante lettre, et je vous
prie de m'en écrire souvent de pareilles.   Votre nation
et votre gouvernement se conduisent également bien dans
cette grave question d'Orient, et il y a en France une
satisfaction très réelle de l'alliance anglaise, et un grand
sentiment de sécurité à se trouver de moitié avec la
Grande Bretagne dans les complications menaçantes de
l'avenir.   C'est une puérilité de rechercher lequel de vous
ou de nous peut avoir plus ou moins d'intérêt matériel
ou mercantile dans cette affaire.   Nous avons au plus
haut point, et au même degré, l'intérêt moral et politique
de l'équilibre européen, (celui-là vaut tous les autres) et
nous ne devons pas permettre que la Russie rompe cet
équilibre à son profit.   Depuis trente ans la Russie, par
la soumission à laquelle elle avait réduit la Prusse et
l'Autriche, dominait l'Europe.   Cette domination va
devenir complète et peut-être irrévocable, si on lui laisse
obtenir un nouveau triomphe dans les circonstances
actuelles, et alors la France et l'Angleterre prendront le
second rang dans le monde.   C'est là un intérêt immense,
sans pareil, et qui vaut tous les autres.   Les nations qui
consentent à déchoir ne sont plus des nations.   Pour
celles qui ont occupé le premier rang passer au second,

---

* Parliament was opened by the Queen on the 31st of January,
and the debates on the Address resulted in a vindication of the
foreign policy of the Government, which did something to restore
popular confidence in it.

c'est passer au dernier. Par malheur beaucoup de vieux royalistes, anciens légitimistes, et nouveaux légitimistes se font Russes, par une vieille faiblesse qui les porte à espérer en l'appui du dehors. Mais ce sont des misères dont il ne faut tenir compte.

Je n'aime pas le gouvernement que nous avons, mais je n'y pense plus dès que le gouvernement est en face de l'ennemi extérieur, et qu'il soutient une bonne cause . . . Certainement si on peut conserver honorablement la paix, ce sera mieux. Pour nous autres vieux constitutionnels la guerre n'a que des chances' ou fâcheuses ou déplorables, fâcheuses si la victoire confirme notre gouvernement dans ses penchants anti-libéraux, ou déplorables si la défaite exposait la France à voir l'étranger sur ses frontières. La paix donc nous vaut mieux sous tous les rapports. Mais si l'intérêt de l'équilibre européen commande la guerre, nous ferons des vœux pour qu'elle soit heureuse. C'est là le sentiment, croyez-le, des gens honnêtes et éclairés en France. Mais il ne faut pas qu'on se fasse illusion, la guerre sera terrible. Les ministres sont des gens habiles et éclairés, et n'ont pas besoin des lumières d'autrui ; mais nous savons quelquefois sur le continent des faits dont la connaissance ne passe pas le détroit, malgré le progrès de la vapeur.

La Russie sait qu'elle va jouer sa grandeur, et elle fera des efforts inouïs.—Mieux vaudrait ne pas commencer que de commencer avec des illusions, et d'entreprendre la guerre sans des moyens suffisants. Il faut d'abord maintenir l'Autriche et la Prusse en état de neutralité, et pour cela ne rien faire en Allemagne surtout en Italie, qui puisse leur donner des ombrages. Nous serions tous perdus si de politique, la guerre devenait révolutionnaire, ce sera bien assez d'avoir à la Russie seule, placée comme elle est sur le terrain de la lutte, où nous ne pouvons arriver qu'avec des vaisseaux. Il ne faut pas nous figurer qu'on puisse faire à son commerce un grand mal. D'abord le commerce extérieur n'est pas chez elle, comme chez vous, ou chez nous, une chose de première nécessité, secondement les Américains résolus à faire tous les profits de la neutralité, vont accourir avec leur pavillon, pour faire tout le commerce russe, et il faudrait bien se garder de recommencer avec eux une guerre de neutralité. A la vérité, les matières navales sont interdites d'après le droit des neutres, (entendu comme l'entendent les Français et les Américains) et ce sera déjà une gêne pour eux, mais il faut prendre garde de se brouiller avec les Américains pour l'exercice du droit de visite. La souffrance commerciale ne sera donc pas aussi grande pour les Russes que vous le croyez.

Il faudra attaquer ses rives fortes pour réduire cet ennemi par les armes. Il faudra une grande armée sur le Danube, il faudra des expéditions en Crimée, et dans les provinces de la Baltique, et ce n'est pas là une petite affaire. Vous pouvez tenir pour certain que la Russie finira par ériger des forts immenses, entre le Pruth et le Danube. La Pologne est éteinte, et ne bougera pas. Vous avez peut-être 250,000 Russes sur le Danube, donnant 180,000 combattants réels. Je ne serais pas étonné que la guerre devenant acharnée ; les Russes envoyassent jusqu'à 300,000 hommes, donnant 200 à 200,000 combattants. Ce n'est donc pas avec des vaisseaux et quelques expéditions de vingt ou trente mille hommes qu'on peut lutter ; avec de pareils moyens nous aurions la confusion de voir prendre Constantinople sans nos gens, et à la honte de nos deux pavillons. Je crois qu'il faut mettre les Turcs avec des subsides, en mesure d'avoir 150,000 hommes de leur nation sous les armes, (ce qui sera une très petite dépense, le soldat turc ne coûtant presque rien) et de plus il faudra cent mille Européens sur le bas Danube. A cette double condition, avec l'appui de nos deux marines, il est probable qu'on aura des succès. Si on y ajoute quelques expéditions navales portant des troupes de débarquement, et allant détenir des établissements maritimes, on peut espérer de réduire l'orgueilleuse puissance, à laquelle nous avons affaire, à une paix raisonnable. Mais si on compte sur de moindres efforts on se trompe, et il vaut mieux ne pas entreprendre une lutte, dont on ne sortirait pas à son avantage.

Vous me demandez si la France pourrait aujourd'hui disposer de 70,000 hommes, et vous ajoutez que la question est peut-être indiscrète. Elle n'est pas indiscrète du tout, et je suis, par la connaissance que j'ai des affaires administratives de mon pays, en mesure de vous répondre. La France n'est pas préparée, mais elle peut néanmoins dans très peu de temps donner les 70,000 hommes, et excellents. Elle a 100 régiments à trois bataillons. On peut très rapidement augmenter l'effectif des régiments, de manière à tirer deux bataillons de guerre de chaque régiment. En prenant 30 de nos 100 régiments, en les portant sur le littoral de la Méditerranée, de Port-Vendres à Toulon, on peut en tirer 60 bataillons de guerre, qui à 900 hommes chacun, feraient 34,000 hommes d'infanterie de ligne. En prenant 6 bataillons de chasseurs de Vincennes à 1,000 hommes chacun, on aurait 60,000 hommes d'infanterie, avec 25 batteries d'artillerie (la batterie est de 6 pièces chez nous) on aurait 150 bouches à feu attelées, et 6,000 hommes d'artillerie, cela ferait 66,000 hommes. Enfin en prenant 20 régiments de cavalerie, sur 54 que nous avons dans l'Afrique à 600 chevaux chacun, on aurait 78,000 hommes, et ajoutant 2,000 hommes du génie, et du train des équipages, on arriverait à 80,000 hommes, qui en les administrant bien, en les nourrissant sainement, en les habillant confortablement, en ayant soin de ne les jamais faire bivouaquer dans des lieux malsains, se réduiraient à l'entrée en campagne à 70,000 hommes, chiffre réel. Si

la moindre négligence dans l'entretien ou les emplace-
ments survenait, ces 80,000 hommes se réduiraient à
40,000, mais en supposant les soins nécessaires, on peut
vous fournir le contingent en deux mois ; il faudrait un
mois au moins pour le transport, en supposant un double
voyage de vos flottes et des nôtres, car les chevaux sont
très difficiles à transporter ; il faudrait un mois pour se
reconnaître une fois sur les lieux. Ce serait donc, si on
donnait les ordres demain, un délai de 4 mois qu'il
faudrait avant d'avoir apporté aux Turcs un secours
efficace. Si à nos 70,000 vous en ajoutiez 30,000, alors
je crois que la Russie pourrait se repentir de sa témérité.
Si non, elle nous couvrira de confusion. Pour que nos
70,000 hommes se maintiennent à ce chiffre, il faudrait
20,000 hommes de renfort par an. Nous pouvons cela
très aisément, si le continent reste neutre, et si on a de
grands soins hygiéniques.

Quant à Sevastopol, je ne sais pas un moyen plus sûr
de mettre la Russie au désespoir, que de la frapper en
cet endroit ; mais je doute de la possibilité d'une telle
opération, sans des troupes de débarquement. J'ai vu et
étudié des reconnaissances bien faites de cet établissement.
J'ai entretenu des officiers qui m'aient été sur les lieux.
L'entrée de Sevastopol est difficile même pour les Russes
entrant en amis, et chez amis, mais entrer sans balises,
sous le feu, serait un grand danger. On serait probable-
ment échoué sous des batteries formidables. Pourtant
Nelson a fait des choses aussi difficiles. Mais par terre
Sevastopol est tout investi, quinze mille hommes
débarqués l'enleveraient rapidement, aidés par une flotte
puissante.

En coupant ensuite par une suite de retranchements
la presqu'île de Pérékop, on resterait maître de la Crimée,
et la Russie serait annulée dans la mer Noire. Mais cela
ne serait possible, qu'autant qu'une puissante armée sur
le Danube pourrait occuper et retenir le gros des armées

russes, qui sans cela se reporteraient en masse vers la
Crimée, pour réjoindre un établissement qui est aussi
important pour eux que Portsmouth pour l'Angleterre,
et Brest pour la France.

Voilà, mon cher ami, une longue réponse à vos
questions.   Il faut éviter la guerre si on le peut
honorablement, (ce dont je doute) et si on décide à la
faire, la faire sans illusion, et avec le développement des
moyens nécessaires ; vigoureusement faite, la guerre peut
rétablir l'équilibre européen, peu entamé depuis vingt
ans ; mollement faite, elle nous couvrira de confusion, et
achèvera la rupture de l'équilibre, en augmentant la
puissance déjà trop grande de la Russie.   Voilà, mon
cher ami, l'avis d'un vieux philosophe, qui a beaucoup
réfléchi sur tout cela, et le vœu d'un bon patriote qui
aime avant tout la France, et presque autant que la
France l'Angleterre, parce qu'en ces deux nations se
résume l'univers civilisé.   Tout à vous de cœur, donnez-
moi des nouvelles.

A. THIERS.

Mr. Hayward to the Duke of Newcastle.

MY DEAR DUKE,   Jan. 9, 1854.

I had this morning a very long letter from Thiers, in
which he sketches out the probable plan of the Czar, and
the armaments required to encounter him with effect.
He thinks you cannot save Turkey by merely naval
operations.   We must subsidise and France send troops,
unless we like to send troops too.   He says that he has
seen plans of Sebastopol, and spoken with officers who
have been there ; and that the entrance is difficult and
dangerous—even when not under fire.   He says Louis
Napoleon could not spare 70,000 men without at least
two months' notice and preparation.   I am afraid, from
what I hear, that things may remain some time longer in

this present state of neither peace nor war, which must
place Government in a most embarrassing condition as
regards the Reform Bill ; for were you to put it off, and
no war were to come, the Radicals would cry treason.
On the other hand, enlightened opinion is certainly
against the resulting agitation during war. I understand
that Kelly has actually got ready a Reform Bill, but
the tone of the Derbyites is against any Bill at present, and I don't think his *ruse* will answer, unless the
negotiations take decidedly a pacific turn. Even then
it will be odd if your Bill be not deemed the best of
the two.

Ever yours faithfully,

A. HAYWARD.

Macgregor says that his constituents (Glasgow), and
the majority of members he has spoken to, are for
postponement of the Bill.

Hon. Sidney Herbert * to Mr. Hayward.

[EXTRACT.]

MY DEAR HAYWARD.   Belgrave Square, Jan. 11, 1854.

Many thanks for your letter : it interested me much.
I think the Emperor† will decline negotiations under
surveillance, will not declare war when blockaded, but
will give a sort of " you be d—d " answer, and leave us
to take such further steps as we choose, he pursuing his
war with Turkey his own way. His notion evidently is
that the party that declares war is necessarily the
aggressor, or at any rate technically so, and that he can
assume the air of a martyr. I do not think the British
public who have holloaed so lustily for war, and con-

---

* Was Secretary of State-at-War in Lord Aberdeen's Government ; *vide post*, p. 237.
† Of Russia.

lemned all attempts at pacification as cowardice, are at
ill aware of the severity, the cold, and the duration of the
truggle in which we shall soon be engaged ; and not a
ew of the noisiest will be the first to quail at the
acrifices to be made, and to reproach the Government
or not having made more efforts to procure peace.

Believe me,

Yours sincerely,

SIDNEY HERBERT.

M. de Rémusat* to Mr. Hayward.

5?, Rue d'Anjou, St. Honoré,

CHER MONSIEUR HAYWARD,   31 janvier 1854.

Je ne saurais assez vous remercier des soins que vous
avez bien voulu donner à mes intérêts littéraires, et je
vous prie de m'excuser si j'ai ainsi abusé de votre
obligeante amitié. Je comprends très bien que les
circonstances sont peu favorables aux entreprises de
ibrairie, et les libraires de Paris, qui me pressaient il y
a quelques jours, vont peut-être à présent ajourner leurs
nstances et leurs projets. Je crois, en effet, que nous
levons perdre presque tout espoir de paix. Le public
commence à s'apercevoir de la gravité de la situation.
Il s'est obstiné à ne pas croire la guerre possible ; car il
a redoute, et le gouvernement absolu n'avait été accueilli
en France, que comme une garantie de tranquillité. Il
est très dur à tous les intérêts engagés avec excès dans
es spéculations mercantiles de renoncer à leur aveugle
sécurité sur l'avenir. Aucune des diverses opinions
politiques qui divisent notre société, n'avait fait entrer
lans ses calculs la possibilité d'une guerre sérieuse, et le
chef du gouvernement est entouré de conseils pacifiques.
Pour moi, je déplore la guerre, mais je ne la blâme pas.

---

* M. de Rémusat, one of Thiers's intimate friends, frequently
corresponded with Mr. Hayward on literary and political subjects.

Je voudrais encore l'éviter, mais si elle est inévitable, je crois qu'il vaut mieux la faire énergiquement, que reculer dans la politique qu'on a suivie jusqu'à présent, et pourvu que l'alliance entre nos deux pays se soutienne jusqu'au bout, je ne suis pas sans confiance dans l'avenir, mais je suis forcé de reconnaître que l'opinion des classes éclairées n'est pas en général d'accord avec la mienne, et que le gouvernement rencontre plus d'obéissance que d'approbation. Nous attendons avec impatience le discours de la Reine : et je souhaite vivement que votre Cabinet le maintienne. Veuillez, mon bien cher Monsieur, agréer encore tous mes remerciments et les assurances de mes sentiments les plus dévoués,

CH. RÉMUSAT.

Mr. Hayward to the Duke of Newcastle.

MY DEAR DUKE,   Feb. 14, 1854.

I made it my business last night to ascertain (particularly for Cooke's* guidance) the first impressions of people on the Reform Bill.† I saw, I think, about fourteen members of the House of Commons, of varying shades of politics, and the general result was in the highest degree favourable. But it is a measure which cannot be appreciated except by persons who have carefully studied the subject, and are capable of taking both deep and comprehensive views of representative institutions. It was not to be expected that such a measure would excite enthusiasm, and I am told that Lord John's manner was more than usually cold. I am quite sure that, happen

* Editor of the *Morning Chronicle.*
† Lord John Russell, taking advantage of the circumstance that war, which had now become certain, had not been actually declared, introduced on the 13th of February his Reform Bill. In the face of graver and more engrossing events it met with but a cold reception, and was subsequently withdrawn.

what may, the Bill will firmly establish the character of the Government, and I am not without hopes that the various interests, adroitly and yet *honestly* conciliated, may ensure its immediate success. It is amusing to see the exasperation of the sufferers, but it is to be hoped that their wounded feelings may be soothed by reflection. The *Times* is evidently waiting to see which way the vane may point. With the sincerest regards,

Ever faithfully yours,

A. HAYWARD.

Mrs. Norton arrived in town yesterday. Members will not speak out till they have consulted their constituents.

M. Thiers to Mr. Hayward.

MON CHER HAYWARD,   Paris, 16 février 1854.

Je vous remercie de vos intéressantes lettres, et je vous prie de me faire connaître, de temps en temps, la marche des choses chez vous. Ici nous n'avons rien de nouveau. La publication de la lettre de l'Empereur Napoléon * a été blâmée par tous les gens sensés, comme un acte inconvenant, et la rédaction par les bons juges n'a pas été admirée. Sur la masse elle a fait un effet favorable. On commence à s'animer en France contre le Czar, et la guerre paraît de jour en jour plus motivée, ainsi le gouvernement ne trouvera pas d'obstacle à son action. Dieu veuille qu'il profite de son immense pouvoir pour finir des préparatifs suffisants, et surtout à temps ! Je crains toujours que les Russes ne fassent quelques gros coups avant que les troupes européennes soient arrivées. S'il y avait seulement 15,000 Anglais, 25,000 Français à Schumla au milieu de mars, tout accident fâcheux serait impossible ; mais je crains qu'il n'en soit pas ainsi. Nous ne pourrons pas tirer d'Alger

* To the Czar, dated January 29.

plus de 15,000 hommes, dont 3,000 d'une Cavalerie admirable, ce sont des Chasseurs d'Afrique. Notre gouvernement devrait avoir le bon sens de prendre la division de Rome, qui est toute formée, habituée au service de guerre, et surtout acclimatée aux pays fiévreux. Elle lui procurerait dix autres mille hommes à ajouter aux 15,000 d'Afrique. Cela lui compléterait ainsi 25,000 hommes tout formés, et ne craignant pas la fièvre qui sera le grand ennemi des Occidentaux sur le Danube. Mais il ne faut guère compter sur une aussi sage résolution, qui aurait de plus l'avantage, de nous concilier davantage l'Autriche.

Le moment des débats d'une alliance de guerre étant le meilleur, on ferait bien d'écrire une convention, pour régler la participation de chacun aux efforts communs que la guerre exigera. C'est le seul moyen d'éviter plus tard des démêlés fâcheux, dont nos ennemis pourront se servir pour nous diviser. Il y aura inévitablement des jours de mécompte et d'humeur, et il ne faut pas que, ces jours-là, il puisse y avoir un sujet quelconque de contestation. Il faudrait convenir de donner les uns les $\frac{3}{4}$ des forces de terre, et $\frac{1}{4}$ des forces navales, les autres $\frac{3}{4}$ des forces navales, et $\frac{1}{4}$ des forces de terre, en convenant que la dépense, calculée après chaque campagne, serait payée par moitié. Sans cette précaution, je crains des démêlés après coup. Quant à vous autres, on admire beaucoup la résolution et l'activité de vos préparatifs, ce qui n'empêche pas, s'il reste une chance de paix, de tâcher de la recueillir précieusement. La paix en effet vaudrait encore mieux que la guerre (Lord Aberdeen a raison de la soutenir), surtout l'Occident ayant obligé la Russie à reculer. Ce serait un beau triomphe de droit sur la force ambitieuse des deux puissances civilisées, sur la puissance conquérante du Nord. Pour moi, je fais toujours des vœux pour l'union de la France et de l'Angleterre, sous quelque gouvernement que ce soit.

L'opinion en France fait, dans ce rapport, de notables progrès.

Quant à votre Reform Bill, nous sommes ici dans l'impossibilité de le juger, mais nous ferons des vœux pour qu'il ne divise pas le parti qui gouverne. C'est là le point capital, et qui est d'un intérêt, j'ose dire européen. Vos Ministres auront acquis une gloire sans pareille, s'ils ont conduit si bien cette crise si grave et si important. Adieu, je vous adresse mes congratulations, et mes vœux pour le *Drapeau-uni*, titre qu'il faut substituer à celui de *Royaume-uni*. Mille saluts affec-tueux,

A. THIERS.

Mr. Hayward's next two letters to the Duke of Newcastle are chiefly interesting as illustrating how statesmen are apt to deal with testimonials. The question arose out of an inquiry which took place, relative to the Duke of Newcastle's appointment of Mr. Stonor as judge at Melbourne.

Mr. Hayward to the Duke of Newcastle.

MY DEAR DUKE,   Sunday, March 18, 1854.

I understand from Merivale that Stonor was merely sent out to supply a temporary vacancy, although doubtless with the expectancy of a permanent appoint-ment hereafter. If this be so, it is a pity it is not made public; for it materially varies the complexion of the case, both as regards the amount of hardship and the extreme degree of circumspection required. An idea has got abroad that none of the testimonials were opened. Now, it appears to me that nothing is more natural than, when a man has been recommended *orally*, to regard his testimonials as mere matters of form and simply to look over the list of them. A printed paper would almost as a matter of course be thrown aside, and if Stonor did not mention his electioneering mishap in his letter, he has only himself to thank for what has occurred. The income he is supposed to have sacrificed is a *gross* exaggeration.

Ever faithfully yours,

A. HAYWARD.

Mr. Hayward to the Duke of Newcastle.

MY DEAR DUKE,   May 13, 1854.

I cannot resist the temptation of writing to congratulate you on the tone, temper and result of your examination before the Stonor Committee yesterday. Nothing could possibly be better done on your part. It leaves a broad impression of manliness, clearness, generosity, and straightforwardness, which cannot fail to tell with the public, who may not be so well acquainted with the distinctive qualities of your mind and character as your friends. Although you have obviously taken upon yourself *individually* everything which even the most adverse critic could throw upon you, you are evidently not to blame, for you did precisely what every one else, anxious for the performance of a grave duty, would have done. No one, in point of fact, does read *through* such documents; and Merivale's recommendation was enough to dispense with the reading them at all. M—— will not be permitted to evade the real issue, to which he is brought back in to-day's *Chronicle*. On the whole the affair will do good, both by doing you credit and by stopping such attacks in future.

Ever yours faithfully,

A. HAYWARD.

Mr. Hayward to his Sister.

The Athenæum, March 20, 1854.

The messenger with the Czar's refusal to the ultimatum is hourly expected, and war will then be declared forthwith.* Telegraphic news is never considered a foundation for actual proceedings. The last published correspondence is considered highly favourable to the Government, and though Lord Aberdeen appears to have been wrong as regards the clerk in the Foreign Office, he is well known to have ample authority, but was unwilling to give up names or refer to what passed in society. No one doubts that ―――― did talk very foolishly of what he had seen in the Foreign Office. It was thought at first that Crowder would be the new Judge, but now Alexander (a relation of Lady Cranworth) is rather the favourite. The appointment will probably be made at leisure, as Gurney is sent down to do the duty. I dined last week with the Bishop of Exeter amongst other diners. I wrote the notice of Talfourd.†

A. H.

Sir William Molesworth to Mr. Hayward.

87 Eaton Place,
May 10, 1854.

MY DEAR HAYWARD,

I am very much obliged to you for the trouble which you have taken about my speech, and am delighted at your liking it. You will see however that it was *Burked*, owing to the fact that nobody would say one word in favour of Adderley's motion, and I could not get up after

* War was declared on the 27th of March.
† Mr. Justice Talfourd, who was an old friend of Mr. Hayward's, died at Stafford on the 13th of March, in the act of charging the grand jury. Mr. Hayward wrote a notice in the *Morning Chronicle*.

Peel or Pakington to repeat in substance what they had already said. What a blunder the Derbyites made last night in insisting upon a division on malt.* They have missed their chance by giving us such a majority; they ought to have surprised us, or at least to have run us very hard. The consequence of the division will be to persuade the country that the House of Commons is decidedly in favour of an increased duty on malt, and that opposition is useless. Nothing could have been more lucky.

Ever yours truly,
WILLIAM MOLESWORTH.

When the Crimean War broke out, Lord John Russell advocated the separation of the offices of Secretary for the Colonies and Secretary for War, which, according to the usual practice, were both held by the Duke of Newcastle.

The Cabinet decided in favour of the division, and thereupon the Duke expressed his readiness "to retain either or neither." It is said that Lord John wished Lord Palmerston to have the Secretaryship for War. But the Duke of Newcastle was put forward for the office; and he assumed it. Some thought the Duke acted unwisely in leaving a department in which he had already effected amendment. But he said in reply, " In leaving the Colonial Office I am well aware of what I have done. I know that in this new department, whatever success shall attend our arms I shall never derive

---

* The Chancellor of the Exchequer in the supplemental estimates had, on the 8th of May, proposed an increase of the Malt Tax from 2s. 9d. to 4s. On the following day, in Committee, Mr. Butt's motion against the increased duty was negatived by 224 to 143 votes. It was agreed in the House that the increased tax should be a *war tax*.

any credit ; and this, too, I well know, that if there shall be disaster, upon me alone will come the blame and the public indignation." It is to the acceptance of this new post that the following letter refers.

Mr. Hayward to Sir John Young.

MY DEAR YOUNG,   May 30, 1854.

I heard last night, on what seemed good authority, that the War Minister question had been settled by the Duke's electing to take it and vacating the Colonial Secretaryship. I should not much wonder at his choice, if forced upon him, for the War Minister would be virtually Prime Minister whilst the war lasted. I don't think Dizzy did you much harm last night.* There is not a word of truth in a prevalent report, that the *Chronicle* has been sold.

Ever truly yours,
A. HAYWARD.

The next letter tends to vindicate the Duke of Newcastle against the charge of indolence and indifference, shortly afterwards brought against him.

The Duke of Newcastle to Mr. Hayward.

MY DEAR HAYWARD,   Portman Square, Aug. 20, 1854.

I am sorry not to see you before you start,† to talk over the events of many days since we met. I have no commission for you, for I fear you will find me in sad disgrace in Vienna, not with the Austrians, but with a

---

* In the debate on the withdrawal of the Canterbury Bribery Prevention Bill, in which Mr. Disraeli made an attack upon the Government, and upon Lord John Russell in particular.

† On a tour abroad for the benefit of his health.

fair friend. I must try to make my own peace by a
written apology for a silence which my labours may, I
hope, be considered to extenuate. I have no hope of
any release. I cannot leave town, except for two or three
days at a time, whilst great operations are pending, and
when any day may bring despatches and require answer.
I wish I had Larcom,* but I fear others would be very
unwilling to give him up.

> Believe me, yours very sincerely,
> NEWCASTLE.

I think Castlereagh is rather unjust. Did he see the
letter to which A.'s was an answer?

Monsieur Thiers to Mr. Hayward.

Cauterets (Hautes-Pyrénées),
Sept. 16, 1854.

MON CHER HAYWARD,

J'ai reçu aux extrémités de la France votre intéressante lettre de Vienne, et je me hâte de vous
répondre, sans savoir où ma lettre ira vous joindre. Je
suis ici enfoncé dans mon travail, et retenu par les
chaleurs, qui sont extraordinaires, mais je vais en partir
bientôt, de manière qu'en me répondant vous pouvez
m'écrire à Paris.

Je n'ai d'ici rien à vous mander; l'expédition de
Sevastopol sera une chose brillante si elle réussit, mais
j'ai des inquiétudes. Si la glace n'est pas enlevée avec
une extrême rapidité, on aura dans peu de jours 80,000
Russes sur les bras, et il faudra s'en aller. Je compte
sur trois choses; la promptitude de nos soldats, la nature
des ouvrages qui sont faits en vue de l'attaque de mer, et
non pas en vue de l'attaque de terre, enfin la mauvaise
fortune des Russes cette année.

---

* The Rt. Hon. Sir Thomas A. Larcom, Bart., K.C.B., then
Under-Secretary to the Lord-Lieutenant of Ireland.

Ces trois raisons ne me rassurent pourtant pas tout à fait. Je trouve qu'on a trop longtemps averti les Russes, et qu'il faudrait, pour qu'ils ne fussent pas prêts, un miracle d'incurie. Toutefois il faut s'attendre à tous les miracles de ce genre de la part du gouvernement. La vraie vigilance gouvernementale est ce qu'il y a de plus rare au monde. Si l'entreprise réussit, il ne faut pas se dissimuler, qu'au lieu d'être la fin de la guerre, elle en sera le commencement, et tout de même si elle ne réussit pas ; car les battus, quels qu'ils soient, ne voudront pas traiter après un échec. C'est ce qu'on a peut-être un peu perdu de vue, en forçant cette expédition. Voilà les conséquences du défaut de préparatifs préalables ! On n'a pu faire quelque chose qu'à la fin de la campagne, et cette fin venue, on a voulu agir à tout prix, n'importe où, n'importe comment. Je souhaite ardemment notre succès, mais l'expédition engage le fer, au lieu de le dégager, et la guerre étant portée sur le territoire russe, aurons-nous les puissances allemandes aussi bien disposées ? J'en doute.* Évidemment la Russie joue en ce moment sur cette carte, et c'est à cela qu'il faut prendre garde. En tout cas, c'est une grande chose que l'union de la France et de l'Angleterre. Tout à vous,

A. THIERS.

Mr. Hayward to his Sisters.

Florence, Sept. 16, 1854.

I got here the night before last. I start for Rome on the 20th and shall be at Naples by the 1st October. My journey has done me a great deal of good, particularly since my arrival in a warm climate. I have come through Venice, Padua, Ferrara, and Bologna. Travelling is both pleasant and cheap for those who speak the languages and fall in with the habits of the country.

---

* Sagacious words.

The English, who are obliged to trust to interpreters, are of course cheated. By dint of hard fagging I now speak French, German, and Italian with tolerable fluency, and take every opportunity of talking with the natives. There is no cholera here nor at any place I have passed through, though half the world believe the contrary, and the hotels are consequently empty. Bulwer,* our Minister *here*, is at a bathing place some way up, but I dine to-day with Lord Normanby, who has a villa close to the town. Write and let me know your plans.

Ever yours,

A. H.

Mr. Hayward to his Sisters.

Paris, Nov. 22, 1854.

I have been staying on from day to day because this is the centre of intelligence, and most of my pleasantest London acquaintances are here ; but it is getting very cold, and their wood fires never warm a room perfectly. I think therefore of starting at the end of the week, and you had better write to me at the Temple, as my laundress will have the earliest intelligence in case I am not arrived. Nothing can be more critical than the state of our army at Sebastopol, though I think they may succeed in destroying one side of the place and the fleet. But they are evidently outnumbered, and our reinforcements arrive slowly for want of ships. Lord Palmerston, just arrived, is in high spirits. The Emperor is said to be irritable and impatient. I have as much society of all sorts as I want. I have dined three times with Thiers, and I go a good deal to the evening parties of the famous Comtesse Kalergy (the niece of Nesselrode), one of the most beautiful women in Europe. She is a great friend of Mrs. Norton.

A. H.

* Sir Henry Bulwer (the late Lord Dalling).

MY DEAR YOUNG, The Athenæum, Nov. 28, 1854.

I returned from Paris late last night. In my train from Paris were General Bentinck and another officer. Bentinck said they had hitherto made no impression on the walls. The French military men think they shall force their way into one side and destroy the shipping at least. The war is not liked in France. All sorts of stories were about in Paris as to Louis Napoleon's conversations with Lord Palmerston, whom the Parisians fully believe to have been deputed by the Government. The truth is, he came over to amuse himself. *He* was speaking very cheerily about results. Hayter was to start last night, and be in town to see Lord John this morning. The *Chronicle* has been sold, and the editor is changed, the former sub-editor having been put in his place. I shall see Cooke to-morrow, and learn all about this, and then I have promised to see Hayter. My conviction is the Government will not suffer by the anticipated attacks in Parliament. If they were deceived as to the Russian force in the Crimea, so was the French Government, and so were the whole English nation, who clamoured for the attempt. No doubt it has turned out a mistake in which we all shared. I expect no good from Austria. In fact, foreign affairs never looked more gloomy.

Ever yours truly,

A. HAYWARD.

MY DEAR YOUNG, Temple, Nov. 29, 1854.

You will see that there has been a disaster in the Black Sea, but no troops have been lost. Bright and

Company are preparing to be very acrimonious, and the discontented Whigs (like Lord Seymour) are talking very violently against the Government. Their grand omission was not seeing, directly after Alma, that great reinforcements would be wanted directly. Thus time was lost. The fact is, everybody was deceived. It seems that Sebastopol was hardly walled or fortified at all on the Inkerman side when the Allies first landed. Cathcart, Brown, and others wanted to storm at once. Burgoyne objected, and undertook to take the place in the regular way in a week. During ten days or a fortnight both France and England were in a fool's paradise. This was when the Emperor sneered at the *timidas aves.* Would he sneer now ? *

I have no fear, however, that the Government will meet with all the party support they want. I am sorry to hear that S. Herbert is quite worn out, and the Duke of N. dreadfully fagged. Lord Monteagle (writing beside me) wants to know whether the first service is to be short and confined to war business. The *Chronicle* politics continue unchanged. This is one condition of the sale, and the same literary connections continue. I will write when I have anything to tell.

Ever truly yours,

A. HAYWARD.

Shortly after Mr. Hayward's return to England from abroad, he was selected by Lord Aberdeen to fill the

---

* After having made good their 'flank march,' the Allies had safe ground for inferring that, at a sacrifice of men which Burgoyne did not estimate at more than about 500, they at once could lay hold of Sebastopol ; but Science stepped in representing that such a loss, even though small, was one that ought to be spared, because she said, in less than three weeks she could carry the place in an easier, smoother way, breaking down its resistance at once by means of a strong cannonade delivered with heavy siege guns. (Kinglake's 'Crimea,' vol. vii. pp. 95, 96, 6th edition.)

office of Secretary to the Poor Law Board in succession
to Lord Courtenay, who had been offered a Commissionership of Woods and Forests. A portion of the
Press, notably the *Morning Herald*, violently opposed
the appointment, raking up the old Bench affair against
Mr. Hayward, and accusing the Government, especially
the Duke of Newcastle, of jobbery and favouritism.
Lord Courtenay, after hesitating, at the last moment
declined the commissionership on very good personal
grounds. Mr. Hayward's chances were thus extin-
guished; but the offer having been definitely made
and accepted, the Government lay under a distinct
obligation to provide him with another post. Notwithstanding this, Mr. Hayward, fearing that any such
attempt might embarrass his friends in their position of
daily increasing difficulty, intimated with characteristic
loyalty and unselfishness that he had no desire to press
his claims, and the loss was in fact never made good to
him. Allusion is made to this matter in several of the
following letters.

Mr. Hayward to Sir John Young.

MY DEAR YOUNG,   The Athenæum, Dec. 4, 1854.

Lord Aberdeen has offered me the place of Secretary
to the Poor Law Board, which I, of course, accept.
Lord Courtenay takes the Commissionership of Woods
and Forests, vacated by Kennedy, as in case of Lord
Devon's death he would not be able to hold the Poor
Law Secretaryship. I shall say nothing, however,
except to a few well-wishers till I am installed. I don't
think much will come of this treaty with Austria, and
I see no prospect of peace, for neither party will

give up the Crimea. He left on the 18th, and up to that time he heard none of these clamorous calls for reinforcements. I dined yesterday at the Molesworths with Charles Villiers. Lady Molesworth gave me a bad account of the Duke of Newcastle, who had dined there on Wednesday. He then complained of the return of an old heart-disease, and said he could not get up a staircase without pain. I have not seen him myself. He is killing himself with work and anxiety. The fact is the rest of the Cabinet left him almost alone during the greater part of the vacation.* I breakfasted on Saturday at Milman's with Macaulay and Lord Lansdowne. Lord Lansdowne looks better than he has been these two years, and was in excellent spirits. Macaulay is better, but the history will hardly be carried further in 1855. Best regards to Lady Young, and believe me

Ever truly yours,
A. HAYWARD.

Gladstone wrote to the *Times* to contradict the statement, that he would be driven to a loan.

Mr. Hayward to his Sisters.

Dec. 5, 1854.

The statement in some of the papers of to-day is correct. I am to succeed Lord Courtenay as Secretary to the Poor Law Board. The place is permanent and the salary one thousand a year. The offer has been formally made to me and formally accepted.

Ever yours,
A. H.

---

* "It seems clear that there was a languor, not to say hollowness, in the support which the Duke got from his colleagues." (Mr. Kinglake's 'Crimea,' vol. ii. p. 74, 4th edition.)

Mr. Hayward to the Duke of Newcastle.

MY DEAR DUKE,   Temple, Dec. 6, 1854.

I cannot doubt that I am largely indebted to you for
the offer made me of Lord Courtenay's place, which I
gladly accepted, having paid much attention to the Poor
Laws. I enclose you a letter from Mrs. Norton. I was
sorry to be unable to give a cheering answer to her
inquiries about yourself, but I hear on all hands that
you are dreadfully overworked. Your difficulty will
be to state your case fully without appearing to throw
blame on others. I have no doubt you* Raglan asked.
People are talking now precisely as if they had all along
been aware of that which the battle of Inkerman has
brought out into full relief.† For more than a month
after the affair at Alma, *both* Governments and both
nations were equally in the dark—Sebastopol was to fall
forthwith, and the bulk of the army was to be in winter
quarters at Constantinople before Christmas. If *at that
time* you *had* foreseen the necessity of the extraordinary
steps to which you have since resorted, you would have
had no concurrence.‡ You would have been thought
extravagant if you had talked of stripping important
garrisons of nearly all their troops or of preparing winter
barracks, &c., for the Crimea. I can positively aver
that, until the necessity had actually arisen, no one at
Paris foresaw it any more than in London. Neither
could any one have foreseen that the Turks, who had
begun so well, would end by being worse than useless,

---

* Some words are missing here ; the letter was damaged in the
fire that occurred some years ago at Clumber, when a large portion
of the Duke of Newcastle's correspondence was destroyed, including a number of letters from Mr. Hayward.

† The vast reinforcements that Russia proved able to bring up.

‡ Kinglake's ' Crimea,' vol. ii. p. 74, 4th edition.

and if they had done well, either on the Danube or in
the Crimea, none of our disasters could have occurred.
I had a good deal of talk with Lord Lyndhurst the day
before yesterday. He vehemently deprecated any kind
of division in Parliament, and said that we should take
care to appear as a united nation. At the same time he
was not sparing in his criticisms. Perhaps these hints
may not be altogether useless to you. But I will occupy
no more of your time, and of course this needs no
answer.

With the most grateful feeling,

Ever faithfully yours,

A. HAYWARD.

Mrs. Norton to Mr. Hayward.

MY DEAR AVOCAT,   Paris, Dec. 8, 1854.

I do assure you I have seldom been so glad of *any*
piece of news as to hear that you were to have the
Secretaryship of the Poor Law Board. As a recognition
of ability and power to serve, it is pleasanter even than
as an acknowledgment of past services, in a *different*
and political literary way, and I am sure no man ever
deserved more from his friends, either for his energy in
their behalf or the patience and generosity in all matters
concerning himself. I suppose it is a very " hard place,"
as the maids say, but you have spirit and energy for
anything, and have proved yourself labour-proof, a
veritable salamander in the hot forge of hard work!
All the better too is it that what you have at last been
offered falls in with what you had written and occupied
yourself about, as there can be none of the discontented
growling which generally attends like a Greek chorus on
occasions of *anybody getting anything.*

The Kalergy* is under "orders to quit," a ceremony which was to have taken place on the 8th, and is deferred to the 16th. I do not know that even the dishevelling of her golden tresses will produce a longer delay ; but she seems very sorry to depart. As to my return, I linger, I scarce know why ; in the conviction that I shall only be tormented, without the balance of friends having "time" for me, and my small drawing-room, or of my sisters being in town, and the belief that everyone will disperse after a few days of Parliament. I have nothing here—except the sort of dark security from trouble the mole has, who is underground ; instead of ferretting about where a trap may pinch his neck and squeeze his bead eyes out of his head (N.B. Not that my eyes are "bead" eyes). I meant to have gone home the week after I arrived here. I am vexed to hear poor accounts of the Duke of Newcastle's health. I wrote to him, but I dare say he will hardly have time to read my letter. A "Colonel" writes (not publicly) that if they will but subscribe *men and artillery*, all other matters which they are fussing their subscriptions about would come right of themselves ; and that the army could not re-embark if it would, so there is only Hobson's choice for them, and sin and cruelty on the part of all who would fetter the hands of Government by a cursed and dogged opposition and by the recollection of party disputes. I scrawl yet another line, and say that poor Lady Ellis seemed very anxious about Sir Henry, who has taken drearily the news of Lockhart's death.

Yours ever truly,

C. CLIENT.

* The Comtesse Kalergy, referred to *supra*, p. 224.

Mr. Baines to Mr. Hayward.*

[EXTRACT.]

MY DEAR HAYWARD,

13 Queen's Square,
Dec. 10, 1854.

I understand that Lord Courtenay's Patent for his new office will be ready to-morrow afternoon, and he will then formally resign the Secretaryship of our Board. If that should be the case, and I hear nothing further from the Government (as I now presume I shall not) upon the subject of your appointment, I will give directions for the formal completion of that appointment immediately. I will send you a note as soon as everything is ready for your reception at Gwyder House.

Allow me to add, that it will give me great pleasure if my influence at the Board can be of service to you in any way whatever, and that it shall not be *my* fault if we do not always co-operate in the discharge of our public duties with the most frank and perfect cordiality.

Yours very truly,

M. T. BAINES.

Mr. Hayward to his Sisters.

Dec. 14, 1854.

I have heard nothing more, and I have no doubt the affair will remain in its present uncertain state for some days. I should not care myself if I were sure you would not fret, for I have a full conviction that it will come right in some way, or that some good will come out of it. I send you an extract from Baines's note to me on the 10th. The Lord Chamberlain (Lord Breadalbane) met me yesterday, and said they *must* make it up to me in some way if the hitch could not be got over. The offer to me was broad and unconditional, nothing being said to me of any contingent resignation.   A. H.

---

* The Rt. Hon. M. T. Baines, President of the Poor Law Board. This letter clearly shows how far the appointment had gone.

Dec. 15, 1854.

I was very glad to get your letter, for I was afraid of your being hurt, and if it had not been for the newspapers I should never have mentioned the matter to you till it was decided. We shall know nothing more till something is settled about the Woods and Forests Commissionership, as to which Shelley gave a notice last night. Lord Courtenay was not to blame if he was promised £1,500 a year. But the offer to me was not conditional. I was told he had positively accepted his new office. My case has not a hitch in it. All we want is the vacancy, and the Government can't leave things as they are. The attacks on the Ministry have come to nothing—Disraeli has made a dead failure.

A. H.

Sir E. B. Lytton to Mr. Hayward.

MY DEAR HAYWARD,   Saturday night, Dec. 16. 1854.

I looked out for you the other evening in the House, but you had vanished with E. Bruce. I merely now write a line to say, that if your appointment be confirmed and questioned in the House of Commons, you may rely on my vote in favour of that disposal of patronage.*

Yours truly,

E. B. LYTTON.

Mr. Hayward to the Duke of Newcastle.

MY DEAR DUKE,   Dec. 17, 1854.

A military friend just now suggested to me, that the strength of the Ministerial case for the Foreign Enlistment

---

* This generous offer of support, from a political opponent, was warmly appreciated by Mr. Hayward and his Peelite friends.

had not appeared, and he gave me, from memory, the following list of foreign troops in our service in 1814.*

1. The German Legion.
2. Chasseurs Britanniques (French).
3. $\left.\begin{array}{l} \text{Rolls} \\ \text{Welterville's} \\ \text{Mirons} \end{array}\right\}$ Regiments or Battalions—Swiss.
4. The Corsican Rangers.
5. Some Greek Regiment.
6. The 60th, of which five battalions German.
7. Colonial Corps of various nations.

He said that a reference to the Army List of 1814 would make all clear. It is the disadvantage of a Government like ours that explanations may be given which are information to the enemy. Could not this be obviated in some way by telling the opposition leaders what the case really was, and then throwing the responsibility of publication upon them?

My own affair has turned out unluckily, but I am not the less grateful to my friends.

Ever faithfully yours,

A. HAYWARD.

Lord Ernest Bruce† to Mr. Hayward.

St. George's Place,
Monday night, Dec. 18, 1854.

MY DEAR HAYWARD,

I am very glad to receive a copy of Bulwer's note, which must be very satisfactory to you even now, and at any rate does great credit to his feelings. You will see that the *Morning Herald* this day devotes three mortal

* On the 12th of December, the Duke of Newcastle introduced the Foreign Enlistment Bill in the House of Lords. The Bill was opposed by Lord Derby as dangerous in principle, but it was carried.

† The late Marquis of Ailesbury. (Died, October 1884.)

columns to you and the Duke of Newcastle. Very complimentary, but in truth I do believe totally undeserved by His Grace! for beyond wishing you well in every respect I cannot but think that his mind was far too much occupied at the moment with weightier matters to enable him to turn much attention to the extraordinary intrigue in your favour of which he is accused. You of course know, that the warrant for Lord Courtenay's appointment was actually sent down to Windsor for the Queen's signature; that it was only late on Tuesday afternoon that Lord Courtenay sought an interview with Lord Aberdeen, at which Gladstone and Wilson were present, and requested a delay of twelve hours in making out the patent, which was acceded to ; and that only an hour before the House met on Wednesday he finally sent in his refusal of the Woods and Forests. At that interview Gladstone stated his fixed determination, to abide by the appointment and propose for him in the estimates the difference of salary. Lord Courtenay's answer was, " But after what has occurred respecting Mr. Hayward's appointment, how can you guarantee to me that you will carry it ?" This I know to be the truth.

Yours ever,

E. B.

Mr. Nassau Senior to Mr. Hayward.

South Cliff House, Tenby, South Wales,

Dec. 24, 1854.

MY DEAR HAYWARD,

Two little pamphlets on the Poor Law appointment have reached me here. In this remote corner we know so little of what is going on, that I infer only from the last that there has been a hitch about Lord Courtenay, and that things remain *in statu quo.* If so, I sincerely regret it. Taking great interest in the administration of the Poor Law, I was delighted with your appointment. You would have brought with you knowledge and talent, and sound principles and courage in applying them. When you have time, pray tell me how things stand now—what was the difficulty, and whether and how it is likely to be got over. I stay here till the 9th January, when I pass through town on my way to the Grange.

Ever yours,

NASSAU W. SENIOR.

Mr. Hayward to his Sisters.

[EXTRACT.]

1854.

I have nothing new to tell you, and the best thing now is to dismiss the late affair from our minds as much as possible. Considering all things, it has most decidedly improved my position in every way. The attacks on Lord Raglan are not wholly without cause, but greatly exaggerated. All depends on the weather. If that has been good for the last fortnight, things will get on well. It seems, too, that Austria is now really about to take part, which will speedily settle the whole business. As for the prospects of the Ministry, nothing can damage them but internal disagreement, and I hope they will have the sense to keep clear of this.

A. H.

On the 23rd of December Parliament was adjourned, after a short session (in which the Foreign Enlistment Bill was passed), and was to reassemble on the 23rd of January, 1855. Public opinion toward the close of 1854 had been much excited by reports, published in the *Times*, of the suffering of our army in the Crimea. Indignation was aroused at home against Lord Aberdeen and the Duke of Newcastle, and abroad against Lord Raglan and his staff-officers. In the pages of the

Morning Chronicle, Mr. Hayward endeavoured to meet or turn aside the various charges, and to do all he could to extricate his friends in the Government from the torrent which was surging around them. During the recess, well-founded rumours of dissension in the Cabinet combined with their other difficulties to weaken the Government. As soon as Parliament met, Mr. Roebuck gave notice of motion for a committee, " To inquire into the condition of our army before Sebastopol, and into the conduct of those departments of the Government whose duty it has been to minister to the wants of that army." Lord John Russell, thinking that this resolution could not be resisted, resigned his office without waiting for the Division, on January 29, which showed a majority of 157 against the Government, and caused their immediate fall from power.* The task of forming a new Cabinet, unsuccessfully attempted both by Lord Derby and Lord John Russell, was at length achieved by Lord Palmerston, after considerable difficulty in winning the support of the Peelites; their adherence, however, was only temporary; for when the Prime Minister found himself compelled to yield to the continued clamour for the inquiry demanded by Mr. Roebuck, Sir James Graham, Mr. Gladstone, Mr. Sidney Herbert, and the other Peelites retired from office. Thus

---

* "The actual cause of the dissolution of the Cabinet was the sudden resolution of Lord John Russell, when he refused to meet Mr. Roebuck's motion of censure and threw up the game. This abrupt determination of the Whig leader placed Lord Palmerston at the head of affairs, and terminated the official career of Lord Aberdeen." (" The Correspondence of Lord Aberdeen," *Edinburgh Review*, October 1883.) The Peelites were naturally exasperated with Lord John Russell for his conduct.

ended the separate existence, as a party, of those friends
and followers of the late Sir Robert Peel, with whom
Mr. Hayward had for so many years been connected.

Mr. Hayward to Sir John Young.

[EXTRACT.]

MY DEAR YOUNG,   Jan. 3, 1855.

I don't like the aspect of things at all. My only hope
is that what is stated in to-day's *Chronicle* about the
treaty with Austria may come true. I fear the state of
things in the Crimea is wretchedly bad, and all depends
on the weather. If the weather has been fine during the
last fortnight they may have got their road* into order
and the things distributed. If not, Heaven help them.
It is quite true that Lord Raglan sits all day long writing
in his house, though no one can guess to whom he writes,
for the Duke (I hear) gets no private letters from him
longer than his public ones. The quartermaster and
adjutant-generals are considered very inefficient. There
is no general system of management emanating from
headquarters, and the difference in the accounts arises
from the difference of position and the varying energy of
commanders of brigades and regiments. Thus the letter
from P.'s relation in to-day's *Chronicle* proves nothing,
because he is quartered at Balaclava itself, and Sir
Colin Campbell (an old soldier) has managed to hut his
men and make them comfortable. The best defence
cannot be stated, for it will offend the French ; who have
had hardly any of the hard fighting, and not half of the
worst duty. Besides the trenches we have had the
Inkerman heights to guard, and *our* road from the sea is
seven miles with a high hill, and *theirs* less than four with
a flat. Compare the amount of our losses with theirs

* From Balaclava to the front.

since the landing.   I hear that a French soldier is not in
the trenches more than one night in nine, an English
soldier two nights out of three.   Hardinge and Raglan
have never liked each other,* and do not co-operate
cordially.   Of course the poor Duke is made the scape-
goat ; and one hears it daily and confidently announced
that he and Lord Aberdeen are to go out.   I believe the
Whigs would not be sorry if they thought the Government would hold together after such an operation.
Opinions float as to whether Lord John Russell or Lord
Palmerston or Lord Lansdowne would be the new
Premier.   Will the other Peelites stand this (the going out
of Lord Aberdeen and the Duke)?   They know the Duke
is not at all to blame, and that Lord Aberdeen is simply
guilty of foreseeing the real nature of the struggle.

I have got my matter pretty well off my mind now. . . .
The last I heard of my abortive appointment from any
member of the Government was what you witnessed at
the House of Commons.   I have been left to infer Lord
Courtenay's final refusal, and not so much as an expression of regret or explanation has one member of the
Cabinet addressed to me directly or indirectly.   Yet the
offer to me was broad and unconditional, and no contingency depending on salary was coupled with it.   Best
regards to Lady Young, &c.

Ever yours,
A. HAYWARD.

Lord St. Germans† to Mr. Hayward.
[EXTRACT.]
Vice-Regal Lodge, Dublin, Jan. 5, 1855.

I earnestly hope (not on my own account, for I
would rather be in Dover Street than here), that our

---

* Lord Hardinge was Commander-in-Chief.   This is a mistake.
† Lord-Lieutenant of Ireland in Lord Aberdeen's Government.

friends* will not quarrel among themselves, and thus give
our opponents the only chance of getting into office. A
change of Government would produce a very injurious
effect abroad, to say nothing of the mischief that it would
do at home. The enrolment and organisation of militia
in this country is proceeding very satisfactorily. There
has, generally speaking, been no difficulty in getting
recruits, and with regard to the officers, there has been
only that of selecting from among the country gentlemen
the best qualified for this service.

Sir John Young to Mr. Hayward.

MY DEAR HAYWARD,   Feb. 2, 1855.

Speak † kindly and respectfully of Lord Palmerston,
but point out the difficulty he labours under, the almost
utter, perhaps, impossibility of his obtaining the command of a Parliamentary majority with the Derbyites
compact in front, and Lord John hanging in jealous
observation in his rear—besides the scattered elements
of discontent amongst the R. Phillimores and that dis-
satisfied restless bench. Clarendon is in the same or
rather worse position, being placed in very similar circumstances and without the prestige of Lord Palmerston's
popularity. Ignore the existence of the Peelites *in toto*
—write as if they had no existence individually, or
collectively. This is, I think, enough for you. I
will only add the expression of my belief in the fact,
that Lord John Russell has been sent for. I leave it to
your own known virtue and to public morality in general
to handle this topic. Lords Palmerston or Clarendon
might each present a ministry full and competent, a
good first rank ; but they want parliamentary support on
which they could rely. If Lord John Russell can pro-

* The Whigs and Peelites.
† In the *Morning Chronicle.*

duce a cabinet or half a cabinet of men of any note, then is there an end of truth and honour amongst British statesmen ;* and if a third of the House of Commons vote with or countenance his intrigue, then every political calculation, every one accustomed to count up votes and strength in the House of Commons, is grievously at fault.

Ever sincerely yours,

J. Y.

Lord St. Germans to Mr. Hayward.

Vice-Regal Lodge,
Feb. 2, 1855.

MY DEAR MR. HAYWARD,

Many thanks for keeping me *au courant* of all that is going on around you. One likes to hear what is said and thought as well as what is done. I am very glad that Lord Derby was sent for. Till he had declared his inability to form a new Government, no member of the Aberdeen Cabinet could undertake to reconstruct the old one. Lord Aberdeen and the Duke of Newcastle have been cruelly and unjustly treated, but in the present state of affairs their Peelite colleagues could not, I suppose, decline to resume office without them. I have given Felton Hervey an Inspectorship of Prisons. I was glad to be able to do this, not only because I have a very good opinion of Hervey and wish him well, but because I was very desirous to oblige Lord Clarendon who had urged me strongly to provide for him if possible. The Orange party complain loudly of (what they think) the want of pluck shown by Lord Derby. They thought that the loaves and fishes were in their grasp, and do not like the prospect of remaining empty-handed.

Believe me to be, my dear Mr. Hayward,

Yours sincerely,

ST. GERMANS.

* Lord John Russell failed, and especially in attempting to secure the co-operation of Lord Clarendon as Foreign Minister.

Lord Lansdowne to Mr. Hayward.

DEAR HAYWARD,   Berkeley Square, Thursday morning.

I have certainly no reason to complain of the leading articles in the *Morning Chronicle*, which are only too civil to me, but I must say I wish the fashionable writer for that newspaper would spare me, and not proclaim me as going to pay visits to the Earl of Derby.* Certainly if there was a day in the year on which I would not have visited Lord Derby, though I might have had pleasure in doing, so on others, it would have been yesterday, and it so happened that though I did see several persons at home, the only person I visited in the course of the day was the Duchess of Sutherland, which was certainly not for the purpose of constructing a Cabinet.

> Believe me,
> Very faithfully yours,
> LANSDOWNE.

Lord St. Germans to Mr. Hayward.

                                        Vice-Regal Lodge,
MY DEAR MR. HAYWARD,   Feb. 4, 1855.

The *Morning Chronicle* has assuredly done yeoman's service in pointing out the men who alone are capable of forming a new Government, and in depicting the evils consequent on the existing interregnum. It might, however, I think, have spoken more strongly in condemnation of the vote of the House of Commons, which put an end to Lord Aberdeen's Cabinet, and thereby stopped the diplomatic and checked the military action of England at a most critical moment. I cannot suppose that any member of Lord Aberdeen's Cabinet will take part in the conduct of affairs till that vote is rescinded.

---

* At the time of the political crisis, when Lord Derby was attempting to form a Ministry.

To prepare that Hon. House for the operation of swallowing dirt would therefore, I think, be a very useful task.   I hope that the rumour that Lord John has been sent for is true.   When he has failed, and fail he must, to form a Government, he will be comparatively harmless as a leader of opposition.   I rejoice to hear that Graham is almost well.

Believe me to be
Yours very truly,
ST. GERMANS.

Mr. Hayward to Sir John Young.

MY DEAR YOUNG,   Feb. 5, 1855.

I have just received a letter from Lord St. Germans. I am convinced that the worst thing that could happen for Lord Aberdeen and the Duke would be the refusal of the Peelite colleagues to resume office without them, and the consequent embarrassment.   It would stop the reaction in their favour.   It is really too bad if they do not consult you, Elcho, Cardwell, &c., before taking such a step.   Pray let me know as soon as things are fixed.

Ever yours,
A. HAYWARD.

In this state of things, I hardly know what to write.

Lord Elcho to Mr. Hayward.

MY DEAR HAYWARD.   Treasury, Feb. 6, 1855.

I disapprove so much of my friends' conduct, that I last night told Lord Palmerston that, although it had been my intention to leave the Government even in the event of Lord Aberdeen having continued in office, as I was tired of my present post, still, I should now be ready if he wished, to retain it for a short time in order to show my disapproval of Gladstone's course.* This morning I saw Lord Aberdeen, who told me I had done right, and expressed his satisfaction at hearing I had joined Palmerston. Palmerston has not offered me any higher office, and I know not if he intends to do so, but I wrote to my father yesterday afternoon, to say that if he did, I should feel myself obliged to refuse it, and retain my present place, lest my motives for separating from my friends should be liable to misconstruction. All hope, however, is not yet lost; Lord Aberdeen is doing all he can to induce them to join Palmerston, and I believe they are now sitting in Council to decide this momentous question. If they still persist, they will have, in every sense of the word, committed the greatest mistake public men ever did. In the present circumstances of the country, it amounts to a political crime. It was the corruption and the discredit into which her public men had fallen which destroyed the Government of France, and led to the *Coup d'Etat.* I wish we may not, if this goes on much longer, see something of the same kind here. We are now politically and nationally discredited, and as I told Gladstone last night, I begin to wish I was a Frenchman. Lord John did not improve his case last night. I don't think I could ever belong to a Government of which he was a member. My only respect for him was on account of his apparent reverence for our Constitution, which indeed is since 1832 of his own begetting, and now he ends by bringing it to a dead-lock and discrediting it in the eyes of Europe when most we need its harmonious working. I hope you approve of the course I have thought it my duty to take.

Yours ever,
ELCHO.

* In hesitating to join Lord Palmerston.

Mr. Hayward to Sir G. C. Lewis.

MY DEAR LEWIS,   Temple, Feb. 8, 1855.

As a London character is sometimes useful in a
canvass, I have written one for you in to-day's *Chronicle*,
which I send.* Things seem settling at last, and I am
glad of it, for I have written the first article of the *M. C.*
for more than a fortnight (being often obliged to re-write
more than once in the day), and I am dead beat. This
paper was getting very like the Crimean army. One
day, about a month ago, the new proprietor, Serjeant
Glover, came to me and said he had broken with all his
staff, and that unless he was helped he should break
down at once or put the paper into other hands. I
thought it best to save it for the party, and so resumed
writing for a period—a period very critical for my
friends; and during the three weeks preceding their fall
I was their only defender. It is, however, a thankless
office. On Monday night I thought the Peelites were
going to make fools of themselves by refusing to join.
In fact they did refuse, and the fact was telegraphed to
Lord St. Germans by Sir John Young, who accepted the
Governorship of the Ionian Islands in the full conviction
that they were out. Lord Aberdeen brought Gladstone
and Graham round on Tuesday. Lord Palmerston will
have great difficulties to encounter, and I don't think
any stable Government can be found whilst this Parliament lasts.† The state of the army gets worse and
worse. By the returns up to the 21st there were only

* In the General Election in 1852 Sir G. C. Lewis was defeated
in Herefordshire by a Protectionist combination, and remained out
of Parliament. But the death of his father, Sir J. Frankland Lewis,
in January 1855, having caused a vacancy in the representation of
the Radnorshire Burghs, Sir George was persuaded to stand, and
was returned to Parliament. In February following he succeeded
Mr. Gladstone, as Lord Palmerston's Chancellor of the Exchequer.

† Parliament was not dissolved till the 21st of March, 1857.

22,000 men of all arms, exclusive of sailors. On the 8th there were 29,000, and reinforcements had arrived in the interim. It is strange that no man of masterly genius has yet emerged in any department. Evans and Napier must be half mad.* Literature is a thriving trade. Moxon has just brought me the account of my fifth (popular) edition of 'Faust,' of which he has sold 1,500 copies. I find myself £6. 2s. 7d. out of pocket. He proposes a sixth on the same terms. Best regards to Lady Theresa, and believe me,

Ever most truly yours,
A. HAYWARD.

I write from the Temple, and have heard nothing to-day.

Monsieur Thiers to Mr. Hayward.

MON CHER HAYWARD,   Février 19, 1855.

Je vous remercie de vos intéressantes lettres, et je vous fais mes excuses pour mon long silence, mais je suis tellement enfoncé dans le travail, que je n'en sors pour aucune chose. Il n'y a ici rien de nouveau. Tout le monde se demande si on fera la paix, et on ne le croit plus guère, après l'avoir cru un moment. La Russie la désire, cela est certain, mais les limites, dont Sevastopol peut être le motif, lui repugnent horriblement. Nous autres (vous et nous) nous tenons à ne pas poser les armes sans avoir pris Sevastopol, et il se peut que lorsque la paix sera possible pour nous, elle ne le soit plus pour les Russes. Pourtant je ne désespère pas tout à fait de la paix. Si on s'enfonce davantage dans la guerre, il faut se dire qu'elle exigera de plus grands moyens que dans la campagne précédente. Les Russes feront les derniers efforts surtout contre l'Autriche, et il

---

* On account of their speeches at the dinner given by the Lord Mayor of London to Sir C. Napier on the 6th of February.

faut se tenir prêt à la secourir si elle est battue, chose qu'il est impossible de dire aujourd'hui.

On vous engage beaucoup à changer votre ministère, et vos institutions administratives. Je ne suis pas sûr que vous obteniez ainsi de grandes améliorations dans les résultats. Sans doute vos institutions militaires et administratives laissent beaucoup à désirer, mais la question est ailleurs, chaque guerre a ses difficultés et ses moyens qui tiennent au progrès du temps. L'homme qui sait prévoir, qui sait approprier les ressources aux circonstances, et qui a cette sollicitude dévorante sans laquelle on ne suffit jamais aux besoins de la guerre, est toujours difficile à trouver en tout temps, et tout pays, et les institutions ne sauraient le suppléer. Dans le doute, j'aimerais mieux garder les hommes qui y sont. Du reste, je vis au désert en philosophe, je regarde passer les astres, je les mesure, et vis heureux dans mon observatoire.

Écrivez-moi quelquefois,

Mille amitiés,

A. THIERS.

Lord St. Germans to Mr. Hayward.

Vice-Regal Lodge,
Feb. 26, 1855.

MY DEAR MR. HAYWARD,

I wrote this morning to Lord Palmerston to resign the Lord Lieutenancy. Whether our friends ought to have yielded and made the best of a bad bargain is a question on which I cannot pronounce a very decided opinion.* I think that in their place I should have acted as they did. I viewed from the beginning (as you know) the proposed inquiry with alarm. At any rate, my course was a plain one. I could not abandon my old friends and colleagues and allow myself to be absorbed in the Whig party. If

* On the question of Mr. Roebuck's inquiry.

it be true that . . . is to be Chief Secretary, I shall congratulate myself on having taken time by the forelock. I could not have stomached the appointment of a Chief Secretary by the Prime Minister without any sort of consultation or communication with me. . . . would not be acceptable to either of the great religious bodies in Ireland, where religion and politics are so mixed up that to speak of a religious body is to speak of a political party. His persecution of the bishops and deans of the English branch of the Established Church will make him unpopular with the Protestants in Ireland ; his vote on the Ecclesiastical Titles Bill (to say nothing of his English birth and education) with the Roman Catholics. I am glad to hear that the *Morning Chronicle* affair * has made some progress, and that there is reason to hope that it will end satisfactorily.

In haste,

Yours very faithfully,

ST. GERMANS.

How strange that the two sons of Sir Robert Peel should be members of a Government to which none of his old friends or colleagues belong !

ST. G.

Lord St. Germans to Mr. Hayward.

Vice-Regal Lodge,

MY DEAR MR. HAYWARD,   Mar. 3, 1855.

In yesterday's *Globe* there is an insinuation, or rather an assertion, that I had a leaning to the Orange party. Now, if I had a leaning, it was the other way. The only act of my government that has been made the subject of discussion in Parliament is the Six Mile Bridge prosecution. On that occasion I acted in direct contravention, not only of the wishes, but also of the instructions of the

---

* The sale and transfer of the paper.

Cabinet. I was desired to order the Attorney-General to put the priests on their trial. This I positively refused to do, and rather than do it would have resigned. Does that look like a leaning to the Orange party? Lord Palmerston, at the instance of the Protestant Association and other similar bodies, has frequently taken me to task for not giving sufficient protection to Scripture-readers and to the distribution of anti-Catholic tracts and handbills. In vindicating myself I have more than once expressed strong disapprobation of the practice of vilifying in public places the religion of the majority of the people, and have declared that those who promoted such a practice appeared to me to be more blameable than those who resented it. Does that look like a leaning to the Orange party? As to the patronage of the Irish Government, I can safely say, that it has been almost exclusively exercised in favour of Liberals, at least I cannot call to mind more than one or two cases in which that course has been deviated from. In short, there are no grounds whatever for such an imputation. The object of the *Globe* is, of course, to serve Lord Carlisle, but he has no right to do this at my expense. A few words to that effect in the *Morning Chronicle* might be of use, without saying anything that might be twisted into making me the mere tool of the R. C. party. To you such a caution need not be addressed, but of the discretion of all the *M. C.* writers I am not so sure.

Always,

Yours sincerely,

ST. GERMANS.

I hope to be in London on the 15th.

The letters which follow refer to the Bill for abolishing the stamp duty on newspapers, one of the first measures taken in hand by Sir George Lewis as Chancellor of the

Exchequer. It simply embodied the recommendations of a select committee in 1851, but was strenuously opposed by existing newspaper proprietors, who feared competition if it were passed. Sir E. Bulwer Lytton's speech was thought to have largely helped the Bill, and Mr. Hayward heartily approved of it.

Mr. Hayward to Sir G. C. Lewis.

MY DEAR LEWIS,   Temple, Mar. 28.

I cordially congratulate you on the success of your measure, which may be considered complete, as the division was taken under circumstances peculiarly favourable to the opposition. It has given the Government a very opportune lift. Bulwer Lytton's was a capital speech. I met him the same evening at the Athenæum, and he was then hesitating for fear of offending his party. I suggested that he had young Stanley* on his side. "Oh!" he said, "that will be deemed bad company. Our people call him the greatest liberal in the House." What little doubts I had have vanished, but I do not anticipate any great immediate change either for evil or for good. The *Chronicle* is angry and foolish.

                                   Ever truly yours,
                                        A. HAYWARD.

Sir G. C. Lewis to Mr. Hayward.

MY DEAR HAYWARD,   Downing Street, Mar. 28, 1855.

The division of Monday night settled the question of the newspaper stamp, and now nothing remains to be decided but the details. Bulwer's was an admirable speech. It even influenced some votes. I have no

---

* Lord Stanley, the present Lord Derby.

doubt it will be read all over the country, and will tend to fix opinion on the subject. Drummond was exceedingly pungent and humorous ; I never heard him so successful. The answer of the *Times* is spiteful without being effective.

Ever yours truly,

G. C. LEWIS.

Sir Edward Bulwer Lytton to Mr. Hayward.

MY DEAR HAYWARD, Mar. 28, 1855.

Many thanks for your kind note. I never quite understood the sudden change in the *Chronicle.* What and how is it? There is, I suppose, no Peelite journal now? I suppose there will be. I thought my best hit, apart from Walpole, was the old quotation applied to the *Times*—

> " Expende Annibalem—quot libras in duce summo Invenies."

And so it would have been in the old house, but I don't think there were ten men who took it in in this ; that which told most was a concluding sentence about our old friend the *Spectator*, which came into my head at the moment. Our division must have pleased Gladstone ; it is a complete vindication of his scheme.

Yours,

E. B. L.

Mr. Hayward to Sir E. B. Lytton, M.P.

MY DEAR LYTTON, March 29.

You may be pleased to see Lewis's letter. He speaks of the immense impression of your speech (on Newspaper Stamp Act). Your quotations very very happy, as happy as Lord Lyndhurst about Lord John Russell;* but no one seems to appreciate these things now. The allusion to the *Spectator* was very telling, but the fact of its being stopped by a stamp or tax was new to me. The *Chronicle* was sold to Glover some months since. I write an article for it now and then, but this is the extent of my connection, and the Peelite party have nothing to do with it.

Ever truly yours,

A. HAYWARD.

Monsieur Thiers to Mr. Hayward.

MON CHER HAYWARD,   Paris, 29 mars 1855.

Je vous remercie de votre intéressante lettre, et de la spirituelle missive du *Chronicle.* Ces messieurs sont fous en vérité ! Il ne leur suffit pas d'avoir les avantages matériels du pouvoir, il leur faut encore la gloire pour eux, la calomnie pour leurs adversaires, et M. de Morny s'enchaînant à M. Verot. Du reste, on dit que l'Empereur a désapprouvé les provocations de ce tapage. Cela fait honneur à son tact des convenances. Quant à moi, je ne vais pas mal pour un homme qui s'est cassé un membre. J'écris difficilement, bien que le bras droit me reste, et c'est pour cela que, depuis longtemps, je ne vous ai pas donné signe de vie. Du reste, nous sommes dans une obscurité complète. Les gens sensés et patriotes désirent la paix, mais sentent aussi le besoin de tenir les Russes en bride, et de ne pas leur permettre de hausser la voix. Ils ont repris de la morgue, depuis qu'on dit que nous ne pouvons prendre Sevastopol. C'est là ce qui exigera peut-être une nouvelle effusion de sang, bien regrettable, car en prenant Sevastopol, on ne pourra pas avoir la prétention de le garder. Verser le sang pour prendre ce qu'on doit rendre huit jours après, est bien cruel, et peut cependant être nécessaire. Si pourtant les Russes

* 'Life of Lord Lyndhurst,' by Sir Theodore Martin, p. 443.

accordent l'abolition des deux protectorats, celui des Grecs et celui des provinces, la libre navigation du Danube, avec un lieu sur chaque rive de terrain neutre, plus enfin la limite des six vaisseaux dans la mer Noire, on aura fait une belle paix et on pourra traiter sans regret.   Cela ne paraît pas impossible, pourtant la plus grande incertitude règne, et je crois que les Gouvernements n'en savent pas plus que nous.   Du reste, on est tranquille ici.   Tout le monde a les yeux tournés sur Sevastopol.   Je crois que si on s'est pourvu d'une artillerie suffisante, surtout en personne, et qu'on fasse taire les feux de la place, on viendra à bout de cet épouvantail ; autant qu'on peut en juger à distance, la difficulté est loin d'être invincible.   Adieu, je vous serre la main, et vous remercie de votre constante amitié.   Je crois, comme vous, que l'état des partis chez vous ne permet pas un autre ministère.

A. THIERS.

The following letter refers to the debate on Mr. Disraeli's motion expressing "dissatisfaction with the ambiguous language and uncertain conduct" of the Government, in reference to the great question of peace or war.   Sir F. Baring proposed an amendment to this motion, simply expressing regret that the second Vienna Conference had not put an end to hostilities, but promising support for the war.   The motion was submitted on the 24th of May, and after a three nights' debate was rejected by a majority of 319 to 219.

Mr. Hayward to Mr. Gladstone.

MY DEAR GLADSTONE,   Athenæum Club, May 23, 1855.

Robarts (member for Cornwall) seemed just now very anxious to know what course you meant to pursue to-morrow, and whether there was any chance of a *tertium quid*, as neither Disraeli's motion nor Baring's amendment would meet the views of himself and others who were unwilling to bring the negotiations to an abrupt conclusion, or to declare all hopes of peace at an end. He computes the friends of peace in the House of Commons, who would be likely to follow you at not less than 50. This needs no answer, but I thought you might as well know that this state of feeling exists. Disraeli's resolution is a vote of censure on Austria and want of confidence in France.

Ever faithfully yours,
A. HAYWARD.

Mr. Hayward to his Sisters.

May 24, 1855.

Politics get more and more tangled, but I do not anticipate any immediate change. Lord Palmerston had a meeting this morning and satisfied most of his supporters. On the other hand, some of the leading Derbyites, such as Lord March and Lord Granby, will not vote with Disraeli. I was at Lansdowne House on Saturday last, and I dined yesterday with Lord Londonderry. All patronage at present must go in the Whig direction, but it is to be hoped that we shall have another turn of the wheel some time or other. If you can get on comfortably I can.

Ever yours,
A. H.

The Duke of Newcastle to Mr. Hayward.

MY DEAR HAYWARD,   Portman Square, June 12, 1855.

I return Young's * letter. I trust he may succeed in a very difficult post. If he does not, his appointment will

---

* Sir John Young had accepted the post of Lord High Commissioner of the Ionian Islands.

be well remembered, as mine; if he does, he, like the Transport Corps (vide *Economist* et alios ubique), will be set down to my successor. I should now have been in the Crimea in the midst of this intense interest and success, but for that greatest curse of life—a governess! I am still in search but cannot find, and till I do I am tied by the leg to the school-room. I cannot, till I see it, believe that the Roebuck Committee will pander to the *Times* and bring in a verdict of guilty. Cowardice could no lower go.

Ever yours very sincerely,
NEWCASTLE.

Lord St. Germans to Mr. Hayward.

Port Eliot, Devonport.
June 23, 1855.

MY DEAR MR. HAYWARD,

I return Young's letter with many thanks to you for letting me see it. He may be a little bored at Corfu, but he must be very glad in his heart to be out of the mess in which he would have found himself had he remained in Parliament. The loss of office would have been a serious thing for him, and yet he could not well have retained it. When he took the Ionian Islands I thought that he did wrong; but I am now satisfied that he did right. The Peel party is, I am afraid, nearly defunct; a little sooner or a little later, one or other of the stronger parties will have absorbed all its members. We have had no war cry since free trade ceased to be one, and without some war cry no party can go on long in this country. It is true that the talents of some of the leaders secured for them a certain number of adherents, but it is diminishing fast; indeed the peace or war question has, I think, been the *coup de grâce* to the Peelites. I have not seen the *Chronicle* since I left town. I left off reading it when you left off writing in it. How melancholy the tidings from the Crimea! Not that I despond or despair of the ultimate fall of the place, but the loss is fearful. Every list of casualties that I see reminds me of that which nearly broke my heart,* and prevents time from producing its natural effect on my mind. I am, however, always glad to receive from you an account of what is going on in the political world, and am very sensible of your kindness in keeping me *au courant* of it.

Believe me to be yours, very faithfully,

ST. GERMANS.

Mr. Hayward to his Sisters.

July 23, 1855.

In consequence of Lord John Russell's conduct,† the Government are in considerable danger, though I think they will pull through. At the same time I do not much care how politics go for the present, but it is as well that Lord John should be damaged, as the split between him and my friends is final. Balls are quite out of my line, but I went to Lady Clanricarde's because it was the night of the division, and I wanted to know how things were going. I passed yesterday at Lord Lansdowne's villa at Richmond with Macaulay, Mrs. Norton, Colonel Rawlinson and some others. I dine with Lord John Manners on Friday. But party-going is now coming to an end. My plans are still uncertain. My article‡ has been very successful. The one in the

* The Honourable Granville Charles Cornwallis Eliot, of the Coldstreams, fell in action at the battle of Inkerman. He was second son of the late, and brother of the present, Lord St. Germans.

† Lord John Russell's resignation in the face of Sir E. B. Lytton's notice of motion condemning his conduct at the Vienna Conference.

‡ On "The Life and Writings of Sydney Smith," *Edinburgh Review,* July 1855.

Quarterly is a mere abstract of the book by a man who never saw Sydney Smith.

Ever yours,

A. H.

The Duke of Newcastle to Mr. Hayward.

MY DEAR HAYWARD,   Constantinople, Nov. 18, 1855.

Your letter of 20th September had seven weeks' rest in the Crimea whilst I was making a most interesting and instructive tour in Circassia, and from which I returned to Sebastopol for only five days. I am now on my way home, and, including a delay of three or four days at Malta and two in Paris, hope to be in London at the end of the first week in December. Many thanks for your "slip." I fear the opinion, very flattering —and too favourable—is much further from being that of the country than you suppose. Never in my recollection was the whole London *daily* press so dishonest, and never had a man who seeks no interest but that of his country so little chance of fair play; whilst the great mass of the people, having neither leisure nor mind to form their own opinions, found their political judgment upon the trash they imbibe with their tea and coffee, or their gin and bitters, as the case may be.

I shall probably see you soon, and therefore will not begin a yarn, which might easily become as long as the electric wire which Panmure* is making the leading string of old babies in the Crimea.

Poor Molesworth ! Curious that he should have died just as he was about to test the soundness of the judgment of critics, who studied his champagne more carefully

* Secretary of State for War.

than his ideas.   He had some great failings, but I regret him much.*

Ever yours most sincerely,
NEWCASTLE.

The following letter refers to the Count de Montalembert's work ' De l'Avenir politique de l'Angleterre,'† which was published in two parts in *Le Correspondant* of the 25th of November and 25th of December.

Mr. Hayward to the Count de Montalembert.

Temple,

MY DEAR COUNT DE MONTALEMBERT,   Dec. 24, 1855.

I wrote to you on the 21st (the date of the very welcome letter I have just received from you), so that our letters must have crossed.   Of course, no exertions shall be wanting on my part to bring about a due appreciation of the service you have rendered, not only England, but civilization, by leading what on the Continent is (I know) almost a *forlorn hope*, but you need be under no misapprehension of being misunderstood.   In the case of a man whose reputation insures his being read or listened to, the comments of the press amongst us are of very small importance.   He is sure of a fair hearing, and *that* in your case is tantamount to a great success.   So soon as the essay appears in a separate form and in a readable translation, misrepresentation will be impossible.   At

---

* Sir Wm. Molesworth, who became Secretary of State for the Colonies in Lord Palmerston's Government, died on the 22nd of October, 1855.

† " A book in which he indicates with instinctive sagacity the felicitous concurrence of circumstances, habits, and modes of thought that have made the British Empire what it is." (' Eminent Statesmen and Writers,' by A. Hayward. ' Montalembert,' vol. i., p. 320. Murray, 1880.)

present it is known only by garbled or broken extracts. The editor of the *Examiner* has stated openly, that all he knew of it was what he saw in a French newspaper. When I first heard of it I tried in vain to get a copy. There was not one at the English publishers of the *Correspondant*, and this review is not taken in at any of the clubs. Monsell lent me his copy, or I could not have seen it at all. Everybody is running about asking for it. I will-get the *Morning Post* for you, if possible, but the notice is beneath contempt—a mere compound of ignorance and vulgarity. It is now an admitted fact, that the French and the Emperor desire peace ; and this is the cause of no trifling anxiety to our Government, whose existence depends on war. The English of the less reflective order want to go on to recover our military prestige. It is not expected that Russia will accept the conditions. In the *Times* of to-day (the Berlin Correspondence) it is admitted that the English are really discredited in Germany.* I will write again so soon as the second part, or the complete *brochure*, arrives.

Ever most sincerely yours,
A. HAYWARD.

Lord Brougham to Mr. Hayward.

MY DEAR MR. HAYWARD,

Château Eléanore,
Christmas Day, 1855.

Many thanks for the Xmas Box† you have given me, more especially that part of it in which you advert to Law Amendments. I need not say how sincerely I

---

* After the fall of Sebastopol Austria proposed terms of peace, which were accepted by France and sent to England for approval. England, however, insisted upon an alteration in the terms, and the Austrian ultimatum as amended was borne to St. Petersburg by Count Esterhazy. Fears of France breaking with England at this critical moment were very strong in some quarters.

† ' Juridical Tracts,' by A. Hayward, Esq., Q.C.

feel your kind mention of my labours. But I am chiefly
gratified at the prospect of your publication rendering
important service to the cause, and it really, under the
blighting influence of feebleness, and also jobbery, requires
to be helped. Let me suggest how valuable it is to keep
in the minds of men, especially of men favourably disposed but apt to be discouraged, the great proportion of
measures we have actually carried. I verily believe that
a volume might be made of Acts and parts of Acts which
have been passed since Sir S. Romilly's death in 1818,
all of which he had attempted to carry, and many of
them repeatedly, or had urged the principles wholly or
in part adopted in them, or had in his writings strongly
recommended. They related chiefly to mitigation of
the Criminal Law, but also to other subjects. He hardly
lived to see one of them passed. Yet now they are
reckoned as clearly just and true as that two and two
make four. Another volume might be made of the Bills
which I not only urged but brought in and carried: for
example, of the nine which I brought in one session
(1845), five or six, the greater number, are now law;
including the great reform—I may almost call it revolution—in the Law of Evidence, allowing parties to be
themselves examined in civil cases. I have sometimes
thought that, but for the appearance of self-glorification,
the best service I could now render would be to publish
a list of these and similar measures to encourage the
faint-hearted.

Mrs. Norton's* is as clever a thing as ever was written,
and it has produced great good. I feel almost certain
that the Law of Divorce will be much amended, and she
has greatly contributed to it. Your projected additional
republication of accounts of Codes and Courts, is also
very important with a view to improvement of procedure.
It was partly with this view as to *Political Improvement*

* A letter to the Queen on Lord Cranworth's Divorce Bill.

that I laboured for so many years on my 'Political Philosophy,' for there was really no work that deserved the name.   It is a useful and easily-consulted repertory of information and history, on constitutions and their weakness and their faults.   Yours apparently will do this service to the judicial system, giving *its* comparative analogy as that did of governments.

Many thanks for your information.   The Duke of Newcastle always, both in public and private, has acted nobly, and I dare say he did right also prudentially in refusing.*   He has, God wot, been treated with injustice, but nothing to Aberdeen.   However, my delight was great to see in a weekly paper called *Saturday Review*, just published, an admirable article on this subject.   John Bull is gone clean mad, and we shall be quarrelling with Louis Napoleon on peace.

Yours very truly.

[Lord Brougham frequently, as here, omitted his signature.]

Mr. Hayward to Mr. Gladstone.

MY DEAR GLADSTONE,   Temple, Dec. 31, 1855.

Perhaps you will like to see the enclosed letter. Fitzroy has been several weeks in the south of France. His account is abundantly confirmed by others, and the last time I was at Lady Palmerston's it was an admitted fact that Louis Napoleon was *most inconveniently* pressing for peace.   The Government think they have nailed him by getting him to agree to terms which Russia is not expected to accept, but if the Czar shows any inclination to treat, Louis Napoleon may insist on lightening them. I hear that he is short of money, that he cannot get another loan, and does not dare to increase the taxes, as the people are suffering very much from high prices

---

* Probably the Governor-Generalship of India.

already. C. Greville (just arrived from Lord Clarendon) tells me that Esterhazy is to *intimate* merely, that if Russia chooses to treat, Austria has reason to believe that such and such terms may be had. The answer is to be *yes* or *no*. If *yes*, an armistice to be declared. If *no*, Esterhazy and suite to leave. He is to wait nine days, and then (if he has got no answer) to demand one, and wait ten more. When Montalembert was in England, I had a good deal of talk with him on the subject of his essays, 'De l'Avenir politique de l'Angleterre.' He writes, " I feel sure that no one in England will better understand my opinions than yourself. But what you cannot understand is the depth and extent of hostile feeling towards England in France, and throughout the Continent." His first part was excellent ; his second part is full of passages and allusions calculated to excite prejudices. Thus, by way of compliment, he calls our Established Church *une pépinière* for Roman Catholicism. He has also fallen into one or two curious errors, as when he says that the names of *all* our contemporary celebrities are to be found on the list of Cambridge and Oxford honours. A London bookseller had proposed a translation, which I offered to revise, but I now fear it would do more harm than good. Have you seen these essays ? If so, pray tell me what you think of a translation.

> Ever faithfully yours,
> A. HAYWARD.

*Mr. Hayward to Mr. Monsell.**

MY DEAR MONSELL,   Temple, Dec. 31, 1855.

Montalembert's essay (part 2) abounds with passages calculated to provoke attack.† Take, for example, his

---

* The Rt. Hon. Wm. Monsell, now Lord Emly, then Clerk of the Ordnance.

† He was bitterly assailed on both sides the Channel, especially

remark (p. 344) that the Established Church is *une pépinière de Catholiques ;* and (in reference to the Convocation) that all emancipation of the Church will tend to the development of the elements which draw it towards Catholicism. Nothing can be more annoying or injurious to the so-called Puseyite members of the Church. His preference of the Roman Catholic working clergy on the Continent (well-founded or not) will equally offend, and I have heard many contend that his alleged defence of England is a covert attack. Reeve thinks so, and I much fear an *Edinburgh Review* article in that sense. For every reason, therefore, he should be as correct in matters of fact as possible ; and he should be requested to modify the passage in which (p. 32) he says that the lists of honours comprise "tous les grands noms de l'Angleterre contemporaine.". What could possibly have put this into his head? For the number is singularly rare at present. Brougham, Lord John Russell, Campbell, Lord St. Leonards, Bright, Cobden, Disraeli, &c., were never at a University. Palmerston, Lord Lansdowne, the Duke of Newcastle, Graham, Molesworth, the Bulwers, Lord Derby, Lord Stanley, C. Villiers, Lord Clarendon, Lord Ellenborough, Lord Panmure, did not take honours. On looking over the lists of honours for the last twenty years, you will hardly find a name distinguished in Parliament, literature, or the Bar. As minor errors, he places Pitt (who was at Pembroke) at Trinity, and Burke (educated at Trinity College, Dublin) as not having been at a University at

---

for what he said about the churches ; and we have a letter now before us, dated La-Roche-en-Breny, January 3, 1856, in which he writes, "This act has been, and deserves to be, looked upon as an act of foolhardiness. I have to contend both in Europe and America with the whole weight of *religious* prejudice against Protestant England, and of *political* prejudice against English freedom or English ambition." ('Eminent Statesmen,' vol. i. p. 320.)

all.   I learn from Jeffs that the one volume edition is
delayed, so that perhaps there may be time to get these
things altered.   The truth is, the Universities contribute
next to nothing to the working mind of England.   Men
take their honours to gain tutorships or fellowships, and
then drop into obscurity.   Dr. Twiss (a first-class man)
confirms this view, and says that the enjoined course of
study disqualifies for the world.

In haste,

Ever yours truly,

A. HAYWARD.

There are admirable passages, which makes it the
more provoking that their effect should be spoiled by
the prejudices he will rake up.

The letters of Mr. Hayward and his correspondents on the negotiations for peace have not been omitted ; but it must be understood that they, all of them, wrote in the dark on this subject, because uninformed of the separate negotiations which Louis Napoleon had been secretly carrying on with Russia behind the back of England.*

In the autumn of 1856 we find Mr. Hayward mentioning, in a letter to Mr. Gladstone, one of his numerous visits to Lord Palmerston at Brocket. If there is any truth in the statement, that he was at one time disliked by Lord Palmerston as an active ally of the Peelites, it is clear that the estrangement had already vanished, and been replaced by a friendship which continued without interruption in the future. It was at Lord Palmerston's special request that Mr. Hayward's article on de Bazancourt's 'L'Expédition de Crimée,' in the *North British Review*, was translated and circulated in French, for the express purpose of counteracting the false impressions created on the Continent by de Bazancourt's semi-official work.

His insight into the workings of political life during his connection with the *Morning Chronicle*, and with several of the members of Lord Aberdeen's Government, had done much to raise the value of Mr. Hayward's literary faculty. For he was not only a forcible writer, but a man of experience and matured judgment. He had, moreover, a practical way of looking at things that oftentimes made his opinion of no small value to men engaged in public life. On this point the late Mr.

* See the separate negotiations fully given in the second volume of the 'Diplomatic Study,' an official work issued by the Foreign Office of St. Petersburg.

W. E. Forster has written that, such men "were glad to get his opinions by reason of his personal qualities, his experience, his accuracy, his clearness of vision, unobscured by party preferences, though perhaps sometimes warped by personal likings or dislikings, for which however allowances could be made, and especially his absolute independence both in thought and speech. There was also a rare, I may perhaps say unique characteristic of his political thought and experience which was to me both instructive and attractive, the result of a curious combination of a hard worldly, even cynical appreciation of men and things, with strong sympathy with popular movements, and ideal aspirations. This made him an optimist when he might have been expected to be a pessimist ; and a believer in the future, though a severe critic of the present."* These traits, so distinctly portrayed by his friend, earned for Mr. Hayward an unique position in political circles, and among those who were engaged in public life.

Mr. Hayward to Mr. Gladstone.

MY DEAR GLADSTONE,   Temple, Jan. 2, 1856.

I send you Montalembert's first part ;† I have lent the second to Sidney Herbert, but I will forward it to you as soon as I can get it back. They are to appear in a single volume shortly, but are at present not to be had in London. If the second had proved equal to the first, they would have done much good. I believe the notion of a translation is given up. I also send a publication of mine‡ which my friends are not ex-

---

* Private MSS.   † 'L'Avenir politique de l'Angleterre.'
‡ 'Juridical Tracts' : essays originally published in the *Law Magazine*.

pected to read, as its sole object is to put in my claim to rank as a jurist and law reformer when law reformers were scarce. I have written to Thiers and Mignet, as well as to Montalembert, but I build more upon Brougham, who will soon be in Paris. He always *forces* his way into the Tuileries, and gives his advice without ceremony. They should understand that this war-cry is transitory and superficial. I have never met with a sensible man who, after five minutes' conversation, did not admit that the sooner we are out of the mess the better.

The alliance is in much more danger from the continuance of the war than from peace, for the French will attribute all their resulting sufferings to our selfishness, and we shall never get them to act cordially in concert. At this very time the Government cannot put forward their real defence for abandoning Kars, which was that Louis Napoleon would not hear of detaching any part of the allied army, because the French think all movements in that direction have reference to our Indian empire. The French are in the highest degree exasperated at the comments of the *Times* on Pelissier,* and nothing has kept us friends hitherto but our suppressing, or touching lightly, what was wrong in their camp, and constantly giving them the best in every comparison. When I was last in Paris, I grew impatient at their boasting and lying, and declared I would publish the truth if I could find an organ. "There is an end of the alliance," said Thiers, "if you do. *You* may bear the truth; *we* can't." Again, Louis Napoleon has got what he wanted from the alliance—recognition and position, and (if Russia is not foolishly obstinate) he will not refuse reasonable terms for fear of English anger, though I dare say he would be glad to keep Lord Palmerston

* Marshal Pelissier, Duke of Malakoff, commanded the French army in the Crimea.

in office. What I dread is Russian pride. Suppose they act as after the burning of Moscow?—tell us to do our worst, and bide their time. Who can tell what fresh combinations may arise within two years? The *Morning Post* (more Louis Napoleon's paper than Palmerston's) had a furious attack on Prussia on Monday. The key to this is that there have been dealings between Austria and France contemplating, if the war is to go on, an attack on Prussia by France, which is to guarantee Italy, Hungary, and Poland to Austria. The occupation of the Rhenish provinces would at once make the war popular in France. What becomes of the balance of power then? We want an organ to bring the British public acquainted with these contingencies. The *Saturday Review* had a capital opening, but has left the common sense of the question to the *Press,** which only tells half the truth. In fact, Disraeli has been told that his principal followers are for war. The landed interest think it as good as a corn law. I dined yesterday in company with C. Villiers, who had come that morning from the Grove. He agrees with you about the Revenue, and said that both Lewis and Lord Clarendon were *low.*

In the Cabinet I hear Lord Palmerston and Lord Lansdowne give the tone. Canning alone made head. Poor Molesworth told me that the entire character of their deliberations was changed after you, Graham, and Sidney Herbert left. There is no longer anything deserving the name of discussion.

Did I mention the letter to Elcho from his brother, the Colonel, in the Crimea? He describes Russell † as an amusing fellow, with a brogue. They had him to

---

* A weekly newspaper, the organ of Mr. Disraeli, who was believed to contribute leading articles to it.

† Mr. W. H. Russell, the *Times* correspondent in the Crimea.

dinner, and he stated openly that his letters had been so altered in London that he could no longer recognise some of them. Meyrick, of the Guards, who had seen them, and lives much with him, confirmed this statement.

Since the *Times* breach with Lord Clarendon and Reeve, they are no longer so well up in information as they used to be. Molesworth is another loss to them. In Scotland and the far north, the cheap papers have gained enormously on the London press; but this is more owing to the telegraph than to the reduction of the duty. Within a given radius round Aberdeen, for example, you get all the most interesting news twenty-four hours before the arrival of a London paper; and so in proportion round Edinburgh, Glasgow, Newcastle, &c. &c. I myself actually ceased taking in a London paper whilst I was in Scotland. I have dotted down these things hastily, under the impression that some of them may interest you. I will keep you *au fait* if I hear anything whilst you are in the country. Don't trouble yourself to answer.

Ever most truly yours,
A. HAYWARD.

Mr. Hayward to the Count de Montalembert.

Temple, Jan. 5, 1856.

"If I might give a short hint to a public writer, it would be to tell him his fate. If he regards truth, let him expect martyrdom on both sides, and then he may go on fearless, and this is the course I take myself."—*De Foe.*

MY DEAR COUNT DE MONTALEMBERT,

These few sentences from De Foe might serve as a motto for your book, at least for the second part which is most calculated to provoke attack. If, in defending ordinary people (and nations are made up of ordinary people), you admit their faults, they are angry with the admission and hardly thank you for the defence. This has happened to me a hundred times on a minor arena, and I do not at all wonder at your suffering from the same cause when writing on subjects which so strongly excite men's passions and prejudices. There never was a period when the Roman Catholics (I do not use the term invidiously) were the object of more violent fear and dislike than at present—thanks to the violence of certain Irish members of the Catholic Church, who want to be persecuted. If the English Catholics stood alone, they would inspire respect at all times. The association with Ireland is their bane, and the irritation against Wiseman* was aggravated incalculably by his being a vulgar pushing Irishman. It is hardly possible now to get into Parliament through an English or Scottish seat, without a pledge against Maynooth, or some other Shibboleth of illiberality. This has kept me out, and will continue so to do. The *perverts* are constantly run down. *Puseyism* is still a most mischievous term of reproach to any public man, and the most injurious charge that can be brought against the Anglican Church is its tendency to assimilate with Rome. All your most eloquent and most profound remarks on the Anglican Church will therefore most probably be turned against it: as where you say that, *sous certains rapports*, it is a *pépinière* of Catholicism; or where you point out the tendency of Convocation. I mentioned this yesterday to the Bishop of Oxford, and he entirely agreed with me.

Other passages will give offence : such as your pre-

---

* Cardinal Wiseman had appealed to the people of England on the Pope's action in restoring the Catholic hierarchy in 1850.

ference (well or ill-founded) of the Continental working clergy in point of zeal, &c., and your praises of the Spanish population at the expense of the English. You are aware, of course, that all Protestant writers connect the tyranny of the Spanish monarchs, since Ferdinand, with their bigotry, and argue that the Spaniards are not free because they are not Protestants.

What you say of the foreign policy of England in the first paragraph of your conclusion is, I presume, what people have in their minds when they accuse you of attacking England *under the notion* that you are defending her. Most assuredly you cannot be accused of doing anything *covertly*, and I do not believe that this was meant. Beyond all question you have brought out into bold relief all that is most honourable and distinctive in our habits, institutions, and modes of thinking; and you have made fewer mistakes than any foreign writer that I am acquainted with in the same number of pages about us. When you do go wrong, it is where you necessarily depended upon authority and had been mis-led as to the facts: as in the importance you attach to our two Universities. They have been gradually losing influence, despite of the very laudable efforts to adapt them to the age.

I have sent you my Tracts, but I fear they will be too repulsive by their technicality except parts of that on Criminal Law. Hopes of peace do not rise. If the war lasts much longer, I do not believe that the alliance will. All the sensible part of the nation are rapidly sober-ing down, and would be glad if Louis Napoleon would drag our Government into peace.

Ever faithfully yours,
A. HAYWARD.

Mr. Hayward to Lady Morgan.

MY DEAR LADY MORGAN,   Temple, Jan. 9, 1856.

There is an article on Beyle* in the forthcoming *Edinburgh Review*, and you will easily discover the writer; but it would have been a breach of faith in him to announce himself beforehand. I was much too tired to accompany the Fords (with whom I dined at Sir Hugh Campbell's yesterday) to your party. You have more strength and spirit, as well as more genius, than any of us. We must go back to the brilliant women of the eighteenth century to find anything like a parallel for you and your *soirées*.

                Ever faithfully yours,
                        A. HAYWARD.

Mr. Hayward to Mr. Gladstone.

                        The Athenæum,
MY DEAR GLADSTONE,   Jan. 12, 1856.

C. Greville (who has seen the Granvilles since their return from Windsor) says that Prince Albert thought the answer of Russia might arrive at any moment. The great interest is how Austria will act, whether she will treat any counter-proposition as *no*, or commence a negotiation. If Austria leans towards the modified proposals, it seems not unlikely that France may do so too. If Russia won't listen to reason, there is much fear of France agreeing with Austria to attack Prussia and bring her into the war. How they are to make her neutrality a *casus belli* does not appear. We set out with enforcing the obligations of international law. Are

---

* Henri Beyle, author of 'La Chartreuse de Parme,' 'Promenades dans Rome,' &c., who wrote under the pseudonym of "de Stendhal." He died in 1842, and his works were reviewed by Mr. Hayward in the *Edinburgh Review*, January 1856.

we to break through them by way of enforcing them?
I was sorry to hear that our Court is by no means anti-
warlike. The *Press* is stronger for peace than it has
been of late, and declares the chances to be favourable.
E. Bulwer says that on seeing the peace articles in the
Press, he wrote to Disraeli to state that, if such were his
opinions, he (Bulwer) was afraid they would not act
together. Thereupon Disraeli denied all complicity or
agreement with the articles. This is odd, and therefore
I mention it. I believe he will be for whatever turns up
trumps. I hear that the French are now looking forward confidently to peace. Bulwer said he thought the
peace party were gaining ground, but that he thought it
impolitic to advocate such views in Parliament. Lord
Clarendon says the Czar is waiting to see what impression the peace party will make in Parliament. He (the
Czar) also thinks that he may as well procrastinate till
the time for active operations is at hand. Have you
seen Cobden's pamphlet, *Next, and what Next?* His
arguments are badly put, but there is a great deal of
truth and sagacity mixed up with them.

Delane (of the *Times*) has been laid up by a bad fever
for several days.

Ever faithfully yours,
A. HAYWARD.

Mr. Hayward to Mr. Gladstone.

The Athenæum,

MY DEAR GLADSTONE.   Jan. 14, 1856.

The tone of the Government is to treat the partial
acceptance as a nullity, and go on with the war. It
remains to be seen whether France will do so. At
present, it would seem that every point in which
Turkey can be deemed deeply interested is to be
conceded.

Are we to go on with the war for the mouths of the

Danube, and the neutralisation of Bomarsund ?   *That,*
if the reports of Russian acceptance are right, is now the
question.   The Government people have got into their
heads that they are to be vehemently assailed by the
Duke of Newcastle for the misconduct of the war.   How
far this may be a well-founded apprehension I cannot
say ; but I know his conclusion, from what he saw in the
East, to be that the war has been misconducted.   I hear
on good authority that a Kars blue-book is in preparation, and that Lord S. de Redcliffe will appear principally
to blame.   Macneil's report is also printing.

Ever truly yours,
A. HAYWARD.

In Government circles, they talk of a loan of thirty
millions, and the raising of the income-tax to ten per
cent. as inevitable.   Louis Napoleon's embarrassments
increase.

Mr. Sidney Herbert to Mr. Hayward.

Wilton House, Salisbury,

MY DEAR HAYWARD,   Jan. 25, 1856.

Your dinner is very tempting, but I do not come up
till Tuesday or Wednesday ; indeed, I am kept here by
guests.

There is no doubt of our unpopularity throughout
Europe, nor any as to its cause.   It requires a large fleet
and standing army to enable us to bully and vilify every
other country in Europe in every paper we read over
our muffins ; and our public opinion ends by being as
arrogant and as ignorant as our instructors themselves
are.   I saw a great deal of this feeling in Germany last
year.   It extends to all classes.

I think peace will be, though the terms in the one
essential point are less good than the Vienna proposals

T 2

of last year. Circumstances prevented the Government adopting them then, and they, I suppose, think themselves precluded from taking them now ; and we must be content with neutralisation, which we have no means of enforcing, and which in the nature of things can be but a temporary arrangement.*

> Believe me,
> Yours sincerely,
> SIDNEY HERBERT.

The Duke of Newcastle to Mr. Hayward.

MY DEAR HAYWARD,   Clumber, Jan. 25, 1856.

I am ashamed to see ' Juridical Tracts ' lying on my table and to reflect that I have not yet written to thank you for sending them to me. Day after day I have delayed doing so, in the hope of a vacant hour or two to peruse them. As yet they lie with Macaulay's two volumes, reproaching my preference for Agents, Lawyers, Bailiffs, Coalviewers, Tenants and a host of enemies to literary leisure. I suppose peace will absorb every other topic at the meeting. Do you hear of any hostile motion either on that subject or on the war in Asia ? Does the Opposition mean to attack at once, or to lie by till after Easter ? I have heard the latter, but my means of information are very small. I have no correspondents in either camp. I shall go up to town on Tuesday night, but I shall not remain in London more than a week unless something is to come on immediately. I can occupy my time more profitably and more agreeably here. I have excellent letters from my son† in the

---

* The article in the Treaty of March 30, 1856, providing for the neutralisation of the Black Sea, was abrogated by the Conference of the Powers in London in March, 1871.

† Col. Lord Edward Pelham-Clinton, of the 60th Rifles.

Crimea, where they have had fine, clear, though cold weather, My sailor son* is in despair at the prospect of peace.

Believe me,

Yours very sincerely,

NEWCASTLE.

M. Thiers to Mr. Hayward.

MON CHER MONSIEUR HAYWARD,   Paris, 30 janvier 1856.

Je veux depuis longtemps vous écrire sans en trouve jamais le tems. Enfin je prends un moment, entre deux épreuves d'imprimerie, pour vous remercier de votre dernière lettre déjà fort ancienne, et pour vous dire le très peu que nous savons ici. Comme vous le pensez bien, la paix est le sujet dont tout le monde s'occupe. On la désire généralement, et on y croit. Sans doute on aurait pu continuer la guerre, mais après avoir annoncé la paix, et avoir mis en quelque sorte le pays en possession de ce beau présent, le lui retirer est impossible, ou serait du moins dangereux. Il faut donc qu'on ne songe pas à y mettre obstacle. Après tout, on a atteint son but autant qu'on peut y prétendre dans l'état du monde, et des caractères généralement un peu affaiblis. La marine russe dans la mer Noire est supprimée, le prestige de la puissance grecque est détruit avec le protectorat des chrétiens, enfin la rectification des frontières aux bouches du Danube a plus d'importance qu'on ne l'imagine, sous le rapport militaire surtout. Avec la possession des bouches du Danube, les Russes étaient maîtres des deux rives du fleuve, tandis qu'aujourd'hui ils seront obligés de venir le passer à l'un des points de la ligne brisée, qui s'étend de Galatz à Rassova, de Rassova à Rustchuck, et ce n'est pas une petite opé-

* The late Lord Arthur Pelham Clinton.

ration.   Les résultats obtenus sont donc considérables ;
pour obtenir davantage, il aurait fallu une guerre qui
aurait peut-être embrasé l'Europe, et changé le but et le
caractère de la lutte.   A tout prendre, il faut se contenter de ce qu'on vient d'obtenir.

Je crois, moi, que la France et l'Angleterre réunies
peuvent immensement, qu'elles auraient même pu à elles
deux, et à elles seules, accabler la Russie, mais avec la
tournure que les opérations militaires avaient prise, on
ne pouvait plus l'espérer.   Si, comme je vous l'avais dit
dans le tems, les moyens eussent été préparés à propos
dans la mer Noire, on aurait dû faire perdre à la Russie
les provinces du Caucase et la Crimée.   A ce prix, on
aurait obtenu tout ce qu'on aurait voulu d'elle.   Mais on
n'a rien fait que des sottises en Géorgie ; en Crimée on
n'a pas su préparer les moyens d'une campagne active,
de manière à faire tomber le nord de Sevastopol.   Dès
lors, dégoûtés de cette guerre dans la mer Noire, nos deux
gouvernements ont songé à porter leurs forces dans la
Baltique.   Dès ce moment j'ai tremblé, et souhaité la
paix.   Dans la Baltique on aurait rencontré la tête du
taureau, tandis que, dans la mer Noire, on n'en avait que
la queue à combattre, et on aurait pu s'exposer à un
désastre.   Il fallait dans la Baltique agir avec des moyens maritimes, exclusivement maritimes, et immenses,
mais dans la mer Noire il fallait porter toutes ses forces
de terre.   De la sorte on ne courait aucun danger, et on
pouvait avoir de grands résultats.   Les choses ayant pris
un autre cours, il vaut mieux la paix.   Elle sera belle ; et
la paix faite, il faudra s'occuper de maintenir l'alliance.
Tout l'avenir est là.   Si la paix faite, on se divise, tout
est perdu.   Les Russes seront très flatteurs à Paris ; si
les Anglais, sans être flatteurs, ne sont pas au moins
bienveillants, Dieu sait ce qui pourra arriver, au surplus
cela ne me regarde pas plus que vous.   Je fais des vœux,
et n'y pouvant rien, je regrette presque d'en parler.

Adieu, mon cher Hayward, au revoir, et mille souhaits pour votre santé.

A. THIERS.

The following letter opens a correspondence between Mr. Hayward and Mrs. Grote, with whom his friendship, born of 'letters,' grew to be strong and intimate. He sincerely admired the excellence of her literary judgment, and found in her a constant and trusty critic of his work, especially of his articles for the *Quarterly Review* in later years. Mrs. Grote, on her side, greatly respected Mr. Hayward, admiring his independence of character, unspoiled by the favour with which society treated him, his simple habits of life, his great literary attainments, and his constancy in friendship.

Mrs. Grote to Mr. Hayward.

DEAR SIR.   Savile Row, Feb. 9, 1856.

I have now read the remainder of your paper upon H. Beyle, and must say that I dislike the man more than before. At the same time, I have learnt the cause of the admiration borne him by M. Balzac.* "Il est du métier." M. Mérimée,† it appears, did not much like Beyle personally, although he naturally felt sympathy with the works of a writer who cultivated the same vein of composition as himself; viz. that of investing profligacy, vice, selfishness and hypocrisy with a dramatic interest and captivation.

That the writings of Stendhal should be exhumed by caterers for Parisian appetites, furnishes but a question-

---

* In an article entitled "Étude sur H. Beyle," in the *Revue Parisienne*, September 1840.

† He wrote the introduction to Beyle's 'Correspondance inédite.'

able proof of their genuine value. But so far as my knowledge of them goes, I should say that the "remains" of Beyle exhibit traces of moral poison in every limb and *viscus.* Still, as many individuals continue to live, though a prey to disease, so Beyle managed to enjoy existence notwithstanding his entire ignorance of the pleasures and advantages of a wholesome mind. The "moral" of his story seems to me to lie in showing how well and agreeably one may pass through life without rendering the smallest service to any other being, except perhaps that of dissipating ennui by the stimulant of freethinking and cynical conversation. (I use this last word in the old English, not in modern French, sense.) I shall be happy to talk over this topic with you at a convenient opportunity. Meanwhile, believe me, dear Sir,

Truly yours,

H. GROTE.

*M. Mignet * to Mr. Hayward.*

MON CHER MR. HAYWARD,   Paris, 15 février 1856.

J'ai fait, tout de suite, votre commission auprès de M. Mérimée, ce que j'aurais dû vous dire plus tôt, mais vous l'aurez su en recevant la copie que vous désiriez avoir de la lettre de lord Byron à Beyle.

Mérimée qui ne l'avait pas, l'a trouvée, et vous l'a envoyée. J'ai beaucoup connu Beyle, qui avait de l'esprit, mais qui n'en avait pas assez pour être simple et naturel. Il affectait la singularité, et n'étant pas né original, il s'était fait bizarre. Aussi n'y avait-il guère plus de vérité dans ses livres que dans son nom.

Tout le monde est ici pour la paix. La guerre a été glorieuse, mais onéreuse. Elle a coûté plus de quinze

---

* The historian, friend of Monsieur Thiers and Secretary of the Institute.

cent millions, et emporté cent quarante mille hommes. La France n'y mettait aucune passion, et elle n'y avait d'autre intérêt que celui d'arrêter, de concert avec l'Angleterre, l'ambition russe, et de raffermir l'équilibre européen. Or cet intérêt est satisfait, au delà même des espérances qu'on pouvait concevoir, par les conditions qu'on impose à la Russie et que la Russie accepte. Cette puissance ambitieuse et orgueilleuse qui n'a pas cessé de faire des progrès depuis Pierre le Grand, qui s'est étendue à la suite de ses défaites, comme à la suite de ses victoires, qui après Austerlitz, Eylau et Friedland a gagné la Finlande, et obtenu la promesse de la Valachie et de la Moldavie, recule pour la première fois sans avoir subi des échecs très décisifs, dans une guerre de moins de deux ans.

Elle perd la forteresse d'où elle menaçait Constantinople d'une invasion, l'arsenal où tout était préparé de longue main pour opérer cette invasion ; elle n'a plus la flotte dans la mer Noire, qui reste interdite à sa marine militaire, elle renonce au protectorat dès longtemps acquis des deux principautés, d'où elle menaçait constamment par terre l'empire turc ; elle abandonne les bouches du Danube, dont elle dominait la navigation, et laisse écorner son territoire en Bessarabie. Tous les moyens qu'elle s'était astucieusement ménagés pour intervenir dans les affaires de la Turquie lui sont enlevés.

Il faudrait être plus que déraisonnable pour ne pas se contenter d'un affaiblissement aussi considérable et d'un abaissement aussi inattendu. On ne l'est ni en Angleterre ni en France, l'Angleterre obtempère à la paix comme la France, y applaudit. Ici tout le monde la veut par raison, beaucoup la désirent de plus par politique. Les vieux et obstinés libéraux comme moi, et comme une infinité d'autres, qui ne croient pas que le régime actuel soit le dernier mot de la révolution de 1789, attendent la paix pour en montrer l'impuissance.

Nous verrons ce qu'on fera de l'activité de ce pays,
comment on contentera son esprit, et quel aliment on
lui donnera à la place de celui qu'on lui a ôté.   La
France ne se passera pas longtemps de liberté, soyez-en
sûr.   Adieu, cher Mr. Hayward,

> Tout à vous,
> MIGNET.

Mr. Samuel Rogers died in 1855.   Mr. Hayward, who
had known him during the last twenty years of his life,
undertook to write an article on him in the *Edinburgh
Review* for July, 1856.   In compiling it he was assisted
by many friends of the late poet-banker.   Among others
he applied to Mrs. Geale, the niece of Lady Morgan,
whose recollections are noted in his article.   A little
later on, there is a letter from Mrs. Norton on the same
subject.

Mr. Hayward to Mrs. Geale.

11, King's Bench Walk, Temple,
DEAR MRS. GEALE,   March 27, 1856.

Can you be persuaded to jot down for me a few of
your reminiscences of poor old Rogers ?   I have promised to write an article on him for the *Edinburgh
Review*, and I am trying to collect as many anecdotes
and impressions as possible from those who knew him
best.   You were a great favourite of his, and saw a great
deal of him.   Tell me in particular what was the peculiar
quality of his musical taste, and whether he was really a
good judge of all, or what, sorts of music.   I should
really feel much obliged if you will do this.   I saw Lady
Morgan on Sunday ; she looks very well.   The prolonged
east winds make every one look and feel miserable in
London, which is very empty just now.   I see from the

papers that you are very gay in Dublin. With the highest esteem, believe me,

Ever faithfully yours,
A. HAYWARD.

In the following letter Mr. Hayward alludes to his controversy with the late Mr. Croker about the translation of Monsieur de Montalembert's work on England, which was to be subjected to Mr. Hayward for approval before publication. In looking over the proofs, Mr. Hayward found the work had been misunderstood and mistranslated under Mr. Croker's superintendence, and it was finally abandoned at the time. Mr. Hayward discusses some of the mistakes with Sir George Lewis.

Mr. Hayward to Sir G. C. Lewis.

MY DEAR LEWIS,   Temple, May 6, 1856.

It will amuse you to see from the enclosed* how differently the same thing strikes different minds equally well qualified. *Le style, c'est l'homme;* and I think you attach too little importance to changes in style, even when they are merely such. But style can't be changed without breaking the fine logic of thought. Thus when *libéraux attardés* are turned into *hypocritical reformers,* we have the old English Tory of the Reform Bill speaking instead of the Liberal Conservatives of France. The eternal introduction of *reform* and *reformers* would alone be sufficient to convict Croker of being the translator.

You must not suppose that it was merely authorial vanity that made Montalembert protest. One paper remarked, that the French Emperor could not be very

---

* 'The Battle of the Translations'; 'Specimens of an authorised translation from the French.'

illiberal if he allowed his Government to be called *that clumsy despotism.* The expression is *cette théorie monarchique.*

Another (the *Press*) accused M. of obscurity for speaking of the opposite party, and asked what party? The text is *le principe contraire.*

The *Athenæum* assailed him for saying that Dickens took all his characters from the *inferior* classes: M. having said classes *intermédiaires.*

I could multiply such instances *ad nauseam*, and I will undertake to cite from every page at least three mistranslations which every one shall allow to be indefensible. Respect for your judgment must be my apology for troubling you with this. C. de Rémusat speaks in the highest terms of Lord Clarendon's diplomacy. Graham told me on Sunday that he thought the Kars division had completely set you up for this session.

Ever truly yours,
A. HAYWARD.

Allusion has been made before to the squabbles at the Carlton Club between the Derbyites and "Peelites." Without entering into the whole story, the following letter from the late Mr. Charles Greville to Mr. Hayward is inserted, as an expression of opinion on a course of conduct that has often been called in question.

Mr. C. Greville to Mr. Hayward.

MY DEAR HAYWARD,   Bruton Street, May 9, 1856.

I read the letter in the *Morning Chronicle* yesterday. I am not aware that my Whig friends or any of them are heedlessly calling out that "the Peelites ought to leave the Carlton Club." I have, of course, heard the recent scenes in the Carlton often discussed, and I have heard some people express an opinion (not Whigs particularly) that the Peelites would act wisely in withdrawing themselves from a club where they have been, and are likely to be, so uncivilly treated ; but I have heard nobody say they *ought* to do so.   My own opinion on the matter, whatever it may be worth, you are welcome to—no power on earth should induce me, if I were a Peelite member of the Carlton, to be bullied into withdrawing from the Club ; but I think in present circumstances I should abstain from frequenting the Club, not out of any deference to the Derbyite members, but because I should dislike the society of a set of rude intemperate fellows, who don't know how to behave like gentlemen ; and I should be reluctant to expose myself to the effects of their brutality, and to be (however innocently) in any way the means of brawling and coarse behaviour in this Club.   I should, therefore, wait patiently till these heats subside, and a sense of propriety is restored to the majority of the habitués of the Carlton.   Nothing can be so absurd and so un-reasonable as the conduct of these gentry.   People assemble there for social and not for political purposes, although this Club may have been originally a political club ; but it is in the very nature of societies so formed gradually to lose much of their original character.   The great principles may still characterise such a club, but the details are of necessity constantly fleeting, and fresh elements of political opinion are constantly coming in to disturb the unanimity which may have prevailed amongst the original members.   This must always be the case in any club which is not a Military, or Naval, or University club, where membership depends on a profession or a fact.   It is so at Brooks's, the colour of which is *generally* Whig or Liberal, but with much admixture of other opinions ; still, Tories and Derbyites do not come there— to mix with birds of another feather.   Derby has taken

his name off.   Lord G. Bentinck was, I think, a member
to the day of his death.   I suppose the Carlton was
originally formed on a Conservative principle, and when
Peel was endeavouring to revive the Conservative party
after the Reform Bill.   It might be difficult to say what
party or set of men ought now to be considered as the
legitimate heirs of the founders, but I can see no reason
for Derby and his crew claiming the exclusive heritage.
Can't men live at clubs in harmony, and meet there
without quarrelling, as they do in private houses?

Yours very truly,

C. GREVILLE.

*Mrs. Norton to Mr. Hayward.**

MY DEAR AVOCAT,   May 8, 1856.

I have been in such trouble that it is no use my
attempting letters to satisfy friends.   You must forgive
me.   If your article on Rogers was delayed a little I
really don't think it would be 'a pity';—if it comes out
now, it will only be swallowed up in the shoal of reviews
on " Table Talk," &c.   A good thoughtful review a
little while hence—a review of *Rogers*, not of 'Table
Talk'—will really be read and thought of, and will be
curious, for I suppose no man ever was so much attended
to and thought of, who had so slender a fortune and such
calm abilities.   I am sure you will know what I mean :
no man ever *seemed* so important, who did so little, aye,
and said so little, (in spite of table-talk) for his fellow-
men.   His God was Harmony; and over his life Harmony presided, sitting on a lukewarm cloud.   He was
not the " poet, sage, and philosopher" people expect to
find he was, but a man in whom the tastes (rare fact!)
preponderated over the passions ; who defrayed the ex-

---

* Part of this letter has been quoted by Mr. Hayward in his
article on " Samuel Rogers " ('Selected Essays,' i. 112).

penses of his tastes as other men make outlay for the
gratification of their passions ; all within limit of reason,
he did not squander more than won the affection of his
seraglio, the Nine Muses, nor bet upon Pegasus, though
he entered him for the races when he had a fair chance
of winning.   He did nothing rash.   I am sure Rogers
as a baby never fell down, *unless he was pushed;* but
walked from chair to chair of the drawing-room furniture
steadily and quietly till he reached the place where the
sunbeam fell on the carpet.   He must always have pre-
ferred a lullaby to the merriest game of romps ; and if he
could have spoken would have begged his long-clothes
might be made of fine *Mull* muslin instead of cambric
or jacquenet, the first fabric being of incomparable softness, and the two latter capable of that which he loathed,
starch.

He was the very embodiment of quiet, from his voice
to the last harmonious little picture that hung in his
lulled room, and a curious figure he seemed—an elegant,
pale watch-tower, showing for ever what a quiet port
literature and the fine arts might offer, in an age of
"progress," when every one is tossing, struggling,
wrecking, and foundering on a sea of commercial speculation or political adventure : where people fight even
over pictures, and if a man does buy a picture, it is with
the burning desire to prove it is a Raphael to his yelping
enemies, rather than to point it out with a slow white
finger to his breakfasting friends.

I have *no* letters with me—and my first task in town
will be to try and "find" (ungrateful word !) any letter
of Rogers's that might interest—but you know I was
almost always near him—near enough for that, to him,
harmonious pleasure—a well-written *note.*

Yours ever,
C. CLIENT.

The article on Samuel Rogers was republished in 1858 among Mr. Hayward's 'Collected Essays,' and he then received the following letter from Lady Dufferin, to whom he had sent the proof-sheet with a request, that she would add any recollections in her power.

Lady Dufferin to Mr. Hayward.

Dufferin Lodge, Highgate.
Feb. 8, 1858.

My reminiscences of Rogers? Yes, I will endeavour to rub them up for your service. To the best of my recollection, he was a fine, robust-looking man, with a florid complexion and something of a rollicking manner. The heartiness and cordiality of his address had perhaps a tinge of rusticity, which, combined with his peculiar costume (top-boots and cords), and the unkempt luxuriance of his shaggy locks—or am I thinking of the late Archbishop of Canterbury? There is a slight confusion in my ideas on this subject, so I had best go straight to my less material souvenir of your old friend.

Jesting apart—I wish I could find anything either in my papers or my recollections to add to your own interesting details about Rogers. I am loth to say, now that he is gone (what I often said in his lifetime), that I never could *lash myself* into a feeling of affection or admiration for him. This may account for the paucity of my stock of recollections respecting a really remarkable man, to whom my grandfather* had obligations, and who always professed to feel a great attachment to me and my family. To tell the truth, there was a certain *unreality* in him which repelled me. I have heard him say many graceful things, but few kind ones, and he never seemed to me thoroughly in earnest save in ex-

* The Rt. Hon. R. B. Sheridan.

pressing contempt or dislike. I have always heard that he was very liberal in pecuniary matters—although the instances you give (or rather, which your friend gives) do not appear to me to merit the term generous. He gave what he valued least—*money;* he never gave what he valued most—admiration. It seemed a positive pain to him to hear any modern poet praised, and I remember his treating me with a rudeness almost bearish because I indiscreetly avowed how much I admired Tennyson's *Princess.* He was certainly witty; it was wit in the strictest estimation of the term: the produce of a keen and polished intellect sharpened by long contact with the world and hardened by a just confidence in his own powers; but there was little or no *humour* in him, nothing that warmed or kindled fun or sympathy in others, much that provoked retort.

The only "funny" thing I remember his saying was, on one occasion when we were accidentally left alone in the dark, after some jesting remark on the danger to my reputation—" Ah! my dear, if sweet 78 could come again! Mais ces beaux jours sont passés."

He told gracefully, with his usual elaborate simplicity and studied artlessness, a little anecdote about himself. 'They were playing at forfeits. Miss S. had to pay a kiss. " Oh! it was to my uncle, so I paid gladly." "Suppose it had been to me?" "I should have paid it *cheerfully!*" Was not that a bitter-sweet adverb?'

I can remember nothing more, and fear that *this* is hardly worth remembering. I have had in the course of my life many notes from him, much in the style of one you have already adverted to. They generally begin with, "Pray, pray!" A form of exordium which alternated with, "What shall I say?" I have preserved none of them, and the only *letter* I ever received from him is mislaid at present, so I am unable even to subscribe that much to your pleasant article. Pray forgive my poverty—it extends even to my powers of invention, or you should have had some sparkling "mots" which no one else ever heard of.

I return the proofs with many thanks.

Yours very truly,

HELEN DUFFERIN.

Mr. Hayward to Mr. Gladstone.

MY DEAR GLADSTONE,   Temple, July 30, 1856.

I send you by this post the August number of the *North British Review*, which contains an article of mine on the Crimean campaign, being the result of conversations with Lyons, Airey, and various other eye-witnesses of the leading events. The full history yet remains to be written, and it will be long before the impression made by the *Times* and the misrepresentations of the French will be done away.

London is thinning very rapidly. I suppose you know that Lord Drumlanrig's place was first offered to Lord R. Clinton, who took time to consult the Duke of Newcastle and then refused ; and afterwards to Lord Giffard. There was a technical difficulty about the Privy Councillor's berth, or Castlerosse would have been sworn in on Monday. There was an article on the American question* by H. Bulwer in the *Edinburgh Review*, and one by his brother Edward in the *Quarterly*.

Ever faithfully yours,

A. HAYWARD.

Lowe and Delane are going to the United States.

---

* A difficulty had arisen with the United States, in consequence of the enlistment there of recruits for the British Army, which was resented as a breach of neutrality.

The Duke of Newcastle to Mr. Hayward.

MY DEAR HAYWARD, Clumber, Aug. 1, 1856.

Many thanks for the *N. B. Review*—I have read your article this morning with much interest. If I had seen it before it was published, I could have pointed out to you a few mistakes ; but they are of such a nature that they will not be generally detected, and do not materially affect the line of argument. I am very anxious, however, to see something less ephemeral than an article in a Review to counteract Bazancourt's most unfair book.* To do this effectively, however, a history must be written quite free from any bias for or against anybody. I hear Kinglake has undertaken the task. He has a noble opportunity of producing a text-book for future history, but to accomplish this it must be *stoically impartial.* I have never thanked you for a kind sentence in your article on Rogers. If anything brings you this way, I and the fishing-rod will be very glad to see you ; this summer, though, you may find me alone. In the winter, I hope you will come and meet some friends.

Ever yours most sincerely,

NEWCASTLE.

Mr. Gladstone to Mr. Hayward.

MY DEAR HAYWARD, Hawarden, Aug. 4, 1856.

Your gift of the *Review*,† it so happened, came into my hands before your kind letter, and I had at once pitched upon the article and read it with particular interest, though in ignorance who was the author. I do not feel myself able to take quite so favourable a view as

* 'L'Expédition de Crimée jusqu'à la Prise de Sebastopol. Chroniques de la Guerre d'Orient, par le Baron de Bazancourt, Chargé de Mission en Crimée, par S. Exc. le Ministre de l'Instruction publique.' 2 vols. 3me édition. Paris, 1856.

† The *North British Review*.

yours of the conduct of all parties on our side ; but the pith and marrow of your argument lies in what you say of the question between us and the French. It is high time that in a quiet way this part of the subject should be worked through. I have read E. Bulwer's article in the *Quarterly*, but not his brother's yet. There is something ridiculous in an elaborate and ponderous argument about the Mosquitos, ending with a proposal for their deportation. I suppose Savonarola and Grote are both Milman. The latter goes the whole hog too much for me.

I remain, most sincerely yours,

W. E. GLADSTONE.

In the autumn of 1856, difficulties arose touching the execution of the Treaty of Paris. The two points which were then chiefly occupying attention were the dispute with Russia as to the rectification of the Bessarabian frontier, and her occupation of Serpent's Island at the mouth of the Danube ; Lord Palmerston took a very firm tone, and insisted that the treaty should be specifically carried out. The parts taken by France and Austria in supporting the Russian claims were mainly due to the revolutionary aspect of affairs in the Italian peninsula. The atrocities of King Bomba at Naples were also attracting notice, and caused both France and England to remonstrate, and remonstrance proving vain, to withdraw their legations from Naples. Russia protested at this step, on the ground that " To endeavour to obtain from the King of Naples concessions as regards the internal government of his states by threats, or by menacing demonstration, is a violent usurpation of his authority, an attempt to govern in his stead ; and it is an open declaration of the right of the strong over the weak." The letters at the close of the year treat of these matters.

Mr. Hayward to Mr. Gladstone.

MY DEAR GLADSTONE,   Aug. 11, 1856.

I have been since Wednesday last at Brocket. The Clarendons came on Saturday, but I collected no news beyond what has appeared in the papers ; namely, that the Russians are trying to back out of the treaty, and that the French decline to join England and Austria in compelling them.

We, I believe, are taking a very decided tone. The remaining points relate to the boundary line by which their territory was to be restricted, and to some territory near as well as on the river.

Lord Palmerston was in the highest health and spirits. After taking his ride on Saturday, he came down to me as I was fishing on the lake from a boat, took the oars, and rowed for half an hour. I start for Germany to-morrow.

Ever truly yours,
A. HAYWARD.

Mr. Hayward to Sir G. C. Lewis.

                                  Hôtel du Louvre, Paris,
MY DEAR LEWIS,   Sept. 21, 1856.

Where shall you be about the beginning of next month ? I expect to be in England in ten days, and should be most happy to pay you a visit either going or returning from North Wales, where I propose to pass a fortnight before re-settling in London. I have been to Munich, Milan, Turin, and Genoa. To judge from the Sardinian press, one would suppose that an immediate

breach with Austria was inevitable ; but with them, as
with us, the popular feeling is exaggerated, if not mis-
represented, by the journalists.   I do not think there is
any chance of a rising in Italy.   Here the *classe ouvrière*
is very discontented, owing to the scarcity and high rent
of lodging within the walls.   It is a sort of *close parish*
grievance, and admits of no effective remedy.   The
Emperor has not gained an inch of ground with the
educated classes.   Ford, Thackeray, Merivale, Lord
Clanricarde, E. Bruce, H. Baring, Bonham Carter, Mrs.
Norton, Lady Morley, and Lord Walpole are amongst
the English with whom I have fallen in since my arrival
a week since.   I met Macaulay at Milan on his way to
consult records at Venice.   Lord Walpole has been
beforehand, and has luckily got copies of the annual
reports of the Venetian Ambassadors at London from
1714 to 1728, for Walpole's amanuensis writes him word
that Macaulay's arrival has frightened the authorities,
and raised a difficulty as to future access to the documents in question.   This hotel is a curiosity.   I find it
very comfortable ; but I want hardly any attendance,
and the lack of it is the common complaint.   With best
regards to Lady Theresa,

Ever faithfully yours,

A. HAYWARD.

Mr. Sidney Herbert to Mr. Hayward.

[EXTRACT.]

MY DEAR HAYWARD,

Wilton House, Salisbury,
Nov. 1, 1856.

I think our Neapolitan policy beneath contempt.
Bomba must win if he only sits still, for the three inter-
vening Powers have no one object or sentiment in
common in the matter, and we cannot move without
differing.   Austria wants the *status quo ;* France wants

a change of dynasty, but no change of system ; and we want a constitution without caring one farthing whether the dynasty goes or stays.   I think the Russian protest, though evidently not an accurate copy—the language is so undiplomatic—hits us very hard.   We have no moral right, and we denounced Russia for doing exactly the same thing in Hungary—namely, putting down a revolution ; for Bomba's rule is a revolutionary one, being a standing evasion or infraction of existing laws ; and we have chastised Russia for doing the same thing in Turkey, and justly chastised her ; but Palmerston can never resist shaking his fist in the face of any one whom he is not afraid of.   If they show fight he runs away, as in the case of the U. S. this spring—and he has bitten Clarendon.

Believe me,

Yours sincerely

SIDNEY HERBERT.

M. Charles de Rémusat to Mr. Hayward.

52, Rue d'Anjou St. Honoré, Paris,

MON CHER AMI,   30 novembre 1856.

Je suis enfin revenu à Paris, et pendant que j'étais en route, le *North British* m'allait chercher à la campagne.   J'ai donc été un peu tardif à vous remercier de l'article que contient le dernier numéro.   J'y reconnais toute votre indulgente amitié, et je voudrais mériter tout ce que vous dites de l'auteur et de l'ouvrage.   Je ferai mon profit de tout ce que contient l'article, dont l'esprit noblement libéral me convient d'ailleurs si bien, et je vous prie encore d'agréer toutes les expressions de ma gratitude.

J'ai trouvé ici l'atmosphère politique un peu troublée. On ne sait absolument que penser.   Il y a un peu de confusion dans les rôles.   Voilà l'Angleterre qui poussait

à faire quelque chose en Italie et qui s'allie intimement
avec l'Autriche. Voilà la France qui s'amuse à se faire
la cour par la Russie, quoiqu'au fond elle ait la‘ ferme
résolution de ne pas se brouiller avec l'Angleterre. On
dit que votre Cabinet obtiendra bientôt ce qu'il désire.

Quant à nos affaires intérieures, elles sont toujours
fort paisibles, un peu attristées par la cherté des sub-
sistances dans une partie de la France. La guerre et les
achats de grains à l'étranger ont amené une exportation
extraordinaire de numéraire qui produit un peu de gêne
dans les affaires : et le cours de nos splendeurs finan-
cières en est interrompu. Je ne crois toutefois à aucun
changement fondamental dans la situation politique.
Adieu, mon cher Hayward, encore une fois merci.
J'espère vous voir dans quelques mois à Londres.

Croyez en attendant aux sentiments d'affection et de
reconnaissance,

De votre tout dévoué,

CH. RÉMUSAT.

Mr. Hayward to Mr. Gladstone.

MY DEAR GLADSTONE,　　　　　　　　　Dec. 5, 1856.

I dare say you will like to hear how the Italian
(Naples) question stands as to proof of King Bomba's
atrocities, which are still denied by G. Bowyer & Co.

Both Petre and Craven say there is no doubt at all,
that, not more than six weeks since, Poerio was obliged
to undergo an operation, and that they refused to take
off his chains whilst it was performed. Petre told me
last night, at Lady Palmerston's, that he was in hopes of
getting direct evidence of this in the shape of a letter
from Poerio himself. Craven further says, that the
political prisoners, in one place or another, cannot fall
short of 5,000 or 6,000 ; as that was the number named
by the Minister of Police to be transported to the

Argentine Republic in case of a so-called amnesty. I was at Brocket the week before last with Craven, and had several long conversations with him on the subject. He has no notion that any substantial concession will be made.

It seems clear that the appearance of the fleets in the Bay was to be the signal for a *demonstration*, which would have resulted in a revolution. On finding that the cry of *constitution* was to be raised, and that nothing was to be said about the Murat claim, the French drew off, and refused to co-operate in any further movement. Our fleet was already at Ajaccio. The King snubbed Hübner,* and when Craven made a party for him, gave out that any one attending it would be in bad odour at Court. The effect was that hardly any of the leading people dared to come. This intervention is almost universally condemned, everybody seeming to think that to intervene to this extent was to compromise the country and mislead the Italians. This is Lord Lynd-hurst's view, with whom I had a good deal of talk at Paris.

The notion, that governments with such totally different views could co-operate for such a purpose, seems preposterous.

The understanding at Lady Palmerston's last evening was that the Russians had complied with the requisitions of the Allies, and were to carry out the treaty in our sense. In fact, Lord Palmerston as good as told me that he had carried his point.

He seems in the best health and spirits. A French translation of my article on the Crimean campaign is about to appear at Brussels. I have carefully corrected it, after consulting again with the generals, and have struck out everything that could give reasonable offence to the French, or indeed to any one.

Ever faithfully yours,
A. HAYWARD.

* Austrian plenipotentiary.

I have just got a letter from C. Rémusat, in which
he speaks of the financial difficulty of the Empire as
transitory, and likely to lead to nothing serious.

No doubt, however, L. N.'s popularity is altogether at
an end.   The workmen are singing songs about Caligula,
and posting *Le Roi s'amuse* on the walls.

The Duke of Newcastle to Mr. Hayward.

MY DEAR HAYWARD,   Clumber, Dec. 5, 1856.

I am really ashamed to think how long I have
delayed my notes * ; but each day brings its own
business, and it is not easy to find time for the *extras.*
You will probably think my remarks not very important
after all, but I have scrupulously noted every point in
which I could detect any error, and I think I have as
scrupulously stated nothing but what I know to be
correct.   I have made figures in the margin of the
Review, which I return, corresponding to those in my
paper.   You ask me for the number of transport
animals which Fildert† had available when the Expedition
sailed.   I cannot from memory tell the exact number,
but I know he had in Bulgaria more than 5,000 transport horses, and when the Expedition sailed, upwards of
4,000 were ordered to be gradually removed down from
Varna by land to Constantinople.   Many of these died
on the way, from want of care ; but so late as the
beginning of January 1855, when he had only about
400 in the Crimea, he had 1,100 at his depôt at Constantinople.   Of course these animals could not have
been taken *with* the Expedition, and were not wanted

---

* The Duke revised Mr. Hayward's article on the Crimean
Expedition before it was translated into French.

† Commissary-General in the Crimea.

for a *coup de main.* Why they were not sent for after-wards is quite another matter.*

If you ever say anything to Kinglake respecting our conversation at the Athenæum, pray take care that he does not conceive the idea, that I object to my private papers coming before the world, *so far as I am concerned;* all that I require is, that if any are used *all* should. I am quite prepared to abide by an impartial examination of all I did, but I do think it monstrous that letters written in the spirit, not only of official but private confidence, should be given for publication without even the knowledge of the writer. I shall take no step to prevent publication. If, when they appear, I think they do not give a fair explanation of events, I shall publish for myself; and if I do I shall spare nobody, though I shall strike at nobody.

Believe me,

Yours very sincerely,

NEWCASTLE.

Baron Audrian to Mr. Hayward.

MY DEAR MR. HAYWARD,　　　　Vienna, Dec. 7, 1856.

I am very much indebted to you for the pleasure your letter of the 29th last gave me, and for its very valuable and interesting contents. Extracts of your article on the Crimean campaign I have caused to appear in the *Wanderer,* one of our best Vienna papers, and I think the whole should be published shortly. I expect with great impatience the revised and improved copy you have the kindness to send me, and shall with great pleasure do my best to make it generally known. I think that nothing should be omitted to put the events of the last war into their true light, and to counteract

---

* *Vide* 'The Invasion of the Crimea,' by A. W. Kinglake. Sixth edition, vol. vii. "The Winter Troubles," p. 109, *et seq.*

the effects of so many intentional misstatements. People here do not much like the idea of having Conferences again, when everything that appears to be settled may be open to discussions again.   There is one point upon which Austria seems decided not to yield, and that is the union of the Principalities.   We cannot allow a Wallachian Piedmont to be created on our Eastern frontier, as a *foyer* of Russian intrigues and predominance, which it would be impossible to balance, united as these provinces are to Russia by so many ties, religious and others.   In this respect, as in so many others, the interests of England and Austria are identical, and their efforts should be united.

Sir H. Seymour * is generally liked and esteemed here, and seems to be gaining ground every day.   The Emperor has been well received at Venice.   Of course there was no enthusiasm to be expected, but the last administration improvements, the amnesty, and the restitution of the sequestrated property to emigrants, have produced a good effect.   Similar measures are expected in Hungary, where the convocation of a Protestant Synod for next May has also made a very favourable impression.   Baron Jellachich is dying.   Prince Metternich, on the contrary, grows younger every day.

> Believe me,
>
> Ever faithfully yours,
>
> AUDRIAN.

Pray give my best compliments to Mrs. Norton.

Mr. Hayward to Mr. Gladstone.

[EXTRACT.]

MY DEAR GLADSTONE,   Temple, Dec. 17, 1856.

The Government anticipate a quiet session, after a little hostile criticism on their foreign policy.   They

* English Minister at Vienna.

have been getting ready the measures they intend to bring forward, which accounts for the frequent Cabinets. C. Villiers told me, last evening, that Lord Palmerston would have no Reform Bill unless Lord John Russell tried to get the start.   It is rumoured that Lord John has been getting up materials for an anti-Ministerial display on Italy.   I had a long talk with Lord Lyndhurst yesterday. His opinion on Naples coincides with yours.

Our Cabinet give out that the Conferences will not extend beyond one short sitting, in which judgment will be immediately given against Russia.

Such, however, is not the opinion of foreign Ministers. France has a strong leaning to Russia, and Sardinia will not be easily brought to concur with Austria *in anything*. Louis Napoleon's prestige is entirely gone, and he now depends on the military, and on public apathy.   The Duke of Newcastle complains of being overwhelmed with work, but he found time to look over my *brochure* and gave me some useful hints—Airey has carefully gone through it.   I have materially strengthened and *softened* the main argument, that is, the English case as against the French.   I am very glad to hear that your Homeric labours are progressing.

Ever faithfully yours,
A. HAYWARD.

Mr. Hayward to Sir G. C. Lewis.

[EXTRACT.]

MY DEAR LEWIS,   Temple, Dec. 29, 1856.

I hope you will make up the Persian difficulty. Nothing that costs much, or postpones the repeal of the Income Tax, will please.   People won't care about Naples.   Gladstone (from whom I heard last week) thinks there will be a strong Session.   He thinks the

Neapolitan interference most ill-advised in the state of uncertainty how far France would co-operate. Some good, however, has resulted, for the King has let out some really important prisoners at last. So Craven (who knows them all) tells me.

I met Lord H. Lennox yesterday. He gave an amusing account of his and the Disraeli dinner at the Tuileries. Lennox was talking of the advent of his people to power as a certainty, if anything happened to your chief. But I do not see how they could either form a Cabinet or get a majority.

London was never emptier at this season. A general indifference seems to prevail, which proves how little the English know or care about foreign politics, which are certainly in a very doubtful condition. Lowe has given me all the documents, pamphlets, &c., he brought from America, and I am writing an article from them. Best regards to Lady Theresa,

Ever yours,
A. HAYWARD.

The difficulties as to the mouths of the Danube and the Bessarabian question had been settled ; and the Neufchâtel question, though threatening at one time to involve Switzerland and Prussia in hostilities, was eventually disposed of peacefully.

The War with Persia terminated favourably for our arms, and the independence of Herat was guaranteed by the Shah, in a treaty signed at Paris in March 1857. The English people, under the direction of the press, were inclined to grow more and more distrustful of Louis Napoleon ; and the visit from the Grand Duke Constantine seemed to argue that the court Russia was paying him was intended to undermine the strength of the English and French alliance.   A war with China was impending, in consequence of Sir J. Bowring's conduct in regard to the lorcha " Arrow."   On a question connected with these proceedings Lord Palmerston's Government were defeated on the 3rd of March, 1857, and Parliament was dissolved shortly afterwards, but the General Election returned the Prime Minister with a larger majority than before.   Most of the following letters refer to these matters.   But some few discuss Mr. Hayward's pamphlet or *brochure*, 'Expédition de Crimée,' * as the translation of his article on the Crimean War in the *North British Review* was called.

Mr. Hayward to Mr. Gladstone.

MY DEAR GLADSTONE,   Jan. 4, 1857.

The belief gains strength daily, that France will have a dash at Prussia.   The object of the military council (to meet at Paris) is to separate the allied forces, and enable each nation to act independently of the other.

Colonel Rawlinson, who was with Lord Clarendon yesterday on Persian matters, says that the Herat affair is an old story revived with exaggerations.   It was known three months ago that the Government there had changed hands, but the usurper is in the English interest, not in the Persian or Russian.

Mortgagees are beginning to raise the rate of interest, as I know to my cost.   They want four-and-a-half or five per cent. on the best fee-simple security.

I believe Louis Napoleon is well informed of the true state of English feeling, and is not misled by the press.

* ' Expédition de Crimée.—Quelques Éclaircissements relatifs à l'armée anglaise.' (Bruxelles, 1857.)

Strzelecki,* who returned from Bowood yesterday, says
that Lord Lansdowne was more peacefully inclined than
some months since.

Ever faithfully yours,

A. HAYWARD.

Sir James Graham to Mr. Hayward.

MY DEAR SIR,   Netherby, Jan. 11, 1857.

I have read with interest the *brochure* which you
kindly sent to me, relating to events in the Crimea. I
know that the facts are accurately stated ; and the
inferences are drawn with precision and perfect fairness.
The French, who have hitherto triumphed at our expense
and in defiance of truth, will be very angry ; but I care
less for their anger than for their insidious vain boasting,
and the period has arrived, when history must vindicate
her rights, and when the truth must be told. Your con-
tribution is valuable in this sense ; and the fair fame of
England will rise in proportion as the real facts are
brought to light. The Historian of the Russian War
has British triumphs in reserve ; the Historian of the
Russian Embassy, in the person of —— † does not shed
much glory on our country, or reflect the brightness
of an illustrious name. Such exhibitions are degrading
and painful in the extreme.

I am,

Yours very faithfully,

J. GRAHAM.

---

* Count Strzelecki.

† A lecturer who had referred with some merriment to the
coronation ceremony at St. Petersburg. His comments were
taken up and severely criticised.

Mr. Gladstone to Mr. Hayward.

MY DEAR HAYWARD,   Hawarden, Jan. 16, 1857.

I ought, several days ago, to have thanked you for your letter and the interesting budget it contained ; but I have in hand a work about Homer which ought now or never to come to something, and it makes me slack in the duty of writing political letters, though not at all unthankful to receive them.

I always hear of Naples with the greatest interest, but I could wish to have heard better news. With good intentions the Government have made a mess of it. The *least* that would have warranted interference in point of prudence would have been thorough oneness of spirit and intention with France, *plus* at least acquiescence on the part of the other great Powers. Less than this was sure to fail. And even if an amnesty could have been had, it would only have been the mercy, though the great mercy, of a moment, without the abolition and complete security for the non-revival of the extra-judicial and anti-legal system of Government.

The point about Bolgrad* I take to be the question who is the judge rather than who shall have the capital of the Bulgarian colonies.

I am glad to hear your article is coming out in a corrected form. I should have liked also to see it enlarged.

In five-and-twenty years I cannot recollect a Parliamentary recess such as this has been : so constantly agitated and disturbed with rumours and quarrels in every shape and in every quarter. It looks as if we were to have a very rough and uneasy Session.

* In delimiting the new Russian frontier, a dispute arose concerning the identity of a small village referred to in the Treaty of Paris as Bolgrad, with a town of the same name considerably further south.

We are to be here till the old year strikes his last, and then we meditate a fortnight at Hagley on the way to Oxford, Wiltshire, and London.

Sir J. Graham has had sad anxieties about his wife, but she is better. Lord Aberdeen, to judge from his letters, is in excellent health and spirits.

Always
Most truly yours,
W. E. GLADSTONE.

M. Thiers to Mr. Hayward.

MON CHER MONSIEUR HAYWARD, 16 janvier 1857.

Voilà bien longtemps que je ne vous ai écrit. Je vous adresse quelques mots aujourd'hui pour vous remercier de l'envoi de votre brochure. Je n'ai pas eu encore le temps de la lire, j'ai seulement jeté les yeux sur quelques pages. J'en devine l'intention, et je la regrette. L'avantage de relever l'armée anglaise, qui n'a pas besoin de l'être, sous le rapport de la bravoure, et de la bonne conduite, ne vaut pas l'inconvénient de nuire à l'alliance de la France et de l'Angleterre. On est ici fort susceptible, on trouve (à tort selon moi) le gouvernement anglais très exigeant, et il suffirait de la moindre piqûre, pour faire éclater de fâcheux sentiments ; or sachez que l'alliance rompue, le monde serait bouleversé. Nous avons besoin de vous, mais vous avez tout autant besoin de nous. Le jour où vous serez brouillés avec nous, les Américains vous traiteront durement. Ne jouez donc pas, de grâce, avec un intérêt aussi grand que celui d'une telle alliance. Un peu de gloire militaire n'est rien auprès d'un intérêt de cette importance. Adieu, je suis pressé, et ne puis vous en dire davantage.

A. THIERS.

M. de Rémusat to Mr. Hayward.

MON CHER AMI,   2 février 1857.

J'ai reçu la traduction de votre écrit, et je l'ai relu avec un grand plaisir. Je suis convaincu que vos rectifications sont exactes. Il est certain que la presse anglaise a exagéré les choses au détriment de votre nation, et que la nôtre, courtisant à la fois l'amour propre du maître et celle de notre pays, ne mérite pas une entière créance. L'ouvrage de Bazancourt a peu d'autorité, mais il a dû être assez lu, et méritait peut-être une réponse. Saint-Arnaud était un charlatan et un général des plus médiocres. La vraie faute a été dans l'indécision de nos deux gouvernements, qui ont, je crois, envoyé nos armées en Orient, sans savoir bien ce qu'elles y devaient faire. Quant aux qualités des deux armées, je crois bien que la nôtre est plus marcheuse, parce que c'est une qualité de la race française, et que son éducation militaire y contribue. Des officiers dignes de foi m'ont dit, qu'ils ne trouvaient à redire l'armée anglaise que deux choses, un certain défaut de célérité, dans la marche, et l'absence d'ingénieurs qui eussent l'expérience de leur état. Quant aux souffrances, il se peut que la première année votre administration ait encore plus mal fait que la nôtre, qui ne s'est pas fort distinguée ; mais la seconde année, c'est à dire pendant tout l'hiver de 1856, l'armée française a horriblement souffert, sans qu'on en ait rien dit, et il est certain que l'armée anglaise a été bien pourvue et bien portante.

Mais vous savez toutes ces choses mieux que moi, et je ferais mieux de vous remercier encore de l'intéressante et instructive lecture que je vous dois. Je ne sais où en est notre alliance. Je puis vous assurer que tout ce qui a ici une vraie sagacité politique, et quelque sentiment libéral, la regarde comme plus que jamais désirable et

X 2

même nécessaire. Je crois même que notre gouvernement y tient beaucoup, surtout l'Empereur. Mais l'infatuation de l'amour propre, et les intérêts privés des Morny et autres ont fait faire quelques fautes qui ont compromis l'alliance. Que votre Cabinet ait une bonne majorité à la session qui va s'ouvrir, et je vous réponds que le Cabinet français sera comme il faut. C'est D'Israeli qui a persuadé ici que le ministère anglais ne pouvait durer. De votre côté, je pense que vous ferez bien de fermer les yeux sur les "blunders" du gouvernement français, et de songer, avant tout, à la grande utilité de l'accord de nos deux puissances. Mais la place me manque. Adieu, mon cher Hayward. J'espère être à Londres au mois d'avril. Ne m'oubliez pas, et croyez-moi bien cordialement à vous.

CH. RÉMUSAT.

Lord Howden * to Mr. Hayward.

MY DEAR HAYWARD,   Madrid, Feb. 7, 1857.

I was glad to see your caligraphy, and I have obeyed your instructions. I have sent one of your pamphlets to Narvaez,† the other to O'Donnell,‡ our Castor and Pollux, not in union but in refulgence—(after writing this I find that nothing on earth can be so inapplicable as my mythology, for most certainly the *quorum simul alba Stella refulsit, . . . Concidunt venti, fugiuntque nubes* § is not the trade of these worthies.) The French ignore

---

* English Envoy in Spain from May, 1850, to March, 1858, when he was recalled.

† Marshal Narvaez, Duke of Valencia, a soldier and a statesman of Spain.

‡ Leopold O'Donnell, Count of Lucena and Duke of Tetuan, espoused the cause of the Queen-mother Christina, and had, during the previous year, caused the dismissal of the Cortes and proclaimed martial law.

§ Horace, 'Odes' I. xii. 27.

us at their feasts, but that is, at least, negative. *Here* we are declared to be a fifth-rate military power, and the position of an English Minister here is proportionately agreeable. The Spaniards (*le coup de pied de l'âne* if you like) are glad to have a fling at us on all occasions, but especially on this, to revenge a good deal of injustice done to them, (or at all events a vast amount of *supercilium*) by our writers on the Peninsular War, who never forgave the Spanish Commissariat for not feeding John Bull better, while the Don was living (and marching his forty miles a day) very contentedly on bread and olives. I thank you very much for your little epitome of English politics. I have nothing to return to you in that way, for we are quiet for a wonder ; but anything is on the cards, and unfortunately there are no trumps in the pack. There is a good deal of fear entertained of the eventual designs of France, whenever the time comes that it shall suit L. Napoleon to throw off the English alliance and make another. To the north, the French are pushing a railroad on a point for evidently pure strategical and political purposes. The Crédit Mobilier even says so openly. On the south, comes information from all the consuls in Barbary, that the French are laying down in Africa a base of operations against Morocco, with which power a quarrel can be picked any day. I don't know how England will like this, but as to Spain she will get up some day completely enveloped, and go to bed, perhaps, completely Gallic. When you see Mrs. Norton, make her, I pray, my respectful salutation, and believe me

Truly yours,

HOWDEN.

Mr. Hayward to Sir G. C. Lewis.

Athenæum Club,

MY DEAR LEWIS,   March 16, 1857.

Gladstone and S. Herbert have come to an explanation * which has ended very like the lovers' separation in Little's poems:

> "You may down *that* pathway rove,
> While I shall take my way through *this*."

Sidney Herbert takes the Liberal, and Gladstone the Derbyite turn. I know no one likely to follow Gladstone's lead in the matter, except perhaps Lord A. Hervey. Sidney Herbert's address will speak for itself, and I hear he is to be furiously opposed by the Derbyites.

Ever truly yours,

A. HAYWARD.

Sir G. C. Lewis to Mr. Hayward.

Downing Street,

MY DEAR HAYWARD,   March 17, 1857.

In my opinion, Gladstone has made a wrong decision. He does not agree entirely with either party, but I strongly suspect he has much more in common with the Derbyites. Unless Gladstone changes his side of the House, and openly separates from his friends, his adhesion to the Derbyites will be of little value to them—for he is sure to differ with them from time to time.

Ever yours truly,

G. C. LEWIS,

The Dissolution will probably be on Saturday.

* In view of the general elections, a suggestion had been made that the Peelites and Derbyites should not actively oppose each other's candidates. Mr. Sidney Herbert rejected the proposal from the first, while Mr. Gladstone was more favourably disposed towards it. Cf. Lord Malmesbury's 'Autobiography,' vol. ii. 63, 64.

Mr. Hayward to Mr. Gladstone.

8, St. James's Street,
MY DEAR GLADSTONE, March 26, 1857.

I hear that great offence has been taken both by Roman Catholics and Dissenters at the expression "Scriptural Established Church" in Sir S. Glynne's address. S. Conway is hesitating whether he shall not propose Mostyn after all, some explanation having been offered.

Lord Palmerston's speech at the Mansion House and his address have given great offence, but the farmers cannot understand why their member voted with their natural enemy, Cobden. This is the real hitch, not China.

I think Lord John will win, but it is very doubtful. Currie asked Grote to propose him (Currie), and Grote replied that he should *plump* for Lord John.

The Duke of Newcastle writes that his son will walk over the course, and that his brother is safe, though there may be a contest. Elcho writes from Venice that he got my letter (explaining how parties stood) the day after he had despatched his address.

The troops * are not to be sent for some time, for fear of their arriving in the unhealthy season. Why were not they and Lord Elgin † despatched two months ago?

Ever truly yours,

A. HAYWARD.

Mr. Hayward to Mr. Gladstone.

8, St. James's Street,
MY DEAR GLADSTONE, April 6, 1857.

The statement touching the Emperor's repudiation of Yeh ‡ is, as you may have guessed, a fiction. I had a talk

* The troops for China.
† Special Ambassador to China. He negotiated the Treaty of Tientsin. ‡ The Chinese Governor of Canton.

with Lord Elgin this morning, who thought the chances of a satisfactory settlement as far off as ever. Yeh made a flourishing report to the Emperor, and the Emperor told him not to be too hard on us if we were properly humbled. *Voilà tout!*

The isolation of Canton by the Government of Pekin creates the great difficulty, in Lord Elgin's opinion, of effecting any arrangement on a broad or Imperial basis. He starts in about a fortnight. The troops could not act till past the middle of August if they were there. Their departure is consequently postponed. What excuse have the Government for not sending Lord Elgin and the troops two months ago? The majority is begining to be thought more favourable to Lord John Russell's views than to Lord Palmerston's.

Ever faithfully yours,

A. HAYWARD.

The Duke of Newcastle to Mr. Hayward.

MY DEAR HAYWARD,   Clumber, April 10, 1857.

Viewing the elections from a distance, and as an outsider, caring little for men but much for measures, I come to the conclusion, that Palmerston will be disappointed with his new Parliament. The gain to *Liberal opinions* is very great, and the Derby party is for the present smashed; but in these very facts are to be found the Premier's disadvantages. Nobody *can* fear the alternative of a Derby Ministry, and unless Palmerston *rises* to the occasion he will soon find his popularity gone and his Government in danger. It is all nonsense to suppose that the China vote has really influenced the decision of the country, but there is a question which alone Palmerston cares about (and that in an *adverse* sense), which has gained ground everywhere and is now established as the question of the day—Reform of Parliament—and I have no belief in a *good* measure coming from unwilling men ; and *how* unwilling are the influential men in the present Cabinet my former association with them pretty well informs me.

I am ever,

Yours very sincerely,

NEWCASTLE.

Lady Dufferin to Mr. Hayward.

DEAR MR. HAYWARD,   July 9, 1857.

I am much gratified by your kind notice of Frederic's book,* and I greedily swallow every scrap of praise it receives, as I confess to admiring it myself, and yet I am a stern critic of all he does, for much love casteth out flattery.   The one sentence which gives me no pleasure in your letter is the allusion to an idea, on the part of some of his readers, that I have had any share in *writing* it.   I think it is rather hard upon him that he is always to be suspected of borrowing from an intellect in *every way* inferior to his own.   You may remember, perhaps, that a speech of his (when he first came of age) was a good deal noticed, and I was immediately accused of writing it : although upon that occasion he was so sensitive on the subject of help, that he would not let me know beforehand what he meant to say, and his speech was as new to me as to his other hearers.

In this instance (the book) he, with some misgivings, allowed me to revise and correct the greater part of it in the proof-sheets (for it was in the printer's hands before I returned to England), and I exercised my functions in cutting out a great deal which I thought rather too flowery and romantic for a simple narrative, although a great many of the expunged paragraphs were literally extracts from his real letters to me ; and so far from his being

* The present Lord Dufferin's ' Letters from High Latitudes.'

willing to accept assistance, when I took the trouble to write a very fine page in my best English to be substituted for one of his which I had objected to, he would not accept it, but compromised the matter by cancelling both. Some of these days, I shall show you one or two of the original letters from which these are compiled ; to my mind, they are even more original, racy, and spirited than these holyday-dressed epistles—but they would not have done for the public eye for many reasons. Pray do me the service of contradicting, in the most positive manner (*on my authority*), the assertion that I did more than I have said. Nothing would annoy me more than to know that such an idea got into his readers' heads. What a spirit of contradiction possesses one's kind friends! I, who have never done anything, am supposed to be capable of doing much ; it is a great lesson, which I shall lay to heart. I will never give the measure of my shallowness ; I will go on labouring in my vocation ; I will "do nothing" more energetically than ever. Perhaps, by dint of frequenting your society, and keeping my own counsel in the same determined manner, I may get to be suspected of certain articles in the *Quarterly.* Who knows ? *En attendant,*

I am, yours sincerely,

HELEN DUFFERIN.

Mr. Hayward to his Sisters.

July 31, 1857.

I have nothing whatever to do with politics or political writing. I am staying in town to finish an article on a literary subject for the *Edinburgh.* I go on Tuesday next to Knebworth, for four days. About the tenth, it is just possible that I may be able to run down to see you.

I am much pressed to go to Sheridan's,* and though

* Frampton Court, Dorchester.

it is hardly worth while to make the journey for one visit, the being able to see you will determine me, if I can manage it.   Let me know whether there is a coach from Taunton, and at what hour, or whether the best way is from Dorchester.

Ever yours,
A. II.

Sir John Young had written to Mr. Hayward complaining of the reports published by the *Daily News* on Ionian affairs.   He feared these reports would discredit him in the eyes of the Government, by whom he had been but lately complimented for his conduct.   So he wrote to ask Mr. Hayward whether the reports were likely to damage his reputation.   Mr. Hayward probably replied, that the House of Commons was too much occupied with graver matters to pay attention to Ionian affairs. It is a curious thing that Mr. Hayward's correspondence contains so few allusions to the Indian Mutiny, which kept the country in a ferment of savage indignation in the years 1857–58.

The Duke of Newcastle to Mr. Hayward.

MY DEAR HAYWARD,   Clumber, Nov. 24, 1857.

A man does not much like to be told that his safety lies in his insignificance, which seems to have been your crumb of comfort to poor Young ; but you told him the truth, and unless he were to crown King Otho in Corfu, or head his Parliament against the Queen's troops, the House of Commons is not likely at this moment to spend much time in criticising him or his Government. Perhaps, by flogging as many women as Ward did men, he might establish a fair reputation for " vigour and energy."

The tide is beginning to turn against Government in the matter of India.* The country papers are expressing *doubts* whether Palmerston had any right to boast of his activity and foresight at the Mansion House. I think the coming short session will sow the seeds of much mischief to his popularity and power. I am laid up with an accident out hunting, having dislocated my left shoulder by a bad fall, it will be some time before I can use the arm again. I shall be at the meeting.

Believe me,

Yours very sincerely,

NEWCASTLE.

Mr. Hayward to Mr. Gladstone.

8, St. James's Street,

MY DEAR GLADSTONE,   Nov. 27, 1857.

The papers announce your speedy return to London ; but perhaps you may like to hear a little of the political gossip. The *Times* (speaking, I suppose, by authority) announces the abolition of the double system of Indian Government ; but I dined with Rawlinson yesterday, and I am convinced that the Directors had no certain intimation of their fate. Only last night, too, I was talking on the same subject with C. Villiers, who was equally in the dark, and said that you were the only man in the House of Commons who could carry through a well-considered and comprehensive scheme of government for India. As for Vernon-Smith,† it will be (to borrow Curran's metaphor) the feeble hand thrown to a distance by its attempt to grasp a globe too large for its comprehension. . . .

---

* This was the year of the Indian Mutiny.

† President of the Board of Control.

It is expected that the Speech will promise a measure of Reform, trusting to the chapter of accidents for the evasion of the promise ; and fling the Bank question as a bone of contention before the House in general terms.

It is somewhat remarkable that no one, not even the warmest of their supporters, expects anything sound or good from the Government. Two days ago I met Lord St. Germans, who told me that he had accepted the office of Lord Steward mainly because he wanted occupation, and the Queen was very kind about it. He was completely in the dark as to future measures of the Ministry he was thus pledged to support. Although Lords Palmerston and Granville stood up gallantly for Lord Canning at the City dinners,* the Government here refuse to take the responsibility of the proclamation, and in consequence of that refusal the Direction have formally required Canning to state his grounds.

The Government will be called to account for—first, not sending some of the troops overland ; second, for not sending them at once by steam. I hear that Lord Stratford had procured the assent of the Porte, but Lord Clarendon did not like to set the example of crossing neutral territory. The truth is, the pressing urgency of the crisis was not seen in the first instance, or all minor objections would have been set aside.

The commercial panic in London has abated ; but Kirkman Hodgson told me that the Americans owed us £32,000,000 on the balance, much of which would never be paid. Peabody was very hard run, having £800,000 to pay on one day.

The Duke of Hamilton is a large shareholder in the

---

* At the Lord Mayor's banquet on the 9th of November (*vide* 'Life of Lord Palmerston,' vol. ii. p. 349, by Hon. E. Ashley).

Western Scotch Bank,* which may account for his coming forward. I do not believe Keating will be the new judge, nor consequently that the Solicitor-Generalship will be vacant. There was a talk of the judgeship being offered to Wortley. Lord Lyndhurst has returned in full vigour. He told me that he had received the usual summons from Lord Derby, but *lithographed* this time. Hayter tells his people, that he is not aware of any pressing reason for their attendance at the short session.

In literature the most notable event is Buckle's ' History of Civilization in England.' His range of reading is quite unprecedented, and his style is clear. His views may be wrong, but the book is instructive and suggestive to a most remarkable extent. He is a self-educated man, of recluse habits, of about forty. The best article on India is in ' The *London* Quarterly Review.' With compliments to Mrs. Gladstone,

Believe me,

Ever faithfully yours,

A. HAYWARD.

* On the 9th of November, the Western Bank of Scotland closed its doors. This led to many other commercial failures and a financial panic. The crisis was chiefly due to the over-trading of the Americans, and became so severe that the Government suspended for a time the Bank Charter Act of 1844.

END OF VOL. I.

LONDON: PRINTED BY WILLIAM CLOWES AND SONS, LIMITED,
STAMFORD STREET AND CHARING CROSS.

www.ingramcontent.com/pod-product-compliance
Lightning Source LLC
Chambersburg PA
CBHW020933030726
47496CB00005B/1175